INTRIGUE

Seek thrills. Solve crimes. Justice served.

Killer In The Kennel
Caridad Piñeiro

The Masquerading Twin
Katie Mettner

MILLS & BOON

KILLER IN THE KENNEL
© 2024 by Caridad Piñeiro Scordato
Philippine Copyright 2024
Australian Copyright 2024
New Zealand Copyright 2024

First Published 2024
First Australian Paperback Edition 2024
ISBN 978 1 038 93550 2

THE MASQUERADING TWIN
© 2024 by Katie Mettner
Philippine Copyright 2024
Australian Copyright 2024
New Zealand Copyright 2024

First Published 2024
First Australian Paperback Edition 2024
ISBN 978 1 038 93550 2

This is a work of fiction. Names, characters, places, and incidents are either the
product of the author's imagination or are used fictitiously, and any resemblance to
actual persons, living or dead, business establishments, events, or locales is entirely
coincidental.

MIX
Paper | Supporting
responsible forestry
FSC® C001695
www.fsc.org

Published by
Harlequin Mills & Boon
An imprint of Harlequin Enterprises (Australia) Pty Limited
(ABN 47 001 180 918), a subsidiary of HarperCollins
Publishers Australia Pty Limited
(ABN 36 009 913 517)
Level 19, 201 Elizabeth Street
SYDNEY NSW 2000 AUSTRALIA

Cover art used by arrangement with Harlequin Books S.A.. All rights reserved.

Printed and bound in Australia by McPherson's Printing Group

Killer In The Kennel
Caridad Piñeiro

Books by Caridad Piñeiro

Harlequin Intrigue

South Beach Security: K-9 Division

Sabotage Operation
Escape the Everglades
Killer in the Kennel

South Beach Security

Lost in Little Havana
Brickell Avenue Ambush
Biscayne Bay Breach

Cold Case Reopened
Trapping a Terrorist
Decoy Training

Visit the Author Profile page at
millsandboon.com.au.

New York Times and *USA TODAY* bestselling author **Caridad Piñeiro** is a Jersey girl who just wants to write and is the author of nearly fifty novels and novellas. She loves romance novels, superheroes, TV and cooking. For more information on Caridad and her dark, sexy romantic suspense and paranormal romances, please visit www.caridad.com.

CAST OF CHARACTERS

Sara Hernandez—Sara was the head of an agency responsible for search-and-rescue efforts in state park and forest lands in the Northeast. She is experienced at search and rescue and is an accredited trainer for not only SAR, but also for training dogs to be used for security. Joining SBS to become their lead K-9 trainer is a dream come true.

Jose Gonzalez Jr. (Pepe)—Pepe has been living in the shadow of his family's SBS Agency and tries to stay out of their oftentimes dangerous business. Instead, he's made his own success as a Realtor. But when the family asks for his help in finding a location for their new K-9 training center, Pepe steps up to the challenge to help his family.

Ramon Gonzalez III (Trey)—Marine Trey Gonzalez once served Miami Beach as an undercover detective. Trey has since retired and is now the acting head of the SBS Agency and hoping to expand it with the addition of a K-9 division.

Mia Gonzalez—Trey's younger sister Mia runs a successful lifestyle-and-gossip blog and is invited to every important event in Miami. That lets Mia gather a lot of information about what's happening in Miami to help Trey with running the SBS Agency.

Josefina (Sophie) and Robert Whitaker Jr.—Trey's cousins Josefina and Robert are genius tech gurus who work at SBS and help the agency with their various investigations.

Ricardo Gonzalez (Ricky)—A trained psychologist, Ricky helps SBS with their domestic abuse cases.

Chapter One

The chatter of restaurant diners bounced off the walls like marbles ricocheting off pinball machine flippers.

Shiny slabs of white and chrome gleamed from the spotlights beaming down on the walls and colorful splashes of carefully placed modern art.

Jose Gonzalez peered around the restaurant as the waiter brought over the first vegetarian dish of their tasting menu. The place was busy for midweek, likely because of the star the restaurant had recently earned and the sighting of a few celebrities dining there the week before.

He suspected that's why his date had insisted on coming here to eat the flowers, fruits and vegetables for which the restaurant had earned some fame. He'd met Marta a few weeks earlier at a popular hangout in the Fontainebleau where celebrities also liked to linger.

Marta was cover-model beautiful with her perfectly highlighted hair, pouty bee-stung lips and a body with all the right curves. So why did he feel like something was lacking?

As he chowed down on the salad of red and golden beets, arugula, pistachios and a vegan goat cheese, he had to admit it was rather tasty. But after another dish of nothing but vegetables emerged from the kitchen followed by a third, he glanced lovingly at a nearby table where a delicious-looking filet mignon sat next to golden roasted potatoes and Broccolini.

"Isn't this delicious?" Marta said, a false trill of delight coloring her voice and a piece of something green stuck to her lower lip.

"Delicious," he replied, hoping she wouldn't pick up on his boredom with the meal and surprisingly, with her.

Fail, he thought as she narrowed her gaze and peered at him. "Jose?" she said, voice rising in question.

His phone rattled against the hard, gleaming white surface of the table.

He glanced at the screen and saw that it was his cousin Trey calling on his office line. Jose normally avoided anything to do with his family's South Beach Security agency but taking the call this time was a welcome interruption.

"Who is it?" his date asked, clearly annoyed by the phone's buzzing.

Holding his hand up in a request for her silence, he answered.

"*Hola*, Pepe," Trey said, using his childhood family nickname.

"*Hola*, Trey. How can I help you?" he said, and hoped it would give him an escape so he could go grab himself a Cuban sandwich somewhere to satisfy the hunger gnawing at his belly.

"I need your help with a new project," Trey said.

Jose nodded. "Hold on a second. I'm on a date," he said, and placed his hand over the phone to muffle his voice.

"I'm sorry, but I have to take this," he said, shot to his feet and headed for the patio where the restaurant had a bar and outdoor dining area. It was quieter there, the sounds muffled by the verdant spill of plants down the exterior walls of the building.

"What do you need, *primo*?" he asked, and hoped it wouldn't be something that dragged him into the Gonzalez family business. For years he'd struggled to build his own path without his well-known family's influence as well as the dangers often faced by his cousins at SBS.

"This must be some date if you're taking my call," Trey teased.

Jose turned and peered through the glass door to where his date sat, her full lips thinned in aggravation at his absence. The bit of green gone.

"You could say that," he said, not wanting to be unkind. Marta was nice in her own way. She just wasn't his type, whatever that type was.

"You're not going to ghost her, are you?" Trey asked, the faintest hint of accusation in his voice.

"You know me better than that, *primo*. I'll let her down easy," he confirmed and pushed on. "So why are you calling?"

"We need your help—"

"You know I don't want anything to do with the agency," he interrupted quickly.

A frustrated sigh drifted across the line. "I know, Pepe. We need your help finding a property."

Finding a property? "That's it? Nothing else?" he said, surprised at the simplicity of the request.

"*Sí*, just that. Our K-9 business has been growing and we'd like to set up a training center for our people and dogs. We need to find a location for that center," Trey advised, and continued explaining what they wanted to have on the property and roughly how much acreage they would need.

"That's a nice-sized property," he said, and in his mind the dollar signs spun like the reels on a slot machine.

"It is, but I know you're the perfect person to find us a place," Trey said, rousing unexpected guilt.

"Why me, Trey? You know I try to avoid getting involved in SBS business and this sale... I don't need to tell you that my commission on a property like that—"

"Will be a very nice one. You're family and family sticks together," Trey said without hesitation.

Full-blown guilt erupted at Trey's words as if the trust Trey was placing in him wasn't deserved, but he intended not to disappoint.

"We *are* family. I'll find you the perfect spot. Don't worry."

"I won't. I know you'll do right by us," Trey said, and ended the call.

Jose lowered the phone and stared at it for a long time. Trey and his SBS cousins always managed to do right by whoever they helped.

He intended to do the same with SBS and after a quick glance at Marta, with his date.

Once they finished dinner, he'd end it like a gentleman. After that, he'd head to Little Havana for a tasty Cuban sandwich packed with roast pork, baked ham and Swiss cheese to satisfy his hunger pangs.

Finally, as soon as he was in his South Beach condo, he'd settle down in his home office and get to work on finding Trey a perfect property for his new venture.

TREY LAID HIS phone down and stared across his desk to where his siblings sat expectantly.

"He said yes?" his baby sister, Mia, asked, obviously surprised by their cousin's response.

"He did and I'm surprised as well," Trey admitted.

"Was it just about the money?" Ricky asked.

Trey wished he'd had Ricky on the line during the call. As a psychologist, his younger brother might have picked up on Jose's motivation, although Trey considered himself a good judge of people. He'd needed that a lot to survive his time in the marines and later as an undercover police detective.

Trey shook his head. "I don't think so. I got the sense he really wanted to help because we're family."

"Surprising," Mia said with the arch of a manicured brow.

"Pepe is a good guy and I understand why he wants to make his own way. It's tough being part of a family like ours," Ricky said, ever the mediator and sometimes the outsider since he was more of a feeler and not a doer like Trey and Mia.

Trey had no doubt about how hard it was to be part of their family. They had buried their roots deep into the Miami soil and flourished beyond expectations. But that success brought many demands, and Trey could understand Jose's desire to forge his own life and success removed from those demands.

Because of that, he said, "Now that we know Pepe will look for the property, do you agree Sara Hernandez is the best candidate to run the K-9 training center?"

He handed the résumé across the desk to Ricky to refresh his memory of their possible new employee.

"Her work history is impressive. She's responsible for the search and rescue teams in several state parks," Ricky said, as he in turn passed the résumé to Mia.

Mia took a quick glance at the paper and said, "I agree. She's very impressive and she's also a certified K-9 trainer. I'm all for asking her to take the job."

"Great. I'll reach out to her, and hopefully we can move on this quickly. The K-9 Division has really taken off, and I'd love to be able to train our own agents and canines," Trey said, and took another look at the résumé and Sara's headshot. She was pretty with that kind of girl-next-door look that was the antithesis of Jose's artfully groomed and manicured fashionistas.

Perfect, he thought, and picked up the phone to call her.

THE WOMAN CRASHED through the underbrush in the thick hardwood hammock he'd released her in earlier.

He always gave his women head starts to make it a fair fight.

This one was literally like the proverbial bull in the china shop, leaving a trail of crushed brush and broken branches, enabling him to track her easily.

He caught a glimpse of her bright red blouse as she darted behind a tree, probably thinking she could hide there until he gave up the hunt.

Laughing lowly, he picked up his crossbow and tucked it tight to his shoulder. It was lubed, loaded and ready to fire. He never took chances anymore because he'd almost lost one of his women when he'd misloaded an arrow.

Never again. If she'd gotten free…

Don't think about that, he told himself, and focused on the tree and the tiniest bit of red peeking out from the edge of it.

Waiting. Watching. Patient.

His mother had always told him to be patient. To take care of his things. To watch out for wicked women.

I'm doing just that, Mommy, he thought.

As the bit of red became a larger target, he let the arrow fly.

It struck flesh with a resounding *thunk*.

The woman dropped to the ground like a stone.

He walked over to where she lay face down, motionless. Blood leaked from the arrow embedded deep in her back, a darker crimson against the red of her shirt.

Laying a booted foot on her back, he tore out the arrow, wiped it clean with some leaves and slipped it back into his quiver.

Never let a good weapon go to waste, he thought.

Flipping the woman over, she stared up at him with sightless eyes. Blue like the sky above, but bloodshot and old-looking despite her youth. Drugs and hooking would do that to you, he thought. A wounded wasted life that he gifted peace with his benevolent kill.

After all, you wouldn't let a wounded animal suffer.

He knelt and slipped off her earrings. Cheap little wire ones with bits of fake crystals. Tucking them into his pocket, he was about to haul her off to her final resting place when the sound of a car engine intruded, loud in the quiet of early morning. A pricey car if he was any judge.

Sounds traveled far out here. It was why he used to do his hunting at night when the kennels had been open. In the years since greyhound racing had been banned in Florida and the kennels had closed, he'd had the entire property to himself.

Until today, he thought, and crept silently toward the kennels to see who had ruined his pleasure. It took him nearly ten minutes to reach the edge of the forest that bordered the abandoned buildings. He carefully hid in the underbrush to see who had arrived on the property.

He had been right about the car. An expensive Maserati SUV sat in the driveway in front of what had once been the kennel owner's home. Beside it stood what his mother would have called a "rather dandy fellow" thanks to her love of Regency romances.

Raising the crossbow, he used the scope to get a better look.

Handsome. Possibly Latino. Sharp dresser. If he had to guess, the suit was as pricey as the expensive Italian car.

A sinking feeling filled his gut as the man looked around and began inspecting the property.

This was not good. Having people here, in his playground, could only bring problems.

He told himself not to worry. Who would want these abandoned buildings way out here?

But as the fancy man smiled and nodded, he worried that trouble would soon be coming his way.

Chapter Two

The receptionist led Jose into Trey's office and when he entered, he realized it wasn't just Trey inside, but also Tio Ramon, Mia and Ricky as well as a twentysomething woman he would best describe as pixieish. At her feet was an immense black-and-tan bloodhound who raised its head as he entered and eyed him with somber deep-set eyes before lazily lowering its head again to rest it against huge paws.

Jose walked over to Trey and hugged him hard and then did the same with his cousins Mia and Ricky.

He shook his uncle's hand and said, "You look great, *tio.*" In truth, his uncle looked years younger, as if the weight of the world had been lifted off his shoulders, and maybe that was the truth now that his son Trey had joined the agency and taken over many of its responsibilities.

"You look well also, *mi' jo,*" Tio Ramon said, and clapped him on the back. A second later, his uncle swung his arm out in the direction of the young woman and what he assumed was her dog.

"This is Sara Hernandez. She's going to head up the new division and live at the facility. We were hoping you could show her the property and work with her to get everything up and running. You do know contractors and the like, right?" his uncle said with the arch of a thick, salt-and-pepper brow.

Tio Ramon looked so much like Jose's father that he suddenly felt as if he were five years old again and in trouble.

"*Sí*, I know contractors. I can recommend one as soon as Ms. Hernandez checks out the property and lets me know what's necessary."

SARA DIDN'T KNOW what to make of the very handsome man who was clearly being put on the spot by his family members.

His discomfort at working with her was apparent, but that didn't stop her from holding out her hand as she rose and said, "Sara Hernandez. It's very nice to meet you. This is Bongo, my K-9 partner."

He took hold of her hand and his gaze locked with hers. His eyes were the blue of the Caribbean Sea, and he had the same Roman nose and dimpled chin as his cousins. There was no denying they were family no matter how much this man might want to forget that.

"Nice to meet you also despite the circumstances," he said, and shot his family members a scathing glance before peering at Bongo with obvious reluctance. "He's big and…drooly, isn't he?"

She didn't blame him for not liking surprises. "It's a 'she' and yes, she is. A characteristic of the breed unfortunately. If today isn't good for you—"

"No, it's fine. I knew Trey wanted you to look at the property. If you want, I can drive you there and take you home afterward."

Pointing her index finger upward, she said, "I'm staying in the penthouse temporarily. We were hoping the owner's home on the property could be fixed up quickly."

Jose tilted his head from side to side, as if considering. "It didn't look too bad, but I'll let you decide. Maybe Mia could even help get it ready," he said, and looked in his cousin's direction.

"I'd love to help. Just let me know when you need me," she said with a broad smile and a quick look between the two of them.

"Great," Jose said, and clapped his hands as if to end any discussion. Facing Sara again, he said, "If you're ready to go…"

"I am," she said, and after bidding goodbye to all the family members, he and Sara walked out of the room and to the elevators.

Jose had his hands stuffed in his pants pockets and shifted back and forth on his heels as he said, "I don't mean to make this sound…negative, but I'm not normally this involved in my family's business."

Which she took to mean once again that he wasn't all that eager to work with her, and she was okay with that for a number of reasons. She'd grown up around men like Jose with their bespoke suits and fancy cars. Or at least what she assumed would be a fancy car, and she wasn't disappointed as they reached the parking level, and he directed her toward an elegant and sporty Italian SUV.

"I hope Bongo won't be an inconvenience for you."

Jose laughed and shook his head. "If I was worried, we'd have taken one of the company cars," he said, and tossed a hand in the direction of several vehicles in the garage that bore the SBS emblem.

Considering Bongo's size and drool factor, maybe that was a good idea, she thought. "Maybe we should take one of those," she said, and gestured toward an SBS SUV.

JOSE DIDN'T KNOW WHY, but he'd gotten the sense that she saw him as some kind of snob. He also didn't know why that bothered him. Shaking his head, he said, "No, that's okay. I think Bongo will be comfortable in the back seat."

Even if that meant having dog hair and drool all over his expensive Italian leather.

She hesitated, eyeing his pristine vehicle and then the SBS SUV, but gestured to his car and said, "If it's okay with you."

Hoping he wouldn't regret it, he opened the back passenger door so that the bloodhound, who was easily a hundred pounds of loose skin and ears, could hop in.

He turned to open the door for Sara, but she had already climbed into the passenger seat.

A liberated woman, he thought, and totally not the pampered type he normally had in his life.

He pulled out of the parking lot onto Brickell Avenue and as he checked for oncoming traffic, she caught his attention yet again.

She was dressed casually in a pale blue blouse that brought out the hints of blue in her gray eyes and embraced her generous breasts. As he slipped into the driver's seat, he noticed how the faded denim of her jeans clung to her shapely thighs.

His gut tightened unexpectedly, and he pushed away his awareness of her because this meeting was all about business. The last thing he wanted was to be involved with anyone connected to his family's SBS business. Reminding himself of that, he said, "I hope you'll like the property."

She shot him a quick look and nodded. "I think I will. Trey was kind enough to send me the photos you took of the location."

"Trey is a good guy. I think you'll like working with him," he said without hesitation.

"But *you* don't normally work with him?" she asked, head cocked to the side as she waited for his response.

He tightened his hands on the wheel and held his breath as he considered how to explain their awkward family dynamic. After a long exhalation, he said, "The longer you stay in Miami, the more you'll realize how well-known the Gonzalez family is and how much power they have."

"I gathered as much from some of the research I did when I decided to apply for the job," she said, and nervously drummed her fingers on her thighs.

"It's normally a good thing unless you want to take your own path," he said, and shifted his hands on the wheel again as he turned onto the expressway that would take them to where the kennels were located. The property was forty minutes outside of Miami in an area mostly known as the home of various fruit orchards, flower farms and a racing horse stable that his SBS family had helped protect several weeks earlier.

"IT IS A good thing, but not necessarily easy," she said.

Sara knew all about trying to choose her own destiny. Her family, owners of a successful New Jersey financial investment firm, had wanted her to follow in the footsteps of her father and brothers and join the family business. Only Sara had no interest in stocks, bonds and finances or the kind of attention that came with such success. She'd almost reconsidered taking this job with SBS because of the attention it would bring. But from an early age she'd loved the outdoors and dogs, and this job was the way to follow her dreams.

She admired that Jose was of a same mind, and it made her reconsider her earlier thoughts that he was a lot like the men who'd orbited in her family's rarified circles. Their primary goal had been to take advantage of her family's success and connections to boost their way up the corporate ladder, but Jose was apparently trying to make his own way.

Jose shot a quick look in her direction, his gaze questioning.

"My family is…well-off," she said and left it at that. Let him draw his own conclusions about what that might mean and why she might not like it.

He did another quick peek at her and shrugged, but she

wasn't sure if it was a shrug of confusion or acceptance. Since he turned the discussion back to the property, she sat and patiently listened as he explained the history of the location and the various buildings on it.

"I think it's perfect. There are already kennels for the dogs, a training ring, and a small oval track that you could maybe convert to an obstacle course. I understand that's a thing," he said and paused, as if waiting for her to confirm his understanding.

"That's a thing. I love training dogs on the obstacles, especially the little ones," she said with a laugh.

Jose chuckled and pointed his thumb in the direction of Bongo, who sprawled across his back seat, drooling. "I imagine you need some activity with a dog as laid-back as Bongo."

Sara shook her head and likewise laughed. "Actually, bloodhounds were bred to track scents for hours so they like being active despite their laid-back look. I normally exercise Bongo a lot to keep her in shape for assignments."

"Hopefully this job won't be so crazy that you won't have time to do that," he said, and turned off the expressway onto a small road that ran through flat fields and scattered homes and farm buildings on either side of the narrow street.

"How did you get started with the dogs and search and rescue?" he asked.

"I just had an affinity for dogs and I loved the outdoors. I loved helping people, so it seemed like a natural way to go," she said and quickly added, "What about you? Why did you become a real estate agent?"

A look filled with joy entered his gaze as he said, "I remember the day my family moved into their first home. It was so special. My parents had worked so hard for it. And I love architecture. Like you, it seemed like a natural way to go."

A few miles down the road, Jose slowed near a wooden blue-and-white sign that read Florian Kennels.

The bright Florida sun and damp humidity had taken its toll on the sign over the years of abandonment. The colors had faded, and paint peeled here and there, exposing wood cracking from the elements.

She hoped the buildings and kennels wouldn't look as bad and was pleasantly surprised as they pulled up in front of a home and an assortment of other buildings.

HE'D BEEN TAKING a nap after tending to his garden earlier that day when the alarm tripped to warn that someone had come onto the property.

Since the fancy man's visit, he'd rigged a simple driveway alarm by the kennel sign so he would know when company was calling. The tall grasses there had made it easy to hide the device, especially since its green color blended in.

Grabbing a set of digital binoculars, he slipped on a long-sleeved camo shirt, snagged the remote for the surprise he'd installed the night before and headed through his fields to the hardwood hammock, careful to move silently through the woods to remain undetected.

He sneaked to the edge of the trees, crouched silently in the underbrush and raised his binoculars.

The man was back but with a woman this time who held the leash to a very large bloodhound.

A beautiful woman, he thought, and snapped off a few photos with the camera built into the binoculars.

He waited, patient, as the two and the dog entered the home, probably to inspect it.

It was a nice place. He'd visited a few times when the Florians had invited him to various events, but the home had reminded him of his mother too much. Made him too lonely and angry at the same time, so he avoided visiting. Luckily, he preferred his place with the peace and privacy that he needed for his games.

Barely half an hour later, the couple emerged, smiling, the bloodhound trailing after them. The couple unfortunately seemed satisfied that the home would be suitable for them.

He hadn't been happy about that possibility when he'd seen the man, but this woman...

He might be able to have some fun with her. If she survived that was.

Watching, he followed them through the binoculars as they walked through the kennels and training ring and then visited the remains of the old racing track and outbuildings.

Holding his breath as they neared the outbuildings, he waited, finger rubbing almost lovingly across the remote.

That's it, he thought. *Just a little closer.* "Almost there," he said out loud, and held the remote up to make sure nothing would interfere with the signal.

Chapter Three

"The place is in good shape. Just some cleaning, fresh paint and minor repairs," Jose said as he gestured Sara in the direction of the small track once used to train the greyhounds for racing.

They strolled toward the track and paused at the low white fence surrounding the oval.

"This will make a great course. There's plenty of room for the different obstacles," Sara said, and pointed to one spot. "I could see a nice long tunnel tucked against that far side," she said, knelt and rubbed Bongo's ears. "Right, Bongo?"

The dog let out a low woof and shook her head, sending her floppy ears and drool flying into the air.

Sara wiped some drool off her jeans and laughed. The sound sparkled in the quiet of what was becoming a sultry afternoon thanks to the Florida humidity and heat.

Jose joined in her laughter, enjoying her easygoing nature and lack of guile. It was refreshing after the women he'd been around where every action seemed intentional and planned. But he reminded himself that she worked for SBS, and getting involved with her meant being drawn closer to the family business.

When she stood, she grabbed hold of Bongo's leash and pointed toward the outbuildings several yards away.

"What are those used for?" she said.

Jose peered in their direction and shrugged. "I don't know.

I assume you can use them to store whatever equipment you'll need for the obstacle course," he said, and walked toward the outbuildings.

Sara and Bongo walked beside him, but he was only about ten feet away when something caught his attention. A strong smell. Like nail polish.

Something Trey had once said about a police raid on a meth lab ripped through his brain a second before a flash inside the outbuilding registered.

He wrapped Sara in his arms and hauled her to the ground as the outbuilding exploded, sending shards of glass and wood raining down on them.

Ears ringing and back stinging where shrapnel from the blast had torn into him, Jose slowly got to his feet and helped Sara to hers. Yards away, a fire was eating up one outbuilding and threatened to spread to the two nearby structures.

Bongo, who had apparently run off at the first hint of the blast, raced back to Sara's side.

"Are you okay?" he asked and peered from her to Bongo.

She nodded shakily. "I am thanks to you." Kneeling, she examined Bongo who had avoided any injuries.

Rising, brows knit together in worry, she said, "Are you okay?"

Jose looked back over his shoulder and winced at the sight of the blood leaking through the tears in his shirt. "Not really."

She raced around to examine his shoulder and gasped. "We need to get that cleaned up."

As another little explosion drew their attention, Jose said, "We need to stop that fire from spreading first. I saw a hose somewhere."

She nodded. "Back near the fence for the track," she said, and jerked a thumb in the direction of the old oval.

"I'll call for help," he said, and dialed 911.

They located the hose and water spigot and raced back to

the outbuildings to wet down the two nearby buildings to try to save them. Barely minutes after they had started, the sounds of sirens filled the air.

A fire truck pulled into the driveway followed by a police cruiser.

The firefighters spilled from their vehicle and raced to work, reeling out yards and yards of hose. As the firefighters approached, Sara and he stepped aside to let them extinguish the flames threatening the remaining structures.

While they walked back toward the house and driveway, two police officers strolled up to them. One officer pulled her notepad from her duty holster and took out a pen.

"Mr. Gonzalez? I'm Officer Rojas. This is my partner, Officer McAllister," she said, and flipped a hand in the direction of the older man.

Jose nodded. "This is Sara Hernandez. She's a new South Beach Security K-9 agent."

"Nice to meet you. Can you tell us what happened?" Officer McAllister said.

Jose half turned toward the outbuildings, which earned an immediate comment from Officer Rojas. "We need to call some EMTs to take a look at you." She immediately jumped on her radio to call for medical assistance.

Jose peered at his back again, grimacing at the throb of pain that traveled across his body as he did so. "*Gracias.* I appreciate it."

"You mentioned on the 911 call that there had been an explosion," Officer McAllister said.

"We were approaching the outbuildings when I smelled something like nail polish. I remembered my cousin Trey mentioning acetone and a meth lab. He used to be a cop."

Officer McAllister nodded. "Detective Gonzalez. I've heard about him, and acetone *is* used in meth labs."

"And it's highly flammable. When I saw a flash through the window of the building, I knew I had to act," Jose said.

AND HE HAD acted to protect her over himself, Sara thought, and glanced over at Jose's back where several bits of wood had torn into his flesh.

She grimaced at the pain he must be feeling and how much worse it might get once the adrenaline of the moment wore off.

Standing beside him, she offered what little info she could as the officers continued their questioning. They were just finishing up when a team of firefighters came by, hauling their hose back to the truck.

One of the firefighters walked over to them. "Looks like a meth lab, kind of."

Officer Rojas said, "Kind of? What does that mean?"

"There's definitely some beakers, what's left of rubber tubing, clamps and stuff, but if it was a meth lab, it was a small one," the firefighter said, and with a nod of his head, he walked off to join his crew as they packed up to leave.

A second later, an EMT truck pulled in followed almost immediately by an SBS SUV.

"If you don't mind, my partner and I want to take a look at the damage, and you should have the EMTs work on your back," Rojas said. With a jerk of her head in her partner's direction, they walked toward the outbuildings.

From beside her, she heard Jose mutter a curse as he caught sight of Trey and Mia walking toward them. Shooting a glance at him, she said, "What's wrong?"

"This is exactly why I never wanted to get involved in SBS business," he muttered, and took off in the direction of the EMT truck.

She followed, clicking her tongue to get Bongo, who had been resting at her feet, to follow her to Trey and Mia as they stood by Jose at the EMT truck.

"Are you okay, *primo*?" Trey asked as Jose sat on the back ledge of the truck while one of the EMTs cut off his shirt.

"You know how much this guayabera cost?" Jose said, and tugged at the front of the Cuban-style shirt that was made from expensive linen. She recognized the pricey fabric since her father and brothers had often had custom-made linen shirts.

"I'll buy you a new one, but I'm more worried about your back," Trey said, and gestured to where the EMT had grabbed hold of some forceps.

"He's got about four or five wood shards in his shoulder. It won't take long to get them out and clean up the wound," the EMT said as she tackled the first of the splinters.

"*Gracias a Dios* it's not that bad," Mia said, and laid a hand on Jose's uninjured shoulder, but he shrugged it off.

"Easy for you to say, Mia. It's not your shoulder," Jose groused, but his complaint lacked any real sting. Unlike the splinters piercing his skin. Jose winced as the EMT removed each one.

"You kept me safe," Sara said, her mind traveling back to that fateful second when he'd covered her body to protect her.

With a shrug that had the EMT admonishing him to keep still, Jose said, "You should be thanking Trey. It was a story he told one *Noche Buena* that made me react."

Sara was impressed with Jose downplaying his role. In her earlier life, the men she knew would have been only too eager to take credit for something like that to improve their position with her family.

"The one about the meth lab? Is that what the police say was back there?" Trey asked, and peered in the direction of the two officers who were walking around the burned and broken shell of the outbuilding.

"The firefighter said it was likely a small one," Sara said, which earned a scowl from Trey.

"They must have been using the property while it was

empty. Very few people come out this way normally," he said, and looked around as if to confirm it.

"Hopefully they'll be long gone now that we're here," Mia said, and quickly added, "But for now, you should stay in the penthouse until we can secure this place. You too, Jose. We want to make sure you're okay since you were hurt."

A fleeting look swept across Jose's face. A combination of anger and resignation that she immediately understood from their earlier conversation and his comment just moments before.

Jose hadn't wanted to get involved in his family's SBS business, but with this explosion, she suspected he had no choice but to go along with whatever was happening until he could gracefully extricate himself.

And she had to brace herself in case the explosion made more than the local news. If it did, she knew her mother would be calling, worried about her chosen profession and pressing for her to leave her career for a safer life with the family business.

CROUCHED LOW, he kept an eye on the police officers and people gathered around the back of the EMT truck.

His explosion had gone off just as he'd planned, only the dandy fellow had somehow realized what was happening and kept them from getting close enough to be killed, or at least, severely wounded. But he was satisfied that the dandy had gotten a taste of pain.

It was all about the pain. The more he inflicted the less he felt it himself. It was what kept him going along with the belief that he was putting these women out of their misery and sending them to a better life. Ending the pain of their pitiful existences.

And these people weren't going to stop him.

As the police and EMTs left, the others lingered for only a few short minutes before heading to their vehicles.

He watched with satisfaction as the dandy got into the SBS SUV together with a man who had to be a relative. The resemblance couldn't be denied although from the looks of it this man was a warrior. The beautiful woman and the dog got into the vehicle with them while another gorgeous woman slipped into the pricey Italian SUV.

Having the men around was a problem.

Having the women around…

Well, that could be quite exciting, he thought, reconsidering just what he would be doing on this property.

But he had to be ready for them just like he would be for any hunt. And he had to protect his garden and hunting grounds at any cost. Any.

This group would soon find out that he wasn't someone to be messed with, and while he was busy showing them that, he intended to have his fun.

Chapter Four

It had been a surprisingly silent ride back to Brickell Avenue and the South Beach Security building.

Jose had expected Trey to pepper both him and Sara with questions about the explosion and the property, but he hadn't said much other than to ask how they were feeling.

"Achy," Sara said, making Jose feel immediately guilty.

"I didn't mean to tackle you so hard," he said, regretful about possibly injuring her.

"No need to apologize. You kept me from being hurt. How's the shoulder feeling?" she said, and leaned forward to see his face as he answered.

He turned slightly to meet her gaze and couldn't control the grimace of pain as he did so. "Tender, but it'll heal," he said, trying to downplay the injury, especially in front of Trey, who'd experienced far worse injuries during his service as a marine and a detective.

"I'll look at it in the penthouse. Wounds like that can be tricky," Trey said with a quick peek in his direction.

"Sure," he said, nodding as Trey pulled into the parking lot for the SBS building. Seconds later, Mia parked Jose's SUV right next to them.

"Sophie and Robbie are in the penthouse so we can discuss security at the location. Ricky will be coming by later—"

"Because you think we need some therapy to deal with our near-death experience?" Jose challenged.

With a reluctant nod, Trey said, "It might help to talk to Ricky."

Jose sucked in a breath to bite back another angry reply because underneath it all, he knew Trey was truly worried about them. "I appreciate it, but it's not necessary. For that matter, I'm not sure I'm really needed to discuss security and whatever else is happening at the property," Jose said as he felt himself being inextricably pulled into the SBS family business.

THERE WAS NO mistaking the mix of reluctance and anger spilling off Jose, and given their earlier discussion on the way to the kennels, Sara understood.

"I'm sure Jose would be better off going home and getting some rest," Sara said, not wanting to pressure Jose into something he clearly didn't want to do.

"Pepe does need rest, but we also have to find out as much as we can about what happened today. Plus he probably knows more about the history of the location than the rest of us, so it would be good to have him around until this all gets resolved. Isn't that right, *primo*?" Trey said, and eyeballed Jose in challenge.

Jose literally squirmed in his chair and was saved from answering as Mia rapped her knuckles on the passenger-side window.

"I'll meet you upstairs," she said, and pointed a perfectly manicured index finger upward before hurrying away while she took a call.

"We should go. The sooner we chat with Sophie and Robbie, the quicker they can work on a security plan for the location and the sooner you both can get some rest up in the penthouse," Trey said as he exited the car, brooking no disagreement.

But Jose delayed, making Sara say, "I'm sorry. I know you didn't want to get sucked into your family's business."

"I don't but Trey is right. I'm the one with the 411 on the

property, although it might help to talk to the prior owners also," Jose said, and opened his door, clearly going along with Trey's plan despite his reluctance.

She followed his lead, left the SBS SUV, and Bongo jumped out beside her. They walked into the SBS building, badged themselves in, and over to the elevators that would take them up to the penthouse level that the agency used for clients' overnight stays or when one of their staff worked a late night or needed lodging, like she did.

"Hopefully we can get through the business quickly and get some dinner," Trey said, and used his badge in the elevator to unlock access to the topmost floor.

"That would be great," Jose said, but everything about his body language told a different story.

Jose had his hands clasped in front of him and he rocked back and forth slightly, obviously on edge.

The elevator swept straight up to the penthouse floor since it was well past the time when most people would be heading home at the end of the day. On the topmost floor, the doors opened into the luxurious suite that SBS was lending to her until the kennel owner's home was ready.

His cousins Sophie and Robbie, the SBS tech gurus, were setting the table in the expansive open space while Mia removed dishes from a large box. As she did so, the earthy aromas of beans mingled with the citrusy and garlicky scent of roast pork.

"Smells great," Jose said as he walked in and did a slow turn to examine the space. "Place looks great. You've furnished it nicely."

Sara had assumed that Jose would have been in the penthouse before, but clearly not. "It's very…" She hesitated, struggling to find the right word.

"Luxurious. Decadent. Over-the-top?" Jose said with a boyish grin.

"Definitely more than what I'm used to. Log cabin is more my style," she replied with a chuckle. She'd left luxuries like this behind when she'd opted not to join her family's successful business.

Trey stood next to them with his hands on his hips, also perusing the space. With a shrug, he said, "We like to be comfortable here."

"Especially since we use it when we need a place to chill," Mia said as she walked over and hugged Jose. "Sorry you were hurt, *primo*."

"I'LL BE FINE," Jose said, unable to say more, considering Mia had been shot months earlier during one of the SBS cases and had nearly died. His injuries couldn't even compare, making him feel lacking as he so often did around his SBS cousins.

Sophie and Robbie walked over then and likewise offered their regrets.

"Once the place is secure, we'll hopefully keep anything else from happening," said Sophie. Robbie and Sophie's mom was his dad's baby sister.

"I'm sure you will," he said, well aware that Sophie and Robbie had inherited the technological smarts that made their parents top NSA operatives.

"We will," Robbie said, and shook his hand before dipping his head and smiling in Sara's direction.

It was definitely a look of interest, which surprised Jose. Computer nerd Robbie had always struck him as asexual, so this was a new side to his cousin. On top of that, an unexpected pang of something reared up as well. He couldn't call it jealousy because he didn't really know much about Sara yet, although he liked what he did know.

"Maybe we should get to work," he said because the sooner they did, the sooner he might get some rest and maybe even make an exit despite his cousins' wishes he stay overnight.

"Dinner first! I'm starved!" Robbie said, and wrung his hands eagerly.

"You're always starved," his baby sister Sophie said with a roll of her eyes, dragging chuckles from everyone in the room.

Jose followed Mia to the island separating the kitchen from the rest of the open space and was about to help her finish unpacking the dishes when Trey stepped out of a nearby room holding a sweatshirt.

Trey handed it to him and said, "This might be better than what's left of your guayabera."

He shot a look at his bloodied shirt and the cuts the EMT had made at his shoulder so he could clean and dress the injury. "You're not wrong," he said, and gestured with the sweatshirt toward the nearby room. "I'll be back in a second."

He hurried to the room, a well-appointed bedroom, shut the door, took off his shirt and shrugged on the sweatshirt, grimacing as the motion pulled at the wounds in his shoulder.

Muttering a curse, he walked back out to the kitchen and helped Mia uncover the last of the dishes they'd ordered. As he did so, Mia said, "We got these from our local Cuban place. I think you like it too, right?"

The restaurant Mia had chosen was located halfway between his cousin's office building and Jose's real estate company's home base.

"It's a good place and I like supporting local," he said, and placed a large dish of black beans next to a heaping plate of white rice.

"Local is always good," Sara said, and helped them uncover the rest of the dishes while Sophie, Robbie and Trey set the table. She must have fed Bongo since the dog had her head buried in a large dish and was busy chowing down.

In no time they had served themselves buffet-style and sat around the table, enjoying the food. Bongo lay nearby, her large head pillowed on equally large paws. Long ears flowed over her paws to almost carpet the floor.

"This is delicious. My mom would approve," Sara said as she forked up some roast pork.

"Your mom is Cuban?" Jose asked, wanting to know more about her.

"*Mami* is Cuban. *Papi* is about as Irish as you can get," she said, and faked a brogue as she tacked on, "Hails from County Clare."

Which possibly explained the hints of red in her golden-brown hair, like cinnamon dusted on hot chocolate. It could also explain the shards of green in her unique gray-blue eyes and the smattering of freckles across the bridge of her nose.

And oh damn, he was paying too much attention to her, he thought, and looked away as he ate some of the rice and beans.

"Tasty," he echoed, and decided to get to business in the hopes of making a speedy exit despite his cousin's desire that he stay overnight. "What are your plans for securing the place?"

Sophie shot him a puzzled look, clearly surprised by his question. "You want to know?"

With a shrug he regretted as pain flared in his shoulder, he said, "I'd feel more comfortable knowing Sara will be safe at the kennels. Especially after what happened today."

"We agree, Pepe. Sara won't be living there until we feel it's safe," Trey said, and lifted his chin in Sophie's direction, as if to prompt her to continue.

Sophie did so with a quick nod. "We can run through our plans *after* dinner."

"We also have a crew coming in tomorrow to clean, especially in the kennels. There are a lot of weeds and leaves that have piled up there over the years. The training ring also, although it wasn't as bad," Mia said.

"No, it wasn't. But I'd like to get some new artificial turf in there for better cushioning and footing if the budget allows," Sara said, and delicately picked up a piece of fried yuca to eat like a french fry.

The crunchiness of the yuca had him grabbing a piece, which he swirled through some citrusy mojo sauce before taking a bite.

"Will you need that surfacing for the obstacle course too?" Jose asked.

SARA NODDED AND popped the last of the yuca fry in her mouth. Hastily swallowing, she said, "That surface would be good for the obstacle course. That is if you want to have that kind of training at the location."

Mia and Trey shot a quick look at each other before Trey said, "Whatever you want or need, Sara. We told you that when we hired you. We want this to be a first-class facility for our people and if you'd like, for anyone who wants to have their K-9s trained."

"But the first thing to do is get it secured," Mia said, which had everyone around the table murmuring their agreement.

"For sure," Trey said, and looked at Sophie and Robbie. "I'd love to hear more about your plans *after* we finish dinner."

It was clear to Sara that Trey wanted the rest of dinner to be business-free. She had no doubt Jose wanted to finish the business part and rush out the door, but Trey clearly had other plans. Because she wanted to know more about the family in general, she said, "How long have you all been working together?"

The cousins peered at each other before Trey said, "I just joined the agency several months ago. Like Pepe, I avoided being part of SBS for a long time, but when they helped Roni—"

"Your new wife?" Sara asked.

Trey nodded. "We weren't married at the time. She was

a Miami PD detective and SBS helped us during a difficult case. I realized the good the agency does and that it was time to help out."

Mia added, "I was pretty much the same. My cousin Carolina and I were doing well as social influencers, but I felt like I needed to do more. Carolina and I still do some gigs, but SBS truly feels like home now."

Interesting, Sara thought before glancing in the direction of the other cousins. "What about you two?"

Sophie and Robbie shared a quick glance. "Our parents are with the NSA and were hoping that we'd follow them there right after college, but we had other ideas."

"Like creating some games and things at first, but like Trey and Mia, we eventually realized the good that SBS does," Robbie added.

Beside her Jose squirmed a little, understandably so. Feeling his discomfort, she said, "Not everyone's path is the same. My family has a successful financial company, but I preferred to go my own way especially after my family had some problems that made the news."

"You're talking about your dad?" Trey said.

It didn't surprise her that Trey knew. He'd probably researched her and her family before offering her the position. "Yes, my dad. He was accused of embezzling but was cleared. That didn't matter to the press. It's why I avoid that kind of publicity."

"It's not easy to do. We understand why Pepe steers clear of us," Trey said, and risked a quick glance at his cousin.

"It's not you, *primo*. It's the danger you're always in. We can't all be action heroes," Jose said, and there was no denying the anger and frustration in his voice.

"No, we can't, and we will try to free you from this as soon as possible," Mia said, her tone mirroring Trey's.

"Good. I'd appreciate that," Jose said, and dug into his food with some force, his fork scratching the plate beneath.

The exchange of words cast a pall over the meal, and silence fell over the table until the plates were empty.

"I'll clean so you can get started," Mia said, and sprang out of her chair.

"I'll help," Jose said.

Trey laid a hand on his uninjured shoulder and said, "No need. You should rest after that injury."

"I'll be fine," he said, and shot to his feet, but Sara caught the slight wince as he did so.

She helped as they all cleaned off the table, put away what was left of the takeout and Trey prepped a large pot of coffee.

In no time the table was clear, and Sophie and Robbie had popped open their laptops to demonstrate what they planned to do.

Sophie turned on the large television on the opposite wall of the room, and a second later an image from one of the laptops filled the screen: a satellite view of the kennels.

"If you're ready, we'll get started," Robbie said, and with a few keystrokes a dotted line appeared along the edges of the woods behind the main buildings on the property.

With a laser pointer, Sophie highlighted the line on the screen. "As we mentioned before, perimeter cameras should work here like they did at the *Buena Suerte* stables a few months back. I'm not sure we need security guards working the area at this time."

"I agree," Trey said, and gestured for Robbie to continue.

"We can place a driveway alarm on the new sign you plan on putting in," he said, and an X showed up by the entrance to mark the location of the alarm.

"Sounds good so far," Trey commented, and Robbie switched to a view that displayed the owner's home, kennels, training ring and outbuildings.

"For the house, glass break, entry and motion sensors as well as hazard sensors for smoke, fire and water leaks. Sirens, of course," Sophie said.

"Of course," Jose muttered beneath his breath, but Sophie pushed on with her suggestions.

"We'll also have security cameras and floodlights positioned to monitor the area around the house, kennels and training ring."

She stopped and glanced at Trey and seemingly knew what he was about to ask since she said, "We can get the house done tomorrow. The other locations will take a few days."

"Good. How about prepping the house so Sara can live there?" he asked Mia.

"As I mentioned before, we have a cleaning crew scheduled in the a.m. The house first and then the other areas," Mia replied and then continued. "Painters are coming tomorrow and once they're done, I'll call for the delivery of the furniture Sara and I selected."

"It seems like you've thought of everything," Sara said, grateful for their thoroughness in getting the location ready for her.

"We've tried. I just wish we'd thought about any possible dangers on the property before sending the two of you there unprotected," Trey said, regret in his voice.

"You couldn't have known," Jose said, his earlier anger and frustration missing.

"*Gracias*, for that, Pepe. It was probably a freak explosion, but we should have checked everything at an abandoned location like the kennels. From now on, we don't assume anything. We take every step as if we're on a case. Understood?" Trey said, and peered around the table at everyone.

Chapter Five

"Understood," Jose said half-heartedly, echoing what everyone else said and surprising Sara with his agreement.

With that decided, Mia, Sophie and Robbie went off to work while Trey hung back with her and Jose. "I want to take a look at that shoulder."

"What about Ricky? When will he psychoanalyze us?" Jose said with an arch of a brow.

Trey tightened his lips into a thin slash. "It didn't sound like you were too keen on talking, so I asked him to come by another night."

"You called him off?" Jose said, anger surging to the forefront at his cousin's controlling actions.

"Isn't that what you wanted?" Trey challenged.

Sara felt as if she was watching two rams in rut going after each other and so did Bongo, who raised her head in response to the vibes. Sara stepped in to lower the temperature of the discussion. "We appreciate that, Trey. I know I'd like to get some rest, and I'm sure Jose feels the same way. Right?"

Her words had the desired effect as the tension in their bodies melted before her eyes and Bongo laid her head back down on her paws.

"I'd like to get some rest. Maybe after you take a look at my shoulder, Trey," Jose said to further defuse the situation.

Trey nodded. "Sure thing. I have some first aid things in

the bathroom," he said, and motioned in the direction of the room where she had been staying.

Because of that, she trailed after the two men to make sure she hadn't left anything too personal out in the bedroom or bathroom.

Luckily all was in order as the two men hurried into the bathroom where Jose peeled off the sweatshirt, revealing a nicely sculpted chest and lean six-pack abs.

Heat ignited in her core. There was no denying Jose was a very attractive man but at this point in her life, she wasn't interested. Her entire focus was on getting this K-9 center up and running. Nothing else, she thought, but couldn't pull her eyes away as Jose turned so that Trey could inspect his injuries.

"The EMT did a good job. There's a little swelling, but it should go down soon. I'll check again in the morning," he said and continued. "I keep some sweats and things in the other bedroom you can use tonight. I'll bring by more clothes for you in the morning."

"I'd rather head home tonight," Jose said, but Trey shook his head.

"And I'd rather we kept an eye on you until we know there are no other repercussions from the explosion," Trey insisted.

Jose hesitated, clearly not happy, but then relented and nodded. "Fine. I'd appreciate you getting some things from my condo," Jose said, and thankfully jerked the sweatshirt back on, hiding that too tempting masculinity from her gaze. Once he had done that, he reached into his pants pocket, took out some keys and handed them to Trey.

"We'll be at work for a while on the security details, but you can call me at any time if you need something," Trey said, and waved his cell phone in the air in emphasis.

"Anytime?" Jose said with an arch of a dark brow.

"Anytime. I am always here for you, Pepe," Trey said, and with that he rushed from the room, leaving the two of them standing there in awkward silence. Staring at each other through the reflection in the bathroom mirror.

"He sure knows how to make me feel guilty," Jose said, and faced her.

"I don't think that was his intent," Sara said, feeling as if she'd stepped into a minefield of family dynamics.

"Probably not. Trey has always been up front but that doesn't change how I feel whenever I'm around this side of the family," Jose admitted with a stilted shrug.

Not that she wanted to play psychologist like Ricky, but she wanted to know why this seemingly successful and handsome man had such issues with his cousins.

"How do they make you feel?" she asked as they walked out of the bathroom and back into the living room area.

Jose whirled to face her, a surprised look on his face. "You really want to know?"

She nodded. "I do. If I'm going to be working with them and you, I'd like to know what makes the Gonzalez family tick."

Jose shook his head and chuckled. "It may take all night."

"Then maybe I should get us some drinks," she said, jumped to her feet and walked to the wet bar at one side of the room.

Jose tossed out his selection as he settled himself on the couch. "Scotch over ice, if there is any, *por favor.*"

There was definitely scotch, top shelf at that, as well as several bottles of other high-quality liquors. The Gonzalez family didn't skimp on anything for themselves or their guests.

She poured two fingers of scotch into a highball glass with ice and then a glass of wine from a bottle she'd opened the day before. She walked to the sofa, handed Jose the glass and sat opposite him in a large comfy chair.

He raised the glass and said, "To the new K-9 center."

Tapping her glass against his, she said, "To working together."

His lips quirked into a twisted smile as he said, "For now."

It bothered her he was in such a rush to leave, not that she should be bothered. After all, she barely knew him and yet... She wanted to know him better. He had possibly saved her life after all.

"For now," she echoed and pushed on. "So tell me. How do your cousins make you feel?"

A sharp blast of laughter escaped him. "Seriously?" he challenged and sipped his scotch.

"Seriously," she said, and cocked her head to peer at him, not wanting to miss any nuance of his answer.

He tilted his head from side to side, as if searching for an answer. But then the words burst from his mouth in a rush. "Guilty. Sad. Needy. Inferior."

"Wow," shot from her mouth before she could control it.

Jose shook his head and murmured. "*Sí*, wow. A lot to unfold, right?"

Since he'd shared and she got where he was coming from, she said, "I feel the same way sometimes. Guilty that I didn't go into the family business. Sad that they don't get me. Definitely inferior since I'm not hauling in some six or maybe even seven figure salary."

"But you're doing something you love, which means way more than money," Jose said.

Sara barked out a laugh. "Tell that to my bank account."

Jose leaned toward her, glass cradled between his hands. "Seriously, Sara. It does mean more, and you know it."

This close, she could see the rays of green in his amazing blue eyes and the dark stubble of an evening beard along the strong line of his jaw. As his gaze locked with hers, her stomach did a little flip-flop, and she took a sip of her wine to settle it.

"I know it does and so do you. It's why you have your own business instead of working with SBS."

"Well, that and the bullets," he teased and sat back.

She got it. Her dive into the family history before taking

the job had warned about how risky SBS business could be in more ways than one. The bullets, of course, but also the regular exposure to the limelight with both their cases and the scrutiny that came from being that well-known. Such scrutiny had almost destroyed her family. But that worry hadn't stopped her from the opportunity of a lifetime. All she had to do was stick to her job and not get too involved with the Gonzalez family.

Or Jose, the little voice in her head warned.

"I was sad to leave my family in New Jersey, but I knew it was the right thing to do."

"Do you miss them? You're a long way from home," Jose said.

She nodded. "I do, but I'll go home for Thanksgiving in a few weeks, and I have some cousins in Miami. I'll visit them once I get settled."

"Because family is important," he said, sadness evident in the tone of his voice.

"Why does that seem to make you sad?" she asked.

He ripped his gaze from her to peer down into his glass as if it held the answer. With another awkward shake of his head, he said, "I sometimes wish I did want to be part of SBS. Work with them. Understand why they do what they do."

"Now's your chance." The words escaped her before she could bite them back.

Chapter Six

A chance? Jose wondered, and the words echoed in his brain, on and on and on. A chance he'd never wanted to take, only he'd promised his Tio Ramon he would help. But this woman presented another level of risk that had him reconsidering so much.

With a dip of his head in a semi-nod, he said, "I did sell them the property after all."

"You did," she said, and raised her glass in a toast.

"I will help you get the place ready. I know some good contractors who can assist with any work that needs to be done, like the new surfaces in the training ring and obstacle course."

She smiled, seemingly pleased that he'd remembered. "Help with the surfaces would be greatly appreciated."

He grinned and nodded. "A good real estate agency always remembers what a client wants."

Her smile faded, which made him quickly add, "Not that you're just a client."

"I'm not sure how to take that right now, but I'll assume it's a good thing," she said, and her smile brightened a bit.

"It's a good thing," he replied although he was still uncertain about what he was feeling around her. She was attractive, but not his usual type. Smart. SBS only hired the best, and he had to assume she fell into that category. Compassionate and maybe that came from dealing with animals and sensing what was going on without words being spoken. Or maybe it was because of what had happened with her father and the scrutiny she'd had to survive.

But as their gazes locked and his gut tightened with a very physical sign of desire, confusion erupted again about what was going on between them.

He shot to his feet and drew Bongo's attention with the sudden movement.

"I'm going to call it a night," he said.

She gave the dog a hand gesture, as if to reassure Bongo all was fine, and slowly came to her feet. "Good night, then. I'm going to take Bongo for a walk before we turn in."

"I'll go with. It's not as busy in this area at night, and I'd rather you didn't go alone," he said, and even though it was the truth, it was also in part that despite his earlier words, he wasn't ready to leave her just yet.

"*Gracias.* I'd appreciate that until I'm more familiar with the city," she said, and signaled to Bongo.

At the door, she grabbed a leash she'd set on an entry table and clipped it on. Using her security badge, she opened the elevator doors.

"Who else has a badge besides Trey?" he asked.

"Only Trey and Mia, and they've been really good about respecting my privacy after hours."

Good to know, while also being a challenge that the two of them were here alone with complete privacy.

Not that he was a hookup on the first date guy. Not that this was a date, which made him wonder what it would be like to take her on a date.

They rode down to street level, cleared the security desk in the main lobby and strolled out to Brickell Avenue.

MUCH LIKE JOSE had said, the area was not as busy as it had been during the day, Sara thought. "I guess this is mostly a business area?"

"Mostly although there are some residential buildings farther up," he said, and walked beside her and Bongo, matching his longer stride to hers. He'd tucked his hands into the pockets of his dress pants, which were smudged with dirt and grass from when they'd hit the ground earlier that day. Which reminded her of his injuries.

"How's the shoulder?"

"A little tender but getting better. How about you? Still achy?"

She had been sore immediately after the blast, but like him, the aftereffects were passing. "Better. Not so bad, but I suspect I may have a few bruises in the morning."

A wry smile crept across his lips. "You and me both. Hopefully tomorrow won't be as eventful as today."

"Hopefully," she said as Bongo sniffed at a spot on the curb and then paused to relieve herself.

She pulled out a poop bag but as she bent to clean up the mess, Jose said, "Let me."

He took the bag from her, secured the waste and tied the bag.

"*Gracias.* You didn't have to," she said as they walked back toward the SBS building.

"Not a problem. I do it for my *mami* all the time when we walk her dog," he said but held the bag gingerly, clearly not a fan.

Much like she wasn't much of a fan of being lumped in with his mother, who she assumed was a wonderful lady. It was as bad or maybe worse than being friend-zoned. Mom-zoned. So not good even though it was way too early to be thinking of him like that. Or maybe not too early as an image of him bare-chested filled her brain.

He dumped the bag in a trash can at the sidewalk's edge, they entered the lobby, cleared security, and went up to the penthouse. Once there, she unclipped Bongo's leash but her dog remained close, obviously uncomfortable with Jose, although bloodhounds were generally not protective.

Jose seemed uneasy around the dog since he kept some distance between them once they were in the center of the large living space.

"I guess this is good-night. Get some rest," he said, and with an awkward wave, he rushed off but then stopped as he neared her bedroom door.

"I never got where I'm supposed to sleep," he said sheepishly.

Sara pointed down the hall. "There are two bedrooms farther down. The spare clothes that Trey mentioned are in the one right past mine."

"Great," he said and walked off, leaving her alone in the immense space with Bongo.

She knelt and rubbed the dog's ears. "He's a good guy, Bongo. No need to worry," she said, and reached into her jeans pocket to pull out a treat for her dog.

Bongo quickly took the treat, leaving slobber all over her hand. She laughed and shook her head. "You are drooly, but you're my drooly baby. Let's get some sleep."

She signaled to Bongo who followed her into the bedroom where she'd set up a big circular dog bed for the bloodhound. As soon as she closed the door, Bongo went to the bed, circled around a time or two, and finally lay down, satisfied that everything was fine.

Except, of course, for the fact that Sara had nearly gotten blown up and still had a little soreness from being hauled to the ground. Soreness that a nice hot shower would help.

She went into the bathroom and turned on the hot water in the shower. Water spewed from not only a rain shower feature, but from the side walls and as she stepped in, the heat of the water soothed the physical remnants of the explosion.

The emotional remnants would be harder to handle.

She could have died. Jose could have died.

Jose had saved her life. Jose who didn't think he could be an action hero like his cousin Trey, and yet he had been just that this afternoon.

He was complex, she told herself while she showered, running soapy hands across her body, lingering at the tender spots.

Unfortunately, he was also a lot like the men she'd grown up with. Privileged and pampered. Part of the SBS family, no matter how much he denied it. Getting involved with him meant being more involved with the family, which had its own issues. But despite that, he was intriguing her more than he should.

But she reminded herself that he was only there because of a sense of obligation to his family. Once he finished doing whatever they expected of him, he'd be gone just like the boyfriend she'd had when her father had been accused of the embezzling. He'd run at the first hint of trouble.

That was a good thing to remember, she told herself as she let the heat of the water calm her jumbled thoughts about Jose.

When she finally left the shower, peace had settled over her. She slipped into her pajamas and bed, but as soon as she climbed beneath the sheets, her phone rang.

Her mother was calling.

She was tempted to ignore it, but knew she'd only keep on calling.

"*Hola, mami,*" she said.

"*Hola*, Sara. Your *Tia* Rosario called—"

Tia Rosario who was a terrible gossip and had likely seen the news about the explosion on the local Miami news. "I'm okay, *mami*. It was nothing big."

"It was an explosion, *mi'ja*. I thought this work was supposed to be safer than the search and rescue you were doing," she said.

"It is. It will be. Not to worry," she said, and quickly tacked on the one thing she knew would placate her mother. "I can't wait to see you in a few weeks for Thanksgiving."

Her mother's harrumph burst across the line, but she'd been mollified by Sara's words. "See you soon, *mi'ja*. Love you."

"I love you too, *mami*," she said, and swiped to end the call.

She flipped on the television to relax, lay back onto the pillows and sleep slowly claimed her. But with sleep came unexpected dreams about Jose until the chirp of her phone warned it was time to start the day.

She brushed her teeth and hair, dressed quickly and rushed out to make a pot of coffee, but Jose had beaten her to it.

He stood by the counter, bare-chested in sweats that hung loosely on his lean hips.

When he saw her, he ran a hand through the rumpled locks of his hair and beamed her a smile. *"Buenos dias."*

And damn, she had to admit that waking to him there was definitely a good start to the day.

JOSE UNLOCKED THE door to the owner's home and did a quick look around the empty interior on the first floor as Mia, Sara, Bongo and a trio of cleaning people followed him inside.

A fine layer of dust covered everything along with some dirt on the floor. The air smelled musty, a testament to how long the home had been empty.

"The owners renovated about ten years ago to create this open space and a half bath," he said, easily slipping into real-estate-agent mode to describe the spacious ground floor, which was relatively clean considering it had been vacant for nearly three years.

"There is also a home office on the other side of this floor, a large, finished basement with a playroom and workshop downstairs, and three bedrooms upstairs with two bathrooms. They're not as updated as this area," he said with a wave toward the stairs.

Mia jammed her hands on her hips and did a quick look

around the space. "This is a nice layout. Maybe we should start upstairs?" she said, and turned to the cleaning crew.

"Makes sense since we may track dirt through this area as we clean," replied an older woman with the cleaners. She gestured to the other two women to head upstairs, leaving him alone with Sara, Mia and Bongo, who sniffed around the edges of the room.

He held the keys to the home up in the air. "I guess you should get these. There are three keys to the front door. They also open the back door. You might want to change out the locks, though."

Mia nodded and took the keys. "That's a good idea. I'll call someone to come in today."

"*Gracias*, for everything," Sara said. She laid a hand on his arm and smiled.

"*De nada*. I'm sure the two of you have things to—"

A bloodcurdling scream cut through the air and echoed in the emptiness of the home's rooms.

One of the cleaners, a young woman barely out of her teens, ran down the stairs, stumbling so badly on the last one that Jose had to reach out to stop her from face-planting onto the floor.

"*Brujeria,*" the young girl said, seemingly worried about witchcraft, and glanced back up the stairs as the older woman came down carrying a garbage bag filled with something.

"It was a few doves. A Santeria sacrifice probably. Nothing to worry about," she explained, and hurried out the door.

Jose was a little freaked out about the sacrifice but even more worried about the fact that someone had had the time inside the house to do it. "It's a good thing Sophie and Robbie will be securing this place," he said, and gave his attention to the young cleaning girl.

"*No te preocupes. Todo estará bien,*" he said, telling the young woman not to worry just as her boss returned and commanded her to go back to work with a sharp jerk of her head.

The girl timidly went along, but not before shooting him a look mixed with gratefulness and fear.

"Sophie and Robbie should be here soon," Mia said and as if they'd heard her, his cousins entered with a duo of the SBS techs.

Sophie and Robbie came over to hug them all—family always came first even on a job—and then Sophie asked, "Is the cleaning crew here?"

Mia gestured with a perfectly manicured finger in Barbie-pink. "Upstairs."

Sophie nodded. "We'll start on this floor and then outside. We'll be done by the end of the day."

"Great. I'll feel better knowing this place is secured," Sara said, and signaled Bongo back to her side since the bloodhound had drifted toward the back of the kitchen with her sniffing.

Bongo hurried back and dutifully sat at Sara's side. The dog's head nearly reached Sara's waist, making Jose wonder how she controlled such a large animal, but clearly she was the boss, sparking admiration for her skills and that dangerous curl of interest again.

"Maybe we should tour the rest of the grounds so we can see what else needs to be done," he said, needing space. Despite the stale air inside the home, Sara's clean and flowery scent had drifted over to him, making him want to bury his head in the sensitive crook of her neck to see if it was either her skin or the waves of silky hair that smelled so good.

"That's a great idea," Sara said, and almost raced out of the house.

Mia shot him a wondering look and he shrugged, trying to play it cool as he held his hand out and urged Mia to follow Sara.

SARA SUCKED IN a deep breath, clearing out the dank smell inside the home and thoughts of what else besides doves might have been inside the garbage bag the cleaning woman had brought out and tossed by the back of her crew's van.

Being part Cuban, she heard about Santeria, and her mother had on more than one occasion done something that hinted to at least a passing belief in some things, like leaving a tasty treat for a patron saint during the holidays. But sacrifices were a whole different thing and the fact that someone had done it in the house...

She shuddered and hoped there wouldn't be more unwelcome surprises.

"You okay?" Jose said, and laid a comforting hand on her shoulder.

She nodded shakily. "Not a fan of animal sacrifice."

"I get it, but as awful as we think it is, it could have been done for good reasons. Maybe to help heal someone," he said, trying to relieve her worries.

"Still not a fan," Sara said, and Mia echoed her reaction. "Totally agree. Not a fan."

"Let's check out the rest of the grounds," Jose said.

"Let's," she concurred and glanced at Mia to see if she intended to join them.

"I'm going to hang back here in case Sophie and Robbie need anything or the painters arrive early," Mia said.

"Sounds good, *prima*. We won't be long," Jose said, and gestured for her to lead the way.

"I want to measure the training ring first since that's the most important thing for now," she said, then clicked her tongue to get Bongo moving and walked toward the building directly opposite the former kennel owner's home. As she did so, she caught sight of Trey who was directing a cleaning crew in the area.

Something pulled her in that direction, and she motioned to the kennels and said, "Do you mind if we check first?"

"Not at all. Whatever you need," Jose said, surprising her

with his willingness considering how opposed he had been to helping his SBS family.

When they arrived, the cleaners were armed with rakes and brooms to clear out the debris in the enclosures where the dogs would be housed.

A man entered an enclosure and raked the leaves when a loud clang rang out in the empty kennels and was chased by his cry of alarm.

The man stepped back with the rake or rather, what was left of the rake as the head of it had been snapped off.

Trey urged the man aside so that Jose and she could see what had happened.

A large bear trap had bitten off the bottom of the rake. Fear shivered through her at what the trap might have done if the man had stepped into it.

"So not good," she murmured.

"Totally agree," Trey said, and then called out to the cleaning crew.

"Everyone please clear out until we can confirm it's safe in here."

"Are you worried about more traps?" Jose asked, face set in harsh lines.

Trey nodded. "There's no reason for a trap like that to be in here."

"Or for that Santeria offering to be in the house," Sara said.

"What offering?" Trey asked, worry coloring his tones.

"Some doves in one of the upstairs bedrooms," Jose said, and waved a hand in the direction of the house.

Trey shook his head. "This is not right. We need to get everyone out of there," he said and took a step toward the house, but then a loud bang erupted from a chimney on the exterior wall of the house and smoke billowed into the air.

Chapter Seven

Before Jose's eyes the chimney crumbled, bricks raining down on the overgrown grass beside the house.

A second later, Mia, Sophie, Robbie and their crews raced out of the house, thankfully uninjured.

Trey and Sara took off in their direction, Bongo loping behind them, ears flapping.

Jose paused for a moment, frozen by shock, followed by his mind asking *Why?*

Why was this happening, he thought as he likewise rushed across the yard to where everyone had gathered outside the home.

Mia, Trey and Sara had peered at the pile of bricks that had once been the chimney. Sophie and Robbie drifted over after apparently giving their crew some instructions as they walked to the SBS vehicle.

He joined them and said, "I'm assuming this wasn't some kind of freak accident again."

Trey knelt and peered intently at the ruined chimney. He pointed to a blackened area close to the ground. "That's where the clean-out door for the ash dump would be. They probably put the bomb in there knowing it would take out most of the support for the chimney."

"If it was a bomb, does the same go for the outbuilding that blew up?" Jose said, still trying to grasp that someone was working real hard to hurt them.

Trey slowly rose and faced them. "I'm going to call my contacts at the police department. See if they have anything else on that outbuilding explosion."

"HOOWEE," HE MUTTERED in low tones as he delighted in the destruction he'd wrought.

A pile of bricks was all that remained of the chimney, and he had to admit that he hadn't thought the small bomb he'd placed there could do so much damage.

He'd only intended that and his other little surprises to scare them off but if the looks on their faces said anything, it was that they had no intention of leaving.

Muttering a curse beneath his breath, he took a last look at the group gathered around the ruined chimney.

He was going to have to up his game with this crew, he thought, and skulked away back through the hardwood hammock, careful to hide his trail as he did so.

ALTHOUGH THE EXPLOSION had taken out the chimney, it had surprisingly done minimal damage inside the home.

To make sure there weren't any more surprises waiting for them, Trey had done a careful inspection of the home with Sara and Bongo trailing after him. Besides being great at search and rescue, Bongo had received basic training in locating explosives and cadavers and would hopefully pick up on any other dangers in the home.

After declaring it safe, the cleaning crew returned along with Sophie, Robbie and their team.

While the tech team secured the location, the rest of the team, including Jose, gathered on the first floor.

They all had their serious faces on, especially Jose whose arms were tucked tight across his chest, obviously in defensive mode. She understood. Everything that was happening was probably his worst nightmare since it made it harder to pull away from SBS. It was her worst nightmare also because it would bring media scrutiny and possibly put her in the spotlight. Maybe even revive stories about her father and his problems.

"They say the simplest explanation is usually the right one," Trey said.

"And the simplest explanation is that someone wants you off this property," Jose said, obviously getting where Trey was going.

"Can you think of any reason for that?" Trey asked, skewering Jose with his gaze.

Pursing his lips in thought, Jose nodded and said, "There had been a developer with some interest, but he lowballed the owners."

"Did he try to outbid us?" Mia asked and narrowed her gaze to consider Jose as he answered.

Jose shrugged and shook his head. "As far as I know, we were the only bidders after the owners turned him down, but I can find out."

Trey nodded. "When you do that, can you ask them if they had anything weird going on while they were here?"

"Do you think they would admit it?" Sara asked, fairly certain that a seller wouldn't reveal anything that could possibly dissuade a prospective buyer.

"They'd have to tell us about major issues, but minor harassment…" Jose said and dipped his head in doubt.

"Not sure explosions are minor harassment," Mia challenged, obviously worried about all that was happening.

"I'll find out," Jose told her, everything about his demeanor in defensive mode. Without waiting for any other comments, he whirled and strode out the door, his choppy strides matching the fact that he was clearly upset.

"It's not his fault," she said to the family members in the room.

"We know it's not," Trey said, but then wagged his head from side to side. "We get a little intense when we're on a case."

"Is that what this is now? A case?" she said, although she had no doubt that buying this property had somehow become more than just setting up the new K-9 center.

"It is, but don't worry. We will handle it," Mia said, and everyone around echoed her comment.

"And I will as well. I'm part of the team now, and I'll do whatever you need on this case," she said despite her worries about being in the public eye. She rubbed Bongo's head as her dog sidled up to her and bumped Sara with her head, sensing her upset and the tension in the room.

Mia reached out and laid a hand on her arm. "*Gracias*, Sara. We knew we'd hired the right person to join us."

"*Sí, gracias.* We appreciate anything you can do. In the meantime, I'm going to call the local PD and see what they have on the outbuilding blast," Trey said, and walked to the far side of the room to make his call.

As he did so, Jose marched back in, body set in stiff lines. Face all sharp angles. His gaze locked with hers, the sunny blue of his eyes now the stormy blue of turmoil.

He approached the group gathered there and said, "I spoke to the Florians. They confirmed a developer had put in a bid but dropped out once we expressed interest. As for anything funky, not a thing as long as they lived here."

"Unless they're not saying. Did you doubt what they told you?" Mia asked.

Jose shook his head. "Not at all. They struck me as honest people when we were negotiating, and nothing's changed my opinion."

"We trust your opinion. *Gracias* for reaching out to them," Mia said, mindful of Sara's earlier comments about Jose's role in what was now a case.

JOSE APPRECIATED MIA'S gratefulness and trust but that barely diminished the guilt he was feeling at getting his family involved in a property that was causing them so many problems.

"Whatever I can do, *prima*. We need to figure out what's going on."

"We?" Mia asked, her perfectly manicured brows narrowed in question.

"We, *prima*. I got you into this mess, and I plan on helping you get out of it," he said, feeling at fault for their current situation.

Trey returned to the group at that moment, face set in dour lines. "No fingerprints anywhere, but PD thinks they found the bits and pieces of a detonator as well as trace amounts of ammonium nitrate."

"Which is found in fertilizer, right?" Sara asked while Bongo sat dutifully beside her.

"It is, and I'm assuming we'll have traces of that in what's left of the chimney," Trey said, and glanced at Jose. "The simplest explanation is that this developer wants us gone."

"And any of his landscapers would have access to fertilizer," Jose stated.

"I guess we have our first suspect," Sara said.

"LET'S WORK ON securing the location," Trey said, and peered at Jose intently.

"Are you sure you want in on this?" he asked his cousin.

Jose nodded. "I'm in on this. I'll call around discreetly and try to find out more about this developer."

"That would be great, Jose. We appreciate anything you can do," Trey said, and there was no doubting the gratitude and support in his voice.

"I'll call the painters and hold off on any work until we secure this location," Mia said, and stepped away to phone the company.

"What can Bongo and I do right now?" Sara said, needing to do something while the rest of the team was at work.

Trey nodded and smiled, clearly pleased by her request. "I think the two of us should patrol the perimeter of the house and the remaining grounds."

"I want to go with," Jose said, earning a hairy eyeball from Trey.

"I need to know what's going on," Jose insisted.

"What about those calls?" Trey argued.

Jose raised his phone and said, "Mobile, remember?"

Trey sucked in a breath, as if preparing to challenge him again, but then relented. "Just keep back and don't distract us."

Sara knew he didn't mean the words to cut Jose down to size but as Jose drew his shoulders back and stood straighter, she had no doubt that's how he'd taken it. Despite that, Jose followed them outside, and Sara released her hold on the leash to let Bongo walk ahead and sniff around the outside of the house.

The dog moved decisively in the overgrown grasses, shifting from the foundation of the building to a few feet away under Sara's guidance.

Her dog did nothing to signal that there was something to worry about as they zigzagged from the house to the grass over and over until they reached the rubble of the chimney. There Bongo shifted to the bricks and took a long time to sniff before finally laying down close to the house.

"She smells the explosive," Sara said, and glanced past Trey to meet Jose's gaze.

"That's amazing. Did you train her to do that?" he said.

"I took classes with another trainer so that Bongo and I would be certified for that and cadaver location, but my main focus has always been search and rescue operations and training people to do that," she admitted, not wanting to misrepresent her skills.

"Still amazing," he said.

Trey repeated the compliment and pointed to the kennel area. "Do you feel comfortable checking the kennels?"

Sara examined the area. There was thick grass in and around the building, presenting the biggest danger if their assailant had laid more bear traps there, but otherwise the area seemed manageable.

"I do. Let's clear it so we can focus on the other buildings after," she said, and the three of them hurried there but slowed as they neared.

As she had before, she instructed Bongo to search, but kept her on a short leash and carefully perused the area before she let Bongo move in just in case.

Jose stayed close while Trey was a few feet away, inspecting the ground ahead of them. As he did so, he said, "We should get all this overgrown lawn cut down so it's harder to hide anything and to keep down the mosquitos."

"I have a landscaper we can call in once we know it's safe," Jose offered.

"Appreciate the help," Trey said, clearly trying to calm the waters with his cousin.

Chapter Eight

Jose tried not to take Trey's words as being condescending. His cousin had always been an upfront guy, and he took his statement at face value.

"Where do we go next?" he asked Sara.

She looked at the grounds and said, "Let's go near the woods and work our way back toward the training ring."

"I'll follow your lead," he said, not that he wouldn't be on his toes considering all that had happened in the last two days. He only hoped he wouldn't end the day with even more injuries.

They moved cautiously toward the line of trees surrounding the property. They were part of the parcel that SBS had bought as well as some farmland beyond the hardwood hammock. It made him wonder whether whoever was leaving them the little surprises was located in those woods or beyond.

Because of that, he said, "There's more land beyond these trees that belongs to the kennels. Do you think Bongo could pick up our suspect's scent and track it there?"

Sara peered over her shoulder at him and nodded. "If we can identify the suspect's scent, Bongo can track it for miles."

"Good to know," he said, and followed her as they slowly moved to the tree line, vigilant for any traps. When they neared the woods, Sara stopped and pulled Bongo back. Kneeling, she examined something, then rose and pointed to the ground.

He leaned forward and noticed a thin wire running about six inches above the ground. "Is that a trip wire?" he asked, not that he would know a booby trap from any old wire.

"Or a remnant of an electrical fence. Can you call the former owners to see if they had anything like that?" Sara asked.

"I can. What about in the meantime?"

Sara pulled a brightly colored waste bag from a pouch on her leash and tied it to a small branch near the wire. As she rose, she pulled out her cell phone. "I'll call the others to warn them."

He waited as she did so, and then they worked their way to the training ring.

As she had before, Sara kept a tight leash on Bongo until she had determined there weren't any dangers in the area. Everything went smoothly until Bongo reached a spot directly behind the building. The bloodhound hesitated at that point, eagerly sniffing around the foundation before tugging Sara away from the building to a spot several feet away.

"What's wrong?" he asked as Bongo circled around and around a spot, nose down in the thick grasses growing there. A second later, the dog lay down, signaling Sara that she had found something.

"What is it?" Jose asked, a puzzled look on his face.

Sara didn't know what to make of Bongo's behavior unless a lot of fertilizer was in the area or worse, a cadaver was buried there.

She didn't discount that maybe someone had skipped the proper routes to bury a dead dog, but there was only one way to find out.

"Bongo is scenting either fertilizer or a decaying body. Did you notice a shovel anywhere?"

"I think the cleaning crew left one by the kennels. I'll go get it," he said, and carefully retraced their steps to avoid any surprises.

While he got the shovel, she cautiously parted the grass in the area Bongo had identified and noticed there was one section where the ground seemed slightly mounded, as if it had been dug up and patted back down.

Kneeling there, she rubbed Bongo's head and fed her a treat from a pouch on the leash. "Good girl, Bongo. What did you smell?"

Her dog let out a low woof and rubbed her head against Sara's leg before pawing the ground before her again.

Sara hoped it was just fertilizer, but the way the ground had been torn up had her worried about what they would find.

She stood, inspecting the area once more as Jose approached, shovel in hand.

"Where should I dig?"

She gestured to the spot where she had yanked away the overgrown lawn.

"Right there but be careful. It could be more than just fertilizer."

He drove the shovel into the ground gingerly and picked up a large clump of grass and the red clay prized by the farmers in the area.

Tossing it aside, he dug into the earth in small chunks mindful that it could be another bomb. He flung clumps of grass and soil to the side until he was about a foot deep. So far there had been nothing, to Sara's immense relief.

"Should I keep going?" he asked as they peered into the hole he'd made.

She wanted to call off the digging, only Bongo once again pawed the ground and looked up at her with mournful eyes, as if to say, "Why don't you trust me?"

"Sara?" he prompted, waiting for her instruction.

"Bongo says we should dig some more," she said, and rubbed her dog's head almost apologetically.

Beads of sweat dotted Jose's forehead. Dark rings of perspiration marred the armpits of the new guayabera shirt Trey had brought him that morning to replace his ruined one. With a nod, however, he drove the shovel in again, wincing. Reminding her of the injuries to his shoulder.

"I can dig if you want," she said, feeling guilty, but he just shook his head and jammed the shovel in a little more forcefully.

A slight thunk, as if he'd hit wood or something, had Jose pausing and glancing down at the hole. More carefully, he used the shovel tip to clear the soil and after he did so, he reared back and muttered a curse.

Sara rushed to his side and peered down.

The empty orbital sockets in a skull peeked up at her from the dirt.

THE SBS CREW huddled around the excavation and the near dozen police officers working in and around the hole.

CSI officers, suited up to prevent contamination, carefully removed bones and placed them in evidence bags. Every now and then bits and pieces of fabric emerged from the soil that had kept its secrets for so long.

Beside him Sara wavered a bit and Jose wrapped an arm around her shoulders, offering support and comfort.

He understood how she was feeling. He felt as if the ground beneath his feet was disintegrating and threatening to swallow him whole.

"What do we do now?" he said, and shot a look at Trey, who stood beside him, body tense. Arms wrapped across his chest.

"We wait for the ME's report and see what they have to say about the victim," Trey said.

But then one of the CSI officers, possibly having heard him, called out, "Victims. There are two."

The man held up a second skull.

Jose's stomach turned and a sour taste filled his mouth.

As if sensing that it was getting to be too much for everyone, not just Jose, Trey said, "Let's head back to the house and brainstorm this."

The group ambled toward the home, heads occasionally turning to look toward the training ring and the police officers assembled there.

Inside the building, they drifted toward the kitchen. Trey and Mia leaned on one set of counters while Sophie and Robbie snagged stools at the island that separated the kitchen from the rest of the open concept space.

Sara and Jose stood opposite them with Bongo tucked close to Sara's side.

Trey motioned toward the bloodhound. "Bongo did a good job."

Sara nodded and rubbed the dog's head. "She did only... We just sit and wait for the ME's report?"

Trey tipped his head to one side, as if considering his answer, but then finally said, "Once we have information on the victims, we see what connection they have to the kennels."

Firmly settling his gaze on him, Trey said, "Pepe. You said you'd call the owners for info."

Jose nodded. "I will, not that they'll admit they know about a grave with two women."

"How do you know it's women?" Mia immediately challenged.

"It almost always is, isn't it?" he said sadly and quickly added, "But I also noticed one of the CSI people pulling out what looked like a bra."

"Good catch," Mia said.

"Let's run with that. Two women, and they've been missing for some time given the state of decay," Trey said.

"How hard will it be for the police to ID them?" Jose asked.

Trey shrugged. "It depends."

"On?" Jose queried.

"On whether anyone even cared that they were gone," Mia said sharply and as he met her gaze, he noted the mix of sadness and anger there.

Puzzled, Jose said, "I don't get it."

It was Sara who piped up with an explanation. "They could be runaways, maybe sex workers. Women living on the fringes of society."

"Women no one would miss," he said, finally understanding the sadness in Mia's gaze.

"Let's start with that," Trey said, and jerked his chin in the direction of their tech guru cousins. "Can you get lists and photos of any women who were reported missing in the last five years?"

"What about the sex workers?" Jose said.

"Harder to do without knowing where they might be strolling. Can you ask the owners about their former employees? Especially any young female workers who might have suddenly 'quit,'" Trey said, using air quotes on the "quit" part.

Jose nodded. "I'll call as soon as we're done here."

"*Bueno.* We'll leave Sophie, Robbie and their crew to finish up while the rest of us head to the office," Trey said, and pushed away from the counter.

The rest of the team flew into action, but Sara hesitated and said, "What if there's more than just these two?"

Chapter Nine

He wanted to howl out his frustration, but instead all he could do was mutter repeated curses as he stared through the scope of the crossbow at the crowd gathered around the garden home for his first two kills.

He shouldn't have planted them so close to the training ring only he'd been lazy, and when some plumbers had made the hole to fix a problem with the drain, he'd figured, "Why not?"

As soon as the plumbers had finished and gone, he'd dumped the women he'd been keeping at his place and filled in the hole.

No one had been the wiser.

Until now...

The stream of curses escaped him, audible only to him thanks to the distance to the property.

He had hoped that the little gifts he'd left for the dandy and his friends might have discouraged them from staying. Especially the traps he'd laid around the perimeter, only the pretty woman with the bloodhound had discovered one of them.

That was bad.

If they bypassed those traps and used that bloodhound to search the woods...

He couldn't let that happen.

As he watched one of the SBS equipment vans drive away, he leaned back against a tree trunk to wait them out.

Once the rest were gone and night had fallen, he'd work on protecting his garden.

SARA SCROLLED THROUGH the photos of the missing women that Sophie and Robbie had pulled together while also overseeing the techs working on the location's security.

So many faces, she thought. Young ones. Old ones. Every race.

So many lost souls.

The snick of a door opening had her staring toward the back bedroom where Jose had gone to call the former kennel owners.

When he exited the room, he wore a troubled expression, his handsome face all sharp lines, full lips drawn tight.

Smudges of reddish dirt marred his new shirt, and his hair was tousled, as if he'd been raking his fingers through it in agitation.

"How'd it go?" she asked, and stroked Bongo's head as the dog, possibly sensing her unrest, laid her large head in Sara's lap. It didn't take long for her to feel the wet of Bongo's drool as it soaked her jeans.

"Good, I think." He walked over and sat on the stool next to her at the large island in the kitchen.

He swiped his phone open and laid it on the quartz countertop.

She leaned over to see a photo of what looked like a crew of people in blue-and-white uniforms. At her questioning look, he said, "The Florians always took a group photo before the start of every racing season. This one was taken the last year greyhound racing was permitted in Florida."

Leaning close, he used two fingers to enlarge the photo and focused on a young girl in the second row. Tapping the screen with his index finger, he said, "That's Teresa Hansen. They called her Terry."

Something about the girl's face clicked with her, and she scrolled to the top of the photos she'd just been viewing.

"What did they say about her?" she asked.

"She was seventeen. A runaway who came to them through

a halfway house that helps troubled teens. She was reliable and always willing to help, and then one day she didn't show up. They didn't worry at first, but when days passed without her, they reached out to the halfway house who said that Terry was missing."

Sara shook her head in disbelief. "And that's it? Terry goes missing and no one does anything?"

With a shake of his head, Jose said, "Apparently the people at the halfway house asked around, but no one knew where Terry might have gone. Her things were still at the house, which worried them, so they reached out to the police who told them to file a report."

Which could account for the photo she'd thought she'd seen. She raised an index finger in a stop gesture. "Hold on a minute."

Turning her attention to her laptop, she scrolled through the photos, those missing and lost faces tugging at her heart until she reached one she thought looked familiar.

She turned the screen so that Jose could see it. His shocked gasp confirmed that he also saw the resemblance to Terry.

He brought his phone close to her screen for a better comparison and that left no doubt in her mind.

They'd possibly identified the one woman and made a connection to the kennels.

Sara whipped out her phone and snapped off a photo showing the two screen images. She quickly sent it to the rest of the SBS crew and got immediate replies.

Fantastic! Mia texted.

Awesome! came from both Sophie and Robbie.

Great job. Let's convene in the penthouse for dinner and planning, Trey responded.

Dinner and planning? Was Jose in favor of that? Sara thought, and showed the response to Jose.

She didn't think it was possible for that knife-sharp slash

of his lips to get even more severe, but it did. He looked away, shook his head and blew out a harsh breath.

Laying a hand on his arm, she said, "It's not too late for you to pull out of this. You've done what Trey asked."

With another abrupt shake of his head, he said, "No way. I'm not leaving you alone to deal with this."

Something in her heart trembled at his words, but she worried this was way out of his comfort zone. Hers as well. "I'm not alone. I've got the entire SBS crew with me."

"And now you have me as well. I got us into this mess—"

"There's no reason for you to feel guilty," she said and stroked his arm, trying to reassure him.

"I recommended this property, Sara. Maybe I should have done more due diligence."

"You know better than that. There's no way you could have known. None of us could have, not even Trey with all his experience," she said and at that, the tension left his body like a balloon losing its air.

He nodded. "I'm not leaving. Not until we figure out what's happening, and I know you're safe. Plus, I imagine you would rather not be plastered across the news," he said, and cupped her cheek.

"I wouldn't. People don't understand how hard that is," she said, and leaned into that caress, drawing comfort from it and something else. That something else that she'd been feeling about him since the moment she'd laid eyes on him.

"I do. I understand," he said as she reached up, cradled his jaw and ran her thumb across his lips, the gesture as intimate as any kiss.

He smiled and leaned close. Ran his thumb across her lips as his gaze traveled over her face. "You feel it too," he said.

At her nod, he shifted closer, so close his warm breath spilled across her lips, but just then the whoosh of elevator doors had them jerking apart guiltily.

JOSE SUCKED IN a breath, savoring her fresh floral scent as he slipped off the stool and jammed his hands in his pockets to keep from touching her again.

Trey's observant gaze drifted between the two of them as the elevator doors opened and he led the rest of the South Beach Security crew into the penthouse. But joining them this time were Mia's new husband John Wilson and Trey's pregnant wife Roni, whose baby belly was really showing. He guesstimated she was at least six months pregnant by now, and wondered how she handled being pregnant and actively working as a detective with Miami Beach PD.

To avoid Trey's continued observation, he hurried over and hugged Roni, and then shook John's hand. "It's good to see you. What brings you two tonight?"

A wry smile slipped across Roni's lips, and she grabbed hold of Trey's hand and swung it playfully. "With the hours we both work, it's sometimes the only time we get to spend together."

"Ditto. The new start-up is consuming me so I try to sneak time with Mia whenever I can," John said, wrapping an arm around Mia's waist and dropping a kiss on her cheek.

"And we want to help. Too many women go missing and their families never know what happened to them," Roni added, her smile fading.

"We think we identified one," Jose said, referring to the photo they'd sent to the team earlier.

Trey whipped out his phone and took another look at his text message. "It definitely looks like the same girl. First thing to do is check in with local PD to see if anything they have so far might help confirm that."

"But first, dinner. I'm always hungry lately," Roni said, and stroked her hand across her baby belly.

"And all that digging makes for a hungry boy," Jose said as

his stomach growled loudly, earning a big woof from Bongo, as if in agreement.

"Sorry, girl. It is time for me to feed you," Sara said, and with a hand gesture directed the bloodhound toward the fridge.

While Sara dished out fresh food and filled Bongo's water bowl, the rest of the team shuffled around menus for the restaurants in the area before settling on a local Mexican place.

Once the order had been phoned in, the team settled in around the table and shared reports on what they had accomplished that day.

"All the windows and doors on the house are secure. We've got the cameras on the house installed and will finish connecting them tomorrow," Sophie said.

Robbie added, "We couldn't access the training ring, but did finish securing the kennels. Tomorrow we'll add the driveway alarm and perimeter cameras."

"Great. We'll assign an agent to monitor the feeds until we feel it's secure and Sara can move in," Trey said.

"And that 'we' includes Sara feeling it's safe," Mia said, and shot a quick look at her.

"That sounds good," Sara said, but Jose wasn't convinced she was serious. He knew what it was like to be railroaded by his SBS family and feel trapped.

Laying a hand on hers beneath the tabletop, he squeezed and focused on her. "Are you sure that's what you want?"

She nodded emphatically. "I came here to do a job and I intend to do it. I trust the team, and if they say it's safe, I'm ready to move in."

"We won't push Sara to do anything she's not ready to do," Trey said, obviously reading his vibes.

He bit back the question about what they would push him to do. In truth, he could have extricated himself from this investigation, but he was committed now. Committed to Sara and exploring what he was feeling about her, he told himself.

"I'm good, Trey. You're doing everything you can to make sure the kennels will be safe for me and for everyone," Sara said.

"Unlike the two people in that grave," Mia said with a sad shake of her head.

"We will find out what happened and bring peace to those women," Trey said.

Jose had no doubt the SBS team would do just that. It's what had made them Miami's premiere security and investigative agency.

Trey's cell phone chirped, and he answered. "Sure. I'll be down in a second."

Skipping his gaze across everyone gathered at the table, he said, "Food's here. I'll go get it."

Jose joined the others as they went into action, splitting up to get sodas, cutlery, napkins and plates. All of them acting as if this was an everyday thing, and maybe it was for them. He hoped it never got to be that everyday for him. Which reminded him why he shouldn't let whatever he was feeling for Sara go any further. This was her world now, and he didn't want any part of it.

Minutes later Trey returned, and they settled around the table to eat and plan what they would do the next day. Sophie and Robbie would resume securing the location. Trey was going to coordinate with the local PD on the autopsies and any evidence they had gathered at the scenes of the explosions.

"I'll find out what I can about... Terry Hansen," Mia said, and peered at Sara. "Since you're worried about other traps because of the trip wire you found, let's bring in our other new K-9 agents, Matt and Natalie, to help search. Are you okay with that?"

"I am. I've got a sick feeling there are more surprises there and don't want to search alone," Sara said, and shot him a quick look from the corner of her eye.

"I'll go with you," he said despite all his earlier reservations.

Trey immediately jumped in with, "*Gracias*, Pepe. Hopefully with all of us working on this we'll secure the kennels more quickly. I can join you once I finish with local PD."

Jose did a slow nod in appreciation. He had expected Trey to single him out as not being capable enough to be part of the investigation. He'd always thought his cousin saw him as somehow inferior, unable to be an action guy like he was. It was why Jose had always felt closer to his younger cousin Ricky, a psychologist who had also been trying to make his own way before being sucked into the family business.

Meeting Trey's gaze across the table, he realized now that he'd been mistaken. And when Trey nodded, as if saying "I know you can do this," the years of feeling that inferiority, that insecurity, fell away.

"That sounds like a plan," Jose said.

Chapter Ten

Everyone had filed out of the penthouse except Trey. He kissed his wife and said, "I'll meet you downstairs in a few minutes."

Sara, apparently sensing Trey wanted a moment alone with Jose, excused herself. "Have a good night, Trey. I need a shower and I should call my mother to explain what's happening before my Tia Rosario beats me to it."

When she was gone, Trey flipped a hand in the direction of Jose's dirt-stained shirt.

"Looks like I owe you another one, Pepe," Trey said with a laugh and shake of his head.

Jose narrowed his gaze and examined his cousin carefully. "Why do I think you're liking this way too much?"

"Maybe because I like you. I've always known you had it in you," he said, and tapped the back of his hand across Jose's midsection.

"What? Tacos?" Jose teased, not wanting the mood to get maudlin or too serious.

But Trey was having none of it. "The Gonzalez backbone. Courage. You've got it and I appreciate you helping us."

Jose blew out a harsh laugh. "As if you couldn't handle this on your own."

Trey shrugged broad shoulders and wagged his head from side to side. "Probably. Maybe. Like Sara, I worry those two are just the first ones we'll find. It'll take all of us to solve what's happening at that location. A location you convinced us to buy," he said, his tone teasing.

"Way to make me feel guilty," he said, earning another chuckle from his cousin.

Trey turned and tapped his badge against the elevator access screen before pointing a finger toward the bedrooms. "Sara is an amazing woman, Pepe. But she has her own issues. Remember that."

Before Jose could respond, the elevator doors opened, and Trey walked on.

Jose barely had time to wave goodbye before the doors closed to take Trey down to where Roni would be waiting.

Much like Jose was waiting for Sara to finish her phone call and shower, looking forward to spending what was left of the night together.

But as he sucked in a deep breath, imagining whether they would continue what they had started earlier, he realized Sara wasn't the only one who needed a shower. The stink of the day clung to him, and he wondered why no one had mentioned it earlier while they were eating dinner.

He hurried to his bedroom, stripped off his clothes and quickly jumped into the shower. The heat of the water chased away some of the soreness from the digging. But as he ran soapy hands across his arms and torso, it reminded him of the moment the shovel had hit something hard and white.

Something human.

How long had the two women been there? A year? Two? He didn't know enough about dead bodies, but it clearly hadn't happened recently.

Had it happened while the kennels were open? he asked himself, and the answer came to him instantly: yes.

If one of the women in the ground was Terry Hansen, it had to have happened while she was working there.

She'd been seventeen at the time. Terry had only just begun her life, and someone had taken it from her.

Anger filled him, and he quickly finished his shower, determined to find out as much as he could about Terry. Determined that she wouldn't be forgotten.

In that brief instance, he finally realized why Trey and the rest of his cousins did what they did: so people would get justice. Justice that they possibly didn't receive from the usual law enforcement channels.

He towel-dried himself and tossed on the sweats Trey had brought him along with the other clothes from his condo. When he exited the bedroom and walked into the spacious open area, Sara was seated at the table, working on a laptop. Bongo lay at her feet but raised her head to eyeball him as he approached. Recognizing him, the dog laid her big head back on her even larger paws.

"What are you doing?" he asked and walked to the table to lean over her shoulder.

The action brought him so close he smelled her shower freshness and that brought an immediate reaction as he hardened, enticed by that flowery perfume and her natural scent.

He straightened to give himself some space as she said, "I'm just scrolling through this list of missing women. So, so many."

"Too many," he said, wondering why no one had cared or if they had, why the women had remained missing.

"And it may not even be Terry or any of these women," Sara said, and flipped a hand in the direction of the laptop screen.

"My gut says one of those bodies is Terry," he said, but quickly tacked on, "Not that I'm any expert."

"You're not and I'm not either, but it's just too much coincidence that she was working there and just disappeared," Sara said, and closed the laptop.

"Done for the night?" he asked but got his answer even before she spoke as she pulled over a notepad and pen.

She peered over her shoulder at him, the gray of her eyes the color of a stormy winter sky. "Would you mind calling the Florians again?"

He shot a quick look at his watch. The night had flown between dinner and their showers. It was nearly ten. "I don't, but maybe in the morning. I'm not sure they'd welcome a call at this hour."

Nodding, she said, "You're right. I lost track of time. I should take Bongo for her last walk of the day."

"Easy to do when so much is happening. I'll go with you."

She leashed the bloodhound and together they hurried downstairs, let Bongo do her business, and then returned to the penthouse, where Sara gave her a treat and unleashed her. The dog immediately sat near the table where they had been working earlier.

He gestured to the pad and pen and then over to the nearby sofa. "I know you're not done for the night. Why don't you get comfortable, and I'll get us something to drink while we work on those questions together."

"That sounds nice. A finger of that aged rum neat would be appreciated," she said, and slowly rose from the table, pad and pen in hand.

When she walked to the sofa, Bongo followed and sat by her feet.

At the wet bar at the far side of the room, he poured a finger of a twenty-three-year-old rum, took some ice from the small fridge there and poured himself a scotch. He walked over to the sofa, handed Sara her rum and sat close, wanting to be able to read what was on the pad as they worked together.

Sara sipped her rum but then set it aside so she could write down their questions. "Did the Florians notice anything different about Terry in the days before she disappeared?"

"Did she hang out with any of the other workers and who were they?" he said.

She raised an index finger. "We should get a list of everyone working there at the time."

"If they'll give it to us and the police. I'm guessing some people might want a warrant before they do that," he said, recalling what little he knew based on the police dramas he'd watched.

"Hopefully it won't take that. Like you said, the Gonzalez family has a lot of pull—"

"And the Florians won't want to piss us off," he said.

SARA HELD BACK from commenting on it being an "us" now.

"No, they won't. What else can we ask them?" she said, and they rattled off a few more questions that Sara jotted down on the pad before finally setting it aside and grabbing her glass of rum again.

She sipped the rum and the heat of it traveled down her core, but it wasn't as comforting as the warmth of his body along her side. It seemed almost natural to lean into him, and he reacted by wrapping an arm around her shoulders to hold her close.

They sat there in companionable silence, sipping their drinks. Each lost in their thoughts about today's gruesome discovery and what it might mean.

"This wasn't quite how I pictured my first few days at work," Sara finally said, needing to share the questions racing around in her brain in the hopes of quieting that unrest.

"What did you picture?"

"Puppers. Lots and lots of puppers," she said with a laugh and rough shake of her head. She reached down to the floor, where Bongo lay by her feet, and rubbed the dog's head. "Right, Bongo?"

A low woof answered her, as if the dog knew exactly what she had asked, and sat up to lay her drooly head on the edge of the sofa.

"How long have you been partners?"

"About six years. Before Bongo I had a German shepherd but when she died, I decided to get a bloodhound because they have more scent sensors than other breeds," she answered, and stroked the dog's head and ears.

"Was it hard to train her?"

Sara eyeballed him, as if to judge if he was truly interested. Satisfied that he was, she said, "Not too hard. Bloodhounds are quite smart."

"Is she protective?" he asked, and from the tone of his voice, she sensed that he thought that the dog wasn't all that keen on him.

"Not really. Bloodhounds are very easygoing, and they think everyone is a friend," she said, and almost as if Bongo knew they were talking about her, the dog raised her head and looked at him.

JOSE TOLD HIMSELF it was a friendly look even though he felt like Bongo was their very determined chaperone. He sipped his whisky, falling silent as he considered what to do next.

Sara spared him by asking, "I'm sure this isn't how you pictured this sale going."

"You can say that again," he said with a rough laugh and rattle of the ice in his glass. But the emotions that had been building in him reared up and he blurted out, "I sure didn't expect you."

Her hand trembled as she set her glass on the coffee table in front of the couch, and she shifted to face him.

"Me? You didn't expect me?" she said and tapped her chest with her finger.

He nodded and caressed her cheek. Ran his thumb across

the creamy skin there and then drifted it lower to trace the edges of her lips. "I didn't," he said, before leaning forward to finally do what he'd wanted to do for hours.

He kissed her.

Chapter Eleven

His lips were hard and mobile. Soft and demanding. Needy and gentle all at the same time.

Her head spun with the whirlwind of emotions swirling through her, as conflicted as the vibes she was getting from him.

That was confirmed as he expelled a rough breath against her lips and shifted away slightly as he said, "Like I said before, I didn't expect you. This."

"I didn't either. It's...confusing. There's just so much going on," she admitted, but even as she did so, she slipped into his lap, straddling his legs so that they were face-to-face because she didn't want to miss any nuance of what was happening.

He smiled, a lopsided smile, and cradled her jaw before easing his hand around to cup the back of her skull. Tangling his fingers through her hair, he applied gentle pressure to draw her close.

"It is confusing. It's hard to separate the craziness of this situation from what I'm feeling," he confessed, and his warm breath spilled across her lips. This close, it was impossible to miss the crystals of darker teal in the aqua of his eyes or the stubble of his evening beard on his face.

"What are you feeling?" she asked, raising her hand and running it across that sandpapery stubble, and then dipping her thumb to rub it across his lips.

IT TOOK ALL of Jose's willpower not to cup her buttocks and draw her against the proof of what he was feeling.

He was too much of a gentleman to do that, and he had no doubt Trey would whoop his ass if he did. He tempered that need and instead stroked his hands across her back, gentling her as he said, "I'd be lying if I said I didn't want you, but that want is way too soon."

And it was way too complicated because of her connections to his family and SBS.

"It is. I'm not the kind to just hook up," she said, and quickly slipped off his lap. "And I'm not a tease either."

This was going from so nice to so wrong so quickly, and he tried to smooth things over. He faced her on the sofa and said, "I know you're not. I'd like to see if this—" he paused and pointed back and forth between them "—can go somewhere. If that's what you want."

She nodded her head shakily. "I think it's what I want only... Being involved with you and your family—"

"And the business."

"And your business. When I first heard about the job posting, I did an internet search and you came up a lot also at a number of events."

He tipped his head from side to side, considering what she said and finally said, "I hit a lot of social events, but a lot of them are for charities I support."

"What kinds of charities?" she asked, as if hoping the cause was worth the publicity.

"Ones that help renovate homes for injured veterans and people in need."

"Good causes," she said, but then quickly tacked on, "But I just want to train the dogs and stay out of the news. I've already lived through that."

And he knew it hadn't been a good thing based on what

Trey had said earlier. "Mind telling me more about what happened?"

"My father was wrongfully accused of taking a client's funds. My family…there was a lot of media coverage until he was cleared of wrongdoing."

"And now you're in the news—"

"Again. I'd rather live a low-key life, but first we have to work on this investigation."

"You're right. The sooner we finish that, the sooner we can explore whatever it is that we're feeling," he said, and cradled her cheek again, the caress meant to comfort and not entice.

She covered his hand with hers and offered him a regretful smile. "First thing in the a.m. you call the Florians and we take it from there."

With a last stroke of his thumb across her smooth cheek, he said, "I will. Maybe that will help us decide what to do."

She nodded. "I'm a little tired and need to be alert tomorrow. I'm going to turn in."

"I agree. I'll see you in the morning," he said, then shot to his feet and held his hand out to help her from the couch.

She slipped her hand into his and rose. With a slight hand gesture to Bongo, the dog came to her feet and tucked herself tight to Sara's leg.

Sara and Jose walked hand in hand to her bedroom door where she paused and faced him, hesitant. "Good night," she said, then dropped a quick kiss on his lips and rushed into her room. She would have slammed the door in his face, but Bongo's big body was in the way. As soon as her dog was inside, she closed the door.

Jose stood there, staring at the polished wood, teak he guessed. As a Realtor he noticed those kinds of things, and maybe he should think about how to use those skills to help Sara and the SBS team in the future.

Or maybe even now, he thought, doubling back to the sofa

to grab the paper and pen to review the questions they'd come up with and maybe add some more.

Later in his bedroom, he lay on the bed and turned on the television to see if there was any coverage of today's discovery. Flipping from one local news show to a hyper local cable news channel, he listened as one reporter after another gave only the barest info on what the police had found at the kennels.

Possibly not surprising since the police probably had very little so far.

Trey had said it would take a few days at least to determine cause of death, much less identify the two bodies.

Although Jose was sure that one of them was poor seventeen-year-old Terry. Since he knew from all those TV crime shows that the killer was most likely someone Terry had known, he was going to press the Florians to find out who had been Terry's friends and more importantly, who hadn't been.

He added a question to the list to find out who might also have after-hours access to the location and how someone could have dug a grave without anyone noticing.

A grave filled with bones, he thought, as the image of what he'd found that day rocked him. The off-white skull against the reddish-brown Florida soil. A few inches away, thin finger bones poking upward, as if trying to claw free of their prison.

Shoving away those images, he forced himself to think about what he'd seen on the property, trying to remember if there had been anything that had seemed out of the ordinary on his various visits to the location before recommending that Trey buy it.

Or if there had been anything unusual about the sale itself. There had been interest from that other buyer, but he hadn't thought anything about that since it wasn't unusual to have multiple bidders on a project. But maybe this buyer hadn't liked losing the property. Maybe because they had been hiding the bodies at the kennels? he thought.

That and so many other ideas came to mind, and he jotted them down, determined to help find out what had happened to those two women and why someone clearly wanted SBS off the property.

SARA HAD TRIED her best to fall asleep and get a good night's rest, but sleep hadn't come easily. The images of the last two days had tumbled over and over in her brain, rousing more questions than answers.

Answers that wouldn't come easily, she thought as she placed the espresso pot on the stove, needing the caffeine that a good cup of Cuban coffee would provide. Hopefully it would help make up for her restless night.

The coffee was just bubbling up in the pot when she heard Jose's door open and his soft footfalls as he walked down the hall.

Bongo raised her head as he came in and barked a "Good morning."

He walked over, knelt and rubbed Bongo's head and ears. "Good morning, Bongo. Sara," he said, and beamed a smile in her direction.

She shut off the stove and raised the coffee pot. "Do you want some?"

"Sí, por favor," he said, and strolled to where she stood by the stove. He laid a hand on her waist, bent and dropped a fleeting kiss on her cheek.

She placed the coffeepot back on the stove, rose on tiptoes and brushed a kiss on his lips as she said, "Good morning, Jose."

"I think I like starting the morning like this," he said, and deepened the kiss, but a second later her phone chirped, shattering the moment.

"I have to get that," she said, and snagged her phone from the counter.

"It's Trey," she said and answered. "Let me put you on speaker. Good morning, Trey."

"*Buenos dias.* I was hoping the two of you could come down in about an hour."

She met Jose's gaze and he nodded and said, "I just need to call the Florians, and then we can come down."

"*Bueno.* We're bringing in some breakfast, so don't worry about making your own," he said, and ended the call.

Sara laid the phone on the counter and Jose said, "I'll go make that call."

She nodded. "I'll bring in your coffee."

"Sounds good," he said, and hurried off to phone the former kennel owners.

THE SBS TEAM sat around the conference room table.

Trey had already given them a brief on what the police had so far, "brief" being the operative word, Jose thought again.

"Hopefully PD will have something in the next few days. Roni will keep on them to give us any info, and we promised to keep them updated," Trey said, and peered in Jose's direction. "Do you have anything, Pepe?"

Jose nodded. "I spoke to the Florians this morning. They weren't too keen on me waking them that early, but they cooperated once I explained what we'd found."

"Did they have anything useful to add?" Mia asked.

He nodded again and provided his report. "Apparently there was some kind of plumbing issue that forced them to dig up the area behind the training ring. The contractors had fixed the problem and were supposed to fill and grade the area but when they arrived the next day, someone had already done the work."

"Like whoever killed those women," Trey said, and glanced around the table where everyone nodded in agreement.

"How long ago was that?" Trey asked.

"About three years ago. Around the same time that Terry Hansen disappeared."

"Any idea who Terry's friends were? Enemies?" Trey said.

"I have some names. I assume someone can check them out," Jose said, ripping a piece of paper from the pad and passing it to Trey.

"Robbie and I can do that while our crew finishes up the security details," Sophie said, and took the paper from Trey.

As she did so, Jose said, "There's one name I think we should focus on—Barry Metz. He was a caretaker of sorts. Lives in a cabin at the far side of the woods. He's been watching the property since the kennels closed and was supposed to move after the sale. The Florians aren't sure that he did."

"Let's hope he did, otherwise it might be an issue. I don't like the idea of kicking anyone out of their home, even if they are a squatter," Mia said.

"I agree. If he's still there and not a threat, we can consider how to handle it," Trey said and finished with, "Our other K-9 agents, Matt and Natalie, will meet us there to finish the search of the property. If there's nothing else—"

"Just one thing. The developer who was bidding against us is…a little shady. Nothing concrete, but I heard he had connections to some underworld types," Jose said, earning a sharp look from his cousin.

"Talk about burying the lede," Trey said with a shake of his head that ruffled the longer strands there.

"His name is on that sheet as well, Sophie. Just be careful who you talk to about him," Jose said, worried about what might happen if the rumors were true.

"Got it. We'll keep the search to our sources for now," Sophie confirmed.

"If the developer is dirty, maybe the bodies are connected to him, which would explain why someone wants us off the property," Mia said, connecting the dots to a possible motive.

"Or he could just be pissed off we outbid him, and he wants to make us sell," Robbie said, offering a different explanation.

"Seems to be a lot of trouble when he could have just bid more for the property," Jose said, not feeling Robbie's motive for what was happening.

"Or maybe whoever buried those bodies wants to keep his secrets safe," Sara suggested.

"My money is on that reason," Mia said.

Trey echoed his agreement and said, "I think so too, which worries me because like Sara said, I think we're going to find more bodies."

Chapter Twelve

Sara had met the other SBS K-9 agents a few days earlier when she'd first arrived. Matt was now engaged to the owner of the *Buena Suerta* stables whom he met on an earlier SBS case. Natalie had likewise met her new fiancé, an Everglades tour boat owner, and his son on another investigation. Both agents lived close to the kennels and with their past military experience in addition to their K-9 partners, they would be a big help in defusing any dangerous situations.

She walked the perimeter with Matt, Natalie and Jose and identified five possible trip wires along the edges of the woods. They'd carefully marked the areas with bright yellow caution tape and were just finishing up the last one when Matt said, "We should trip it from a distance to see what we're facing."

"How will we be able to do that?" Natalie said, peering at the wire and then back toward the buildings that were a good thirty yards away.

Jose tracked her gaze and said, "I used to be a pitcher. I think I could nail that wire from sixty feet away."

Matt shook his head. "*Mano*, that would be quite a feat. I think thirty feet is more than enough."

"Done," Jose said, and looked around for something he could toss. Several feet away were two baseball-sized rocks. He walked over, picked one up and hefted its weight in his hand.

Satisfied, he walked about a dozen yards away with the

rest of the team. Matt and Natalie stood off to one side, and he waited until Sara and Bongo were slightly behind him.

"Ready?" he asked.

"Ready as we'll ever be, but maybe we should let the others know," Sara said. She tightened her hold on Bongo's leash, and called Trey to warn him they were tripping the wire.

After Sara finished with the call, he nodded, and slipped into his familiar pitcher's stance. Focusing on the yellow tape around the wire, he went into his wind up, then released the rock.

It sailed just high of the trip wire.

"Close but no cigar," Matt teased.

"Next time," Sara and Natalie said, almost in unison.

He didn't intend to disappoint. Picking up the second rock, he tested its weight and assumed the position, wound up and hurled the rock.

It nailed the wire.

A second later, a semideflated volleyball studded with sharp wooden spikes sailed down in an arc that would have nailed anyone tripping the wire.

"Wow," Jose said, and took a step toward the area, but Natalie swung out her arm to hold him back.

"Wait. Sometimes a booby trap has a delayed secondary trap."

Barely a few seconds later, a small explosion sent shrapnel peppering the trees and ground in about a ten-foot circle.

Jose let out a low whistle. "Whoever this is means business."

THE SOUND OF the blast reverberated across the land, pulling him away from tending to his garden.

He lay down the hoe at the edge of a row of onions and looked toward the kennels in the distance with a smile.

Someone had tripped one of his surprises.

Eager to see the damage it had done, he raced to his front

porch and grabbed the loaded crossbow he kept by the front door while he was working the land.

Racing across the fields, he threaded his way through the trees, moving as quickly as he could without disturbing his other garden or setting off any of the traps he'd set in the area to chase off trespassers. It made his passage slower than he would have wanted, but he had to be patient.

Whoever had tripped the booby trap would still be there, delightfully shredded if he'd devised the mace-like device and explosive correctly.

But as he neared the area, he noticed the duo of men walking around in bright white hazmat suits. Raising the crossbow, he peered through the scope.

No body even though he'd heard the explosion, and the spiked volleyball was still swinging back and forth in a deadly arc.

He gritted his teeth at his failure and shifted the crossbow to look toward the group gathered several yards away from what he guessed was a CSI team.

Three beautiful women stood there along with another woman he hadn't seen before and a Labrador retriever. They were chatting with the warrior and dandy. There were also two other men, a nerdy looking one and another military man who had a shepherd at his side.

The pleasure he'd been experiencing with the sound of the blast and the expectation of carnage slowly ebbed and was replaced by anger at his failure.

A failure just like his mother always told him he would be.

His finger tightened on the trigger as he contemplated the arrow burying itself deep into the luscious flesh of one of the women.

Pleasure slowly returned with that image, but he had to be patient.

Before pleasure, it was time for fear.

THE SOUND OF the blast had ripped the CSI team from the training ring and had also brought his cousins and the rest of the SBS crew hurrying in their direction.

As soon as the head crime scene investigator arrived, Jose said, "We need to call in the bomb squad. Maybe they can defuse the other traps and collect evidence as well."

"How did you trip it?" Trey asked and skewered the four of them with his gaze.

"You forgot I could throw a strike from the outfield," Jose said with a laugh.

Trey shook his head and patted Jose's flat midsection. "Good to know you haven't let yourself go to flab."

"Glad I could help, but I'm not sure what else I can do now," he said, watching the CSI team split up, one group heading toward the tree line to collect evidence while another returned to finish their work at the training ring.

"You can help brainstorm. The installation team found an alarm by the kennel sign. Combined with these traps, the explosions and the bodies, we need to regroup. You were always good at thinking on the fly, Pepe," Trey said, and clapped him on the back.

THE TENSION IN Jose's body was undeniable, but Trey was clearly not about to give Jose an excuse for bailing, not that Sara thought he would. It surprised her again, as many of the men she'd met through her family would have run by now, including the man who had been her boyfriend at the time her father's problems had become so newsworthy.

"We'll do whatever you think is best," Jose said.

"Great. Matt and Natalie have to head to their current assignments, but the rest of us can convene in the house," Trey said.

But as they turned to go, something flew through the air and an arrow embedded itself in the ground at Sara's feet.

Jose immediately stepped in front of her while Matt and Trey urged Natalie, Mia and Sophie behind them.

The two CSI officers reacted, moving toward the forest, but Trey called out to them in warning.

"There are other booby traps," he yelled, which made the CSIs stop in their tracks.

Sara peeked around Jose's body, searching the forest, but she didn't see anything. But the arrow was something that might be useful.

Loosening her hold on Bongo's leash, she let the bloodhound sniff the arrow, hoping she could pick up some kind of scent.

The CSI officers came over at that moment. "We'll have to take that as evidence. It may have fingerprints or DNA," one of them said.

Sara gestured for him to take it, hoping Bongo had gleaned what she could from the arrow.

"Let's go plan," Trey said, and looked over at Matt and Natalie.

"You have your assignments, but we may need your help later if you're up for it."

"Whatever you need," Natalie said, and Matt echoed her words.

"Good," Trey said, and with a quick look around to the others that said so much despite its brevity, they all walked toward the house.

At the driveway, Matt, Natalie and their K-9s peeled off to their cars while the rest of the team entered the house.

As Sara walked in, she realized someone had brought in a foldable six-foot table and chairs so that they would have a workspace.

Sophie's and Robbie's laptops were there along with a map and a greenish rectangular box.

"What is that?" she asked, peering at the box and trying to figure it out.

"It's a driveway alarm," Sophie said, and pointed to a sensor on it. "This detects motion and heat. I'm guessing it sends a signal to either a phone or laptop once it's tripped."

"Our team found it hidden by the weeds near the old sign when they went to install our driveway alarm," Robbie explained.

"And since someone just shot an arrow at us, I think it's safe to assume we're being watched," Sara said, and a shiver traveled through her body.

Jose laid a hand on her shoulder and gave a comforting squeeze, but it did little to calm the fear running through her body.

"And they always seem to be one step ahead of us," Mia said dejectedly.

"That just means we have to step up our game," Trey said, and leaned over the table to gesture at the map. "We've secured all the buildings except the training ring. We have one perimeter camera installed but have to put in more once we defuse the traps."

"Do you think the camera picked up whoever shot at us?" Jose asked and stroked his hand across Sara's shoulders, sensing her continued discomfort.

Sophie shrugged hesitantly and shook her head. "Not sure. The camera is intended to record anyone coming onto the property."

"We'll check and let you know," Robbie said.

Sara hoped they had gotten something. Anything really because as Mia had said, they seemed to be one step behind whoever was causing these issues.

"I'm hoping Bongo picked up a scent from the arrow, but it's a long shot," she said and quickly added, "No pun intended." The arrow shaft was narrow, and she suspected their assailant had been smart enough to wear gloves.

"It's worth a try. It's also worth it to explore those woods and see why someone wants to keep us out of there, but first I'd feel better knowing more about our possible suspects. Sophie and Robbie have been doing some digging around," Trey said, and held his hand out to invite the two tech gurus to provide their information.

Chapter Thirteen

Sophie whipped out a mini projector, and a second later broadcasted an image from her laptop onto the wall.

"This is Anthony Delgado, the developer who was trying to buy the property. Rumors say he paid off local politicians to change the zoning to permit residential housing on this property," Sophie began.

"Rumors also have it that Delgado has connections to local mobsters. They've apparently invested in his projects in exchange for what no one knows," Robbie added.

"Maybe in exchange for burying the bodies," Sara said, the image of the women's bones still vivid in her memory.

"Easy enough to do when you're doing major construction," Mia said with a shrug.

"But is there any connection to the contractors working to repair the training ring problems? The owners said they seemed surprised that the hole had been filled," Jose asked.

Sophie smiled and held up a finger. She flipped another image onto the screen. "This is Guy Sasto, the owner of the contracting company. He used to work for Delgado before he went out on his own. He occasionally works on Delgado's projects."

"So, Delgado's suspect number one," Trey said, and it was clear to Sara that he felt there were other possibilities as well.

"Who else do you have in mind?" Sara asked, worried that they weren't getting any closer to solving this investigation.

"Before we move on, do we all agree Delgado might be responsible for those bodies and any others in those woods?" Trey asked.

As everyone around the table nodded, he gestured for Sophie to continue.

JOSE HAD HEARD the rumors from his colleagues about Delgado but having them confirmed by his SBS family was a completely different thing. Knowing what he did now, he had no doubt Delgado could be behind the attacks, but he tried to keep an open mind as Sophie pulled up another photo.

He recognized the face from the photo the former kennel owners had previously sent.

"This is Barry Metz. He's the one the Florians let live in the cabin on the other side of the woods," Sophie said, and with a tap of the keys, a mug shot featuring Metz displayed on the wall.

"Four years ago Metz was arrested for the sexual assault of a thirteen-year-old in nearby Homestead," Robbie said, tag-teaming with his sister.

"So why was he free a year later and working for the Florians?" Jose asked.

A tight smile flitted across Sophie's face. "The parents of the girl didn't want to subject her to a trial and the media attention."

"He wasn't prosecuted?" Sara asked, just to confirm.

Robbie nodded. "He wasn't prosecuted. Homestead PD kept an eye on him for months, but he kept off their radar."

"And came to murder here," Jose said with some bite.

"It's easy to judge, but women get victimized twice in cases like this. First when they're attacked and then after, when the defense attorneys go at them," Mia said, obviously sympathetic to the parents' decision.

"It's a big escalation to go from sexual assault to multiple murders," Sara pointed out.

Trey dipped his head in agreement. "It is. That's why I'm asking Ricky to look at this and give us his opinion."

While Ricky was a psychologist, Jose didn't think this was generally in his cousin's wheelhouse, but maybe he had added it to his specialties with all the work he did for South Beach Security.

"What do we do now?" Jose asked, troubled by everything that was happening and the fact that they were only a little closer to solving the puzzle.

"We need to talk to Metz and Sasto," Trey said with no hesitation.

"Not Delgado?" Sara asked.

Jose stroked a hand across her back as he said, "That's the last person we want to talk to, trust me. To be honest, if I had known it was Delgado, I would have pulled out of this buy."

"But you didn't know and that's okay. We will get to the bottom of this," Trey said.

Mia added, "This is a great location, and in a weird sort of way, I'm glad about what's happened. Those two women, and any others if we're right, deserve justice and their families need to know what happened to them."

Jose understood what she was feeling. "Agreed. No one should be tossed away like trash."

With that, Sara looked at him, smiled and slipped her hand into his. "You're both right. We will get justice for those women."

"I guess it's time for us to go talk to Metz and Sasto," Jose said.

"Do you know Sasto?" Trey asked, obviously aware that he worked with a lot of different contractors on behalf of his real estate clients.

"I do. I can set up an appointment with him," Jose said with a dip of his head.

"After we talk to him, we'll see about meeting Metz," Trey confirmed.

"Sophie, Robbie and I will mind the fort here. The CSI team said they'd be releasing the training ring to us later today," Mia said, and skipped her gaze over to her tech cousins.

"Robbie and I will keep trying to get more info on our suspects," Sophie said.

"*Bueno*. It seems like we've got our work cut out for us," Trey said, and with that the team went into action.

SASTO WAS OUT of the office when Jose called, but his assistant said he'd be back shortly and arranged for the meeting.

"Why does it bother me that he's out of the office at the same time someone is shooting arrows at us?" Sara asked as they drove to Sasto's location in nearby Homestead.

"And that he can make the trip to the kennels in only about fifteen minutes, maybe less in the early morning or late at night," Jose said.

"Too much coincidence," Trey added.

It was a short distance to Sasto's office, and as they pulled into the parking lot, a fortysomething man was stepping out of a large white pickup that had a company logo on the door that read Sasto Contracting Company.

Jose pointed in the man's direction. "That's Guy Sasto. His father founded the company, and he took it over about ten years ago when the old man retired."

The man hesitated as he noticed them parked a few spaces away. When he spotted Jose in the front seat, he waved and smiled, but that smile dimmed as Trey slipped from the car.

Sasto sauntered over to them, shoulders pulled back in a way that reminded Sara of a bantam rooster trying to appear bigger.

Jose got out of the car and so did she, taking Bongo with her in the hope she'd sniff around Sasto and maybe pick up a familiar scent.

Approaching the contractor, Jose held out his hand and said, "Good to see you, Guy."

Sasto's gaze moved from Jose to Trey before giving her only a cursory glance. "I wish I could say the same. What do you want?"

The contractor ignoring her and Bongo was maybe a good thing, she thought as she maneuvered so that the dog could nose around Sasto's legs.

Finally taking note of her and the bloodhound, Sasto got spooked and stepped away.

Sara bent to rub Bongo's head and said, "Don't worry. She's friendly."

"Not a fan of dogs," Sasto said and then returned his attention to Trey and Jose. "I'm in a rush. My assistant set up a meeting this afternoon."

"With us," Jose said.

Sasto narrowed his gaze. "You need some work done?"

"We do. We need you to fill a hole for us. Heard you did the original digging for the Florians," Trey said, his voice as tight and tense as his body.

"I did some work at the kennels. Is that a problem?" the contractor said and lifted his chin in a defiant gesture, but he was several inches shorter than both Trey and Jose and with a waist going to flab. He wasn't going to scare off either of the two men or her and Bongo either.

"They pulled two bodies out of a hole. A hole you dug and filled in," Trey said.

Sasto's face turned a sickly green and he waved his hand back and forth. "No way. I had nothing to do with that."

"But you did the work, didn't you?" Jose said, his tone friendlier and sympathetic.

"We had to fix a broken drainpipe causing backups and weakening the foundation. My guys did the repair but when they went back in the morning, the hole had already been filled."

While the men had been talking, Sara had loosened her hold

on Bongo's leash again to let her get close to Sasto, who had been too upset to notice. Bongo had nosed around his legs, but then returned to calmly sit at her side.

She rubbed Bongo's head as Trey continued with the interrogation. "You had access to the equipment that night, right? Easy enough for you to go back—"

"I had nothing to do with those bodies," Sasto insisted, not that it dissuaded Trey.

"What about Delgado? He have anything to do with them?" Trey challenged.

Sasto turned that unhealthy seasick color again, leaned close to Trey and in low tones said, "You don't want to mess with him. I know your family has clout, but Delgado. He's one scary guy."

"Scary enough that you would do whatever he asked? You can tell us. Like you said, our family has clout. You know my dad is with the DA's office," Jose said, his voice also pitched lower so only their small group could hear the exchange.

Sasto made the sign of the cross against his chest. "On my kids' lives, I had nothing to do with those bodies. Delgado either."

Sara was inclined to believe him. Only a sick man would swear an oath on his kids' lives.

That seemed to placate Trey and Jose as well since Trey said, "If you find out anything, will you let us know?"

Sasto nodded and Jose shook his hand, clearly wanting to keep things friendly.

"We'd appreciate that," he said.

As she was climbing into the SBS SUV, she noticed something hanging from the pickup's rearview mirror. Something that looked like it had been made by a young child. On the back window of the pickup were vinyl decals depicting a mom, dad, two kids and a cat.

Sasto was likely telling the truth, but if he was, where did that leave their investigation? she thought.

Chapter Fourteen

By Jose's guesstimate, the cabin on the far side of the property was a little over a mile away from the other buildings at the kennels. A wide swath of a hardwood hammock offered privacy. There was also another fairly large stretch of land beyond the cabin that was part of the kennel property but leased to a local farmer.

When they pulled up in front of the cabin, the door slowly opened, and a large overall-clad man walked out cradling a shotgun. From what he could remember of Metz's mug shot, it was him although way older and heavier.

As Trey killed the engine, he shot a quick look back at Sara and Bongo.

"Can Bongo restrain him if we need her to?" he asked.

Jose faced Sara, who was shaking her head vehemently.

"No. Bloodhounds are too friendly and gentle to be trained to attack. She's more likely to lick him to death than anything else," Sara said, and rubbed Bongo's ears. The dog immediately licked her hand as if to prove her point.

Trey muttered a curse just as the man called out, "You've got to the count of five to either leave or tell me why you're here."

Trey opened the window of the SUV and called out, "We're the new kennel owners. We just want to chat."

Metz rocked on the balls of his feet and mumbled something to himself that Jose couldn't quite make out.

A second later, Metz laid his shotgun against the side of the cabin, but close enough to reach it if he needed to.

"Stay here," Trey said in a low tone, but Jose shook his head.

"Where you go, we go," Jose said, and Sara joined his chorus with, "We're going too."

Trey looked from him to Sara and Bongo, then nodded. "No quick moves and don't get too close."

"Got it," Jose said, carefully opening his door and stepping out.

Sara joined him a second later with Bongo at her side, not that the bloodhound would be of assistance.

Trey took a step toward the cabin, but stopped by the front of the SUV, maintaining a few yards between himself and Metz. Hands held slightly upward, as if in surrender, he said, "I'm Trey Gonzalez. My family bought the Florian kennels."

"I heard. I have until the end of the month to vacate," Metz said, and spit out a stream of something brown that landed on the floor of the cabin porch. That action probably explained the splatters of indeterminate shades of brown on his overalls.

"I hope that move won't be problem," Jose said, trying to be conciliatory in the hope of defusing the situation.

"I still got a week to go," Metz said, and jammed his hands in his pockets.

Jose raised his hands as if pleading. "We're not here to rush you. We just want to ask you a few questions."

Metz hesitated and then pointed at Bongo. "What's with the dog?"

"She's my K-9 partner. She's going to help me train other dogs," Sara explained and rubbed Bongo's head and ears. "She's friendly," she added, as if also trying to calm any unease that might make Metz act violently.

Metz grunted and then glared at Trey. "You're a cop, aren't you?"

Trey shook his head. "Not anymore. I work with my family now."

"If you're not a cop, why are you here and asking me questions?" Metz said, narrowing his gaze as he focused on Trey.

Since it seemed that Metz had an issue with cops, Jose said, "You used to work for the Florians, right?"

Metz shifted his gaze to Jose and said, "And who are you?"

"I'm Jose Gonzalez. I'm the real estate agent," Jose said, hoping it would continue to defuse any tension.

Laughing, Metz said, "A real estate agent? That's a good one. I'm afraid now. Real afraid."

Jose's gut tightened with anger at being so easily discounted but forced a smile to his face. "Just a real estate agent. You worked for the Florians?"

After another slight hesitation, Metz nodded. "I did. Just some general handyman stuff around the kennels."

"They let you stay here once it closed?" Sara asked.

Metz dipped his head and said, "They wanted to make sure nothing happened to the place since they weren't around."

"Did you notice anything out of the ordinary?" Trey asked.

Metz shook his head. "Nothing. It's pretty quiet out here."

Jose peered at Trey, needing his confirmation to continue. At the slight nod of Trey's head, Jose faced Metz and said, "Do you remember Terry Hansen?"

Metz frowned and peered upward, as if searching the sky for an answer, but then he nodded with some conviction and said, "Pretty little thing. She was around for a while and then just up and left."

"Left? Where did she go?" Sara asked, playing the innocent even though they were all well aware of Terry's fate.

With a casual shrug, Metz said, "Got me."

"Did Terry get you? You like pretty little things like her, don't you?" Trey challenged, getting an immediate reaction.

Metz jabbed his finger in Trey's direction. "I didn't touch Terry just like I didn't touch that girl. She lied about her age and lied to the police because she didn't want her parents to know she liked it."

"She liked it? She was thirteen!" Trey shot back.

Jose knew his cousin well enough to know Trey would like nothing better than to lock Metz up, but to do that they needed evidence.

To lower the temperature again, Jose said, "We found Terry, Barry. We know where she is."

Metz smiled and pointed in Jose's direction this time. "You hear that, Trey? Why aren't you asking her about what I didn't do?"

In a deadly calm tone, Trey said, "Because we found her in a hole in the ground."

METZ ROCKED BACKWARD and Sara feared he was reaching for his gun, but then the man just collapsed into a rocking chair on the porch. The wood of the chair creaked with the weight of him and crazily tilted back, worrying her that it might crash to the ground, but Metz stabilized it with his feet.

If she read his face and actions correctly, Metz seemed truly shocked by what Trey had just said. He either was an award-worthy actor or an innocent man.

"You knew Terry. You liked her. You want us to figure out what happened, don't you?" Sara said, exploiting what she was reading in the hopes he might reveal more.

"Where did you find her?" he asked and peered at Trey almost pleadingly.

"You know where, Metz. Only one hole big enough on the property around the time Terry left," Trey said.

Metz's eyes widened as if the answer had suddenly come to him. It struck her again: actor or innocent?

"The contractors dug a hole to fix a drainpipe," he said, his tone almost defeated, she thought.

"And you filled it up after putting Terry in there, didn't

you?" Trey said, charging into cop mode the way he might have in an interrogation room.

Metz slapped his hands on the arms of the rocker. "I didn't kill Terry. Like I said, she just up and left."

"Right around the time the contractors were doing the work," Jose said and then added, "Who filled up the hole, Barry?"

With a shrug and shake of his head, Metz said, "I thought the contractors did it, but they acted surprised that it was filled."

Which confirmed what Sasto told them, Sara thought.

"Who else had access to the property?" Trey prompted.

Metz spread his arms wide. "Look around. Not much here. Almost anyone could come and go on that property without anyone noticing."

Sara peered around and hated that he was right. Between the wide-open spaces and the woods, it would be easy, especially at night, for someone to enter the property and not draw much attention.

"Was there anyone else working at the kennels who was friends with Terry? Who maybe showed too much interest?" Jose asked.

Besides yourself, Sara thought, and somehow wasn't surprised by Metz's answer.

"Everyone loved Terry. She had her issues, but she was a good kid," Metz said.

"What kinds of issues?" Jose asked, his tone sympathetic once more.

"Rumor had it she did some hooking in the South Beach area. Heard her pimp wasn't too pleased with her coming to live and work out here," Metz replied.

"Know his name?" Trey asked.

Metz shrugged and shook his head. "No. Are you done now? I got some packing to do."

Trey nodded and said, "We appreciate your help."

He was about to turn and walk back to the car when Jose asked, "By the way, do you own a bow of any kind?"

Chapter Fifteen

Jose braced for Metz's reaction, but the man merely gestured to the shotgun and then raised hands with knuckles swollen by arthritis. "Do these fingers look like they can use a bow? I can barely pull the trigger."

Jose's grandmother had suffered from the disease, so he recognized how debilitating it could be. But that didn't necessarily eliminate Metz from the earlier killings.

"If you think of anything—" Jose began, but Metz cut him off with a barked laugh.

"Yeah, sure, I'll let you know."

Jose shared a look with Trey and then Sara. Together the three of them turned, but before they headed back to the SUV, Sara swung back toward Metz and said, "Do you mind if I walk Bongo? She's been in the car too long."

Metz delayed, but then did an almost regal wave of his hand. "Walk away. It's your property after all."

Jose was surprised by his easy acquiescence and pleased by Sara's quick thinking.

With a click of her tongue, she strolled with Bongo to the stand of trees. The dog was active at first, but then paused to lay on the ground. Sara seemed surprised by that and urged Bongo to her feet to let her sniff some more. Bongo lay down again, forcing Sara to tug on her leash and get her working her way toward the cabin. As she did so, Metz rose to watch, appearing a little more anxious as the dog nosed around the edges of the small cabin. Luckily, Bongo stopped at one point to relieve herself and Sara responsibly picked up the waste.

Once she did so, she walked Bongo toward the front porch where Metz stood at the edge, peering down at her.

Bongo stopped to scent him, and he stumbled back from the bloodhound.

"Don't worry, she's friendly," Sara said again, but Metz kept his distance.

Sara walked toward them and once she was at their side, they all hopped back into the SUV, but remained silent until Trey had turned out of the driveway and onto the narrow road that ran along the edges of the kennel's property.

Jose swiveled in the seat. "Bongo scented something close to the cabin?"

Sara nodded. "She did. Something dead."

Whipping his head around to gaze at Trey, he said, "What do we do now?"

Trey tightened his hands on the wheel, knuckles white from the pressure of his grasp. "The police need probable cause to search Metz's home and I'm not so sure that we have enough right now."

"But you own the property. Can't we give them what they need?" Jose asked, unsure how things like that worked in Trey's world.

Sara laid a hand on his shoulder and squeezed. "It's a fine line to walk. We don't want a defense attorney claiming we were acting on behalf of the police and doing a warrantless search that violates Metz's civil rights."

"What about the rights of those women? And any others that may be buried in that forest? Don't they have rights?" Jose shot back, angered that the criminals had more rights than their victims.

"You're preaching to the choir," Trey said, and turned off

onto the road leading to the highway. "Let's head back to the offices and regroup. Discuss how to proceed."

JOSE SHOOK HIS head in disgust. "How to proceed? I'm all for finding out what Bongo is smelling," he said, and glanced back in Sara and Bongo's direction.

Sara was all for that also, but it wasn't that easy, she thought, and rubbed Bongo's head and ears. "If there is a dead body there, we don't want to compromise any evidence that might be in that location," she explained, and at his exasperated sigh, she added, "But maybe we can consider identifying areas where Bongo scents something."

Trey nodded and said, "That's a possibility but only if we proceed with extreme caution. For all we know, there are other booby traps in those woods."

Sara had no doubt there were other surprises waiting for them. Because of that, she said, "Safety is a top priority. We don't want any of the team to get hurt."

Jose and Trey were silent for long moments, and it worried her.

Trey was likely running through all the scenarios for how the SBS team should proceed as he drove them to Miami and the SBS offices. As for Jose, was he reconsidering his involvement? Had this gotten to be more than he bargained for when he'd agreed to help?

She leaned back in her seat, also thinking about all that had happened and how different it was from what she thought she'd be doing in her new job. She'd thought she'd be comfortably settled in the former owners' house and getting the place ready for a new batch of agents and their dogs.

Not this, she thought, and sighed as it brought worries about the kind of exposure she'd had with her family's earlier problems.

Beside her Bongo also sighed, laid her head on Sara's lap and looked up at her with those mournful brown eyes.

Sara smiled and stroked her hand across the dog's smooth loose skin, shifting the folds with her caress. "It's going to be okay, girl," she said, more to reassure herself and not the dog.

"It is," Jose echoed from the front seat. "We will figure out what's going on."

His words alleviated her earlier worry since it didn't sound as if Jose was going to run from whatever was happening, impressing her again with his resolve.

It eased some of her anxiety as did running her hand back and forth along Bongo, taking comfort from that connection to her partner and to the man who was proving to be more than she imagined when she first met him.

As for Trey, although he kept quiet, she had no doubt he was mentally running through all the likely scenarios for how to find out who had murdered Terry Hansen and the other woman in the grave, as well as any other bodies they found.

When they reached the SBS building, they hurried up to the office where Mia had arranged for assorted sandwiches to be brought in so they could work through dinner.

Sophie and Robbie were already in the conference room as well as Trey's pregnant wife, Roni, and Mia's multimillionaire tech husband, John Wilson.

At nearly six months, Roni's baby belly was well-pronounced, and she looked pale and a little tired. It made Sara wonder how she was handling the demanding job of being a Miami Beach detective and helping out the SBS team as well.

Trey immediately went to her side, hugged her and then rubbed his hand across her belly in a tender caress. "How are you feeling?" he asked, worry alive in his gaze.

"Tired and I have a backache. I just need to get some rest," Roni said with a forced smile.

"Maybe you should head home," Trey suggested, but Roni shook her head.

"I've got some info from local PD. Not much, but some," she said, and sat.

Mia walked over and rubbed her hand across Roni's shoulders. "Help yourselves to the food and drinks so we can get this meeting going," she said, and eyeballed everyone to get them moving along.

Sara did as she asked, grabbing some lean ham and cheese as a snack for Bongo until she could feed her later. Setting that on a plate for her dog, she then grabbed a sandwich, chips and a soda for herself and sat.

A second later Jose joined her, offering her a weary smile. Once the rest of the team had settled down, Trey started the meeting.

"Why don't you go first so I can get you home, Roni."

"Your suspicions about the identity of the one woman were accurate. The local police were able to ID Terry Hansen thanks to dental records her family provided," Roni said.

"What about COD?" Sophie asked.

Jose gave her a puzzled look that vanished as Roni said, "The ME couldn't be sure about the cause of death, but both women had bone damage indicative of being shot by a broadhead arrow. There was also a piece of a shirt that the ME could match up with the skeleton, and the damage on that was also indicative of an arrow wound."

"Like the arrow someone shot at us today?" Jose asked, brow furrowed with worry.

"Very similar to that arrow. By the way, the ME found traces of human blood on the arrowhead, but no viable prints," Roni said, and peered in Sara's direction. "I understand Bongo scented something."

Sara nodded. "Possibly, and if we're relying on that, Sasto is not a suspect any longer."

"I ran the suspects through my probability program, and it confirms that. The probability for Sasto to be the killer is only 35 percent," John Wilson said, and passed around copies of a report his program had generated.

Jose peered at it and said, "This is what your secret program does?"

With a shrug, John said, "Not so secret anymore since I've offered a version of it to Miami Beach PD to test."

"A version of it?" Sara asked, also wondering what the program did and why someone had almost killed John and Mia in order to get it.

John peered around the table and at Trey's nod, he explained. "A scaled down version. My program sucks in data from pretty much everywhere and uses that to determine probabilities on who might be a crime victim or who might have committed the crime."

JOSE SCRUTINIZED THE report that John had provided, trying to make sense of what he was seeing based on what John had just said. Waving the paper in the air, he said, "According to your program, Sasto is out and the probability that Metz is our suspect is only about 65 percent. Failing grade, isn't it?"

John nodded. "A failing grade because Metz is on disability due to his RA."

Jose confirmed it, saying, "I saw his hands today. They were in pretty bad shape."

"And he didn't stand for long. He plopped down in that rocker really quick but it could have been because of what we said about Terry Hansen," Sara added.

"Plus no bomb-making experience," Roni said, then winced and rubbed her belly, in obvious discomfort.

"Which leaves us back at square one," Trey said, with a frustrated sigh before turning his attention to his wife. "Maybe I should take you home."

Roni shook her head, and the shoulder-length strands of

her sun-streaked light brown hair shifted with the action. "I'm okay. Let's just finish up."

"Let's," John said, and whipped out more copies that he handed to everyone.

As Jose peered over the report, John explained. "This is a list of sex offenders in a sixty-mile radius who have some kind of experience with explosives and/or military tactics."

Jose's eyes widened at how many names were on the list. It seemed like way too many but beside each name was a number. He gestured to the number and said, "Is this the probability of them being connected to the murders?"

"It is," John said and quickly added, "And I don't need the program to know that this is probably a serial killer and there will be more bodies on that property."

"Bongo thinks so too," Sara said, and hearing her name, Bongo sat up at Sara's side. She rewarded the dog with a rub of her ears and a treat from her jeans pocket.

"What do you want us to do?" Sophie said and laid down the list she had also been perusing.

Trey smoothed his hands across the report as it sat on the tabletop. "You and Robbie should take the top five suspects on here and do a little more digging. No pun intended."

After, he looked toward Mia and John. "This is great, John. *Gracias.* We have a list of missing women, and maybe you can do something to see if any of them have interacted with our suspects."

John nodded. "I can run their data, locations, etcetera and see where they intersect."

Trey turned his attention to Jose and Sara. "I guess we can work with Matt and Natalie in the morning to identify any areas in our woods where we think we might have a body. But just identify and not touch. We don't want to jeopardize the evidence."

"Or trip a booby trap," Jose added.

With a dip of his head, Trey said, "Or trip a booby trap. Is there anything else to discuss?"

Robbie held his hand up, drawing Trey's attention. "What's up, *primo*?"

"Sophie and I were thinking that we could also send up one of the lidar drones to map the area. See if it's showing any irregularities belowground."

With an affirmative nod, Trey said, "That's a great suggestion. It could confirm whatever the K-9 team locates, and help the local PD once we call them in."

"When will we call them in?" Roni asked, weariness evident in her tones and the droop of her shoulders.

"We can have one of them join us in the morning if you think that's appropriate," Trey said.

"Detective Ray Espinoza is the lead on the murder case. If it is a serial killer, the faster he's in on this, the better," Roni said and quickly added, "I can let him know if you want."

"Call him, *por favor*," Trey said, rose and held his hand out to Roni.

She slipped her hand into his, her actions slow and pained. Trey clearly noticed as well since he eased his arm around her waist to offer support and comfort.

"We'll meet back here at 9:00 a.m. to head to the kennels."

When they all nodded, he continued. "John, thanks for your help. If you and Mia have anything else—"

"We'll let you know. Why don't you get Roni home now?" Mia said, also picking up on the other woman's discomfort.

"I'm okay," Roni said, not that you could tell from the look on her face and the almost stiff way she was moving.

"*Amorcito*, let's go home," Trey said, and kissed her cheek, which dragged a hint of a smile from Roni.

"Time for all of us to get some rest," Mia said, shooting to her feet and grabbing hold of John's hand.

"I guess we're going," John said with a laugh, and followed his wife as she nearly raced out the door.

Sophie and Robbie snapped their laptops close and likewise stood, but Robbie said, "We've still got some work to do. We'll be in our offices if you need us."

"Buenas noches," Jose said, and waved at his two cousins as they left the room, heads bent together while they chatted about the tasks left to finish that night.

He glanced at Sara. "You ready to go? Want to grab some chips and things for the penthouse?"

"I'll never say no to a chip. Bongo either," Sara said with a laugh, and playfully rubbed behind the bloodhound's ears. Leaning close to her dog and wrinkling her nose, she said, "Maybe after a nice bath."

Leaving the table, they grabbed a few bags of chips, strolled to the elevators and badged themselves up to the penthouse, but as they did so, Sara said, "Don't you want to go home?"

With a shrug, Jose said, "As much as I want to go home, it makes sense for me to stay close during this investigation. Unless you want some privacy."

She waved her hands in refusal. "I like the company, especially with all that's happening."

As the elevator stopped and they entered the penthouse, lights from under the kitchen cabinets spilled golden beams onto the countertops, but the real light show was outside the wall of windows that faced the city and Key Biscayne.

SARA WALKED TO the windows and stood there, Bongo tucked beside her.

"Beautiful, isn't it?" she said.

Jose walked to her side and murmured, "Beautiful," but as she met his gaze, she realized he wasn't talking about the sights outside the window.

Heat flared through her and rushed to her cheeks. She

ripped her gaze from his and focused on the beauty beyond. The harshness of the man-made buildings was juxtaposed against the moonlight glittering on the calm waters of the bay.

"I pictured you as a nature girl. It made me wonder why you would come to a place like this," he said, and pointed out the window.

"I'm more comfortable in the wilderness but there's beauty in so many things," she said, and sneaked a peek at him from the corner of her eye.

"There is. Ugliness too, like what we found at the kennels," he said, his tone filled with anger and disgust.

"We will get justice for those women and for anyone else out there," she said, and turned away from the window. "I need to tend to Bongo. Feed her, take her for a walk, and then give her a nice bath. It's important to keep all those folds clean."

He glanced at Bongo and arched a brow. "That's a lot of folds. Need help?"

"Sure, but first food. She's got a healthy appetite," Sara said, and hurried to the fridge for the fresh food she gave Bongo at night.

The bloodhound devoured it, and after taking her for walk so she could relieve herself it was time for the bath, a necessity to keep Bongo clean and avoid any issues with the loose skin on her body.

In the bathroom she prepped a bath, adding a special shampoo to the water.

Bongo licked her face and Sara laughed at the dog's antics. "I know you love your baths," she said, and the dog didn't hesitate to jump in, splashing water over the edges of the tub.

Sara chuckled and washed Bongo, scrubbing her down with the lather. Carefully checking her skin for signs of any irritation and washing beneath any folds to keep them clean and avoid nasty doggy odor.

She had just finished rinsing off the soap and pulled the

plug on the bath to empty the water when Jose came in with an armful of towels.

He sat on the toilet seat cover and handed her one.

"Thank you," she said, and toweled down Bongo who helped her by shaking her head and body, sending droplets of water flying across Sara and the tiles of the shower.

Jose laughed and handed her a fresh towel. "Looks like you might be needing this."

"Thanks, again." She grabbed the towel and wiped the water off her face. Dabbed at the spots staining her blouse and jeans.

Bongo hopped out of the tub, wetting her again as she brushed past Sara on her way out of the bath.

"Looks like you may need to clean up too," Jose laughed, and pointed a thumb in the direction of the open concept space. "I'm going to go shower. Meet you out there after?"

Chapter Sixteen

"Definitely." She liked spending time with him and was excited about where it might lead but also worried about how she might fit into a world like his, filled with so many events and people.

She hurried from the bathroom and after cleaning up from Bongo's bath, showered. The warmth of the water spilled over her, chasing away the tension of the day. Helping to prepare her for what she might face tomorrow when they searched the woods.

She worried they'd find a body in the woods between them and Metz's cabin.

Rushing from the shower, she slipped into an oversize T-shirt and loose shorts, her typical nighttime casual wear. They were comfortable and more so, they wouldn't give Jose the idea that she was throwing herself at him although in truth, maybe that's what she wanted to do despite her misgivings.

Jose was already on the sofa when she exited her room, Bongo sitting at his feet. As she approached, she noticed the highball glass with rum sitting beside his scotch. Scattered around the glasses were the few chip bags they'd snagged from the conference room.

She sat next to him, grabbed a bag of chips and opened it. "Thanks."

Hearing the ruffle of the bag, Bongo came to her side, clearly expecting a treat. "Just one. You know they have too much salt."

Bongo whined but didn't budge so Sara gave her the one chip, and seemingly satisfied, Bongo drifted a few feet away to lay by her bedroom door.

"Really? Just one?" he said as he munched on his chips.

"Just one. She's learned that, and I give her healthier treats when she's working," she said, and tossed a chip into her mouth. The saltiness of it had her reaching for her rum and taking a small sip.

"Maybe I should limit myself too," she said with a laugh, and set the bag down, but kept the rum, holding the glass between her hands, steadying herself. Being close to Jose created too many unsettling feelings.

He held his scotch glass in one hand and eased his arm around her shoulders, drawing her closer.

She snuggled into his side, savoring the warmth of his body and the strength of it. Of him. Of his character.

Most of the men she'd known growing up would certainly have run after the explosions much less the discovery of the bodies. They were men unaccustomed to physical dangers. They lived their danger in the stock market and business ventures.

She'd thought Jose was like them in so many ways but as the days passed, he set himself apart from them in unexpected ways, including hanging in unlike her boyfriend had done.

"You've been a surprise," she admitted, then brought her legs up, knelt and faced him.

He seemed taken aback. "Really? How?"

She scrutinized him, dipping her head before cradling his jaw. "You're still here, for one."

A half smile lifted his lips, yanking free a boyish dimple. "You expected me to run?"

A rough laugh escaped her. "Maybe. When my dad got in trouble, my boyfriend at the time tucked tail and ran. And what's happening now sure isn't what either of us signed up for."

"It isn't, but we're going to see this through, right?" he said, and planted a kiss in the center of her palm.

"We are." She set her glass on the table and slipping onto his lap, she said, "There's something else we need to do."

JOSE HADN'T WANTED to push and certainly hadn't expected that Sara would.

"Are you sure?"

She shook her head and laughed. "No. I'm not normally a risk-taker."

"I'm not either," he said, but didn't hesitate to cradle her against him, his hands stroking the long line of her back as she straddled him.

"What have we gotten ourselves into?" she asked and ran her fingers through the short strands of his hair before dipping her hand down to trace the edges of his lips with one finger.

He watched her, seeing the gray of her gaze deepen to charcoal and her pupils widen as she focused on his lips. "Murder. Mayhem," he said seriously, but then added in a lighter tone, "Romance?"

She smiled, her full lips tilting up playfully at the corners, making it impossible to resist them and her any longer.

He kissed her, savoring the warmth of her lips. Loving the taste of her, especially as she opened her mouth, almost shyly. She danced her tongue out to meet his as they kissed over and over until they were both breathing heavily, and he needed more.

Reaching up, he cupped her breast, her nipple hard against his palm.

She lowered her head to watch him as he caressed her. Moaned and shifted against his legs, settling him at her center. The heat of her bathed him and from somewhere deep inside him came something like a growl and an emotion he'd never felt before with any other woman.

"I want you," he whispered against her lips.

"I want you too," she answered, and with that, he shot to his feet with her cradled in his arms.

He marched with her to her room and paused by the door as Bongo raised her head and eyeballed him guiltily.

Or at least that's how it looked to him, which made him kick the door closed for privacy from the bloodhound's too alert gaze.

Hurrying to the bed, he gently laid her on the comforter and eased beside her as he noticed a few scattered bruises on her creamy skin. He traced one on the tanned skin of her arm and said, "I wish this wasn't how we met."

She ran her fingers through his hair again and cradled the back of his skull, drawing his attention to her gamine face once more. "Tell the truth. I'm not the kind to spend time in one of your typical clubs or parties or all those big social events."

He chuckled and shook his head. "No, you're not and I'm glad for it," he said, bent and kissed her again, rejoicing in that difference. At the honesty of her and her beauty.

Sara stroked her hands up and down the powerful line of his back. Held him close as they kissed and he slipped his hand beneath her T-shirt, caressing her again. The tug of his fingers dragged a surprised gasp, and he tempered his touch until she laid her hand over his and urged him on.

He lost his carefully held restraint, deepening his kiss. Breaking away from her only to ease off her T-shirt and then his so they would be skin-to-skin.

She was so smooth against him, so tender and yet strong.

When she shifted her hips, pressing upward, he dipped a finger beneath the waistband of her shorts and eased his hand between her legs to build her passion until there was no stopping where they were going.

He slipped off her shorts and his sweats, muttered a curse. "Hold on. I'll be back."

Hurrying to his room and his wallet, he ripped the condom out of it, tearing the foil and rushing to roll it on before he fell back onto the bed with her laughing, and urging him over her. Into her.

Dios, he thought as he slipped into her. It was like nothing he'd ever felt before. It was like coming home.

HE STILLED ABOVE HER, confusing her.

She met his gaze and his amazing aqua eyes, normally like Biscayne Bay on a sunny day, were a dark, intense teal. "Jose?" she asked, puzzled by his hesitation.

"You're so beautiful. So special," he said, and bent his head to whisper a kiss against her lips, his touch tentative.

"So are you, Jose. So special," she said, knowing that at times he felt insecure about his place in the accomplished Gonzalez family. She wanted him to know there was no reason for that. He was as special, maybe more so, than his cousins.

He moved then, drawing in and out of her, making her tremble from the surge of passion he roused by that simple movement.

She dug her fingers into his shoulders, struggling for control. Needing his strength as he surged into her again and as desire built, it drew them up higher and higher until with one last thrust, he took them over the edge.

Afterward, they lay there silently, holding each other. Stroking and caressing as they savored the peace and joy that came from their union.

"I won't ever be sorry we met like this," she said, and rose on an elbow to gaze at him.

He grinned and faced her. "I won't either."

"What if we find what I think we will tomorrow?" she asked, worried about what the future might bring.

With a determined dip of his head, he laid a hand at her waist and said, "Then we'll deal with it together."

Chapter Seventeen

She woke wrapped in his arms and greeted the morning with his loving, dawn's hopeful rays bathing their bodies through the wall of windows.

After showering and making a quick breakfast for themselves and Bongo, they took her dog for a walk around the block. Bloodhounds needed a good amount of exercise and activity, and she worried Bongo hadn't gotten enough the last few days.

But she would today, Sara thought, thinking about the search they'd have to conduct and what it would reveal.

"I can see the wheels turning," Jose said, and playfully tapped his temple in emphasis.

"Racing might be a better adjective," she said with a smile and toss of her head.

He nodded and said, "It's going to be a busy day."

As they rounded the last corner before the SBS office building, Jose's phone chirped.

Brows furrowed, he said, "It's Trey."

He answered and his look turned even darker. "Don't worry. We can handle things on our own. The important thing is to make sure Roni is okay."

Fear gripped Sara at the mention of the pregnant woman, and she recalled how she'd looked the night before. Too tired and pale, she thought.

Jose ended the call. "Roni's spotting. Trey's taking her to the hospital."

She laid a hand on his arm, trying to reassure him and herself. "She's going to be fine. These things happen sometimes."

"I hope so. They're both so excited about the baby," he said, looked away and muttered an expletive. "Trey said to go with Sophie and Robbie. He'll meet us there later. Matt and Natalie will be there at ten."

"Let's find Sophie and Robbie," she said, and with a click of her tongue, instructed Bongo to walk with them back to the SBS offices. Inside they found Sophie and Robbie packing the drone equipment to map the woods.

In no time they were on their way to the kennel location. Once they arrived, Jose and she waited while their tech gurus prepared the drone and computer equipment that might confirm whatever Bongo and the other canines found during their search.

"I've heard about using lidar drones to find hidden objects, but I've never had firsthand experience," Sara said as Sophie did a final check on the equipment.

"We've used it several times and I still find it amazing," the other woman admitted.

"Thankfully we have John's supercomputer to process the data. That really speeds things up," Robbie said, and walked over with the remote.

The crunch of tires on the driveway gravel drew their attention.

Matt and Natalie had arrived.

They parked, exited the van and seconds later, their two K-9 partners bounded out of the SUV and raced over to Bongo. The three dogs eagerly sniffed each other and tussled playfully until their human partners instructed them to sit.

Matt spoke up first. "Natalie and I were discussing that while our dogs are good trackers, they haven't really had much experience with cadavers."

"We thought we should shadow you and let the dogs get acquainted with the smell if we find anything," Natalie said, and rubbed her Lab's head.

Sara nodded. "Good idea. Honestly, searching for cadavers isn't something Bongo and I usually do, but she's been trained for it."

JOSE HAD BEEN letting the K-9 agents and his tech cousins run the show. But it seemed to him they were losing sight of something important and with Trey's absence, he felt he had to say something.

"I know you're all ready to search, but don't forget someone may have set some booby traps out there," he said, and gestured toward the woods and the caution tape they'd tied around the trip wires they'd already located, and had been defused by the bomb squad the day before.

"You're right. We have to move cautiously and be alert." Sara seconded his warning, earning murmurs of agreement from the other SBS agents.

At their seeming acceptance, Jose said, "I can be a second set of eyes if you want."

"That would be great," Sara said, and stroked a hand down his arm.

"We should get going. The police and CSI units are waiting on us to continue their investigation," Sophie said, and lifted the drone out of the SUV cargo area.

"We've programed this to survey the wooded area and just beyond, to the cabin where Metz is living," Robbie said, cradling the remote in his hands.

"You may hear a buzzing sound as it flies overhead. Don't let it distract you," Sophie warned, and pulled some yellow stake flags from the cargo area.

She handed them to Jose and said, "Can you mark anywhere you get a hit?"

Jose nodded. "I think I can manage that," he said with a self-deprecating chuckle.

"Let's go," Sara said, and with a quick hand signal to her dog, Bongo jumped to life, bounding ahead of her.

Jose fell into step beside her while Matt and Natalie followed, their dogs on a tight leash as they approached the woods.

Sara paused there, searching the edges of the tree line where bits and pieces of the shrapnel in the booby trap peppered the ground. Other pieces had embedded themselves in the bark of the trees along the perimeter.

Jose's gut tightened and grew cold at the thought of what might have happened if they had tripped that trap.

He shared a look with Sara before she drew in a long breath and nodded. "I'm ready."

He wasn't sure he was, but he'd never run from a challenge. With a slow dip of his head, he confirmed he was ready and walked by her side, his gaze glued to the ground and trees in their path. For safety's sake, he grabbed a long branch and used it to poke and prod at the ground before them.

As he did so at one spot, the leaves scattered there gave way, revealing a hole big enough to swallow up a man. Mindful of the risk of a secondary trap, they all quickly retreated the way they'd come in and waited, but nothing happened.

Retracing their steps, they peered into the hole. At the bottom, sharpened sticks would have seriously damaged anyone who fell in.

"Vietcong used traps like this," Matt said.

"Whoever this is, they mean business," Natalie said.

At Sara's side, Bongo whined and tugged on her leash.

SARA WOULD HAVE normally given Bongo free rein to follow the scent, but with the surprises the killer had rigged, she drew Bongo close and kept a keen eye out for dangers.

Bongo tugged her about ten feet away, focused on a scent. As they neared an area a little more concave than the rest of the ground, Bongo jerked on her leash harder, nosed around the leaves and underbrush, and then sat down.

Sara raised her hand and motioned for Matt and Natalie to come forward. Pointing at the ground, she said, "Let your partners scent this area and reward them."

She knelt and rewarded Bongo with praise, her favorite ear rub and a treat. The other SBS agents mimicked her actions as their dogs smelled the area and sat down, copying what Bongo had done.

Satisfied they had located a possible cadaver, Sara motioned to Jose who stuck a yellow stake flag into the ground.

They continued through the woods, allowing Bongo to search and the other dogs to train. Carefully minding the areas for traps.

They found two other spiked pits and marked them as well for the safety of the police and CSI crews who would gather evidence.

After Bongo's third hit, the other two K-9s had seemed to get the hang of it, sniffing and sitting down to notify their handlers of a hit.

"They're quick learners," Sara said, pleased by how well the other dogs had caught on. But then again, Belgian Malinois and Labradors were great dogs for cadaver searches.

"Do you think you can do it on your own?" she asked, examining the large swath of trees they still had to cover. As she did so, she caught sight of the drone flying overhead, also searching the area.

Matt and Natalie shared a look before nodding. "I think we can. We'll keep an eye out for booby traps, go to the top end of the woods, and work our way toward you."

"That makes sense. Call if you need anything," Jose said, and waved his cell phone.

Natalie nodded. "We'll keep you posted."

Matt and Natalie carefully worked their way back to the tree line and hurried to the top of the hardwood hammock to start their exploration.

Jose and Sara resumed their search, Bongo in the lead. As Jose tapped the ground with the stick, a loud snap split the air.

She caught a blur of motion from the corner of her eye and a second later, Jose grabbed her, his hands hard on her shoulders, pulling her against his chest.

Another spiked volleyball split the air in front of her, passing dangerously close to Bongo.

"Down," she called out, and the bloodhound instantly lay flat.

Jose wrapped his arms around her, and they dropped to the ground, Jose protecting her body against any secondary attack.

She held her breath, waiting for an explosion.

Chapter Eighteen

What seemed like an eternity passed, but nothing happened.

Jose raised his head to peer around.

Nothing. *Nada*, he thought.

Despite that, he warily rose to his feet, peering around the area again before he offered Sara a hand up.

She stood, her blouse and jeans stained with dirt and grass.

"Sorry," he said, and brushed away an errant leaf from her shoulder. "I've messed you up again," he said, regret slamming into him that he'd triggered the trap.

She cupped his cheek. "You kept me safe. Again. I owe you twice now."

Turning, she urged Bongo to move away from the spiked ball arcing back and forth, back and forth.

But Bongo refused to move.

She gave Bongo both verbal and hand commands, attempting to move the bloodhound, but her dog wouldn't budge.

"She's scented something there, right?" Jose said and at Sara's reluctant nod, he plunked a stake into the ground.

Seemingly satisfied with that, Bongo came to her feet, and they continued their search, identifying two other areas before their path intersected with that of Matt and Natalie.

Jose jammed his hands on his hips, sweat pouring off him from the heat and humidity beneath the canopy of trees. He did a slow swivel, taking in the sight of the traps they'd identified and worse, the almost dozen flags marking the spots where their dogs had identified possible remains.

No, not just remains. Burial sites. Graves, he thought and met Sara's troubled gaze.

"Is this possible?" he said and waved a hand in the direction of all the bright yellow scattered around the forest.

Sara, Matt and Natalie likewise scrutinized the grounds, disbelief on their faces until Sara locked her gaze with his and in a soft tone said, "It is. Sadly, it is."

THERE WAS LITTLE exuberance around the conference room table that night as the SBS team gathered.

Trey sat at the head, hair rumpled from the constant way he ran his fingers through his hair, clearly troubled.

"Roni will be fine, but the doctors have put her on bed rest. The stress of her job might be what's causing the spotting," Trey said, and skipped his gaze around the room. "Detective Espinoza will be our liaison in her absence."

"We're glad to hear Roni's going to be okay," Sara said since it was clear to see how worried Trey was about his wife.

"*Sí*, she is. She's going to be okay," he said, but woodenly, as if he didn't quite believe it.

Mia took hold of his hand and squeezed reassuringly. "She is, Trey. Believe it."

He nodded and quickly launched into the purpose for the meeting. "What you identified today…if you're right, we're dealing with a serial killer."

"We're right," Sara said without hesitation.

Sophie added support for her statement. "The map we produced from the drone footage confirms there are anomalies at the spots identified by the K-9s," she said, and passed around copies of the computer-generated map.

"The lidar is pretty accurate, isn't it?" Trey asked, and glanced in John's direction as he sat next to Mia.

"It is. It's a proven technology in the right hands," John said.

"And we're the right hands. We did this as carefully as we could," Robbie said to eliminate any doubt.

Trey pursed his lips and nodded. "We'll turn this over to PD who may or may not decide to call in the FBI."

"There's going to be a fire storm of publicity. We should prepare a press release about it. Maybe even do a press conference," Mia said.

Sara cringed at the thought of that, the publicity, and explaining to her mother since she was sure to call again if she heard the news. But she had no choice since she was now part of SBS and was not about to quit her job—or leave Jose—over the public exposure she so dreaded.

Trey blew out an exasperated sigh and dragged his fingers through his hair again. "I'm not sure I'm up for that. Maybe you can do it. Or Pepe," he said, and tossed a hand in Jose's direction.

Sara waited for Jose to say he wasn't part of SBS, but he surprised her with, "Whatever you need. We're all here for you."

Her estimation of him rose ever higher if that was even possible. He'd proven himself time and time again over the last few days, showing her that he was the kind of man you could count on.

"If we're sure about this map and what the K-9s discovered, it's time to move on to the suspects. Do we have anything else?"

John drew out some papers from a pile in front of him and passed around copies.

"We've cross-referenced our list with other data to eliminate suspects. Some were in prison, others were not in-state. Others are dead," John said.

Sara glanced at the list, seeing that many of their original suspects had been scrubbed. "This doesn't leave that many people," she said, disheartened.

"Unfortunately, you're right. Only a few. Hopefully our investigation and any evidence PD finds in those graves will help solve this case," Trey said.

JOSE WASN'T FEELING as confident as his cousin while he reviewed John's report.

"What do we do with this now?" he asked, unfamiliar with what his family would normally do to investigate.

"We continue to dig into their histories," Trey said and glanced around the table, settling his gaze on John, Sophie and Robbie. "Is there anything you can do to eliminate any more of these suspects before we go knocking on doors?"

The trio shared a quick look and then John nodded. "We'll work on it."

"That's it?" Jose blurted out, shocked that's all Trey could suggest. "What about Metz? He's literally living feet away from those bodies. He's been living there the entire time!"

"His RA makes him an unlikely suspect, but you're right about Metz," Trey said, his tone conciliatory despite Jose's disbelief.

"He can't be that close and not have seen something," Sara said, filling in what Trey hadn't said.

"Something or someone. While they scrub the data," Trey said, and jerked a thumb in the direction of the tech gurus, "we'll pay Metz another visit at the same time PD and the CSIs scour those areas you identified."

Guilty that he'd pushed Trey, especially since his cousin had his wife's medical issues on his mind, he said, "I didn't mean to step on any toes, Trey. I'm sorry."

Trey held his hand up and waved it off. "No worries, *primo*. With so much on my mind, all ideas are welcome."

Trey's easy attitude only made him feel guiltier until Sara laid a hand on his and squeezed reassuringly. "It seems like a good time to break."

Everyone nodded and Trey shot to his feet. "I'm going to go see Roni. You're free to have dinner brought in—"

"John and I have a dinner date with Carolina and her new boyfriend. I haven't seen much of her lately and would hate to cancel," Mia said as she likewise hopped to her feet, tugging on John's hand.

Jose glanced toward Sophie and Robbie who waved him off. "We've got work on another case," Sophie said.

He didn't think his family was matchmaking, but regardless, it left him and Sara alone for the night. "It's just you and me," he said, and peered at her.

With a smile Sara said, "Sounds good to me."

THEY REACHED THE penthouse in record time, happy to have time alone and not think about the investigation.

"Do you want to order in dinner or go out?" she said, hoping he'd want to stay in because she was tired after the day they'd had. Also dirty, she thought as she ran a hand across the smudges of dirt and grass on her blouse and jeans.

He took note of her action. "Why don't you clean up and I'll make dinner. The fridge is pretty well-stocked."

She arched a brow in surprise. "You're going to cook?"

Jose laughed and shook his head. "Did I strike you as someone who only makes reservations for dinner?"

With an apologetic shrug, she said, "Sorry to say that you did." Most of the men she'd known, including her father and brothers, would have already been on the phone placing an order.

Raising both hands as if in surrender, he said, "Let me prove you wrong. I'll prep dinner and take care of Bongo while you take a shower."

Bongo had been patiently sitting at her side and at the mention of her name, the dog barked and walked over to Jose who bent and rubbed the dog's head and ears affectionately. In response, Bongo licked his face, making Jose grimace playfully.

"Not sure I'll ever like doggie kisses," he said, and pointed toward the bedrooms. "Go. Shower. Relax."

Pleased that Bongo and he were getting along, Sara went to the bedroom and took a very long and very hot shower, savoring the heat of the water that chased away memories of the day. But as the aromas of what Jose was cooking wafted into the bedroom, her stomach growled.

Steak if she had to guess, and it smelled delicious.

Raking her fingers through the wet strands of her hair, she hurried out to where Jose had already set the table.

Bongo lay near her bowls. There was fresh water in one and evidence that she'd scarfed down the food Jose must have set out for her.

Jose was at the stove, an apron tied around his lean waist. Drops of water marked his T-shirt and the edges of the sleeves, as if he'd scrubbed his arms to wash up.

Cuban-style steaks, thinly pounded and marinated with lemon, minced onions and parsley, were cooking on the stovetop griddle. There were two pots on the stove beside it, and as she lifted the lids, she realized he'd made rice and beans.

"Smells delicious," she said, wrapping her arms around his waist and pressing her head against his back.

He stroked his hand across her arm and said, "You'd better stop distracting me if you want dinner."

After a tight hug, she said, "I'll get some drinks."

"I opened some red to let it breathe," he said, and jerked his chin in the direction of a bottle sitting on the counter.

She grabbed glasses from a nearby rack and poured them generous portions. They needed it after the day they'd had and what they would have to face once the PD and CSI teams began their investigations.

It made her feel helpless in a way because she'd come to jump-start a new K-9 division and that was all on hold with what was happening.

Jose reached out and ran his index finger across the furrows on her brow. "I can tell they're not happy thoughts."

With a twisted smile, she said, "Not happy. Selfish possibly."

"Why is that?" he said and flipped the steaks onto plates.

A second later, he was piling on rice and beans before walking with the plates to the table.

She grabbed both wineglasses and he removed a bowl from the fridge and brought it over to the table: an avocado salad.

"You went all out," she said, but he held up a finger as if to say, "I'm not done yet."

Grabbing a potholder, he opened the oven door, and returned with a plate of fried ripe plantains he'd been keeping warm.

"Wow, I'm impressed," she said as she glanced at the meal, a typical Cuban one much like her family might have had.

"I cheated and used canned beans and frozen plantains, but it works," he said.

They sat to eat, and hunger took over, making for a quick and silent meal. Bongo wandered over and lay down between them, wanting company. As pack dogs, bloodhounds didn't like being alone, and Bongo was used to being at her side for most of the day and night.

As Jose finished his rice and beans, she snagged the very last *maduro*. The ripe plantain was sweet in her mouth with the fried crunchy and caramelized bits.

Jose eyeballed her and jabbed his fork in her direction. "That was *la verguenza*."

She laughed at his reference to the Gallego's curse, namely, taking the last bit of food that should be kept in case company came. In her family, they also teasingly said that whoever took the last bit was bound to be an old maid.

But as Jose's teasing look heated and ignited warmth deep inside her, she didn't think that was going to be her fate.

Voice husky, she said, "You cooked so why don't I clean, and after we can take Bongo for her last walk of the night."

He nodded. "Sounds good."

Rushing off, she cleaned and got ready for the rest of the night, eager for what might happen. Especially if it was a repeat of the night before.

Chapter Nineteen

Night had fallen hard, an almost moonless evening with the barest sliver in the sky sprinkling light through the trees down onto the bright bits of yellow.

The flags almost looked like daffodils poking their heads out of a spring ground, but the stake flags were anything but flowers in his garden.

He tightened his hands on the stock of the crossbow, anger riding high.

Those damn dogs had done their job well, he thought as he counted the flags and noted the caution tape wrapped around his surprises.

A stream of obscenities escaped him.

They'd ruined his garden. His beauties.

They'd also ruined the fun he'd planned to have with the beautiful women who had shown up to work at the kennels.

Now he'd have to redo his plans because he intended to have his revenge, especially after what they'd done to his beautiful space.

But before he did that, he had one other thing to do.

Inching along the edges of the forest, he crept toward the cabin, careful to keep quiet because Metz's hearing was way too keen.

It was how the man had found out about his little games after Metz had moved into the cabin several years earlier.

Metz had been only too eager to remain silent if he got to take part in the fun before he added the woman to his garden.

His willing partner was now nothing but a loose end.

Creeping toward the cabin, he kept an eye out for signs of anyone else because now that Metz had the attention of SBS, someone could be watching.

He didn't see anything or anyone.

Rising on tiptoes, he peered in through a side cabin window.

Metz was asleep in a rocking chair in front of the television. Luckily for him and unluckily for Metz, the television volume was turned way up, but he didn't take any chances.

The first porch step always squeaked and so he skipped it, placing his booted foot on the second. Another step had him on the porch where he avoided another creaky spot until he was at the front door.

He'd have the element of surprise, but not for long.

Making sure the crossbow was ready, he took hold of the doorknob and twisted it slowly. Silently.

You should always lock your door, he thought as he raised the crossbow to his shoulder.

Metz roused then, a surprised look on his face, and started to stand, mouth open as if to ask what was up.

The arrow embedded itself deep in his thick chest.

Metz dropped back into the rocking chair, which groaned from his weight and rocked violently from the force of his fall.

The old man stared from the arrow in his chest to his attacker. He reached up and tried to remove it, but his gnarled fingers could barely grasp the shaft.

"Why?" he managed to say on a strangled breath as the last vestige of life escaped from his gaze.

"You failed me, Barry. You let them ruin my garden," he said, and the calm that had filled him as he had planned his kill fled.

He pulled a knife from his belt and drove it deep into his

lifeless partner, venting his rage again and again until both he and the room were splattered with blood.

Only then did the red haze in his eyes fade.

Time to go, he thought, and hurried from the cabin, but not before preparing another surprise for whoever decided to visit.

Once he was done, he walked to the woods and cut a leafy branch from a nearby pine tree. Retracing his path, he carefully used the branch to brush away his footsteps until he was in the underbrush.

If the SBS team thought it would be easy to track him, they'd be wrong.

Dead wrong.

"SHE'LL NEVER LEAVE you alone if you keep feeding her bacon," Sara said as she caught Jose sneaking Bongo a piece. "Besides, the salt and grease aren't healthy for her," she teasingly chided since she'd been guilty on more than one occasion of giving Bongo a similar treat.

Jose popped the last bit of bacon into his mouth. "Or for us but boy is it tasty," he said with a boyish grin.

She walked over, grabbed his empty plate and skimmed a kiss across his temple, but he wrapped an arm around her waist and hauled her down onto his lap for a deeper kiss.

A rough cough jerked her back to reality, and she pushed to her feet to find Trey standing by the elevator.

"I'm sorry. I didn't mean to intrude," Trey said, an amused flush on his face.

"I'm sorry if we're late," Sara said, and hurriedly grabbed the rest of their breakfast dishes to place them in the dishwasher.

"You're not late. I'm a little early," he said, and skewered Jose with a questioning look.

"We won't be long," Jose said, and picked up the remaining glasses to take them over to the sink.

"No problem. I wanted to warn you that word got out about what we found. I expect a gauntlet of reporters once we get to the kennels, but I know you've handled reporters before," Trey said, and turned his gaze on Sara.

Her stomach knotted at the thought of dealing with the reporters like she had when her father had been accused. She'd dreaded it and even afterward, when one of her and Bongo's searches had become newsworthy. She'd hesitantly dealt with reporters and their questions. But none of those searches could possibly compare to what they'd discovered on the kennel property or the attention it would bring.

Despite that, she acknowledged his statement with a dip of her head. "I have. I can handle them."

"Good. I can use all the help I can get this morning," Trey said, weariness dripping from his words.

JOSE HAD NO doubt his cousin's head wasn't completely in this game, and he understood why.

"How is Roni doing?" he asked.

A barely there smile slipped onto Trey's lips. "Much better. The spotting has stopped, and she'll be home either later today or tomorrow, but will have to continue her bedrest."

Jose walked over and squeezed Trey's shoulder. "That's good to hear, *primo*."

"It is. It'll make her crazy to just lie there, but it's what's best for the baby," Trey said, with a bob of his head.

"We're here for you. Whatever you need," Jose said, and Sara echoed his comments.

"A to-go cup of Cuban coffee and you driving so I can grab a quick nap would be greatly appreciated."

"You got it," Sara said, and while she prepped the coffee, Jose directed Trey to the sofa where his cousin plopped down tiredly.

"Roni and the baby will be fine," Jose said, trying to reassure his cousin.

"It's just…scarier than anything I've ever faced, and I've faced some scary things," Trey said, and after another shake of his head, drove his fingers through his hair.

Trey had faced drug dealers, mobsters and murderers not to mention enemy combatants during his tours of duty. That this scared him more spoke volumes about his love for his new wife.

"We're here for both of you," he said again and patted his hand on Trey's thigh in commiseration.

Trey glanced toward Sara who was just finishing up in the kitchen. "Is it a 'we' now, Pepe? Are you sure about what you're doing?"

With only a quick glance back in Sara's direction, Jose nodded and said, "I'm sure."

Trey blew out a long breath, raked his finger through his hair again, and finally said, "It's not going to get any easier, *sabes*."

In his mind's eye came the image of the yellow flags waving in the slight breeze of afternoon like grisly flowers rising up from the ground.

No, it wouldn't be easier, he thought.

"I understand, but I'm here for the long haul, hard as it may be," he said just as Sara came over to join them.

She sat in a chair across from them and handed Trey the to-go cup of coffee.

He took a sip and sighed with pleasure. "*Gracias.* It's delicious."

Sara smiled. "Glad I could help."

Trey leaned forward, the coffee cup cradled in his hands. "I know this isn't what you signed up for, Sara. I appreciate everything you've done so far."

IT WASN'T ANYTHING like she imagined her first days on the job would be, but she had no hesitation about what needed to be done.

"The women in those graves deserve justice. I will do whatever it takes to make sure they get that," she said, leaving no hesitation about her determination to finish what had been started.

He offered her a grim smile and nodded. "We will make sure they get justice. The first step is to face the press and after, visit Metz. Are you ready for that?"

Chapter Twenty

Trey had warned them there would be a gauntlet but nothing could have prepared them for what awaited their arrival at the kennels.

What seemed like a battalion of news trucks lined both sides of the road, making it almost impossible to drive to the entrance of the property. A police car, lights flashing their warning blue and red, blocked the driveway.

As they drove up, reporters and camera operators swarmed like angry bees around their SUV. The police officer guarding the entrance had to push his way through and once he identified them, he radioed his partner to move the cruiser so they could pass.

A few of the reporters tried to follow them through, but the officer chased them like a beekeeper herding worker bees back to the hive.

In front of the kennel owner's home there was a phalanx of police cars and medical examiner and CSI team trucks as well as ambulances to transport the bodies.

As they pulled up in front of the house and exited the SUV, someone peeled off from a group of CSI people in hazmat suits by one of the ME's trucks.

"That's Sandy Gonzalez, no relation. She's one of the MEs for Miami-Dade," Trey said as they waited for the woman.

When she approached, Trey introduced them. "I wish I

could say it was good to see you, Sandy. This is Sara Hernandez, the new head of our K-9 Division. Jose Gonzalez, my cousin who's helping us out."

They shook hands with the woman who didn't seem all too pleased to be there. That was confirmed with her next words.

"I was hoping your team was wrong, but we've already found human remains in the first area you've marked. I hope you didn't mess up the scene."

Trey's lips thinned into a tight line. "My people are professionals. We preserved the scene as best we could."

"Let's hope so. While we work, Detective Espinoza wants to chat with you," she said, and walked away without waiting for their reply.

"Is she always that friendly?" Jose said with a sarcastic laugh.

"If you've been murdered, she's the one you want on your case," Trey said just as an older man in a rumpled dark suit and wrinkled shirt walked up. His top button was undone, and his tie had come loose from its knot. Everything about him screamed "cop" at Jose.

"Gonzalez," the cop said, with a dip of his head in Trey's direction.

"Espinoza. You're looking good," Trey said, and clapped the man on the back.

"I'd be looking better if I hadn't been here since dawn dealing with the press," Espinoza groused, and faced Sara and Jose.

Trey introduced them. Espinoza pulled a pad out of his inside jacket pocket and immediately started taking notes and asking questions.

"What made you search the property?"

"We had several incidents once we arrived. You should have the records about the explosions, but we also had someone shoot at us," Trey said.

"With an arrow?" Espinoza said just to confirm.

"With an arrow much like the one that killed the two women we found. Your CSI people have the arrow," Jose said, already impatient with the detective's questioning.

"How did you find those women?" he asked, and peered directly at Sara and then Bongo, who was patiently sitting at her feet.

"Bongo," she said, and rubbed the dog's head before continuing. "We were searching the property for any traps and Bongo scented something. We started to dig and found the women."

Espinoza nodded, jotted something down and then motioned with his pad toward the woods where a legion of law enforcement had spread out to recover the remains and any evidence.

"What about the woods? What made you look there?"

"We noticed some wires. We thought they might be part of an old electric fence, but we tripped one and realized that someone wanted us to stay out of the woods," Sara told him.

The detective peered at the dog again. "And your K-9 scented something."

Sara once again rubbed Bongo's head in an almost nervous gesture. "She did."

Espinoza hesitated, tipping his head from side to side as if tumbling around what he'd heard, and then looked at Trey. "You sent over a list of suspects. Wilson help you get that?"

Trey nodded. "He did. Our team is running down those leads right now. We plan on speaking to Metz again."

A low "Hmm," hummed from Espinoza. "You think he's still a suspect?"

Trey dipped his head. "Possibly. At a minimum, he knows more than what he's saying and Bongo smelled something close to his cabin."

Another low hum erupted from the detective before he

slapped his notebook against Trey's chest. "You were the best detective on the force, so you know why I'm telling you this. We need to do everything by the book. Whoever killed all these women," he said, and waved the notebook around in the direction of the woods and training ring, "they need to pay for this."

"We know, Ray. That's why you're here," Trey said, and mimicked the detective's gesture, waving an arm at the police activity at the scene.

"*Bueno.* I'll leave you to issue a statement to the press. Keep it short and sweet," Espinoza said, and then quickly added, "We'll all go talk to Metz as soon as you're done."

The detective briskly walked away to join the ME and CSI teams.

"Keep it short and sweet?" Jose asked, wondering what it was the detective wanted.

"He doesn't want us to give them any info that could compromise the case."

"What's there to tell?" Jose said with a shrug.

"For starters, how many bodies there are," he said.

SARA QUICKLY ADDED, "If it bleeds, it leads. The press just loves sensational stories like this."

She'd only been involved in one murder case, and the press had turned it into front page news for days much like they had milked the accusations against her father for as long as they could.

"Are you ready for that? For them?" Trey asked and at her nod, they walked up the long driveway and past the police car where they were immediately swarmed by the press.

It was almost a physical attack as bodies crowded around her and Bongo, who hugged tight to her leg, overwhelmed by the assault. Jose wrapped an arm around her shoulders and used his other arm to block those who were trying to push closer with their cameras and microphones.

"Please give us some space," Trey said, and held his hands up as if to shove them away and then to ask for quiet.

Two police officers stepped in to offer assistance, shooing away reporters until they were at a reasonable distance.

Once they had some quiet and calm, Trey reached into the pocket of his guayabera and pulled out a piece of paper. He had clearly prepared a statement for the press in anticipation of the circus that was happening.

"*Buenos dias.* I'm Trey Gonzalez, the acting head of South Beach Security. I have with me Sara Hernandez, the new head of our K-9 Division and Jose Gonzalez, my cousin and the real estate agent who secured this property for SBS."

The reporters started tossing out questions, but Trey kept to his prepared statement.

"It came to our attention that this location might be the site of a crime. We immediately called the police to investigate. They are doing that at this time and will provide you with further reports when they deem appropriate. I ask you for patience as they conduct their investigations and that you address any questions to Detective Ray Espinoza, who is heading up the inquiry."

"Is it true your dog found multiple bodies?" one reporter called out.

Sara glanced at Trey who nodded to confirm she should answer, but she kept it discreet. "My K-9, Bongo, scented something unusual. Based on that, we called in the police."

"But is it true it's more than one woman?" another reporter shouted and shoved his mike in her face.

"No comment. You can check with Detective Espinoza for additional information."

The newspeople peppered them with more questions, but Trey ignored them and walked toward the kennel owner's house.

Jose applied gentle pressure on her shoulders, urging her to follow. He leaned close and whispered, "Are you okay?"

As she looked at the crew of people searching through the woods and thought about what they might find, she wasn't sure she'd ever be okay again. But they had to push forward for the sake of those women.

"I'll be okay as soon as we find out who did this."

DETECTIVE ESPINOZA INSISTED on going with them to interview Metz.

Jose stood by Sara and Bongo as Trey and the detective walked toward the cabin.

It struck him as odd that Metz hadn't exited as soon as they'd pulled up. He had to have heard the SBS SUV as it crunched its way up the gravel of the drive.

Beside Sara, Bongo whined and tugged on her leash, seemingly upset.

Hearing the bloodhound, Trey stopped and turned to look at them.

Espinoza stepped onto the porch and time seemed to slip into slow motion.

A sound, like a branch hitting the ground, split the air and the hackles rose on the back of Jose's neck.

Chapter Twenty-One

Trey whirled, wrapped his arm around Espinoza's body and jerked him off the porch.

The action sent the two men tumbling onto the ground with a resounding thud.

Worried about a secondary attack, Jose stepped in front of Sara and Bongo, but nothing happened.

Well, nothing if you ignored the arrow now embedded in one of the porch columns, Jose thought.

Sara, Bongo and he rushed forward to help Trey and Espinoza to their feet. The detective's eyes widened at the sight of the arrow that might have hit him if Trey hadn't acted so quickly.

"I owe you, Gonzalez," Espinoza, said and brushed red clay from his suit jacket.

"You need to watch every step. This guy is determined to take out anyone trying to find him," Trey said, and a second later he walked to the side of the porch to examine the trap that had been set.

Jose and Sara ambled over, and Trey gestured to the make-shift bow and trigger made from a branch. "Basic and rudimentary, but it did the trick."

At Sara's side, Bongo was still antsy, tugging at her leash.

"She smells something," Sara said as Bongo fought to go up the steps to the cabin.

"Let her go, but be careful," Trey said.

Sara gave Bongo a little more leash and followed her up the steps and to the front door.

Jose stayed close behind, ready to act if there were any other surprises left behind by the killer.

At the door, Sara hesitated while Bongo pawed the area near the entrance.

Jose moved forward but stopped dead at the sight of what looked like a bloody boot print.

He waved over Trey and the detective and motioned to his discovery.

"You two stay back while we go in," Espinoza said, making Trey repeat his earlier warning.

"Move slowly and carefully, Ray. There could be other traps."

The two men stood to either side of the door, and the detective grabbed the handle, turned it and threw the door open as they all held their breaths.

Nothing happened as the door flew open and rebounded against the inside wall of the cabin.

Espinoza stepped into the doorway and as Trey, Sara and he moved forward, the detective held his hand up to stop them.

"Stay back. This is now an active crime scene, and I don't think Sara and Jose should see this."

Trey stepped to his side, peered into the cabin and nodded. "You two should step away. Look around for other evidence."

Jose slipped his arm around Sara's shoulders and urged her off the porch, but Bongo continued to fuss, making her issue a sharply worded command.

"Heel, Bongo," she said, and the bloodhound finally responded, walking with them to the ground in front of the cabin.

At his questioning look, Sara said, "It was the blood. With her sense of smell, it hit her right away."

They both looked toward the cabin and while Trey and the

detective were still in the doorway, it was impossible not to see Metz's feet as he sat in a rocking chair and the blood painting the floor of the cabin red.

His stomach turned and cold sweat bathed his body at the thought of what could have made so much blood spill onto the floor.

As he faced Sara, her face was a pale, almost ghostly white. "I've never been good with this kind of thing. It's why I always stuck to search and rescue."

Like him, Sara had been forced into something well out of her wheelhouse, but he wasn't about to let that stop him from this challenge.

"Let's look around," he said, and together they walked back to the trap that the detective had triggered.

As Trey had said, it seemed very basic. Someone had cut branches off a tree and fashioned them into a bow and a trigger that would release the arrow once someone dislodged the wire.

Bending, he noted the fishing line that had been strung across the front porch to act as the trip wire.

"Most anyone has fishing line around," he said to Sara as she let Bongo sniff around the branches.

"I don't see you as the fishing type," she said with a raised eyebrow.

"I have a boat and I like to fish. I'll take you out some day."

SARA SMILED, liking the sound of that since it hinted at something more permanent. "That sounds nice, but I warn you now. I don't clean fish."

Jose grinned and playfully tapped her chin. "That's okay because I do, and I make a mean ceviche."

"I'm game," she said, and gestured toward the arrow embedded in the porch column.

"It's a lot like the arrow someone shot at us, and there's blood on it."

Jose examined the arrow, but then looked toward the cabin. "I'll wager it's Metz's blood."

"Probably," she said, and once again let Bongo sniff around the porch in the hopes of picking up a scent.

Bongo sniffed and then shook her head back and forth, sending her long ears and drool flying every which way.

"Find," Sara commanded.

Bongo glanced back at her as if to say, "Find what?"

"She doesn't look too enthusiastic," Jose said, hands jammed on his hips.

"Not enough of any kind of scent, but sometimes it's not just the K-9 that is responsible for finding someone," she said, and gestured to the ground.

"Someone stood there. See the slight imprints. The ground is too hard and dry for anything more pronounced and..." She paused and pictured the route someone might take into the woods. Gesturing to the ground again, she said, "The dirt there looks brushed smooth. See how different it looks."

Jose peered at the earth intently but shook his head. "I can't say that I do, but I trust you. If you see it, let's check it out."

"But stay clear to not wreck any evidence," she warned, keeping a wide berth of what she thought was the killer's trail while also trying not to lose it.

As with the dirt in front of the cabin, there was a decided difference in a narrow path of grass leading into the woods.

Nearing the tree line, something lighter caught her eye and she gestured to a pine tree.

"Someone cut some branches off that tree. I'm sure CSI can confirm whether it's one and the same as the branches used for the booby trap."

"I'm no expert but it looks the same to me," Jose said, with a nod.

"He went into the woods here, so my guess is he knows

his way around and he either has a place nearby or parked his car close."

"And set more traps along the way?" Jose said, gaze locked on the woods where the happy yellow of their flags and caution tape was a stark contrast to the somber crime scene.

Sara shrugged, unsure. "Maybe, unless he was in a rush or more concerned with hiding his tracks."

Searching the area, she took note of the CSI agents working the scene and then glanced toward where their killer had entered the woods. Shaking her head, she said, "We'll have to keep a close eye out. Are you with me?"

"I'M WITH YOU," Jose said without hesitation. He'd come this far and intended to see it through, no matter what.

Sara loosened her hold on Bongo's leash, giving her bloodhound a freer rein to nose around the underbrush. As the dog entered the woods, they followed at a discreet distance, but as Sara had warned, Jose kept a close eye, vigilant.

They moved slowly, cautiously, and as they did so, the cool of early morning evaporated like dew under the glare of sunlight. In the woods the shade provided some relief, but it was dank, humid and buggy as they trudged along, searching for any signs to point them in the killer's direction.

"He kept to the woods, but along the edges probably because it might be easier to track him in those fields over there," she said, and gestured to the farmland where there were rows of harvested cornstalks and beyond that, an orchard of some kind.

"Is that part of the SBS property?" she asked.

Jose nodded. "About another twenty-five acres or so belong to SBS. It's been leased to a local farmer for quite a long time, and we agreed to let them keep farming. Even dropped the lease price so they could keep it as farmland and avoid developers like Delgado from turning this area into suburbs."

"I'm shocked that a real estate agent like you would be opposed to more development," she said as they started walking again, trailing behind Bongo's lead.

"I'm all for reasonable development, but this area should stay rural. There's already too much encroachment close to the Everglades," he said, determined to protect the fragile area threatened by nearby civilization.

"You are a constant surprise," Sara said with a chuckle and a shake of her head.

Bongo tugged hard on her leash, nearly upending her.

"Easy, girl. What did you find?"

They followed Bongo as she finally emerged from the woods and into an almost five-yard-wide patch of wildflowers. Beautiful and utilitarian since the colorful flowers drew pollinators to help improve the productivity of the crops.

"Heel," Sara commanded as she noted a trampled path across the flowers and into the nearby field of cornstalks.

"Don't you want to follow?" he asked and pointed to the obvious trail.

"I do, but I also want the CSI team to preserve the evidence. Hopefully there's more boot prints. Maybe even fiber and blood to confirm this is the way the killer came."

He nodded. "Got it. I'll call Trey and let him know what we've found," he said, and made the call.

"Good work. We'll have a crew there in a few minutes," Trey said.

Jose stood next to Sara and tracked her gaze as it roamed over the fields in front of them. She raised her arm and pointed into the distance before glancing back at him.

"Is that an orchard?"

He nodded. "Mangos. Also, avocado trees. Good money nowadays thanks to all the hipsters," he said with a chuckle.

"What about a farmhouse? How far away would that be?" she asked, her mind clearly racing with possibilities.

He stood akimbo and peered out, imagining the farmhouse he'd visited while working out the details of the purchase. "Probably about a mile or so to the farmhouse. I could take you there later if you want."

"I want," she said, and her gaze skipped from the fields to the woods behind them.

"A mile or so there. Another mile of woods. Maybe less than that from the woods to the kennels," she said, and it was clear what she was thinking.

"A few miles isn't all that far. Typical walking pace is like fifteen minutes a mile, right?" he said, thinking that he could cover the distance in far less time.

She must have read his thoughts since she said, "You look like a runner. How long would it take you?"

"I do a six-minute mile, but not through brush like that and not while trying to avoid booby traps," he readily admitted, peering at the thick underbrush in the forest and how it might trip up anyone trying to rush.

"Unless you were the one who set the traps. But let's say you started near here. Parked on the road close by. You could easily make it through the woods in twenty minutes and then bam, you're at the kennels."

Definitely bam, you're at the kennels, he thought, and nodded. "The farmer wasn't on our list of suspects."

"He wouldn't be unless he'd committed a crime, but think about how many serial killers were just 'ordinary people,'" she said, emphasizing the words with air quotes.

"I'm almost afraid to ask," he said, deferring to her knowledge of the kind of evil that could commit such crimes.

"BTK. He was even president of his church council. The Butcher Baker. An apparently well-liked small-town baker who hunted his women down in the wilderness, much like what this killer is doing," Sara said, with a toss of her head in the direction of the woods behind them just in time to draw his attention to Trey, Espinoza and a duo of CSI agents.

"What have you got?" Trey asked, and searched the area around them, quickly picking up on the trampled wildflowers in the nearby patch. "Boot prints?"

Sara nodded. "Possibly."

The CSI duo did a closer inspection and the one agent, a thirtyish woman, nodded and said, "Definitely some kind of boot print." Looking around, she said, "Ground is softer here thanks to the irrigation system."

"There may be another one here," Sara said, and swept her arm in the direction of a dirt row along the edge of the cornfield.

"We didn't want to push on to keep from compromising any evidence," Jose said, but quickly added, "Sara has some thoughts on this though."

Chapter Twenty-Two

Sara gave Jose credit for giving her credit. Once again, he was proving himself to be unlike the other men she used to have in her life. But then again, the Gonzalez men were breaking the mold in many ways. Even Trey with all his alpha ways regularly surprised her with his caring and compassion.

Trey peered in her direction and said, "What are you thinking?"

"Whoever is doing this is well familiar with this area and either lives nearby or has easy access. I'm leaning toward lives nearby because while the road leading to the kennels is small, it has a fair amount of traffic."

Trey shook his head. "But not at night, and I'm willing to bet that's when he does his hunting."

Sara nodded. "I agree, but it would be less obvious if he came on foot, and Jose tells me there's a farmhouse not all that far from here."

Trey mulled over what she said, delaying for a bit before turning to Jose. "We met the farmer to discuss the lease terms. Anything rub you wrong?"

Jose's shoulders rose and dropped in a noncommittal shrug. "Can't say that it did although he did seem worried when we said we were buying the property."

"Logical considering you might want to boot him off, right?" Espinoza offered for discussion.

"Logical," Trey said to Sara. "I hired you because of your skills. That includes your ability to read people. Why don't you and Jose go to the farmhouse? Do a meet and greet as if it's just a neighborly visit."

"Makes sense," she said with a quick dip of her head.

"It does. You'd be seeing each other around. It's a perfect excuse," Jose said.

"But don't do anything stupid. If there's anything weird going on get out of there and call us. Understood?" Espinoza warned.

Jose held his hands up in surrender. "Real estate agent, remember?"

That seemed to satisfy Trey and the detective. Trey handed Jose the car keys and they hurried back to the cabin. Along the way she paused to let Bongo relieve herself and gave her a treat along with a good ear rub.

"You did great, girl," she said, and the bloodhound licked her face before they pushed on toward the cabin.

As they approached, it was impossible to miss the yellow crime scene tape surrounding the area.

Through the doorway she could see two agents working on Metz, gathering evidence.

"He was in on it," she said while they walked to the SUV, Bongo hugging her side.

"Had to be. It's why he's dead and I can't say I'm sorry," Jose replied, sweeping out his arm and drawing her close.

The shiver that wracked her body was so strong, he stopped and wrapped both arms around her in comfort.

"It's no way to go," she whispered against his chest.

Bongo, sensing her upset, leaned close and rubbed her head against Sara.

Jose reached down and petted the bloodhound's head, trying to ease her distress at her owner's anguish.

Long moments passed as they stood there, bundled together,

letting overwhelming emotions ebb so they could continue with their investigation.

When Sara shifted away slightly, she wiped tears with a shaky hand.

"You good to go meet your new neighbor?" Jose asked, clearly not rushing her in case she still needed time to compose herself.

"Ready as I'll ever be," she said, and got into the SUV for the short ride to the neighboring farmhouse.

AN OLDER BLACK pickup truck sat in the driveway as they drove up to the farmhouse.

Sara hoped it was a sign that someone was home.

Jose hopped out, walked around to Sara's side, and waited as she unharnessed Bongo and leashed her once she was on the ground.

The building had the clean lines and large front porch typical of many of the older farmhouses in the area. Fresh white paint gleamed in the sunlight while colorful impatiens lined a pea gravel path leading to the front door. Terra-cotta pots sat on the steps to the porch, filled with cascading bright pink petunias.

A painted white porch swing in pristine shape boasted comfy pillows decorated with cheerful, purple pansies. A coir mat emblazoned with the word *Welcome* sat by the front door.

Certainly not a home that screamed serial killer right off the bat. Until she reminded herself of how well people could be at hiding what was really going on inside their heads.

They had just taken a step up the stairs when the front door, which also boasted a floral wreath matching the pinks and purples prevalent in the garden, opened wide.

A handsome older man with a leonine head of white hair and neatly trimmed beard stood behind the screen door. Dressed in an immaculate white shirt and pants, he held a glass of lemonade, and looked like Colonel Sanders had just sprung back to life.

"Nice to see you again, Mr. Gonzalez. How can I help you?" he asked in a cultured voice with the barest hint of an accent that she couldn't quite place.

Jose forced a smile. "It's good to see you again, Mr. Guidry. I wanted to introduce SBS K-9 agent Sara Hernandez since she'll be your new neighbor at the kennels."

Guidry hesitated for the barest second, then stepped out from behind the screen door and held his hand out in greeting.

She shook his cold wet hand and told herself the chill was from the glass of lemonade he'd been holding just seconds before. His touch created an unsettled sensation that made her gut somersault with disgust.

Hiding her reaction, she slapped a smile on her face and said, "It's a pleasure to meet you."

He held on to her hand a little too long if you asked her, and smiled. She imagined it was what a shark looked like a second before it bit you, eyes dead behind that wide grin. As Bongo nosed around his feet, Guidry grimaced and shuffled back a bit, as if to discourage the bloodhound from continuing to sniff.

"The pleasure is all mine, my dear," he said, and slowly released her hand.

When Bongo sniffed Guidry's feet again, he escaped toward the front door.

She urged Bongo back to her side with a hand signal. A second later, Guidry faced Jose. "I understand you've had a bit of excitement at the kennel."

Jose tipped his head from side to side, delaying until he finally said, "Nothing the SBS team can't handle."

"Of course. How could I forget the famous South Beach Security team now owns the kennel? I'm sure they deal with this kind of thing all the time," Guidry replied, his tone so unctuous she imagined him sliding off the porch from its oiliness.

"What kind of thing is that Mr. Guidry?" she asked, wondering what it was that Guidry imagined was happening on the property.

With a careless kind of shrug followed by a slurpy sip of lemonade, he said, "The explosions. A murder? Maybe two?"

"You're right that SBS is handling it," Jose said, his words clipped with anger.

A low hum seeped from Guidry as he digested Jose's words. "If you need anything, just let me know. It's the neighborly thing to do, right?" he finally said.

"Of course, Mr. Guidry. We'll be sure to call if we do," Sara said, and with a gentle tug on Bongo's leash, guided the dog down the steps, but as they hit pea gravel path, Bongo stopped and looked back toward the house.

Guidry lingered on the porch, sipping his lemonade. As he realized he had their attention again, he raised the glass, as if in a toast. The action struck her as challenging rather than friendly.

"Sara?" Jose asked, placing a soothing hand at the small of her back, and likewise peered toward the other man.

"Bongo picked up on something," she said softly, and with a click of her tongue, commanded the bloodhound to move.

At the SUV, she bundled Bongo into the back seat and harnessed her in with a playful rub of her body. "You're a good girl, Bongo."

The dog nuzzled her face and Sara laughed, the dog's loving action wiping away how dirty Guidry had made her feel.

When she hopped into the passenger seat and buckled up, Jose said, "What do you think?"

"He's condescending and gave me the willies."

"The willies, huh? Is that a technical term?" Jose teased,

then started the SUV and did a K-turn to drive away from the farmhouse.

"Definitely," she said with a chuckle, and quickly added, "There's something not right about him," she said, and swiveled to take a final look at Guidry.

He was still on the porch, following them with his gaze, and that earlier sharky grin faded into a knife-sharp slash.

Yep, something was definitely not right with her new neighbor, but did it mean he was a serial killer?

Chapter Twenty-Three

The team had gathered around the conference room, plates with food from a local Asian fusion restaurant sitting in front of them as they discussed the information they had gathered.

"The police have found at least a dozen women, but it will be more since they're still digging. The bodies were in various states of decay, and their best guess is that the earliest of them go back about four years. There are also two victims who are recently deceased, including one that was buried only days ago," Trey said and passed around photos.

Jose peered at the crime scene photo of the woman. Dirt smudged a pretty face with too much makeup that had been smeared in spots. Fake blond hair with obvious roots and a mismatch to her pubic hair. Fake boobs too and a cheap tattoo of what he guessed were butterflies on one ankle.

"We have a tentative ID from a fingerprint—Maisy Moore. Nineteen," Trey said.

"She looks way older than that," Jose stated.

"Makeup can do that. So can a hard life, and Maisy had a hard life," Trey replied, picking up a piece of paper and started summarizing from it.

"Ran away from home at fourteen because she was being sexually abused by her father. Ended up in foster care but also had issues with another of the males in the home."

Mia jumped in. "Issues? You mean he was also abusing her?"

Trey shrugged. "Possibly. He denied it, and she left before the investigation could be completed."

"So, her abuser possibly skates free?" Sara said, clearly upset by that possibility.

"Possibly. We can check him out once we've finished this investigation," Trey said, and continued. "Maisy ends up on the streets after that. Multiple arrests for prostitution. The killer probably picked her up near one of the strip clubs."

"Maybe like he did Terry Hansen, although the only person who said she was a sex worker was Metz. This girl even kinda looks like Terry," Sara said as she peered at the photo.

"He has a type," Jose said as he examined the photo again. Something about the photo made him ask, "If she died so recently, is there a better chance of getting more evidence from her?"

Trey nodded. "Police immediately identified the fatal wound," he said, and reached over his shoulder to gesture to his back. "Broadhead arrow straight through, which likely hit the heart and a nearby artery. There's also evidence of sexual assault and piquerism."

"Piquerism? What's that?" Jose asked, puzzled by the term.

"Some killers need to stick people to experience arousal. Usually with knives, but it could also be pins or razors," Trey explained.

"But the sexual assault means we have DNA, right?" Jose queried, trying not to be shocked by the need to stick someone to get aroused.

"Killer could have worn a condom and sex workers can be problematic because they may have had multiple partners prior to the killer," Trey replied.

He felt like a fool that he hadn't thought about that complication, but then again, sex workers weren't normally the kinds of people in his life. Although he'd met a high-priced escort or two at some of his clients' parties, he thought.

"We'll know more about the exact COD and other evidence once they've finished the autopsy. As for the other victim, no positive ID on her yet, but PD speculates she's been dead for about a month."

Missing for a month and no one cared, Jose thought sadly, thinking that his parents would have been calling other family and friends within an hour if he failed to show up.

"Using facial recognition software on the internet, we think we found the second victim using her profile on Facebook. We've sent the info to PD," Sophie said, and flashed a side-by-side of the police photo with the image from her social media account on a nearby television.

"Tina Rodriguez left home two years ago and took up a life on the streets to support her drug habit. That's also when she stopped posting to her account," Robbie said.

Jose's heart hurt with sadness as he looked at the picture of the seemingly happy and pretty young woman in the Facebook photo and saw what her troubled life had led to. But something struck him at the same time and lightened the sorrow weighing down his heart.

"She's not just some nameless body anymore," he said, and peered around the table, his gaze settling last on Sara, who slipped her hand into his and squeezed.

"She's not," Trey said, and they pushed forward with their review of the case, discussing the additional steps they'd be taking.

"Terry, Maisy and Tina have many similarities. Sex workers. Age. Physical appearance. Those are obvious, but there may be other things we're not seeing. I'll run any info about them through my program to identify additional similarities," John said.

"We'll also refine the list of missing women to try and ID who's in those graves," Mia added.

"We're analyzing satellite photos taken over the last decade for changes in that forest area to hopefully pinpoint when each of those graves was dug," Sophie said.

"If we can do that, we'll match those dates with the list of missing women, again so we can ID the dead," Robbie said.

"What can Jose and I do?" Sara asked, obviously eager to help.

"How did you feel about Guidry?" Trey asked, narrowing his gaze as he peered at them.

"First time I met him, I didn't really get any vibes, but I was only focused on closing the deal," Jose readily admitted.

"And now?" Trey asked with an arch of a dark brow.

Jose glanced at Sara for a hot second before saying, "Smarmy. Off but I can't say why."

Sara quickly jumped in. "I got bad vibes and Bongo seemed drawn to him. Maybe she scented something, and he clearly wasn't too happy about Bongo being near him. Right, girl?" she called out to the bloodhound who had been quietly resting at one side of the room.

"Do you think it's enough of a scent for her to follow?" Mia asked.

Sara peered at Bongo, grimaced and shook her head. "I don't think so. But as far as I'm concerned, he should be a suspect. He's close by and there's something off about him."

Trey sighed heavily. "I get that Bongo didn't have enough scent, Sara. I know you're not a miracle worker and I appreciate your opinion on Guidry."

SARA WISHED SHE was a miracle worker because these dead women deserved justice. Even Metz deserved it, which made her think about the scene of his death.

"Whoever went at Metz left evidence behind. We know

there's a few boot prints. Maybe we can match them to a certain kind of shoe," Sara said, and at that, Trey nodded, yanked a photo from his pile of papers and passed it to her.

"There was a partial print in blood on the porch steps and a full boot print in the field. They were enough to confirm the killer wore some kind of work or duck boot. As wet as the land can get out here, it's a common kind of shoe but the soles can be unique," Trey said.

Sara had seen her share of duck boot soles over the many years they'd done search and rescue. Gesturing to the imprint in the dirt, she said, "L.L. Bean duck boots are some of the most popular, but they have a sole with a chain-like tread. Sperry soles are more circular, like little pods. Sorels have deep herringbone-like ridges."

She ran her hands across the lighter ridge pattern on the photo, trying to recall other boot prints she'd seen over the years but couldn't quite place the soles. "These ridges are lighter. Not as deep as Sorels," she said, and traced the ridges in the photo with her finger.

"It'd be easier to wipe off mud with ridges like this, right?" Jose asked as he also examined the photo.

"It would," she said with a quick nod.

"Mud like a farmer would have on his boots? Just like Guidry might wear," Jose said, eyes opening wide as that occurred to him.

"Definitely more like a work boot a farmer would wear rather than a duck boot. We should start searching the internet to see what we can find on the boots and also on Guidry," Sara said.

Sophie and Robbie added, "We'll do the same."

"Great. Do you think the police will let us into Metz's cabin so that I can take Bongo around. See if she can pick up any kind of scent?" Sara said, eyeballing Trey as he sat at the head of the table.

"I'll reach out to them. In the meantime, the police have released the kennel owner's home, so I'd like for you to run Bongo through there to see if there's anything else," Trey said.

"If there isn't, and if Sara still wants to live there, I'll arrange for the painters to come in," Mia said and looked at her intently, as if trying to gauge how she felt about living in the house.

With a shrug, she said, "The Florians lived there for over thirty years without a problem. I don't see why I can't live there as we had planned to get the K-9 center running. Our K-9s might help stop murders like this from happening or help PD solve them, right?"

"That's why we wanted to start this division. Even civilians might want to train their K-9s for protection or just obedience. This new center might be able to fulfill all those needs," Trey said, his voice sporting the kind of eagerness she'd heard when he'd first approached her about the project. He'd understandably lost that enthusiasm in the last few days with the weight of the murders and Roni's troubled pregnancy dragging at him.

"Are you sure?" Jose said, and tightened his hand on hers, offering support and comfort.

She nodded. "I'm sure. This is what I was meant to do. What *we* were meant to do," she said, and skipped her gaze across everyone seated at the table.

When no one contradicted her, she smiled and Trey said, "Seems like it's time to call it a night so we can be fresh in the morning. I need to take care of my wife."

He shot to his feet and pointed at each of them. "And I meant it when I said get to work in the morning," he said, emphasizing the last few words. "*None* of us can be sharp if we're tired."

"Got it, *jefe*," Robbie said teasingly, and offered up a mock salute.

"Go home. Get some rest. Fresh eyes may make the difference," he said, and without waiting for the rest of them, he made a beeline for the door.

Mia and John were next, arms wrapped around each other. "We'll see you in the morning. Like Trey, I'm looking forward to some time with my new wife."

Sophie laughed and with a sad shake of her head, she said, "It's just you and me and our cold beds, *hermanito*."

"We need to get a life," Robbie teased as he and his sister slipped from the room, leaving her and Jose at the table.

"Time for us to go and get some rest," he said.

She inched up a brow and shot him a knowing smile. "Only rest?"

He leaned close and brushed a kiss across her lips, whispering, "Sex can be restorative, *sabes*."

She didn't know why it bothered her that he'd said "sex" and not "making love." But then again, their attraction had been fast and furious. Had there really been time for love?

He sensed her upset and pulled back, danced his gaze across her face. "Are you all right?"

"I'm fine. Just fine," she said, snatching up the papers Trey had passed out earlier and signaling Bongo to come to her side.

Chapter Twenty-Four

It was impossible not to see that whatever he'd said had upset Sara, Jose thought.

Much like she had done, he grabbed the papers and followed her to the elevator. Once it arrived, she quickly used her badge to access the penthouse, silent the entire time. Bongo was plastered close to her leg, also sensing her mistress's mood.

He let Sara have that silence, hoping that her upset would fade by the time they reached the penthouse a few floors up.

It hadn't.

She walked straight to the table, tossed the papers on it and said, "I know what Trey said, but I don't think I'll be able to get much sleep until I do a few more things."

He chalked her upset off to that restlessness and said, "How about some coffee?"

She nodded. "Sure, but I need to walk Bongo first. I really should have done it before now."

"I'll go with you," he said, but she held her hand up to stop him.

"I need some time alone," she said, and without waiting for him, she grabbed Bongo's leash and rushed toward the elevator.

Not good, he thought, but recognized she needed space. Because of that, he busied himself with making coffee and searched the refrigerator to see if there were any desserts. Maybe something sugary to sweeten her mood, he thought. Something sweet always cheered him up.

Whoever stocked the fridge for Trey must have thought so too because there were homemade flans on one shelf as well as a container of chocolate chip ice cream in the freezer in case you wanted to get chip-faced.

Hoping that would do, he poured himself a drink and sat to wait for Sara.

JOSE'S WORDS SHOULDN'T have bothered her as much as they had, Sara thought as she walked Bongo along the curb in front of the SBS building. Bongo did her duty quickly, but Sara wasn't quite ready to return to the penthouse. Plus her partner hadn't really had any good exercise over the last few days.

She told herself that was the reason she walked right past the entrance and to the corner, and then turned to walk down the block.

The South Beach Security building was primarily in a business area, so foot traffic was light. Just a few office workers either rushing home or out for some late-night food.

She passed the Cuban deli they'd ordered from the other night and considered stopping in for something sweet, but passed on it to keep walking Bongo, who seemed to be enjoying the longer stroll. Rounding the block, she was just past the entrance to the building's garage when Bongo stopped and jerked her in the direction of the entrance.

A heartbeat later, a masked man raced at her from the shadows, wrapped one arm around her waist and pressed a hand across her mouth.

She lost her hold on Bongo's leash, not that her partner would be of much use.

Years of instinct and training took over.

She stomped her assailant's foot hard, grinding his toes into the sidewalk.

Her attacker yelped and lifted her body to keep her from stomping down again.

Jabbing her elbow sharply into his midsection, one, two, three times, loosened the hand at her mouth. She bit down viciously on his gloved hand.

He released her and she stumbled back from him, but he came at her again, tackling her to the ground.

JOSE GLANCED AT his watch for what had to be at least the tenth time in the last ten minutes.

She was taking far longer than when he had gone with her to walk Bongo.

It worried him that something was wrong.

Hopping to his feet, he rushed to the elevator, bouncing on the balls of his feet inside in his haste to find Sara.

It seemed like forever until the elevator arrived at the ground floor.

He rushed past the security desk and through the lobby, almost jogging out the door and to the sidewalk.

It was then he caught sight of Bongo racing toward the corner and his heart stopped cold.

He broke into a run and grabbed hold of Bongo's leash before the dog could rush into oncoming traffic. Bongo hopped up and laid big paws on his shoulders, but he urged the dog down, searching for Sara.

A sharp scream dragged his gaze midblock, and it took him a second to register what he was seeing.

Sara and someone all in black wrestled on the ground.

He muttered a curse and sprinted toward her, dragging a barking Bongo along with him.

The man pinning Sara to the ground looked up, surged to his feet and raced off.

Sara was just sitting up as he dropped to his knees beside her to make sure she was okay.

She pointed to her escaping assailant and commanded the bloodhound, "Find, Bongo. Find."

Jose released Bongo's leash and the dog took off.

Jose scrambled to his feet, chasing after the bloodhound to the end of the block and around the corner, but in just those short few seconds, Sara's assailant had vanished.

He called Bongo to his side, secured her leash and jogged back to where Sara was slowly getting to her feet.

She wavered a little, shaky, and he eased an arm around her waist to offer support.

"Take it easy. I'm here," he said, and she leaned into him, burying her face against his chest. Her body trembled as one shaky breath after another escaped her as she tried to regain her composure.

He stroked a hand up and down her back, offering comfort.

Bongo leaned against their legs, the weight of her also supportive.

With one long controlled breath, Sara straightened. Meeting his gaze, she said, "We need to let Trey know what happened."

He nodded and was reaching for his cell phone but hesitated. "He's got enough on his plate with Roni. We can handle this for now."

Sara hesitated, her gaze troubled. Reluctantly, she agreed. "Let's call Sophie and Robbie. Get them to pull up any video in the hopes we can ID this guy and where he went."

Jose nodded and dialed his cousins. Sophie answered and said, "What's up? I thought Trey said to take the night off?"

"Sara was walking Bongo when someone attacked her right outside the entrance to the parking garage," he said, and turned on the speaker.

"Is she okay? Do you need me to call an ambulance?" Sophie immediately asked.

"I'm fine," Sara said, even though Jose had his doubts about how fine she was.

"Can you pull video from around the building? Maybe we caught him on the CCTV?" she said.

"Robbie and I will work on it. We'll call you as soon as we have something," she said and hung up.

He faced Sara and ran a hand down her arm. It came away wet and bloody.

"You're hurt," he said, and examined her, noticing the angry and bloody scrapes on both her elbows.

She half turned to also inspect the damage, wincing as she did so. "It must have happened when he tackled me."

"Let's go upstairs and get you cleaned up."

When she took a wobbly step toward the corner, he slipped his arm around her waist again, shoring her up.

She leaned on him heavily as they walked back into the building and through the lobby. At the security desk the two guards jumped to their feet, seeing her condition.

"Can we do anything? Do you need us to call the police?" one guard asked.

Sara held her hand up in a stop gesture and offered the guards a weak smile. "I'm okay. We're handling this internally."

"If you need anything, we're here," the guard said.

By the time they reached the penthouse, Sophie was already calling. "We have video. He's masked in all of them, but we think we can calculate his height and weight from the videos. We'll let you know what we find."

"*Gracias*, Sophie. Hopefully you'll have something by the morning," he said, and hung up.

"They will," Sara said more optimistically. "Sophie and Robbie are amazing at what they do."

"Let's hope you're right," he said, and motioned to the sofa. "Get comfortable while I round up some things to clean your elbows."

Chapter Twenty-Five

Sara didn't have the energy to fight with him. The attack had drained her. Shaken her.

A few minutes more...

She wouldn't think about what might have happened if Jose hadn't come along when he did.

Bongo walked up to her then and laid her head on Sara's thigh. She stroked Bongo's head, rubbed her ears and said, "Why do you have to be so friendly, dog?"

As if to prove that point, Bongo licked her hand and drooled on Sara's jeans. She wiped it away with a chuckle and shook her head. "Go lay down, girl."

With another lick, Bongo ambled away to rest by her bedroom door.

Jose returned, hands full of cotton balls, adhesive bandages and bottles. "This may sting," he said as he wet a cotton ball with disinfectant.

She braced herself but still jumped as he gently swiped at her scraped elbows.

"I'm sorry. I didn't want to hurt you."

"I know," she said, and in the second that followed, it became about more than the abrasions on her arms.

He cradled her chin and applied gentle pressure until she faced him.

"I care for you, Sara. It's not just a hookup," he said, sea-colored eyes bright with the light of his happiness.

"I want to say 'I know' only…it's hard to know whether what we're both feeling is real with all that's going on," she admitted, not wanting to place blame on either of them for the confusing emotions.

The light in his eyes dimmed and darkness crept in, stealing his earlier joy. "You need time. I get it. I'll give you all the time you need," he said, and with a butterfly light brush, swiped his thumb across her cheek.

The caress, simple as it was, felt like a kiss goodbye, but she tried to take his words at face value and remain optimistic.

"I know Trey said to get some rest, but I'm too wired. I was going to work on tracking down the boots and finding out more about my new neighbor," she said, then popped to her feet and nervously rubbed her hands across her thighs.

He hesitated, clearly trying to decide what to do, but finally flung a hand in the direction of the bedrooms. "I'm going to shower and then check out some things. Check in with my cousins on what they've got before I bother Trey."

"Sounds like a plan." She stood there, rooted to a spot by the sofa until he walked out of the room. She finally released the breath she'd been holding. A breath that had wanted to call him back and step into his arms. Arms that could excite or comfort. Arms she had come to rely on way too much in the last few days.

Shaking her head to clear away those thoughts, she walked to the table and shuffled through the papers there to find the one with the boot print.

Opening her laptop, she searched various websites recommending footwear for farmers like what Guidry might wear. She whittled down her list to the most popular boots at the websites. The only problem with that was that too many people might own them.

In reality, the only person she was interested in was Guidry.

If he owned a similar boot, it increased the likelihood that he was the suspect they should focus on.

Hopping from one list of "best boots" to the other, there were several manufacturers that made each of the lists. In addition, the same models kept popping up. Grabbing a pad of paper, she made a list of those models and then went to the companies' sites to check out the soles.

The first three boots were no goes. The ridges were either too deep or ran the wrong way.

On the fourth try she got a possible hit, only there were slight discrepancies between the prints. So slight that she guessed the boot had to come from that manufacturer.

Searching through the company's work boots, she finally hit on one that seemed identical. Just to be on the safe side, she printed out an image for a better comparison.

As she laid that image against the CSI photos of the boot prints, she had no doubt she'd gotten the right brand and model.

"I found the boot, Jose. I found it!"

But as she kept reading on the company's site, some of her enthusiasm dimmed.

Jose hurried over and glanced at the photos she had laid out on the table. Picking up the print from the company website, he compared it and nodded enthusiastically. "You did. You found it."

"There's just one problem. It's the company's bestselling work boot for farmers, and it's a big boot manufacturer. That means there could be thousands of pairs out there," Sara said, slumping against the chair dejectedly.

"But we don't have to track down thousands, Sara. All we have to do is find these boots in the suspect's possession. Once we have another suspect although Guidry is on my list," Jose reassured her.

With a dip of her head, she said, "Maybe it's time to call Sophie and Robbie. See what they have."

He nodded. "Sure," he said, then dialed his cousin and put the phone on speaker.

As soon as Sophie answered, she said, "Let me bring in Robbie."

After a slight hesitation, Sophie said, "We have some news."

"So do we. I've tracked down the model of the boot Metz's killer was wearing," Sara said, and met Jose's gaze over the phone sitting on the table.

"That's great. We should send that over to PD," Robbie said.

Leaving that alone for the moment, she said, "What's your news?"

Another uneasy silence followed before Robbie said, "We were able to determine the height of your attacker from the CCTV footage. He's roughly five feet eight inches tall."

"That sounds about right for Guidry. He was shorter than my six feet," Jose confirmed.

Sophie immediately countered with, "But that info doesn't match up with what we got from Florida DMV."

Jose and Sara shared a puzzled look before Sara said, "What do you mean it doesn't match up?"

"DMV records indicate that Guidry is six feet two inches tall," Robbie stated.

"No way. The man we spoke with today was several inches shorter than me," Jose insisted.

"People do shrink with age, but not that much. Plus Guidry is only forty-eight according to the records so he's not of an age to be getting shorter," Robbie said.

"Guidry had a whole Colonel Sanders vibe going on so he looked older than forty-eight, but he could just be prematurely gray," Sara said, recalling how their possible suspect had appeared when they visited.

"Or he could not be Thomas Guidry," Jose said, stating the obvious. "Can you send over a copy of his DMV records so we can see what Guidry is supposed to look like?"

"Sending it right now," Sophie said, and a second later a ding on her phone confirmed she had received a message.

Sara opened her phone and displayed the photo.

The air left her lungs as if someone had punched her in the gut. With a shaky hand she held the phone up so Jose could see the license.

His eyes opened wide, and a curse exploded from his mouth. "That's not Guidry."

"What do you mean it's not Guidry?" Sophie asked.

Jose took the phone from Sara and enlarged the photo with a swipe of two fingers. "It's not the man we met today, although…there are some similarities."

He laid the phone back on the table, and Sara leaned over to take another look at the enlarged photo. "They do look alike," Sara said.

"Enough to be related?" Robbie asked.

Jose tilted his head from side to side, examining the photo and considering the similarities. "Definitely. I'm guessing they could be brothers and close in age. The Guidry we saw could be an older sibling to the man from the license."

"But if the man we saw isn't Thomas Guidry, who is he?"

Chapter Twenty-Six

"You should have called me," Trey said the next morning as they gathered in the conference room to discuss what the team had found after a night of research.

"Blame me, *primo*. I decided you needed the rest and time with Roni," Jose said to avoid Trey ripping into the cousins.

Trey inhaled deeply and ran a hand through hair that was still shower damp. Blowing out the breath, he admitted, "*Gracias*. It was good to have a night off with Roni."

He clapped Trey on the shoulder and said, "How is she doing?"

The first smile he'd seen in days erupted on his cousin's face. "Much better. No more spotting and she's feeling stronger."

"Good to hear," Jose said and with another pat on Trey's shoulder, he walked over to pour himself a big cup of coffee. He needed the rush of caffeine and sugar after the night they'd spent trying to figure out who was posing as Thomas Guidry.

As he turned to go back to the table, he caught sight of Sara hugging Trey and felt an immediate pang of jealousy, which made no sense. Trey was head over heels in love with his new and very pregnant wife, and Sara...

He didn't know what was really up with Sara, only what he wished for and what he'd royally messed up with his thoughtless words the night before. He wasn't sure that his attempt to apologize had worked since they had gone to sleep in separate beds.

He wanted to fix that. Somehow, he would, he thought as he strolled to the table and sat next to where Sara had placed her papers. Bongo lay on the floor a few feet away and at his approach, the bloodhound got to her feet and came over to greet him.

He rubbed the dog's head and ears. "Good morning, Bongo," he said, and after a lick of his hand, the dog went back to her earlier spot.

Making believe he was reviewing his own notes, he nevertheless kept an eye on Sara as she left Trey and got some coffee and pastries.

When she returned to the table, she placed the dish with the pastries in a spot between them.

At his questioning look, she said, "I know you have a sweet tooth."

"I do. *Gracias.*" He grabbed a glazed doughnut from the plate and gobbled it down in a few bites.

At the head of the table, Trey clapped his hands to start the meeting. "Let's get going. I understand you have a lot to share with me," he said, and shot an accusatory eye at his tech guru cousins.

Sophie was not about to be cowed. She lifted her chin a determined inch and said, "We're not apologizing. You looked like you were ready to face-plant yesterday."

"Fair enough," he said, and pushed on. "What did you find out?"

"The man at the farm who claims to be Thomas Guidry isn't. We think it's his brother, Shawn Guidry," Sophie said, and handed Trey the photos they had unearthed the night before.

"This is a very old photo of Shawn," Trey said, eyes narrowed as he examined the image.

"It is. Shawn has managed to avoid notice for a long time, but we ran age progression software against it and made him gray," Robbie said, and handed Trey another photo.

Trey immediately nodded. "This is the man I met to discuss the lease. Jose? Sara?"

"Definitely who we met," Sara confirmed with a swift bob of her head.

"What do we know about Shawn and where is Thomas?" he asked, peering around the table.

"Where Thomas is we can't answer right now. But we do have some info on Shawn," Jose said, and dipped his head in Sophie's direction to ask her to report.

"Misty Waters married Shawn Guidry Sr. in Baton Rouge. Within a few months Shawn Jr. was born, and Thomas followed two years later," Sophie said, and passed Trey some photos they had dug up from an ancestry site.

"Shawn Sr. seems to have abandoned the family when the boys were ten and eight respectively. Two years later, Misty sent Shawn Jr. to a boarding school for troubled children," Sophie said.

"Any indication of what kind of trouble?" Trey asked.

"We plan on calling the school this morning to see if anyone is willing to talk," Sara said.

"What about after? College? Employment?" Trey prompted, eager for more information.

"Shawn was bright enough to land a scholarship to Tulane. Finished with honors and was employed by an investment firm in Miami. Lost the job within a year and from what we can see, he went from job to job for years and then disappeared off the radar," Sophie admitted with a sheepish shrug.

"His falling off the radar coincides with the Guidrys taking a lease on the farmland," Jose said, reading off the notes he'd taken the night before.

"It was too late last night to talk to neighbors, but we plan on doing that this morning," Sara added.

"Mia had a meeting this morning with a prospective client, but once she's free, she can help with that," Trey said, and once again turned his detective's eyes on his team. "What is it you're not telling me?"

Jose blurted out, "Sara was attacked last night."

"We think it was Shawn Guidry based on his general height. Nothing else from the footage since he was wearing a ski mask," Sara said.

"Are you okay, Sara?" Trey asked, his gaze filled with concern.

"I'm okay," she said but that didn't seem to satisfy Trey.

"Are you sure? Your safety is what's most important," he stressed.

"I'm okay. I had Bongo and Jose to help," she said.

Seemingly persuaded, Trey said, "What about Guidry's car? He had to have driven here from the farm."

Sophie pointed toward the large television at the far side of the room. "We got these clips from the CCTV. The same white panel van went around and around the block a few times just before the attack on Sara."

Jose watched as the clips played on the television, but it was impossible to see who was driving, and the license plates had been obscured with the reflective license plate covers used to block red light and speeding cameras from capturing a plate number.

"There is a DMV record for a white van in the name of Thomas Guidry," Jose said.

"That's just too much coincidence in my mind. Shawn was probably scouting the location," Trey said.

"And waiting for me, which means he's been watching us for the last few days, and I didn't see it," Sara said, and pursed her lips in obvious frustration.

Jose laid a hand on her shoulder and offered her a reassuring squeeze. "There was a lot going on. Anyone could be distracted."

"It's my job to see things others miss," she reminded him, still beating herself up about the attack.

"In a forest during a search and rescue. This is not the same thing," Trey offered to ease her upset.

"It won't happen again," she said.

"I know it won't," Trey said, once again reassuring her with his calm, uncondemning presence.

It surprised Jose in a way. The Trey he'd known all his life hadn't seemed that understanding and composed. He'd always imagined him as someone who kicked ass first and asked questions later. But then again, Trey had been a successful leader on the battlefield and as a detective.

Leaders thought about the consequences of their actions, much like Trey was doing now as he said, "It seems like we have our jobs cut out for us to contact teachers and friends and learn what happened in the Guidry family. I trust you all to work together and with Mia. In the meantime, I'm heading to the kennels to coordinate with PD and their CSI teams. I'll keep you posted on anything new."

When he stood, the others around the table did the same thing, but a second later Mia walked in, dressed to the nines in a coral-colored suit that screamed Boss Lady.

Trey strolled to Mia, gave her one-armed hug and said, "The team will fill you in. I'm off to the kennels."

With that Trey left and Mia took over, studying all the materials and information they'd gathered and assigning each of them tasks.

Much like he'd felt with Trey, Jose was likewise impressed with the way Mia handled herself and the team. As they finished, he paused on the way out to share a private moment with her.

"I've never said this, but...you guys are pretty amazing. I never really understood that," he said, awed at the discovery of what his family actually did to help others.

Mia's full lips tilted up in a wide smile. She laid a hand on his arm and said, "We're glad you're here with us."

"I'm glad to be here," he said, surprised by the words as they escaped him and their truthfulness.

"Good. Once you find out more about Shawn, you may want to reach out to Ricky for some advice on his personality traits. That may help us deal with him better," Mia said.

"We will." He hurried out to where Sara waited for him in the reception area, Bongo patiently lazing at her feet.

Mia joined them and motioned down the hall. "There's a smaller conference room where you can work. Make your calls," Mia said.

Chapter Twenty-Seven

Sara was still upset with herself that she hadn't noticed that someone was tracking them.

As Trey had noted a day or so earlier, she was a good read of people and preferred talking to neighbors up close and personal to get a better idea on what they thought of Guidry.

"If you don't mind, I'd rather interview the neighbors in person," she said.

"I'm okay with that if Jose is," Mia said, and peered at her cousin.

"Whatever Sara thinks is best," Jose replied, and ran his hand down her back, offering his support.

"Thank you," she said, appreciative of his agreeing with her decision.

"Just keep me posted and if Sophie and Robbie find anything, I'll keep you in the loop," Mia said, and with a wave, ran off to handle her share of the chores they'd defined during their meeting.

"Are you sure you're okay with going back out to the kennel and farms?" she asked.

He nodded. "I think it's the best way. We're both good judges of people, and there are things you just can't see over the phone or during a video call."

"I agree. Let me just take Bongo for a quick walk and then we can go," she said, and in no time, they were on their way out the door. As she had over the last few days, she walked

Bongo in front of the SBS building only now she was vigilant, searching the crowd and the passing vehicles for signs of a white panel van or anything else that was out of the ordinary.

Satisfied, she joined hands with Jose and tugged him toward the entrance to the parking lot but as they approached, she hesitated, uneasy. Beside her leg, Bongo shifted closer, picking up on her vibes.

"I'm here. You don't need to worry," Jose said, and his words immediately relieved her discomfort.

"I know," she said without hesitation. Jose had her back in so many ways that it filled her heart until it felt like it might burst.

With a smile, he wrapped an arm around her neck and drew her close. Completed the hug by wrapping his other arm around her back, holding her tight, and rocking to reassure her.

Bongo thrust her head against Sara's leg, wanting to join in. It dragged a laugh from her and as they stepped apart, Bongo quickly moved into the gap between their legs, wanting some love also.

They both stroked and rubbed Bongo's head, ears and body, earning happy licks and a series of contented barks before they walked into the parking lot, located their SUV and secured Bongo in the back seat.

After they were moving, she reached over and stroked her hand down his arm, grateful.

He looked her way for a quick second, smiled again and twined his finger with hers.

Hands resting on the console between the seats, they made the half an hour or so drive to the street leading to the kennel. The homes along the road were sparsely laid out, but Guidry belonged to a local farmers' group, and they had pulled up a list of members the night before. Several of them lived along this road and would be the first ones they approached to find out more about Guidry.

At the first farmhouse, a man and woman were in the front yard, heads tucked beneath the hood of a vintage blue Ford tractor. As they drove up, the couple poked their heads out and the seventysomething man pulled a handkerchief from his pocket to wipe his hands clean.

The woman swung around to stand next to him. She was also in her seventies with carefully coiffed gray hair and a smudge of what looked like grease on one cheek.

"Can we help you?" the man said as they walked up after exiting the SUV, Bongo taking the lead, head down as she nosed the ground. Nothing about her behavior hinted at anything off, and she sat calmly at Sara's feet.

Jose held his hand out and said, "I'm Jose Gonzalez with Gonzalez Realty and this is Sara Hernandez, an SBS K-9 agent."

The man's gaze slitted against the sun as he examined them. "Are you the people who bought the Florian kennel?"

"We are. We're just introducing ourselves to our new neighbors," Sara said, and shook both their hands.

"It's a pleasure to meet you," the woman said, and jerked a thumb in her husband's direction. "This is George, but everyone calls him Pappy. I'm Tillie," she said, and laid a hand on her chest.

"I understand you've been here for nearly fifty years," Sara said, recalling what she'd read about Guidry's neighbors to break the ice.

"We have," Pappy said with a bright smile and hugged his wife close. "Came here as newlyweds."

"I imagine you've seen a lot of change in all those years," Jose said, earning a hairy eyeball from the man.

"We have and can't say we like some of what the developers have been doing, so we were glad to hear the kennel property and farm weren't going to change all that much," Pappy said.

"It won't. We plan on sprucing up the kennel to use the location as our new training center. Mr. Guidry will continue to lease the nearby farmland," Sara stated.

At the mention of Guidry, their smiles faded into looks of disgust.

"I gather you're not fans of your neighbor," Jose said, also picking up on the couple's sudden change of attitude.

"He's a bit…" Tilly began, but shrugged and held her tongue.

Pappy chuckled and shook his head. "Tilly's way too nice, but I'm not. He tries too hard to be charming and he's a liar."

"I don't trust him," Tilly added, with a decided bob of her head and jabbed an index finger in Sara's direction. "Especially you. Keep an eye on him."

"We will," Sara said, sensing what Tilly wasn't saying, namely, that Guidry couldn't be trusted around women.

Pappy peered at them intently once more, cocked his head to one side, and said, "Is it true you found bodies in the woods?"

Sara didn't see the sense of lying. "Bongo picked up on a scent and our team located them."

"The police are here now?" Tilly asked and wrung her hands together.

"They are. They'll be removing the bodies to try and ID them. They're also gathering evidence," Jose explained.

Pappy and Tilly shared a look before Tilly blurted out, "Do you think it's possible there are more bodies on our farm? We have woods close to where they're searching."

JOSE WAS TAKEN aback by the question because it hadn't occurred to him that the killer might have been burying bodies beyond the boundaries of the kennel property.

Facing Sara, he said, "Do you think we could search in that area for them?"

"We'd be willing to pay you for your services," Pappy quickly offered.

Sara instantly held her hands up to wave off his proposal. "That's okay. We'd love to help our new neighbors."

"That would be greatly appreciated so we could have some peace of mind," Tilly said, hands clasped in gratitude.

"We understand. We have some more stops to make, but once we do, we'll call to arrange for the search," Jose said.

The older couple's demeanor relaxed with his promise, and they hugged Sara and him effusively.

Once they had bundled Bongo into the back seat, they hopped in and drove off to the next farm down the road. Unlike Pappy and Tilly's avocado and mango orchards, this farm specialized in growing orchids and other exotic flowers. Much like Pappy and Tilly, the owner of the property welcomed them and had little good to say about Guidry.

That same experience occurred at the last two farms, leaving them to report to Trey on what they'd found out and the request for a search of the woods.

When they arrived, Trey was standing by Detective Espinoza and a trio of CSI agents. Trey and Espinoza intently listened to whatever was being said by the CSI folks, but their gazes flitted to a gurney as it wheeled past them.

They waited in front of the kennel owner's home until Trey was done and then hurried over to speak with him.

"How did it go?" he asked.

"Not much love for Guidry from the neighbors. Most think he's not to be trusted," Jose said, consolidating the various comments for his cousin.

"More than one also warned me to watch out, so it's clear they think it's not safe for women to be around him," Sara added to his assessment.

Trey nodded. "Good work. We should run that by Ricky when we get a chance."

"There's something else," he said, mindful of the request from Pappy and Tilly.

"Sure, what is it?" Trey said.

With a quick glance at Sara, he raised his arm and pointed in the direction of the woods. "That hardwood hammock continues across the road into a neighboring farm. Those owners are worried that whoever did the killing didn't stop at the road."

Trey jammed his hands on his hips and glanced at the tree line. With a shake of his head, he said, "The last of the graves stops well short of the road."

"It does, but Pappy and Tilly are very upset about the possibility," Sara said, pleading their cause.

Trey hesitated but as his gaze searched Sara's face, he recognized how important it was to her and to the neighbors. "If you think it makes sense, arrange to do it tomorrow."

"Thank you," she said, and Jose echoed her gratitude.

"It will give them much-needed peace of mind," he said, but at that, Trey muttered, "I wish I had peace of mind."

"What's up?" Sara asked.

"That was the last of the bodies, but it will be another day or so before they'll be finished searching for any additional evidence," Trey stated.

Jose motioned in the direction of where his cousin had been standing earlier. "Is that what you were discussing?"

Trey shook his head. "No. One of the CSIs thinks there's a bit of an anomaly in the last grave."

"An anomaly?" Sara questioned, brow furrowed over her troubled gray eyes.

"The team dug up a pelvis that's clearly masculine. Pelvic cavity was smaller as was the pubic arch. The pelvis was narrower with a higher iliac crest and denser bone," Trey explained, using his hands as well to demonstrate the differences.

"Thomas Guidry?" Jose suggested for consideration.

Pursing his lips, Trey did a reluctant shrug. "Possibly. Once they get all the bones, they'll be able to tell height based on the leg bones. A visual inspection of the bones and bone age test will give us an age range."

"And after that we'll be able to take a better guess if it's Thomas, but if it is, where's Misty?"

Jose barked out a laugh. "My guess is in the grave with Thomas."

"I agree," Trey said. With a last look at the woods, he said, "Let's head back to the offices to discuss what we've got so far."

"Sure, but if you don't mind, I'd like to stop to let Pappy and Tilly know we'll do the search in the morning. Their house is on the way back," Sara said.

Trey smiled and nodded. "Sounds good. I'll see you back at the office."

Chapter Twenty-Eight

Dusk descended over the farmlands, painting the sky in blues, pinks and purples as the sun fled in late afternoon.

Jose turned into Pappy and Tilly's driveway so they could give them the good news about tomorrow's search.

He was almost at the farmhouse when a blur of something big and blue registered in the corner of his eye.

"Hold on," Jose shouted and violently jerked the wheel to the right, trying to avoid being T-boned by the blue tractor the couple had been working on earlier.

The plow on the tractor clipped the left front quarter panel, sending the rest of the SUV smashing against the side of the farm vehicle. The tractor wheels chewed up the side of the SUV with a sickening crunch and screech of metal on metal and the shattering sound of glass as the side window exploded.

Looking up at the driver on the tractor, all he could see was a dark shadow at the wheel. The driver was all in black with a black ski mask.

He struggled to keep the car from being crushed by the wheels as the black-clad driver jammed the tractor against the SUV again.

Realizing he'd never overpower it, Jose slammed on the brakes, sending him, Sara and Bongo reeling back and forth in their seats.

The tractor shot forward, heading straight for a tree to one side of the yard.

The tractor driver jumped off a second before the vehicle slammed into the tree with a sickening thud.

Jose tried to open his door to give chase as the driver sped to the woods, but there was too much damage to the door.

He looked toward Sara to make sure she was okay, but his vision blurred for a moment as wet warmth dripped into his eyes.

"You're hurt," Sara said, and turned in her seat.

He swiped his fingers across his brow, and they came away wet with blood.

Sara tore a piece of fabric from her T-shirt and held it against his brow to stem the flow.

Bongo was barking and shifting from one side to the other in the back seat, making Jose's head pound with the sound.

"Sit, Bongo. Quiet," Sara called out and Bongo whined until she issued the command again and the bloodhound finally fell silent.

The door to the farmhouse opened and Pappy and Tilly came running out.

"Are you okay?" Tilly asked at the same time that Pappy said, "What happened? Damn, look at my tractor!"

"I'm calling the police," Tilly said, and pulled a cell phone from her apron pocket.

"Do you think you can stand?" Sara asked.

"I'm fine, but this door is shot. You go first and I'll crawl out after you."

She did as he asked, exiting the SUV, and then reached back in to help him crawl over the center console. Once he was out, he leaned against the car as Sara got Bongo out of the back seat and did a once-over to make sure the dog hadn't also been injured during the incident.

Pappy walked over to inspect the tractor. Hopping up into the driver's seat, he shouted back, "Someone hot-wired it. Darn front end is toast."

"Don't touch anything in case there are fingerprints or DNA," Sara called out to the older man.

Pappy lifted his hands as if in surrender and hurried back to wrap an arm around Tilly's shoulders as she finished up the call.

"Police are on their way," she said.

Despite the pounding in his head and the chill fear filling his core, Jose forced a smile for the older woman. "Thank you, Tilly."

As if on cue, the scream of sirens rent the air and within a minute, the strobe of red and blue lights traveled across the farmlands as the police cruiser approached.

Sara shifted to his side and laid a hand on his shoulder. Bongo took up a spot at his feet, the dog's weight comforting.

The cruiser cut off its sirens as it came down the driveway and pulled up to the wreck of their SUV. Two officers slipped from the car, and he recognized them from the day of the blast.

He nodded his head in greeting. "Officer Rojas. Officer McAllister."

Rojas shook her head in almost disbelief and said, "Mr. Gonzalez. Ms. Hernandez. I wish I could say it was a pleasure."

McAllister examined the ruined side of the SUV and let out a low whistle and shake of his head. "Who shredded the car?"

Pappy shot an arm out in the direction of his vintage tractor. "Someone hot-wired it. Ran it into the kids' car."

Jose hadn't been called a "kid" in years, but it fit perfectly coming from a character like Pappy.

Rojas pulled her notepad from her utility belt. "Did you see the driver?"

Jose shook his head. "He had a black ski mask on."

Rojas pointed her notebook in the direction of the tractor. "Let's see if we can find anything over there."

With that, McAllister and she walked to the crashed vehicle

and began examining it, searching for evidence. Their flashlights bounced across the vehicle and down to the ground as
they explored in the growing dark.

The sound of wheels crunching on the gravel driveway had
him looking to where an SUV—another SBS vehicle—was
coming down the drive.

As it approached, he realized it was Trey behind the wheel.
Seconds later, his cousin parked and hurried over to them.

"Are you okay?" he said as he took note of the blood on
Jose's face.

He removed the makeshift bandage, but immediately felt
blood welling and reapplied the fabric and pressure to the cut,
wincing at the tenderness at his brow.

"Let's get a butterfly bandage on that," Trey said, and hurried back to the SUV. He returned quickly with a first-aid kit
and went to work on Jose's injury.

"How did you know to come here?" Jose asked.

"I was listening to the police scanner on the way home,"
Trey said without hesitation.

"Because that's what normal people do while they drive,"
Jose said facetiously.

Trey blew out a rough laugh and partially lifted his gaze
toward Sara. "Do you think Bongo can pick up any kind of
scent off that tractor?"

SARA MURMURED A curse beneath her breath because it was
something she should have done right off the bat only she'd
been too worried about Jose's injury.

"As soon as the police are finished, I'll move in," she said,
and turned her attention to watching the two officers as they
scoured the scene. When they shut off their flashlights and
walked back toward them, she went into action.

With a hand signal to Bongo, the dog leaped into action,
leading the way as she sniffed along the ground. At the trac-

tor, she urged Bongo up into the driver's seat and instructed, "Find, Bongo. Find."

Bongo nosed around the pedals and when she patted the seat, did the same there before hopping up and scenting the higher portions of the seat.

"Find, Bongo. Find," she commanded again, and at that, the bloodhound dropped to the ground and sniffed the area before seeming to find a scent.

Head bent close to the earth, Bongo shifted her head back and forth, a clear indication she had something. She moved quickly, tugging the leash as she followed the odor, but it didn't take long for Sara to realize Bongo was leading them straight back to where Jose, Trey, Tilly and Pappy waited.

Barely a minute later, Bongo was sniffing all around Pappy's feet and sat, telling Sara that she had found the source of the scent.

"I'm sorry, Trey. Pappy's scent was way too strong," she said, disheartened at her failure.

Jose immediately came to Bongo's defense. "The guy had on gloves and a mask. No skin visible anywhere so how could he leave behind any evidence."

Sara raised a hand to stop him. "Bongo might have been able to pick up the driver's body odor from the seat even through his clothes."

"Is there anything you can remember about the driver?" Trey asked as Rojas and McAllister returned.

Jose shook his head. "Only that he was all in black and hiding his face. The gloves," he said.

"Leather or something else?" Sara asked.

Jose seemed puzzled for a moment and then said, "No, not leather. Plastic of some kind. And black, but… I could see his wrist. He was white."

She shared a look with Trey since it kept Guidry as a possible suspect. Officer Rojas must have picked up on it since she said, "Is there something you want to share with us?"

"Not at all," Trey said with a shake of his head.

Although Rojas obviously didn't believe him, she held back, instead saying to her partner, "CSI will be here shortly. As first on the scene, we have to preserve any evidence, but you're all free to go."

"*Gracias*, Officer Rojas. If you can, please keep us posted," Trey said, and handed the officer his business card.

She barely shot it a look, held it up and said, "And I'm sure you'll share anything you have when you're ready."

Trey smiled and without missing a beat said, "We will."

They walked to Trey's SUV and piled in with Jose in the front passenger seat and her and Bongo in the rear. She had just finished strapping in Bongo when Trey started the vehicle and did a K-turn to leave.

"Why didn't you say anything to them about Guidry?" Jose asked as soon as they were off the farm property.

"Because the last thing we need is them spooking Guidry into running," Trey said with a quick look in Jose's direction. Wincing, he added, "You're probably going to have a shiner in the morning."

Sara peered at Jose in the dark of the SUV's interior and could see that beside the cut at his brow there was some redness along his cheekbone as well.

"Did you hit the side window?" she asked, worried Jose was hurt worse than it seemed.

He shook his head. "I don't know. All I remember is trying to keep away from those huge tractor wheels and suddenly there was an explosion of glass."

Sara met Trey's gaze in the rearview mirror. "Maybe we should take Jose to the hospital to see if he has a concussion."

"I'm fine. Just a headache," Jose admitted.

"Which is a sign of a concussion. Sara's right. We should have a doctor check you out," Trey said, and immediately programed the SUV's navigation to a nearby hospital in Homestead.

Barely ten minutes later, they pulled up in front of a large Mediterranean-style building dressed in shell pink walls and topped with terra-cotta tiles along all the roofs and porticos.

Trey drove them up to the ER entrance, turned around in his seat and said, "Do you want to go in with Jose while I watch Bongo?"

It made sense since she couldn't leave the dog alone and the hospital might not allow Bongo in since she wasn't technically a service dog.

"That would be great," she said, and hopped out of the car to meet Jose, who was already standing there, waiting.

"This is a waste of time," he murmured as they walked into the ER.

Luckily it was a quiet night at the hospital. A doctor was soon examining Jose, asking him a variety of questions while checking his vision and hearing. Once he finished with that, he had Jose do a series of balance and strength tests. The doctor finished by checking his reflexes.

"The headache is a clue you might have a mild concussion, but all the other tests are good. I don't think it's necessary to do any imaging," the physician said, and glanced in her direction.

"Make sure your boyfriend takes it easy for a day or so including screen time. Your brain needs to rest."

"Got it, Dr. Wright. I'll make sure he gets some rest," she said.

Jose hopped off the examining room bed, came to her side and wrapped an arm around her waist. "Thank you. My girlfriend and I are grateful for your help," he said, playfully emphasizing the "girlfriend" part.

"Come on, babe. Let's go home," he said, and planted a kiss on her temple.

"Remember, rest," the doctor admonished as they walked out of the examining room, stopped by the nurses' station to finish with his health insurance and pay. Once they were done, they strolled out of the ER, arms wrapped around each other.

Trey was standing beneath the portico, Bongo at his side. "I took her for a walk. She seemed a little antsy, but she didn't do anything so you may need to walk her again."

Sara nodded and accepted the leash as Trey handed it to her. "She was probably restless because she's not used to me leaving her alone."

"How did it go?" Trey asked and directed them toward the SUV parked several yards away.

"I'm fine, just like I said," Jose replied.

Trey checked in with her. "Is that what the doc said?"

"Pretty much. He does have a mild concussion and needs to take it easy for a day or two," Sara said, repeating the doctor's instructions.

"And that's what you'll do. No work for you," Trey said, and clapped Jose's back, offering what she supposed was man-style comfort.

"I'm not an invalid. I can help out with the case," he said, but she wasn't surprised.

Despite what he'd originally told her a few days ago, which now seemed like ages ago, Jose was without a doubt part of the SBS team.

Trey nodded. "You can. From behind a desk or the penthouse until we know what that hit did to your head."

Jose was about to argue with him, but Sara laid a hand on his arm to stop him. "It's what makes sense. Let's go home and get some rest."

WITHIN A FEW minutes they were on the turnpike and heading back to the South Beach Security offices. With the detour to the hospital, it was nearly an hour ride back, and Jose found himself drifting off to sleep.

Trey reached over and gave his thigh a shake. "Try to stay awake. I want to make sure there's nothing bad going on."

While he understood, the wear and tear from the crash and all their running around that day was dragging on him. It was a battle to stay awake, but between Trey and Sara, they kept him alert with a shake or questions he tried to answer quickly, not wanting to worry them.

Their actions distracted him to the point that he didn't even realize they were back at the SBS offices until Trey parked in one of the spots reserved for the SBS team.

"Why don't you two head to the penthouse? I'm going to check in with Sophie and Robbie—"

"We'll go with you," Jose immediately said, not wanting to be babied, especially in front of Trey who was the kind of man who would push on in a fight even if severely injured.

Trey met his determined gaze, and something clicked between them. There was recognition of Jose's strength there. Acknowledgment that he too was a man who would do what he had to no matter the cost to himself.

With a nod, Trey said, "Sure. We'll convene in the conference room and order in some food since I'm sure you haven't had a chance to have dinner."

"We haven't," Sara said as she unbuckled Bongo and quickly added, "I should walk her again before we go up since she didn't go earlier."

"I'll go with you," he said, and followed her as she let Bongo stroll up the ramp of the parking lot and onto the sidewalk.

As he walked beside her, she was silent for a long time until she risked a quick glimpse at him and said, "You don't need to prove anything to anyone."

She'd clearly picked up on that unspoken exchange between Trey and him. "I'm not backing down. Trey's handling a lot right now, and I'm not going to add to that."

Chapter Twenty-Nine

Sara couldn't argue that Trey had a lot on his plate, including multiple murders on the property he'd just purchased and the reality that a serial killer was still on the loose and attacking them.

But that didn't excuse Jose's stubborn insistence on ignoring the doctor's instruction to get some rest. "No one is going to think less of you if you take it easy for a day or two."

He jabbed his chest forcefully. "I will think less of me."

The way he had for so long in a family filled with so many successful and courageous people.

She cradled his jaw, went up on tiptoes and whispered against his lips, "I won't."

He groaned as if in pain, hauled her tight against him and deepened the kiss, his hand tunneling through her hair to cradle her skull.

When they broke apart, they were both breathing heavily and he leaned his forehead against hers and said, "No matter how crazy this all has been, I'm grateful for meeting you."

"I am too," she said, thinking that Jose had shown more than once that he was the kind of man who could handle being in a life like hers.

"Let's head upstairs. They're probably wondering why we're taking so long," she said.

"And playing matchmaker," Jose said, a wry smile drifting across his lips.

She narrowed her gaze to gauge if he was being serious, and seeing that he was, she said, "You think your family is matchmaking?"

He nodded and held open the lobby door for her. "I think both Trey and Mia were pushing us together although Trey seemed worried at first."

As she walked with him and Bongo through the lobby, she thought about that first meeting and couldn't argue with him.

"I guess now that they're both happily married—"

Jose interrupted with, "And don't forget Ricky is also engaged."

She hadn't spent much time with Trey and Mia's psychologist brother although they had planned on speaking with him for help with the killer's profile.

"They just want you to be happy," she said, and slipped her hand into his as they cleared the security desk.

While they waited for the elevator, he tugged on her hand to draw her in for another kiss.

"Had to have this before we got upstairs. I don't want to encourage them," he said with a laugh.

She chuckled and shook her head. "Like I said, they only want you to be happy."

HIS HEAD WAS POUNDING, and his face was sore. There were several dead bodies on the property he had just convinced his cousin to purchase, and the serial killer responsible for them had just tried to kill him and Sara. And he hadn't been home in days. He was staying at the penthouse because he wanted to be close to Sara and help his cousins with the investigation.

Somehow, despite all that, Jose was happy, surprisingly. And a lot of it had to do with the beautiful woman standing beside him with her big, drooly dog.

When badged into the now-closed SBS offices, he walked with her to the conference room, slipping his arm around her waist in a very loving and possessive gesture that was not missed by his cousins.

Trey, in particular, let his gaze linger on that caress, but said nothing.

Jose could swear that Trey forced away a smile before he schooled his emotions. It confirmed that he hadn't been wrong to think his cousins had been matchmaking when they'd thrown him and Sara together.

Mia said, "I've ordered in Cuban sandwiches again. Figured it was something we all like."

Like clockwork, one of the deli employees walked in with a big cardboard box and at Mia's instruction laid out sandwiches, assorted sides and sodas on the credenza at one side of the room.

"Sounds good, *prima*," he said, although in truth, he wasn't really hungry since he was nauseous. The ER doctor had warned him that was something he might experience because of the concussion.

The SBS crew must have been hungry since as soon as the deliveryman left, most of them headed straight to the credenza to grab sandwiches.

He hung back, letting those with appetites fill their needs first before Sara and he walked over. Grabbing half a sandwich, he then also scooped up some rice, beans and avocado salad.

As soon as they were all seated, Sara took apart one of the sandwiches and placed some pork, ham and cheese on a paper plate so Bongo could eat before they went to the penthouse.

While she did that, Trey began the meeting. "A couple of hours ago someone attacked Pepe, Sara and Bongo by driving a tractor into their SUV. Luckily, they were unhurt although Pepe has a mild concussion."

That prompted a chorus of questions and commiserations from his other cousins.

"*Gracias*, but I'm fine. Just a little headache," he said, wanting to downplay the injury.

"We're sorry you were hurt. We know you worried about working with us," Mia said.

"Like I said, I'm fine but the sooner we can solve this case, the quicker I can go back to my regular life," he said, with a little more sting than he intended.

Beside him Sara fidgeted, and he could guess why. With the state of their relationship unsettled in some ways, the end of the investigation might mean more distance between them. To reassure her, he laid a hand on hers as it rested on the table.

As he had before, Trey zeroed in on that gesture as did Mia, but neither said anything.

"Do you have any updates, Sophie? Robbie?" he asked, shifting his gaze to their tech guru cousins.

"We've done a lot of digging around and as best we can tell, Misty Guidry disappeared off the face of the earth about four or so years ago. No calls on her cell phone. Her bank account was drained in the months before that," Sophie said.

"We called Misty's brother in Baton Rouge who said they were never close, so it wasn't unusual not to hear from her or her sons," Robbie added.

"We have normal activity on Thomas's cell phone and bank account. In fact, some of the withdrawals from Misty's account match deposits on Thomas's account," Sophie said, using air quotes when she mentioned Thomas since they all suspected Shawn had been posing as his brother for some time.

"We know now that one of the bodies is male. I think we all agree that it could be Thomas," Trey said, and peered around the table to see if anyone disagreed.

"And if it is, I'd put money on Misty being in one of the graves as well," Sophie said.

Murmurs of agreement filled the room just a second before Trey's cell phone rang. "It's the police."

He answered and after a brief back-and-forth, he said, "We appreciate that info. We have some as well that may help you confirm the approximate TOD. We'll send it over shortly."

After he hung up, he addressed the group. "PD has confirmed that the one skeleton is that of a male. Approximately fifty years old and six feet two inches tall. The woman in that grave with him was older. Approximately eighty years old and five feet four inches tall."

"Thomas and Misty. I guess we were right that the man claiming to be Thomas is actually Shawn Guidry," Mia said.

"They were close in age and looked enough alike that Shawn could pass for him with little effort. Except for their mom knowing who was who," Jose said, shaking his head in disbelief at what the man had done.

"It's hard to imagine someone doing that to family," Sara said, and squeezed his hand to offer comfort.

"It seems that was the reason he was sent off to the boarding school," Sophie said, and at Trey's prompting, she elaborated.

"We spoke to the current head of the school who had been there as a teacher when Shawn was admitted. It turns out there were several instances where Thomas was hurt as a young child. Apparently, Shawn Sr. thought junior was responsible, but Misty staunchly defended him. That was part of the reason Senior left."

"What about his behavior at the boarding school?" Jose asked, wondering if his actions there confirmed the father's suspicions.

"The school was highly regimented. Students had little free time and because most were troubled children, there was constant supervision," Robbie said.

"Sounds like a prison," Sara said, and he couldn't disagree.

"What would that kind of environment do to a young boy?" Jose pondered aloud.

Mia suggested, "Might be a good time to call Ricky."

Chapter Thirty

Trey did just that and once Ricky answered, he said, *"Hola, hermanito.* We were hoping to pick your brain. Why don't you fill him in?" he asked, addressing his techie cousins.

Sophie and Robbie reiterated the facts they'd been able to gather about Shawn Guidry and once they'd finished, Ricky said, "It sounds like you may be dealing with an undiagnosed Antisocial Personality Disorder. The parents' rejection and neglect. Their choice of one child over another."

"But it started before he was sent away," Sara said, wondering what could have caused that early behavior.

Ricky immediately provided an answer. "There is strong evidence that both genetics and prenatal environmental factors can cause that kind of behavior."

"So antisocial personality traits are set in stone at birth?" she queried, shocked that it could start that early in a person's life.

"It could be but not everyone with ASPD is bad. It all depends on how they channel those traits. In addition, recent studies on interventions show that certain therapies are effective in curbing antisocial behavior," he explained.

"What about the kind of intense discipline he got at the boarding school?" Jose asked.

A long hesitation followed before Ricky said, "That likely only helped repress the behaviors instead of teaching the individual how to deal with their emotions."

"What would happen once they're out of that kind of environment?" Sara asked, recalling what the cousins had said about Shawn's later life.

"They might be in control for a little while, but in general, people with undiagnosed ASPD have trouble relating to people, holding jobs, and they can be impulsive. But they are highly intelligent and can be very charming," Ricky said.

"Which means he could have charmed his way back into his family's life," Sophie said.

"Very much so when you consider the guilt his mother may have felt at sending him away. He could easily manipulate that guilt," Ricky confirmed.

"Thanks. We appreciate your analysis," Trey said.

He was about to hang up when Ricky said, "I wouldn't just focus on what's happening at the kennels, Trey. You should look into the time immediately after he was fired. It's another rejection that could have set him off."

Trey nodded. "We will. *Gracias*," he said, and finally ended the call.

"We'll work on it. We'll call his employers over those years to see what they'll share. Check for any indications of violence in and around where he was living," Sophie said.

"Perfect. We sent over the boot info to the police as well as our suspicions about Guidry's true identity. They didn't think it was enough to get a search warrant, but maybe now that they have bones that possibly match Misty and Thomas it may be enough," Trey said.

"If it is, when do you suppose they'll ask for the warrant?" Jose asked.

"Probably first thing in the a.m. Until then, we should all get some rest, especially you, Pepe," Trey said, and pointed in Jose's direction.

It was obvious to Sara that Jose wasn't happy about being singled out, but she understood Trey's concern. "You need to get some ice on that cheek and the doctor said to rest."

Although Jose's lips were in a firm disapproving line, he nodded. "We should go. This headache is getting worse."

She noticed then that he'd only eaten half his sandwich, and she worried he was also having some nausea as the doctor had warned. Because of that, she said, "Let's head out. I need to feed Bongo and take her for her last walk of the night."

He didn't argue, only stood, and said, "We'll see you in the morning."

"First thing and feel better, Pepe. We're all proud of how you're handling the mess we pulled you into and thankful as well," Trey said, obviously reading his cousin's earlier distress.

With those words the tension in Jose's body melted away. She slipped her hand into his and grabbed Bongo's leash. The bloodhound immediately came to her feet and followed them out of the office and to the elevator. It barely took a minute for it to arrive and deliver them up to the penthouse.

"Why don't you relax while I feed Bongo?" she said.

JOSE LEANED ON the kitchen counter to watch as she filled one of Bongo's dishes with fresh food and another with water.

Bongo inhaled the food and lapped up some water before the bloodhound trotted off toward the sofa, did a circle or two before settling down to one side of it.

"I'm not sure you're supposed to drink—"

"I'm not, but you go ahead," he said, and waved in the direction of the bar.

She shook her head. "I'm not really in the mood."

He was getting mixed signals from her and decided to clear the air. "What are you in the mood for?"

She smiled, a sexy siren's smile and held out her hand. "Bed. With you."

"Are you sure?" he asked, worried about the tentative state of their relationship, if you could even call it that.

"After all that's gone on today, I don't want to be alone."

He wasn't sure that's why he wanted her to want to be with him, but in truth, he didn't want to be alone tonight either. He wanted to be with her.

Slipping his hand into hers, he said, "Let's go to bed."

They strolled to her bedroom, Bongo following them, but at the door Sara gave the dog a "down" command, and Bongo immediately took a spot by the bedroom door.

"Good girl," Sara said, and closed the door to give them privacy.

Once inside, they rushed toward the bed but slowed once they were there, not wanting to hurry what was about to happen.

SARA TOOK HER time undoing the buttons on Jose's guayabera, which bore traces of the blood from his head wound. It was a glaring reminder of what had happened earlier, but also of his injuries after the explosion. Because of that, as she peeled off his shirt to expose his beautifully sculpted body, she slipped to his side to gently inspect the wounds on his shoulder.

The injuries had scabbed with no sign of any infection, and she said, "They're healing nicely."

She ran her hand up his arm to his shoulder and then faced him. The bright white of the butterfly bandage at his brow coupled with the increasingly black-and-blue area on his cheekbone was a scary reminder of the danger they'd been in that night.

"Does it hurt?" she said, and lightly danced her fingers over the purpling mess on his face.

He grinned, laid a hand on her waist and said, "Only when I smile."

She shook her head and chuckled much as he must have wanted her to. But she understood he hid behind that self-deprecating humor and wanted there to be no doubt as to how she felt about him. "Don't ever think you're not a hero."

His full-lipped smile thinned and grew harder. "I'm just a regular guy."

With a dip of her head, she said, "You're *my* regular guy but the doctor said you need to rest."

HE HATED THAT she was right. "Let's get some sleep," he said.

"Are you sure?" she said, obviously worried that the night wasn't going as they'd expected.

"I'm sure. I'm here, Sara. I'll always be here for you," he said, more certain of her than he had been of anything else in his life.

She smiled and cradled the side of his face. "I love you."

He grinned, taking in those words. Relishing them as he replied, "I love you too."

That released something between them. Something wild and joyful and life-giving.

He may have faced death twice with her, but more importantly, he knew she would be at his side to savor life.

It roused a peace unlike any he'd ever experienced before. Satisfying and rich as they lay down together and then cuddled close, happily tucked in each other's arms.

He was just slipping off to sleep, contentedly lying in her arms when she said, "I don't regret what brought us together."

For so long he'd avoided working with his SBS family exactly because of all that had happened in the last few days. But like Sara, he had no regrets because it had brought them together.

"I don't regret it either," he said, and dropped a kiss on her forehead.

She snuggled closer and he smiled, content. Hoping that contentment could survive whatever was coming their way in the next few days.

Chapter Thirty-One

Sophie had some surprising news the next morning as they gathered at the kennels to finish up security and get the buildings ready. The police had released most of the areas to them since they were finished with their investigations.

As Sara looked around, she noticed that the only areas restricted to them were marked off by the yellow tape around the edges of the woods.

"I reached out to Guidry's past employer. It turns out he was fired from that investment job because of complaints that he had gotten a little physical with one of his female colleagues, but there's more," she said, glancing around as she dropped a literal bomb into the discussion.

"Shortly after Shawn's last known job, 'Thomas' Guidry joined the army and eventually became an Explosive Ordnance Disposal—EOD—specialist. The training for that takes about three years," Sophie said, making it clear that it wasn't Thomas who'd suddenly gotten patriotic.

"Which explains how Shawn seemed to have disappeared for all those years," Robbie added.

"And how he knew to bomb the outbuilding, chimney and set all those booby traps," Sara said with a shake of her head.

"We need to get this to PD. If this doesn't sway a judge into issuing a warrant, I'll be shocked," Trey said.

"I'll email the info to Detective Espinoza," Sophie said.

"While they prepare the warrant, let's work on getting this place ready for Sara and the K-9 center," Mia said, and peered at Jose intently. "Are you feeling okay?"

"Just a headache," he said, downplaying it, but his voice and body were tight, and she had noticed earlier that morning that he seemed a little pale.

"Maybe you can stay here and help out with the painters," Mia said.

"I'm okay," he insisted, and shot a quick look in her direction.

"Mia and I are just going to take some measurements for the flooring, and then we'll be back," she said.

That seemed to mollify him since he nodded. "I'll wait for you and the painters here."

"Great. The rest of us will finish up the security installations," Trey said.

Sophie gestured to the yellow tape along the edges of the woods. "We haven't been able to install the perimeter cameras because of the restrictions."

Trey stood, arms akimbo, and examined the wooded area. With a nod, he said, "We'll finish once they're gone. In the meantime, let's secure what we can."

With that the team went into action, but Sara hung back with Jose, wanting to make sure he was okay.

"Are you fine with staying here? I won't be long," she said, and rubbed Bongo's head as the dog bumped against her leg.

"I'm good. I'll just wait inside for the painters," he said, and without waiting for her, he walked to the house and stepped inside.

Sara stood there for a long minute, a weird feeling in her gut. She was torn between following him and going with Mia to measure for the new floors in the training center and track area.

"Do you want to stay?" Mia asked.

She was being silly. The painters would be here at any moment and Jose would be fine. "No, let's do the measurements," she said, and they walked off toward the training ring.

JOSE STROLLED INTO the house, grateful to be out of the morning sun whose glare had just been making his headache even worse.

Although the doctor had advised against caffeine because of the concussion, he needed a jolt to get going since he felt lethargic even though they'd gotten a nice night's sleep.

He smiled as he thought about the night and how they'd fallen asleep in each other's arms. Woke wrapped together, he thought as he entered the kitchen in search of a coffee machine and hopefully coffee, even if it might be stale after years in the cupboards.

He opened one cupboard, and it blocked his view of the hallway, but sudden motion had him turning in that direction.

A mistake. Something sharp drove into his side, sucking the breath from his lungs.

He looked down to see the short knife buried between his ribs and in a blur of action, Guidry was behind him with an arm around his neck.

"Move or call out and I'll cut your throat," Shawn said.

"What do you want?" Jose said, words choppy since each breath seemed to create fire at the spot where Guidry had the knife buried in his side.

"Satisfaction. You and your friends have ruined my special place. Someone has to pay for that. Maybe those two pretty women I saw walking away," Guidry hissed against the side of his face.

"Leave them alone," Jose said, and pain erupted as Guidry delivered a little twist of the knife.

"Big hero, aren't you? We'll see how much of a hero when I get you alone," he said, and applied pressure at his neck to shuffle him toward a side door in the kitchen.

With a shove, Guidry said, "Open it."

He did, and Guidry led him out the door and through the newly mowed grass behind the house.

Jose almost wished they'd left it longer since it would have created more of a trail to follow. He stumbled on a bit of uneven ground, bringing intense pain as the knife punched into his side again.

"Move," Guidry commanded.

Jose did, hoping the SBS crew would quickly notice his absence but also thinking about how he could save himself, especially since with each step he took, he was feeling weaker, and it was getting harder to breathe.

He was in so much pain coupled with fear, he hadn't really paid attention to where they were going. But as they stopped, he realized they were in the middle of a field that had once held a crop of corn. Now there was only the refuse of chopped cornstalks, leaves, and here and there, verdant vines from a pumpkin patch.

"On your knees," he said, and Jose readily complied, in part because his knees were already crumpling from the loss of blood. It was warm and wet against his side and down toward his waist.

Before his fading eyes the ground opened up, exposing a large four-by-four-foot hole. His surprise was short-lived as with a shove, Guidry pushed him in.

He landed hard and it drove out what little breath he had left.

As he rolled onto his back, his last view was of a crystal-clear Miami fall sky and the ground closing above him.

His last thought was of Sara.

"WHAT'S UP?" Mia asked as Sara stared toward the house through the open door of the training ring.

Sara couldn't say what it was, but she had an unsettling

feeling in her gut that warned they had to rush back. "We're done, right? I'd like to make sure Jose is okay. He was looking a little pale this morning."

Mia nodded. "Sure thing. We're done here."

They hustled back toward the house, meeting up with Trey who had left Sophie and Robbie to finish up with their team.

"Something wrong?" Trey asked, reading her signals clearly.

"Just worried about Jose," Sara admitted, her pace quickening. Bongo quickly walking beside her.

"I'm sure he's fine," Trey said, but fell into step with her, sensing her upset.

She burst through the door of the house and seeing the room was empty, called out his name. "Jose. Where are you?"

He didn't answer.

"I'll check upstairs," Trey said, and took the steps two at a time while Mia checked the far rooms on the first floor.

Sara noticed that a side door in the kitchen was ajar and moved in that direction.

She stopped short at what looked like droplets of blood on the wooden floor.

Tugging Bongo's leash tight, she knelt and examined the floor more carefully. She had no doubt it was blood. Worse, she had no doubt it was Jose's blood.

As Trey came bounding down the stairs and Mia returned to the kitchen, they walked over.

Trey muttered a curse and said, "I'll call the rest of the team for help."

Sara held her hand up to stop him. "No. It'll be too many people mucking up the trail. Bongo and I will find him."

"With what?" Mia said, wringing her hands with worry.

Sara pointed to the drops of blood on the floor. "With that."

Urging Bongo close, she let her K-9 partner scent the blood, and said, "Find him, Bongo. Find him."

SHARP, JABBING PAIN jerked him back to consciousness.

"Good. I don't want you to miss anything," Guidry said, and stepped away, short bloody knife in his hand.

Jose peered at his side and the trio of wounds leaking blood.

Trey's words returned in a flash. *Some killers need to stick people to experience arousal.*

Glancing back at the other man, his joy was evident from the wide smile on his face and the brightness of his eyes, even in the dim light belowground.

"I want you to see how I'm going to kill your friends," Guidry said. He walked to a small table at one side of the space, and flipped on a lamp that spewed a circle of light over an assortment of wires, cans and batteries spread across the table's surface.

Guidry went to work at the table, but Jose wasn't about to let that happen.

He tried to sit up, but his hands were secured behind his back. His feet were also tied to keep him immobile.

That wasn't going to stop him.

He tucked his legs tight to his chest, ignoring the agony that ripped through his side.

Sucking in a few shallow breaths to contain the pain, he somehow managed to get his hands lower and close to his buttocks. Straining even harder, there was enough give in whatever tied them that he could slip his hands past his ass.

A chill sweat covered his body and dark circles swirled in his gaze as oblivion threatened to claim him again.

He inhaled deeply, marshaling his flagging energy, and pushed on. He would not let Guidry hurt his family.

Chapter Thirty-Two

Bongo led them across the narrow piece of woods near the road and then doubled back toward the fields leading to the Guidry farmhouse.

Fields where the only visible things were the stumpy stalks of corn that had been harvested a few weeks earlier. The dried stalks and scattered bits of leaves intermixed with vines, creating a tangle along the ground. Here and there bright spots of orange, pumpkins growing for a late fall harvest, dotted the fields.

They stopped at the edge of the field, searching for anywhere Guidry might be able to hide, but Sara couldn't see anything even though Bongo was pulling her toward the field and not the farmhouse.

Trey peered at the dog's actions. "There's nothing here but wide-open fields. He's probably at the farmhouse."

Bongo jerked at the leash, trying to urge her forward. "Bongo picked up a scent in the field."

"But if she's wrong—"

"Jose could die. Don't you think I know that?" Sara shot the words back at him, fear making her blood run cold. With a deep inhalation, she shook her head and said, "I trust Bongo. She's never wrong."

Trey hesitated, but then relented. "Then let's go."

GUIDRY WAS TOO busy planning his surprise to notice that Jose had somehow managed to bring his hands in front. That let him sit up and shimmy to the dirt wall of the space for support as blood loss made his head whirl again.

There was only a little light from the bare bulb hanging from a wire. It flickered uncertainly and as Jose traced the wire, he realized it was connected to a small device and then a car battery. By the base of the battery were red and black plastic clippings and a wire cutter.

Careful not to draw Guidry's attention, Jose scooted over a few inches and leaned down, reaching for the wire cutter. He grasped the tip of one of the handles and pulled it toward him soundlessly across the dirt floor.

Once secured, he had a difficult decision to make since he was sure the sound of the snip would alert Guidry to what he was doing.

Hands or feet? he asked himself, but the answer came immediately.

With a snip, he freed his legs.

SARA NEARLY RAN to keep up with Bongo as the dog jogged across the cornstalks and vines, hot on Jose's scent. Trey raced beside her, gun drawn in anticipation of a fight.

"Good girl, Bongo," she said in encouragement, hoping that the bloodhound was on the right track since the only thing she could see was a flattened field that led to the avocado and mango orchards in the distance.

They were midfield, surrounded by nothing except the cornstalks and pumpkin vines, when Bongo stopped running. She sniffed the ground, circling around a small area, before she dropped down to signal that she had found something.

Only it looked like nothing to her except dry cornstalks, leaves and pumpkin vines.

"This can't be it," she said, scanning the area and beginning to doubt Bongo for the first time.

Trey stood beside her, examining the area where Bongo had lay down. "Is she sure?"

Sara shrugged and said, "Bongo, please find. Please."

Bongo peered up at her, deep brown eyes almost accusing. She rose up, circled around the space, and then promptly sat again.

Sara muttered a curse and said, "We need to see what she sees."

GUIDRY'S HEAD WHIPPED AROUND, and Jose knew he had to act.

He jumped to his feet and faced the other man, his only weapon the wire cutter.

Guidry smiled and brandished his knife, clearly excited about the prospect of the fight he was sure to win.

Unless Jose had the element of surprise.

Reaching over, he snipped the wire leading to the light bulb, plunging most of the space into darkness. The lamp on the table still illuminated that space and cast light that limned Guidry's body, keeping him visible.

With another snip Jose freed his hands and pitched the wire cutter at the other man's head.

It landed with a loud thunk, stunning the man temporarily, but then Guidry launched himself at Jose.

With the advantage of darkness, he sidestepped the charge, bent, and heaved up the car battery to use as a shield.

Guidry swung out wildly with the knife and it connected with the battery casing, metal scraping against metal.

The other man cursed, giving Jose a clue as to where he stood, and Jose took advantage. He tossed the heavy battery in Guidry's direction.

The pained oomph he heard confirmed he'd hit his mark, but a second later, Guidry barreled into him, propelling him across the room and into the table.

A wild clatter of metal echoed in the space as they fought across the surface of the table, sending cans, wires and batteries flying off its surface.

"DID YOU HEAR THAT?" Sara said and bent closer to the ground.

The noise came again, and Trey said, "I did."

He bent and jerked away leaves and vines with his bare hands.

She saw it then. An almost imperceptible line in the ground not far from where Bongo was sitting. A man-made line.

"There. Look there," she said, joining Trey as he furiously yanked away debris to reveal a rope handle.

He grabbed it and flung open the door, uncaring of whether there was a trap.

The noise of a struggle was evident now and as they peered down, she caught sight of a body flying across the room.

Guidry, his face bloodied, white hair in disarray. He had a wild look in his eye that turned to surprise as he peered toward her.

A second later, Jose came into sight. He was bleeding and held a large wrench that he swung to keep Guidry at bay.

"The cavalry's here, Pepe," Trey said, and scrambled down a ladder on one side of the space, gun drawn.

"Good to hear," he said, grinned and passed out.

LIGHT LEAKED FROM his half-open eyes as he struggled to open them. When he did, an unfocused picture slowly sharpened and became clear.

A family picture, like on *Noche Buena*. They took one every Christmas Eve, he thought, his brain muddled.

Only Sara was in this photo, he realized and tilted his head in her direction. "What are you doing here?" he said, barely able to muster a whisper.

She leaned close, smiling, tearful, and swept a stray lock of hair from his forehead. "You've been out of it since they brought you in a few hours ago."

"Brought me in?" he asked, and shook his head to clear the cobwebs, and finally realized he was in the hospital, surrounded by his SBS cousins as well as Trey's parents and his own mother and father.

"The knife nicked your lung. We had to make sure it didn't cause your lung to collapse," Sara explained, and danced her hand across his face again, her touch comforting.

"You're going to be okay," Trey said, and squeezed his hand.

"Easy for you to say," he teased, and was unprepared for the guilt that flitted across his cousin's face.

"I'm so sorry we pulled you into this, Pepe. We won't again," Trey said, voice filled with anguish.

"That's going to be hard to do, seeing as Sara and I are a thing. We're a thing, aren't we?" he said, smiling as he looked at her.

"We are, Jose. We're most definitely a thing," she said, tears of joy filling her gaze.

"Good," he said, and drifted his gaze across the family gathered around him before he closed his eyes and gave in to the rest he needed to get better.

DAYS LATER HE sat at the table with his SBS cousins, Tio Ramon, and most importantly, Sara and Bongo.

The Gonzales family. For too long he'd run away from them, but no longer.

Trey smiled and rose to give a report on the police investigation of Guidry.

"DNA analysis has confirmed that the man and older woman found in the graves are related to Guidry and are likely his mother, Misty, and younger brother Thomas."

Sara shook her head and murmured, "He murdered his own family."

"And a dozen other women, but not before he and Metz had what they considered fun. Police were able to identify at least eight women, two of them raped before they were killed," Trey added to his report.

"What about the attack on Sara and the tractor incident?" Mia asked.

"General height matches him, but we don't have anything else to connect him to Sara's attack, but it makes sense it was him. As for the tractor, he wore gloves, but must have taken them off to hot-wire the vehicle since PD got a fingerprint that matches his."

"They have enough to charge him?" Sophie asked.

Trey nodded. "They do, and it looks like the district attorney is going to ask for the death penalty."

"So this is over?" Jose asked. He might not have wanted to be a part of SBS, but after all that had happened, he was a part of it now.

"You may need to testify, but you don't have to worry about Guidry anymore," Trey said.

Sara squeezed his hand, and he gripped it tightly and faced her, smiling. The nightmare with Guidry was over, but Sara would soon be a part of his family and no matter what came in the future, they would handle it together.

* * * * *

Don't miss the stories in this mini series!

SOUTH BEACH SECURITY: K-9 DIVISION

Killer In The Kennel
CARIDAD PIÑEIRO
November 2024

Danger In Dade
CARIDAD PIÑEIRO
December 2024

MILLS & BOON

The Masquerading Twin

Katie Mettner

MILLS & BOON

Books by Katie Mettner

Harlequin Intrigue

Secure One

Going Rogue in Red Rye County
The Perfect Witness
The Red River Slayer
The Silent Setup
The Masquerading Twin

Visit the Author Profile page at millsandboon.com.au.

Katie Mettner wears the title of "the only person to lose her leg after falling down the bunny hill" and loves decorating her prosthetic leg to fit the season. She lives in Northern Wisconsin with her own happily-ever-after and wishes for a dog now that her children are grown. Katie has an addiction to coffee and Twitter and a lessening aversion to Pinterest—now that she's quit trying to make the things she pins.

CAST OF CHARACTERS

Selina Colvert—Her past has returned from the dead to hunt her. Selina has to stay off the radar if she wants to remain alive.

Efren Brenna—He prides himself on keeping people safe. Tasked with protecting one of their own, Efren wonders if this will be the job he fails at.

Ava Shannon—Ava is proof that only the good die young. She's returned from the dead, but why is the question.

Medardo "The Snake" Vaccaro—Kingpin of the Chicago Mafia with an ax to grind with Selina and now Secure One.

Randall Loraine—He may be behind bars, but that doesn't mean he's not pulling the strings.

Kai Tanner—A man from Selina's past who may have the answer to her future.

Chapter One

"Getting shot sucks," Selina grumped, shifting to find a more comfortable position. "What's worse is this damn hospital bed. It's like a board with sheets."

Efren glanced up from his crossword puzzle and raised a brow. "Next time, don't walk in front of a bullet."

Her eye roll was epically dramatic. She noticed her reflection in the mirror across from her bed and gave herself a score of twelve out of ten. The airtime before those drugged-up eyes returned to center had earned her the two extra points.

"If I recall correctly, I didn't, but I'll keep that in mind. What were you and Eric whispering about while everyone else tried to save my life?"

His sigh was notably a six out of ten on the exasperation scale. "Has anyone ever told you that you're incredibly dramatic?"

"Not before today. It must be a new skill. You didn't answer my question."

"Nothing," he said pointedly. This time, he didn't even look up from the crossword puzzle.

"Seemed like a lot of nothing considering the time it took. I was surprised you parted ways without a hug or a secret handshake."

When he lifted his head, agitation was written all over his face. Good, she was getting to him. Maybe he'd finally leave her hospital room for more than ten seconds. "Is this contrary banter supposed to convince me to leave?" She raised a brow as an answer. "You'll have to try harder. I've protected kids with more game than you've got."

He was so irritating! Selina forced herself to take a deep breath, or at least as deep as she could without pain.

Don't let him see you sweat. It's bad enough he sees you in pain. He doesn't need to know all your weaknesses.

Efren Brenna had been a burr in her side since the day he started working for Secure One. He'd moved down a spot now that she had a bullet wound in her side, but at least that would heal and the pain would disappear. Not the case with Brenna, it appeared. His reputation was that of a hero, and his ego matched. Okay, that wasn't fair. He was a hero. He'd saved countless lives while bleeding out from a traumatic leg amputation. On the other hand, his ego was too big for her liking. It filled up the room and left no space for anyone else. At least that was her story, and she was sticking to it.

She studied the man who sat engrossed in the newspaper crossword puzzle. Selina knew he was also paying full attention to everything around him in the hospital room and the hallway. She could see his profile from her bed, and she had to admit that some might consider him handsome. His brown hair was cut short in the back with a swoop of hair over his forehead. His skin was the perfect shade of desert tan, and his brown eyes were giant with lashes that any woman would kill for. He was tall to her five and a half feet, but thin and wiry. Under his left pant leg, he wore a high-tech above-knee skin-fit prosthesis with a running blade attached. He always wore his blade when they went on missions, and since he hadn't returned to Secure One, he hadn't changed into his everyday leg. She suspected Eric would return with it soon but wouldn't ask. She didn't want him to think she cared one way or the other about his comfort when she was the one in the hospital bed.

"If you must know," he said, setting the paper aside and leaning forward in his chair, "we were talking about the case—"

Motion caught her eye and she peered through the narrow window in the door. What she saw had her heart rate climbing fast. She put her finger to her lips, her gaze glued to the nurses' station outside her door. Efren swung his head around slowly. Selina wondered if he saw her, too. If she was real. A woman with long blond hair that fell in waves against her back where it blended into her white fur coat stood tapping her bloodred nails on the counter. The door was open a crack so they could hear the discussion between the nurse and the woman.

"I'm looking for Eva Shannon. I was told she was brought to this hospital."

"I'm sorry," the nurse said. "I can only give out information to family. Are you a direct family member?"

"Yes, I'm her sister," the woman answered in a rather bored tone.

Efren raised a brow at Selina in question, and she swallowed hard. There was no way that woman was her sister. She'd put her sister in a body bag eight years ago.

"Let me check," the nurse said, typing into the computer. "I'm sorry, but I don't have an Eva Shannon on this floor. You could try two floors up. That's Med-Surg. She might be there since that's overflow when our floor gets full."

"I'll do that," the woman said.

Selina recognized the signature sass, and sweat broke out on her brow as the woman turned and sashayed toward the elevator. That woman was her sister. The one who was supposed to be dead.

Efren stood by the door until he heard the elevator's ding, then closed the door the rest of the way, jammed a chair under it and spun on her. "Get ready. I'm going to let Eric know we're moving."

"Get ready? Moving? I just had surgery to remove a bullet from my gut. I'm not going anywhere!"

Efren stalked to her bed in a way she'd never seen him move before. A lion patiently hunting prey came to mind. When he stood over her, his entire demeanor had changed. "Did you hear who that woman asked for?"

Selina swallowed before she answered, afraid nothing but a scream of terror would leave her lips if she didn't. "Eva Shannon. I don't know who that is, so I don't know what you're so worried about, Efren."

He braced his hands on the bed and leaned in until he was inches from her face. "You wanted to know what Eric and I were whispering about earlier?" He raised a brow, and she nodded. Having him this close to her was unnerving, and she blinked, afraid to breathe. "It was about the moment before you were shot. Randall Jr. said Ava Shannon right before he put a bullet in you. It was a question, not a statement. Vic also kept mumbling about you being dead, which tells me two things. That woman out there is Ava Shannon, and the woman I'm staring at is Eva Shannon. Cute play on the names. I give your mom props for that. I don't need to know the rest right now, but I need you to stop playing games. Let that fear you keep trying to swallow down motivate you to get up and get out of here before they finish the job!" The growl of exclamation was intense before he turned and picked up his bag, pulling out an encoded phone all Secure One operatives used.

With the phone to his ear, he stared her down, and she closed her eyes because if looks could kill, he'd do a better job than Randall's bullet had. The woman from a few moments ago filled her mind as terror shot through her soul. It was like looking in a mirror in a house of horrors. Ava was supposed to be dead. Selina had been the one to shoot her in the chest. The ME had assured her the bullet had done the trick and ended her reign of terror—all evidence to the contrary. Ava was alive and well, wearing her signature fur. That meant one thing. She was out for blood. Ava did not take well to being wronged, especially by her family.

Her mind warred with what she had just seen and what it already knew. How? Where had she been all these years? That night, the night they raided Randall Loraine's home, things hadn't gone as planned, but Selina wasn't sad to put her twin in a body bag at the end of the night, even if it put a target on her back.

"Listen, Eva, we have to talk about your sister," her police chief said as they strapped on their vests and readied their weapons.

"What's to talk about?" she asked, tightening the straps.

"You can't be a risk to the lives of the team. If she's going to distract you, you need to stand down."

"You should know me better than that by now," she answered, and then lined up with the rest of the team.

Eva could only hope her sister was inside those four ostentatious walls. The task force could prove she knew about the counterfeiting ring, but not that she had her hands in it. She did. They'd find that proof tonight. There was no way Ava Shannon-Loraine would let her husband run the ring alone. She was too controlling— too diabolical—to let an opportunity to manipulate and dominate Randall Sr. pass her by. They should both be behind bars, but first, they had to find the proof. Once they did, Eva had no problem being the one to put Ava in handcuffs.

The team spread out around the perimeter of the Loraine mansion. It had so many doors to cover that they'd had to pull in the SWAT teams from two separate counties. The last thing they wanted was for Randall or Ava to escape and disappear when they'd been building a case against them for over a year. If they went underground, they'd be in the wind forever.

Intel told them the couple spent their evenings in the library. Eva snickered to herself. She was the intel. She's spent enough time inside the mansion to know Ava and Randall's routine. Their sniper on the hill had confirmed they were there. That meant entering the front door, turning right down a hallway, and right into the first door. The room was small, which left them little room to hide, but Eva suspected they had a way out that even she didn't know existed.

With a nod from the chief, they rammed their way

into the house from both ends. Eva tried to tune out the shouting and shrill alarm as she swung into the room where her sister and brother-in-law sat enjoying a glass of bourbon they'd bought with blood money.

"Freeze! You're under arrest!" her chief yelled at Randall as he crawled through a hatch in the floor.

Two SWAT guys hauled him out before he could shut it and handcuffed him before he got a word out. Eva swung her gun around the room. "Where is she?" It wasn't a question as much as a rebel yell at the man who had somehow helped her twin escape.

"Tag, you're it. Run, run as fast as you can, big sister, but little sister can't be caught." Randall's words were spat at her with so much distaste it made Eva laugh.

"You don't know me very well then, Randall." She swept her gun and flashlight down the hatch, but her twin was nowhere in sight. She didn't let that stop her. Eva's feet barely touched the ladder's rungs before she jumped onto the concrete floor below. The tunnel only went one way, so on instinct, she ran, knowing it was leading her toward the property line to the south. Ava couldn't have that much of a jump on her. Maybe thirty seconds. How far could she get in that time? With her gun tight to her chest, Eva noticed movement ahead of her. The swish of long blond hair as she climbed a ladder before popping out into the night.

"Ava, stop! You're surrounded!" she yelled to her twin, but Ava didn't stop.

The adrenaline had Eva's legs and heart pumping as she ran full out toward her twin, knowing that if she escaped, Eva would never be safe. She'd always have to look over her shoulder for a bullet that one day would come. Ava believed in an eye for an eye, but if her family betrayed her, she would burn down the world.

Eva reached out, her fingers grasping Ava's long hair. She pulled her backward and to the ground, where she landed with an oof. "Stay down!" Eva yelled, pointing her gun at Ava's center mass.

"What are you going to do, sis? Shoot an unarmed woman?"

"If she doesn't stay down, I won't hesitate," Eva growled. Her body shook with anger, but her gun remained steady.

"What happened to you?" Ava asked, shaking her head in disdain.

"What happened to me? I'm not the one on the wrong side of the law, Ava."

"You think you're holier than thou because you're a cop. You have no idea what real life is like for me. You're about to find out."

Ava launched herself at her twin but didn't get far before Eva squeezed the trigger. The bullet knocked her back, and shock filled her eyes as she glanced down at her chest, where blood turned her white cashmere sweater bright red.

"You shot me," she hissed, that shock turning to fury. "I can't believe you shot me!"

"I warned you," Eva said, her gun still pointed at her twin. With one hand, she pushed the button on her walkie. "I need EMS on the south side of the property. I have Ava Loraine. She has a bullet wound to the chest."

"Selina!"

She started at the name, opening her eyes to stare right into Efren's brown ones.

"Sorry, what did you say?"

"I said it's time to get you up and dressed. We have to go."

There was a knock on the door, and Efren had his gun out and was next to the door before she saw him move. He opened the door a hair, but Selina couldn't see who it was.

"Quickly," he whispered, and opened the door wide enough for a nurse to slide through. He had the door shut and the chair under the handle before the nurse made it to the side of her bed.

"I have your discharge papers," she said cheerily, as though there wasn't a man with a gun in her room.

"Discharge papers?" Selina asked, her heart pounding in her chest as she pushed herself up in the bed.

The nurse shook the papers in her hand. "Everything you need to finish your recovery elsewhere. Eric told us to be alert for anyone asking about you who looked suspicious," she explained as she busied herself with the machines by Selina's bed. "When that woman looked exactly like my patient, I decided chances were good that was who he was referring to. I know you're an APP, so I'm confident you can take care of your wound, correct?"

Selina nodded, and the nurse smiled. "Good, let's get your IV out and find you something to put on that's a little less memorable." The nurse turned to Efren. "I have enough medication for the day, but she will need more than this."

Efren dug in his bag and pulled out a slip of paper. "Call it into that pharmacy, under that name. We'll pick it up."

The nurse stuck it in her pocket and set about removing Selina's IV and checking her wound. The drugs had made her head hazy, but she forced herself to concentrate. Her twin had returned from the dead, and now Selina and Efren were in her crosshairs. Her gaze drifted to Efren, his backpack on and ready to go while he glared at her in confusion and anger. She was going to have to trust him to keep her safe, but she suspected she was anything but when it came to Efren Brenna.

Chapter Two

Efren's gaze bounced between his mirrors, the road and the woman beside him. Getting her out of the hospital had been a dangerous endeavor that wasn't over yet. This old Jeep bought them time but not safety. It was registered in a way that would take someone more than a few minutes to figure out that Secure One owned it. It would get them where they needed to go, but then it would have to go.

They hit a bump, and he noticed Selina grimace. She was white as a sheet but holding on, and he couldn't ask for more than that. Efren didn't know if it was the pain or seeing her twin again that stole all color from her cheeks, but he would guess it was a little of both. She'd have to tell him exactly what they were dealing with, but it could wait until they weren't running for their lives.

"What's an APP?" he asked, hoping to distract her. She glanced at him in confusion, and he motioned behind him. "At the hospital. The nurse said you were an APP."

"Oh, I already forgot. I'm a little stressed."

"Understandable," he said with a nod.

"It means advanced practice paramedic. I can provide

extensive and advanced patient care on critical patients in the field or in an emergent disaster situation."

"I see. I guess I thought you were a nurse."

"That's what they call me at Secure One to put the guys at ease."

His laughter filled the cab of the small Jeep. "I don't think the guys need to be put at ease when it comes to you taking care of them. Not after the way you cared for Marlise, Charlotte and Bethany. It's easy to see you only want what's best for your patients."

He noticed the shrug from the corner of his eye, but she didn't say anything, so he thought it best to change the subject. "We've been on the road for ninety minutes and haven't picked up a tail, which is reassuring. We're about ten minutes from where we'll pick up your prescriptions, and then it's another thirty to the safe house."

"It's going to be tough to move," she said, her breath tight when she spoke. "Wheelchair or no wheelchair."

He nodded and squeezed her shoulder briefly before putting his hand back on the wheel. "The pharmacy has a drive-through and no monitoring cameras, which is why I picked it. Is there anything else you need? The safe house is stocked with food and supplies."

"First aid supplies?" she asked, shifting in her seat. "I'm going to need gauze and tape."

He was silent as he turned off the highway into a small town. "I'm sure there are first aid supplies, but I don't know how many. Write down what you need, and I'll have them send it out with the prescriptions." He pointed at the pad of paper in the cup holder.

It took effort, but by the time they got to the pharmacy, she had a list that he passed the pharmacist through the window. While they waited, he noticed Selina eyeing him.

"Do you always have fake IDs on you?"

"Yes," he answered, his gaze grabbing hers for a moment. "We work in the kind of business that can leave us injured and on the run. If you aren't prepared, you're dead. As soon as we get the scripts, Michael Fenstad will cease to exist, but we'll have what we need until we can get back to Secure One."

The pharmacist returned to the window and handed everything out to them. Efren gave the pain medication to Selina and money to the pharmacist. As he pulled away, he motioned at the water bottle in the cup holder.

"Take one of the pain pills."

"It's too early," she said, checking the clock.

"Listen. You'll have to walk in when we get to the safe house. The wheelchair won't go over the terrain."

"Where is this place? Canada?"

"Middle of nowhere Minnesota, so just about as bad," he answered, motioning at the water again with his chin. "Take the pill now, so it's on board by the time we get there."

She hesitated only a moment longer before she followed his order. "I'm not immobile," she said defiantly. "I'm just slow-moving."

"And when you're being hunted, slow-moving is a risk factor for death. I do not want you taking another bullet under my guard. I'll never be employed again."

"We can't have that," she muttered with an eye roll that he noticed as he checked the rearview mirror.

He'd kept an eye out since they left the town behind and noticed a pair of headlights follow them out of town.

That didn't mean it was necessarily suspicious, but he couldn't risk driving to the safe house if someone followed them.

"Tag on the rudder," she said, her gaze pinned on her side mirror. "They've been there since we left town."

"Yep, I was just thinking it was time to get rid of them." Efren slowed the Jeep and waited to see if the car went around them. It didn't.

"Next idea?" she asked, glancing at him.

"I hate to do this with you in the car, but they've left me no choice. Hang on and don't scream. It throws off my concentration."

He noted the start of her eye roll right before he yanked the wheel to the right and accelerated into the turn. He had no idea where the road went, but when the car kept going, he pressed the accelerator to the floor to put some distance between them.

"Slow down. They're not following us."

"Yet," he said, concentrating on the road ahead as he drove twice the posted speed limit. "They could be turning around as we speak."

She watched her mirror and let out a rather unladylike curse when headlights turned down the road. "We can't outrun them, and we can't bail," Selina said, her words tight.

"Well, hell, you just ruined all my plans." His words were tongue in cheek, but he heard the frustration in them, too. "Can you shoot?"

"Am I dead?"

"Not yet."

"Then I can shoot. Where's your gun?"

"Take the wheel," he ordered, waiting for her to grip

it before he reached behind him and lifted a semiautomatic from under a blanket.

Selina's whistle was long and happy. "Well, look at you! You came loaded for bear. Keep this up and I might start to like you, Brenna."

She took the gun, and he took the wheel. Rather than give orders, he decided to let her make the plan. Maybe she would start to like him a little if he didn't take all the control away from her the way everyone else at Secure One did. He had to admit that he wanted her to like him, and not because of his ego. Since he returned from the war, he vowed to himself that he'd live his life without caring whether someone liked or disliked him. He was his true self all the time, except when it came to Selina. At the very least, he didn't want her to hate him. "What's the plan, Colvert?" he asked, hoping she had one and that it would stop him from thinking about how much he wished she liked him.

"They're gaining on us fast," she observed. She carefully got herself onto the Jeep floor on her knees and aimed the gun out the window. "When I say now, stomp the brakes. When I say go, hammer it. In between those two words, duck, cover and pray."

Efren couldn't help it. He smiled. Then the first bullet smacked into the back of the Jeep.

"Guess there's no time like the present. Now!"

Efren stomped the brake as she let the first rounds go. He couldn't see if she gained any purchase while he tried to keep the Jeep from careening off the road. Another round of bullets slammed into them, taking out the back window and leaving a sucking wind on his

back. The enemy was outgunned, but Selina had little
time to prove it.

"Don't mind if I do," she yelled, resting the gun on
the back of the seat and pulling the trigger, releasing a
barrage of bullets that definitely hit home. He checked
the rearview mirror again and saw the car headed for
the ditch and a large tree. "Go!"

He threw his arm out to brace her as he slammed
the accelerator, then held her in place until their speed
evened out and she could sit up again. "Great shooting,
partner," he said with a shake of his head. "Once we're
off this road and at the safe house, you've got some
'splaining to do."

THE BRUSH WAS thick and wanted to pull them down with
every step. Selina was tired, in pain and trying to protect a surgical wound. All of that said, she would never
admit to Efren that she was glad he'd made her take that
pain pill. After they found their way to the safe house
using back roads, they had to bury the Jeep in a grove
of trees and walk in. If the people following them had
a team waiting, driving into a trap out here was certain
death, even with a semiautomatic. She knew who was
following them, though she wasn't quite ready to share
that information with her bodyguard yet. If Ava was
alive, then she had the henchmen for Chicago Mafia
kingpin Medardo Vaccaro at her disposal. That meant
one thing—they would never stop coming for her until
she, or Ava, was dead.

Known in the crime world as the Snake, but known to
her and Ava as Uncle Medardo, he was less than happy
when Selina's team broke up his payday by arresting

Randall Loraine and killing Ava. Why did they call him Uncle Medardo? Her father had been part of his lower management for longer than she and Ava had been alive. When her father went into debt to Vaccaro, his boss so kindly suggested that the best way to pay off his debts was to offer one of his daughter's hands in marriage to Randall Loraine.

When her father turned up dead with a cause of death as "indeterminate," that was probably also Vaccaro getting payment for his debts. Selina had been a cop long enough to know a bribe had been accepted by the ME to make Charles Shannon's death an accident. Then again, it was equally possible Ava killed their father for marrying her off. Either way, Vaccaro was once again Selina's problem.

"Please tell me we're almost there," she whispered, trying to slide through the hole in the branches he'd made for her.

"We're here." Efren pointed ahead into the dark.

She squinted but couldn't make out a structure. "All I see is rubble."

"Exactly. That rubble is the safe house. Or rather, underneath that rubble." He flipped his night-vision goggles down and scanned the area. She leaned over, bracing her hands on her thighs to keep her side from spasming.

Getting shot in the side sucked, but Selina knew she was lucky. The bullet had missed all vital organs other than her left ovary. She already knew she couldn't have children, so this would be nothing more than a scar and a memory of another successful Secure One case in a few short weeks. It would be grand if her entire body would stop hurting, though. She'd only been out of surgery twenty-four hours when her twin showed up, and since then, she'd pushed her body to its limit. If she weren't on pain pills, she'd take a stiff drink and a bed. Right about now, she'd settle for the bed.

Efren lifted his goggles and turned to her. "I don't see anyone lying in wait. Let's get you someplace a bit more comfortable. It involves a rung ladder. I'll go down first so I can help you."

"I won't even argue." She followed him through the door of the old cabin with three walls that you could consider upright compared to the back wall, which was in shambles. The roof was gone, and the wooden floor was strewn with bricks, leaves and pine needles. Old mattresses littered the floor, along with cooking pans and metal buckets.

"There's nothing here, Efren."

"At first glance," he said. He slid one of the mattresses across the floor and revealed a hatch.

"A hidden hatch. Okay, but how do we re-cover it?"

"We don't," he answered, motioning her to follow him through the hole in the back of the cabin wall. "The ground cover will hide our footprints," he whispered, helping her around behind a row of trees. "That hatch is there to throw people off."

"What's in the hatch?"

"Pipes that look real but do nothing."

He knelt, swept his hand along the ground between two trees, and lifted a heavy metal door. "This is our hatch. I'll go down first, help you, and then come back up and close it."

Selina nodded and waited for him to climb down the rung ladder. She averted her eyes, because the memory of following Ava down a ladder just like this one eight years ago assailed her. Logically, she knew it wouldn't end the same, but the fear of Ava finding her was intense enough to wipe logic off the table.

An emergency light lit the ladder, and she saw Efren setting the bags on the bunker's floor. Selina prayed she'd make it down without needing his assistance. It would be a mistake to have his hands wrapped around any part of her, and keeping her distance would be the only way to survive any type of forced proximity. She chuckled to herself. Talk about an oxymoron.

"Selina!" he hissed, and she started, forgetting where she was and what she was supposed to be doing. It must be the pain pills. It couldn't be the man waiting for her below.

"Sorry," she whispered. "I was planning out my descent."

Her eyes rolled at herself that time, but she managed to make it down the rung with minimal pain and without falling into his arms. He climbed the ladder again to shut the hatch, and she walked to a bunk bed in the room, sat down and promptly passed out.

Chapter Three

"I need your help, Kai."

Eva could see that the man in front of her was terri-fied, but he finally nodded. "And you're sure I won't get in trouble for this?"

"Positive," Eva promised. "You have to know I don't have any other options. I wouldn't do this if I did."

"I know, but Eva, he's going to be heartbroken. I don't know if he'll ever recover."

"Selina?" a voice asked. "Selina, wake up. You're moaning. It's time for medication."

She blinked several times as the man beside her morphed from Kai into someone else. Someone she didn't know. Had they found her that quickly? "Kai! Kai! Help!"

"Selina, relax!" the man said, his voice frantic. "I'm Efren. You work for Cal Newfellow at Secure One. Your friends are Mina, Marlise and Charlotte."

Efren. Secure One. She blinked again and swallowed down the fear before she sat up gingerly. "Sorry. I got confused."

"I understand," he said, handing her a water bottle. "I remember what that's like when you're tired, sore, tak-ing medication and dredging up the past."

"What time is it?" she asked to change the subject. The last thing she wanted to talk about with Efren Brenna was the past, though she knew it was inevitable.

"It's two a.m. I've been in touch with Cal and taken a nap. I didn't want to wake you until you had a chance to sleep off the pain from walking in. You must be hurting."

"I've felt better, but I'm alive. I can thank you for that both times."

"We're a team, which means no thanks is needed. I wish I could have spared you the pain of getting here, though."

"We're a team, so no apology is needed," she said with a wink. "Besides, you managed to get me the medication I needed and to a safe place before daylight."

"Only because of your scary accurate marksman skills. Does Cal know you're a crack shot?"

"Yep," she answered, taking the pills he held out. After she tossed them back with a swig of water, she took a moment to take in the room. "Where are we?"

"Nice pivot, Colvert," he said with a shake of his head. She smirked and accepted the hand he held out to help her up. "This is the safe house Cal built when he realized if we continued with these kinds of cases, one day we would need it."

"I can't believe he built a replica of the bunker at Secure One."

"If it ain't broke, don't fix it," Efren said with a chuckle. "But you're correct other than the kitchen, compostable toilet and small wash basin. Everything runs on battery power, so you could stay here for a few weeks if you conserve water and power. At least we have the communication equipment available."

"With the amount of equipment here, you could run a small country," she said jokingly. "I need to use that compostable toilet, and then I suppose I need to touch base with my boss."

"Probably would be a good idea," Efren agreed with a wink. He opened the bathroom door for her. "Water, soap, towels and clean clothes are in the cabinet," he said, pointing at the metal locker next to the toilet. "When you're done, you'll tell me everything from start to finish. If I'm going to keep you safe, I have to know what's coming at us."

Fear shot through her at the idea of breaking her silence after all these years. Rather than speak, all she did was close the bathroom door.

WHO'S KAI? That was the only question running through Efren's head. He was obviously someone from Selina's past and someone she relied on when she was in trouble. Was he an ex-boyfriend or an ex-partner? It wasn't a giant leap to assume that Selina, aka Eva, was a cop in her past life. She knew too much to be anything but a cop or a criminal, and he knew Cal didn't hire criminals. He would still make her spell everything out, from her prior career choices to what happened with her sister. Until he understood what they were dealing with, there was no way for him to make a plan to keep her safe. After they talked, they'd contact Secure One as a united front.

The bathroom door cracked open, and Selina walked out. Her steps were ginger, but she'd washed up and found clean joggers in the cabinet. "I have to say, a sponge bath and clean clothes do make me feel like a new woman."

"Maybe some food would, too?" Efren turned from the small camp stove with a pan of hot soup he set at the little two-person table, along with a bag of crackers and her water.

"I hate to admit that you're right, but you're right. Thanks for fixing it for me."

"Remember what I said about thank you?" Efren asked. "Chances are there will come a time when you'll do the same for me. In the meantime, why don't you tell me what we're dealing with here?"

Rather than speak, she focused on the soup and crackers, so he patiently waited for her to finish. Finally, she lowered the spoon and motioned toward the two accent chairs in the corner by the beds.

"If I'm going to give you my life story, we may as well be comfortable. It would be smart to call Cal so I only have to do this once. He knows some, but not all, of my past."

He helped her stand and walked with her to the two chairs in the corner. Once they were comfortable, he addressed her prior statement.

"I have it on good authority that they're sleeping right now, so they can be prepared to help us come daylight. Before sunup, I need a timeline of what happened since the night your sister 'died.'" He put air quotes around that word since they both knew she was alive and well. "Give it to me as you would if you were a witness giving a statement at the station. I'll write it down so we can pull out the pertinent and important information to give the team when we talk to them in the morning."

"You're assuming I was a cop?" she asked with a brow raised.

"Am I wrong?" he asked, raising the opposite brow.

"Unfortunately, no. That said, it's been eight years since I took any witness statements, so you'll have to forgive me if I'm a little rusty." She was going for levity, so he chuckled softly.

"I've got the pad and the time," he said with a wink, motioning at the paper on his lap. "I should ask if we're breaking any contracts with the United States Marshals Service by talking about this?"

"WITSEC?" she asked, and he nodded once. "No. I'm not part of WITSEC."

"Okay, then start whenever you're ready." Efren respected that it would be hard for her to trust him with the truth when she'd kept it a closely guarded secret for so long.

She shifted in the seat, and he got up, grabbed a pillow from the bed and handed it to her. After she slid it along her side, she cleared her throat. "I'd been a Chicago cop for four years when I joined a task force tracking a counterfeiting operation. I was aiming to make detective and knew shutting down the operation would be the feather in my cap to get the promotion."

"How long ago did you join the task force?" he asked, writing on the pad rather than making eye contact. He hoped that would make it easier for her to focus.

"That would be ten years ago now," she answered. "The task force suspected that the counterfeiting originated with Chicago Mafia kingpin Medardo the Snake Vaccaro. I was already intimate with him and his business, so when they asked me to join the task force, I readily agreed."

"Had you worked a case where Vaccaro was involved before the counterfeiting?"

"Nope," she said, popping the *P* harder than necessary. "My father worked for him my entire life. Lower management, if you catch my drift."

His brows went up. "That's wild. A cop's father was a Mafia henchman."

"It wasn't easy being that cop in the beginning. When they found out about my father, my superiors tried to fire me for being a Vaccaro plant. I fought back with the union and won since there was no evidence that I was tied to Vaccaro. I had worked hard to keep myself separated from anything my father did since I was in high school. Then my father got behind on some debts to his boss. The Snake offered him an opportunity to pay them off by giving the hand of one of his daughters to be married to a man within his organization."

"And that daughter sure as hell wasn't you?"

"Nope," she said again, staring at her lap. "My father knew I was working my way to detective, and I wouldn't hesitate to arrest anyone who got in my way of accomplishing that goal, including him."

"Did your sister have her own life by then as well?"

"Nope," she said a third time, much to his amusement.

"I'm sorry for laughing, but I can't help but wonder if this entire conversation will be punctuated with the word nope."

"Nope." This time she gave him a quirky smile. "To answer your other question, Ava did not have her own life. She was a spoiled, entitled debutante wannabe who thought Daddy would bankroll her for life. She never wanted to lift a finger or work for anything. She was fifteen minutes younger than me, and we were identical twins in everything but our work ethic and morals."

"Neither of which is genetically embedded in us," Efren said, and she pointed at him.

"Well said. As a result, my father racked up debts and favors while trying to pay for Ava's every whim. Things like her multiple college degrees that she started and stopped, her spa business that never took off because she was never there, and other random nonsense that my father bankrolled. When the Snake asked for a daughter's hand, it was a no-brainer. If my father could unload Ava, he'd stay out of debt and on the right side of favor with his boss."

"I'm going to go out on a limb and guess that her betrothed was Randall Loraine Sr."

"That's him," Selina answered, practically spitting the words from her lips. "He was twenty-three years older, had three sons and was already a widower. That didn't stop her. As soon as she realized he had money, she readily agreed to warm his bed."

"So, your sister marries Loraine and ends up helping him run a counterfeiting racket?"

"That's a short jump of a long story, but it's the nuts and bolts. Ava married him twelve years ago, and I suspect, though I can't prove it, he was already running the counterfeit operation out of his mansion in Bemidji. The Snake wanted Ava there to paint Randall as the consummate family man who found love again as well as a mother for his boys. Hilarious, since those boys were already teenagers or young adults."

"What happened to your father?"

"He was found floating facedown in the Chicago

River. His death was ruled indeterminate, so I know money changed hands with that death certificate. They also didn't find any water in his lungs, which means he was dead when he landed in the river."

"Nothing fishy about that," Efren muttered, and Selina laughed.

"I can't say for certain that Ava didn't kill him and convince Randall to help her cover it up. She believes in an eye for an eye, and if family wrongs her, she will burn down the world."

"Why would she kill your father? Did he wrong her somehow?"

"I would have no way of knowing that for certain, but if Randall told her Daddy had to die, then she wouldn't hesitate to do it."

"Which explains why she came looking for you as soon as she knew where you were."

"Likely," she agreed, shifting again. She was getting tired, and he had to wrap this up before she was in too much pain to talk. "That or she always knew where I was and was biding her time. If that's the case, then she's smarter than I gave her credit for all these years."

"I doubt she was the brains behind any fake death operation." Efren felt terrible that Selina saw herself as less than her sister when she was the one standing on the right side of the law. "She would have needed help and that help had to come from somewhere."

"More like someone," Selina agreed with a nod. "Vaccaro. I was told that my twin went straight to hell. Obviously, someone got the message wrong."

"Or someone wanted you to think she went straight to hell," Efren pointed out.

"That could be if the EMTs were bought in that town. No way to know now, but I wouldn't put it past Vaccaro to reel Ava back in if Randall had been snagged. The fact that she showed her face now terrifies me."

"Tell me why," he encouraged, leaning forward to show her he was listening and interested in what she had to say. He'd been listening and interested in what Selina Colvert had to say since the day he met her. While she treated him like a second-class citizen and with as much malice as is tolerable in the workplace, he'd always known it was an act. She was scared and hurting, but kept a tight lid on her emotions so as not to rock the boat. Now he understood why. She couldn't rock the boat. If she left Secure One, her life would be in jeopardy again.

"Well, her husband is still in prison, one of her stepsons is dead, another is going to prison, and she could still face charges for the counterfeiting operation. Showing her face again puts her at risk for arrest, if they found evidence she was involved, which I have no way of knowing. My main worry is that she started warming Vaccaro's bed after her 'death' and has become another head of the snake."

"Was there evidence that she was involved in the counterfeiting operation?"

"Before we raided the mansion, we only had circumstantial evidence. You and I both know she was involved, though. She was Randall's wife and secretary. Here's the thing, Ava is lazy, but she's incredibly smart and quick on the draw."

"Just like you are."

"I suppose genetics come into play there."

"You think she knew more than she let on."

"I think she was the brains behind the operation. Randall Sr. is polished, but he isn't smart or talented when it comes to the art of manipulation, if that makes sense."

"Of course it does. He was a puppet of the Snake. A smart man wouldn't allow himself to be controlled that way."

"That sums it up. I spent a lot of time with them as a couple, and Ava ruled the roost. Not just in a spoiled wife kind of way, either. She ruled that house with an iron fist, both with Randall and the two boys still at home. All of that said, we knew the information inside the house held the answers the task force needed to put together a case against them both. I don't know if evidence was ever found to prove she was involved," Selina said with a shake of her head.

"You were on the task force, so wouldn't you know that information?"

"If I had been part of the task force after that night, yes."

"Let me guess. You were put on administrative leave for shooting your sister?"

"Bingo. I was on mandatory administrative leave until the shooting was investigated. I never heard if they found evidence of her involvement, but I know Ava, so I suspect they didn't. If she was the one running the operation, she'd make sure her hands stayed squeaky clean while Randall's were all red."

"Do you think they pulled you because they thought you were a Vaccaro plant?"

"No." Her gaze dropped to her lap before she finished. "I knew being part of that task force would put me in grave danger. I'd be lucky to survive a few days outside of police protection before they'd find me floating face-down just like my father. So I turned in my badge and gun, drove to Wisconsin, and fell off a bluff with the raging Wisconsin River below. That was the last time anyone saw Eva Shannon."

Chapter Four

Selina noted the surprise on Efren's face, but to his credit, he simply glanced up and waited to see if she would continue. When she didn't, he set the pen down on his paper.

"How about we take a break? You can hardly keep your eyes open."

She shook her head. "No. I'm fine. If we're going to call Secure One in the morning, we have to work this out. Then I can sleep."

He picked up his pen again. "You decided falling off a cliff was easier than going into WITSEC?"

"Easier? Not in the beginning. Faster? Yes, and at the time, I needed to disappear quickly. Since I didn't have any family left, it didn't matter if I was in WITSEC or on my own. Besides, I couldn't be sure that the Snake didn't have a plant somewhere in the marshals' office. If I took protection, then I had to trust them and probably would end up with a bullet between my eyes sooner rather than later. I trusted myself and knew I wasn't going to double-cross me."

"Valid. Still had to have been hard."

"It was. I had my search-and-rescue dog to think about. I convinced my friend Kai Tanner to take him for me and to tell the authorities I fell. Since the Wisconsin River opens up into the Mississippi, if they didn't find a body, they wouldn't be surprised."

"He was willing to lie to authorities for you?"

"He may have had a bit of a crush on me," she said. "Maybe if our lives had been different, I could have seen us together, but there was no way I was dragging someone as honest and kind as Kai into something that could get him killed."

"You could have taken the dog and run."

"I could have," she agreed with a head nod, "but then the Snake would know I'd run. Taking Zeus would have been a dead giveaway, no pun intended. It was the hardest thing I've ever had to do to hand his leash over to Kai, but Zeus deserved better than what I could give him."

"Then what happened?"

"I don't know," she answered with a shrug. "I checked the *Tribune* but since I went missing in Wisconsin, it didn't even make the papers. At least not that I could find. The Wisconsin papers reported it as the death of a search-and-rescue agent that was a tragic accident. That told me Kai didn't get in trouble for falsely reporting my death."

"Man, sucked to be him," Efren muttered, making notes.

"Why do you say that?" She snapped her head up, immediately on the defense. "You don't think it sucked to be me?"

"I know it did. It had to be a difficult decision to know your choice was to trust the institution you worked for or go it on your own. It had to be a brutal decision to hand over your dog and walk away. I was simply saying from a guy's perspective, that it sucked for Kai, too. Not only did he have to give up the woman he cared about, but he had to pretend that she was dead for the rest of his life, when he knew you were still out there. It's hard to move on with life when your heart and mind are in a different place."

"Thanks for doing a better job of gutting me than the bullet did." She wrapped her arm around her belly. "I felt like hell asking him, but I had no one, and he knew that. He wanted to be my someone any way he could, and this was the only way he could, so he stepped up."

"What happened after you 'fell off the cliff'?" He put that whole phrase in air quotes, too.

Her sigh was loaded. What followed that day was hard. Harder than anything she'd ever done, and that said a lot when she grew up with a father who worked for the Mafia.

"I was lucky to have money, several new identities and the ability to change my appearance rather easily, but it was still hard to navigate a world where you couldn't trust a soul. You couldn't stay in one place more than a day, visit the same store or restaurant more than once, or even use public transportation. I was lucky the raid happened during the summer or I would have been in much deeper trouble."

"How did you move around?"

"I stole old cars from people's yards, rode ATVs or walked."

Selina stood and paced to her left, stretching her side out carefully. She was relieved it was feeling better after the food and medication. The longer she was down and weak, the easier it was for the Snake to find a way in.

"She was dead, Efren. By the time EMS got to her, she had practically bled out."

"Did you see her code and them call her time of death?"

Selina turned back to him. "No. They ran with her to the ambulance, worked on her, and then I watched them go hands-off," she explained, holding her hands in the air near her chest. "The EMS guys waited a few moments and then one shook his head. They covered her with a sheet and told me she was gone, so they'd take her to the ME. When they pulled away, it was without lights and sirens."

Efren tapped his pen on the pad. "You didn't go to the morgue?"

"No. There was no reason to. I didn't need to identify the body since everyone knew who she was. I was busy dealing with the fallout of shooting her."

"Did they hold a service for her?"

Selina gave him the palms-out. "No way for me to know since I was gone less than twenty-four hours after it happened. I resisted the urge to google anything to do with her."

"Not even from the secure servers at Secure One?"

"Not even then." She shook her head. "You don't understand the ruthlessness that is Vaccaro, Efren. People romanticize the Mafia like they're some kind of antihero who can be redeemed with good morals and making the right choices. If only they knew these guys." She shook her head again in frustration. "They're more likely to be old fleshy men than young, sexy tatted guys in suits. They wouldn't think twice about putting a bullet in you because you're between them and their whiskey bottle. There is nothing romantic about the Mafia, and it's a dangerous ideation to lead women to believe they'd be loved or respected by one. Women are a pawn to these men, and that's why I know Vaccaro had to be involved in Ava's death and rebirth."

"I have to heed to your knowledge on the Mafia as mine is limited to movies and books, but I still agree that a kingpin only does what's best for him, regardless of who is in his way." She lowered herself to the chair and nodded. "I'll have Mina search and see what she can find in the archives."

"You're asking the wrong questions." She sat and leaned over her knees to rub her forehead.

There was no question that the surgery and medication were the reason she couldn't pull all of this information together logically as she usually would. It was frustrating. They were on a timeline that was a matter of life or death. She needed to get it together.

"I wish I knew the right questions, Selina. I'm afraid I'm a bit out of my depth here. I'm a bodyguard, not a cop," he reminded her. "You're telling the story."

Selina slumped over in the chair. "I shot her, Efren. She was dead."

"They wanted you to think she was dead. That doesn't mean she was. If you could have, I know you would have gone to the morgue and checked her cold dead body yourself, right?"

"I would have watched the autopsy." Her words held a bit more fire again, and he smiled.

"Money had to have changed hands."

"If Vaccaro was involved, then there's no question," she agreed. "What I want to know is, was there an autopsy report?"

Efren scribbled it down on his pad. "Because if there was, he paid off more than an EMT?"

"Bingo. Then it becomes a plan rather than a reaction."

"A plan instead of a reaction?"

"Think about it." She grimaced, but it wasn't physical pain. It was the kind of pain a person was in when their world was crumbling around them and they didn't know what to do. The terror inside her had filled her head to toe. There was no room left, but the terror kept coming in waves. As much as she trusted Secure One, her experience with Vaccaro told her she was a dead woman walking. "They knew the task force was closing in, or at the very least, they knew we were looking for that final connection so we could arrest them. Randall and Ava had a plan in case they were arrested or killed."

"Or gravely wounded." Selina tipped her head in agreement to his statement. "Did you keep the task force a secret?"

"From the Snake?" Efren nodded. "We didn't broadcast it, but he was used to being under investigation. It wasn't a stretch for him to know we were looking for the head of the counterfeiting ring. Are you implying there was a mole somewhere? It wasn't me."

"It never crossed my mind that you were," he assured her. "That said, I'm not implying it. I'm assuming it. The Chicago PD is vast in its size and scope. It could have been a beat cop, lieutenant, detective, secretary or janitor. Whomever it was, they were reporting your progress to Vaccaro."

"Could be. It also could be they had a plan in place for every operation he had going on, which was also vast in its size and scope. That's less important now eight years later. What is important is why did she appear now, and how did they know I was working at Secure One?"

"The timing is suspicious. I'll give you that. We already know the Winged Templar killed Howie Loraine, but he had to have Vaccaro's approval to put out the hit. Then, unbeknownst to them, Secure One got involved. Suddenly, there you were, served up on a silver platter."

"I was never visible until the night we tried to rescue Kadie and Vic at the Loraine mansion," Selina reminded him. She hung her head and sat quietly, letting the information roll through her tired, drugged mind. When Victor Loraine's girlfriend Kadie had been kidnapped by his older brother in hopes of getting his hands on Vic's infant son, Secure One had sent Vic in to talk to his brother in hopes of finding Kadie. Instead, Randall Jr. kidnapped Vic too and it was up to Secure One to rescue them. She snapped her head up with her lips in a thin line. "Randall Jr. knew Ava was alive."

"Did he look like he knew she was alive right before he shot you?"

Selina chewed on her lip for a few seconds while she ran the interaction through her mind, forcing herself not to focus on the gunshot, but the seconds before. "No, but all he said was 'you're dead.' He didn't call me Ava Shannon."

"Vic did. Vic specifically said Ava Shannon and that he saw her die."

"Think about it, Brenna." She heard the frustration in her voice, but it wasn't with him. It was with this situation that she couldn't control. "We're twins and I 'died,'" she said, using air quotes, "the day after Ava. Randall said you're dead because he knew I was supposed to be dead, too. Wait." She held up a finger as though she was replaying something in her mind. "Vic said he saw Ava dead?" Efren nodded. "Then he really was knocked silly. He hadn't been to the mansion since he left for college until the day he went there looking for Kadie. I know for a fact he wasn't there the night of the raid."

Efren immediately scratched a sentence on the page and underlined it. "That's a breakthrough."

"That Vic was knocked silly?"

"No. He may have seen her dead. There could have been a service. I'll have Mina contact him and ask about it. It would answer the question of how hard they worked to prove she was dead. Mina is great at digging until she finds those answers, so let's leave it to her. No sense in beating our heads against the wall when we have no way to find out."

Selina pointed at the computers off to her side. "But we do. A little search would give us a lot of these answers."

"It could also open us up for an attack that I can't predict. Until I know how far we can go with those machines, I can't risk it." He set his pad aside and stood, holding out his hand to her. "You've been up long enough. You need to rest. You had a hysterectomy less than twenty-four hours ago."

Selina slipped her hand in his, and the sensation was like silk. He'd touched her before, but this time was different. There was trust there that he was going to help her, even if it were as simple as getting her out of the chair without pain. He ran his thumb over the back of her hand, and the simple motion gave her silent comfort and security that just a few seconds ago she didn't feel. She would never admit it, but whenever she spoke of Vaccaro, the terror was overpowering. Efren was the only reason she wasn't rocking in a ball in the corner. She was a cop, but when you have intimate knowledge about someone as dangerous as the Snake, it was hard not to be terrified.

"Wait," she said, freezing with her hand still in his. "A hysterectomy?"

"The doctor told us he had to take an ovary and without your uterus, you can't have children. I assumed that meant they did a hysterectomy. I'm sorry, Selina. I wish you'd had more time to deal with that before we had to run."

"Time to deal with it?" She pulled her hand from his and lifted her shirt, showing him a healed starburst wound on her abdomen just outside of the bandage from her latest incision. "I'd been a cop about three weeks when I caught a bullet the first time," she explained. "That one ripped through my uterus and tore it to shreds. I was twenty-two. You don't have to worry about me coming to terms with anything. The kid card sailed for me thirteen years ago."

He was silent for a moment as he took in the scars across her belly. "The first time?" She tipped her head in confusion and he traced his finger over the scar. "You said the first time you caught a bullet. How many?"

"The other night made four and the second gut shot. I also took one in my right arm that still has shrapnel left and one in my left thigh. Barely missed the femoral artery. I don't know why I keep cheating death, but there will come a day when I don't."

He took her hand again and tightened his around it. "Not if I have anything to say about it. It's my job to keep you alive, and I take that responsibility seriously. With that responsibility comes the right to order you to bed, and that's what I'm doing. You need more sleep."

When he turned to the bunk, her hand still in his, her eyes were barely open. "I'm relieved to know they didn't remove major organs yesterday. That means you're at less risk of massive bleeding if we have to run again. You need to get as much rest as possible over the next couple of days. I don't know when we'll have to move next."

After straightening the blankets, he helped her down and waited for her to get comfortable before he pulled the blanket over her. "You'll wake me as soon as the team is ready to talk?"

"You know I will," he promised, resting his hand on her shoulder for comfort. "I'm going to doze a bit while keeping an eye on the cameras."

"That's kind of an oxymoron, Brenna," she said, her eyes almost closed and her tongue thick when she spoke. "You need to sleep, too."

"Shh," he whispered, powering down the lantern over the bed area. "Rest now and let your body heal."

"It may not matter," she murmured, and she heard the terror again. "If they find me, all the healing in the world won't help me."

"Not if I have anything to say about it," he whispered, and her tired mind grasped on to that and vowed never to let it go.

Chapter Five

As soon as Selina dropped off to sleep, Efren lowered himself to the chair next to the bunks and leaned over on his elbows to gaze at her. Since the day he'd met her, Selina had intrigued him. The push and pull between them was both frustrating and something to look forward to in his workday. What bothered him the most, though, was knowing she didn't like him. It wasn't his ego that was bothered, either. It was knowing that he *cared* that she didn't like him. A long time ago he'd promised himself he'd never care about anyone enough for their opinion of him to matter. The war taught him that caring about people ends in heartache and pain when they're taken from you in the blink of an eye. The Snake could certainly take Selina in the blink of an eye; he didn't even question that. He was an excellent bodyguard with a stellar record, but he could only do so much as one man.

Still, he had to admit he cared. He wanted to know why she hated him, and wondered if he'd done something to make her so standoffish from the get-go. Everyone at Secure One assured him that it had nothing to do with him, but he wasn't so sure about that. If nothing else, their forced togetherness might afford him the opportunity to discover why she hated him so he could set her straight and put them back on even ground. Whether it was something he could fix or not was another issue. For now, though, Selina needed sleep above all else.

His gut twisted as he stared at her gorgeous face finally relaxed in sleep. She had stolen his breath from their first meeting. Her long blond hair had been pulled back in a no-nonsense ponytail, but the waves still flowed down her back. Her blue eyes were sharp and assessing, but he could easily picture what those eyes would look like when the lights were low and she was relaxed. He wondered if she knew how much terror reflected back at him from those eyes when she spoke of Vaccaro. The answer was no because if she did, she'd use her iron will to shut that down, too. To say Selina Colvert intrigued him was an understatement.

He stood and walked to the computer screen that served as his eyes outside the bunker. The screen had four quadrants, each showing a camera view angled around the old cabin structure. All was quiet, so he clicked the mouse to check the four cameras that blanketed the woods in every direction. Those were quiet, too, other than a family of deer foraging through the underbrush.

Returning to the real reason he was here, he pondered their next move. The Snake had wrapped himself around Selina a long time ago. His goal was to snuff the life out of her to keep his secrets hidden. Efren had every intention of cutting off the head of the snake before he had the chance to do that, though. This was a case of hunting the hunter, but he was prepared to do anything to keep his body count at zero. There wasn't a chance in hell the body to break his winning streak would be hers. He'd make sure it was his body before hers. The idea of losing Selina ran a shiver of fear down his spine as a huff left his lips.

Sure, you want to protect Selina because it's your job, he told himself. *No, you want to protect her because she represents everything you'll never have. As long as she's alive, you can focus on the reasons why she doesn't like you rather than on the reasons why you like her.* Above all, he knew the main reason he wanted to focus on protecting her was to avoid thinking about why the idea of losing her made him instantly lonely. That, above all else, was an emotion he could not afford to entertain.

SELINA STAYED IN bed and watched the man across the room. He had pulled his socket off and was massaging his limb. If she knew one thing about Efren Brenna, it was that he'd never show weakness, and that meant never taking his prosthesis off. In fact, this was the first time she'd seen him take it off longer than to shower or sleep since she met him. The paramedic in her wished he was closer so she could check the skin, but since he wasn't, she'd have to trust that he'd tell her if there was a problem.

She laughed internally. As if he'd tell her anything about himself. Hard-core aloofness was a requirement to be in the boys' club at Secure One. Selina understood it, though. Everyone at Secure One, including herself, dealt with one type of PTSD or the other. You didn't go to war or work in law enforcement and not see things that changed you and stayed with you forever. You learned to compartmentalize it; once you did, you never spoke of it again. It had been heavily debated whether that was a smart way to approach it, but in the end, it didn't matter what anyone else thought was the correct answer. What mattered was getting through every single day trying to live in a society you no longer trusted.

Efren finished his towel massage and then used his pull sock to seat his limb back into the prosthesis. Her practiced eye watched and waited for his facial expression to change when he added the valve to the socket, but he appeared comfortable through the entire process. Since he wore a skin-fit prosthesis, meaning there was nothing between his limb and the socket, she made a mental note to keep an eye on his gait over the next few days. The running blade made him fast when in the field, but walking on it all day was going to be more difficult than on his leg with a computerized knee. Wearing the blade required him to use his limb differently to make the "knee" bend, and that would wear the skin in different places. She hated to admit that there was a weak link in their chain, but there was, and his leg was it. Not because he wasn't competent in his job, but because the situation they were in called for rough terrain that could damage his limb or his blade at any point and leave them vulnerable to Vaccaro.

The name bounced around her brain like a bullet, and she closed her eyes again. Vaccaro had done enough damage to her family and her friends at Secure One. She was happy that the person to take a bullet the other night was her. No one else deserved what Vaccaro doled out to get to her family. Well, namely her, since it appeared her twin was still in good favor with that monster. She and Ava were the last of the Shannon family tree, and she was never more grateful for that.

Selina didn't care what Uncle Medardo had planned for her. She'd beat him at every turn her entire life, and she had no intention of breaking that streak now. Besides, she had all of Secure One behind her, fighting for the answers she'd need before she faced him again. She hoped, anyway. Part of her knew that Secure One would have her back, but the other part worried that her fear the last few months had spread like a virus through the team. If Vaccaro sensed dissension among the ranks, he might be tempted to break them and force people to pick sides.

Since the Red River Slayer had been captured, Selina had been struggling to keep her demons hidden from everyone all the time. Caring for Marlise and Charlotte had been difficult when they first came to Secure One. They were abused and broken, and trusted no one but her. The things they told her and the scars they showed her would never leave her mind or her heart. Then Bethany arrived as they chased the Red River Slayer, and she nearly broke Selina. How did you care for someone who had been held hostage, assaulted repeatedly and groomed to be the sex slave of a madman? Cal and the team knew Bethany needed more help than Selina could give her, but they insisted she try. If only they had spent a few hours in her shoes. She might be an APP, and once a cop, but she was also a woman. She had spent the last three years caring for these women who needed her in the moment, but no one was there for her when she needed someone. That, above all else, was what hurt her the most.

When the Loraines popped back up in her life in a

way that she couldn't escape, her illusions of safety shattered. All bets were off. Her demons came out to play all day, every day, and fighting them back had become a losing battle. She should have run the moment someone said the name Randall Loraine, but she had nowhere to go. Running meant certain death. Sticking with Secure One gave her a fighting chance.

"I'm not going to let him get to you," Efren said once he stood in his socket again.

His voice startled her, and she jumped. "I never thought you would."

As he walked toward her in the bed, she'd never felt more vulnerable, so she sat up and swung her feet to the floor. "Nice try, Colvert, but your fear filled the room and stole all the oxygen. How do you think I knew you were awake?"

"Eyes in the back of your head?" The question was sarcastic, just the way she wanted it. She had to keep Efren at arm's length if she was going to get through this with any kind of dignity.

"You don't know how often I wish that were the case. How are you feeling?"

After stretching side to side and gingerly probing her abdomen, she looked up at him. "It's better this morning. It still feels bruised, but the burning pain in my gut from the incision is mostly gone."

"Good, I'm happy to hear that. It won't stay that way if you overdo it, though. While in this bunker, I need you to be down more than you're up. If we have to move quickly, you'll need your reserves to get through it. The terrain out there is tough to traverse when you're in top form, much less recovering from surgery."

"Speaking of terrain. How's the leg?" she asked, nicer this time, as she rubbed her eyes. "I noticed you had your socket off."

If he thought she didn't notice the way his eyes widened when she said that, he didn't know her very well. His "it's fine" was also not an acceptable answer.

"Run it down," she ordered. "Skin, pinch points, pain, function."

Efren threw his hand onto his hip with a huff. "I've been an amputee a long time. I don't need help with managing my situation. My leg, or lack thereof, will not be a factor in keeping you safe."

"That might be true, but I need help managing my situation, and the only help I have is standing in front of me," she said, her voice full of fire. "So run it down and be honest. I have the skills to keep small problems from becoming big problems."

"The skin is fine, there are no pinch points, I'm managing my phantom pain by keeping the limb compressed and with towel massage, and the function is superb. I could run this leg at half function and it would still be more than we'd need to get your surly backside out of trouble."

"Ego much?" She stood and straightened completely, finally able to take a deep breath.

"Honesty isn't ego."

She lifted a brow and pinned him with an assessing gaze. "I'm surprised they didn't bring your other leg to you at the hospital before they left town."

He shook his head as though he was thoroughly fed up with her questions. "Eric intended to, but Mack took mobile command back to Secure One before he got there to get it. They were headed back with it when we had to bail. It's not a problem, Selina. Walking through that terrain last night on the computerized knee would have been much more difficult. The blade is thinner and easier to maneuver in those situations. They both have their pros and cons. Well, look at you. Standing up straight is an improvement."

Selina accepted that he wanted to change the subject, so she didn't push. "The faster, the better, if you ask me."

"In this situation, yes, but don't overdo it. This is a marathon, not a sprint."

"Speaking of, have you heard from anyone?"

"Cal contacted me. They're ready to meet when we are. Mina has been working for a few hours already."

"Good. Hopefully, she'll know something to help unravel this situation. I'll be right out." Selina closed the door to the small bathroom and stripped off her shirt. She had little time, but the most important thing was to check her incision and ensure there was no sign of infection. As she peeled back the bandage, the incision slowly revealed itself, and she couldn't help but grimace. She had seen it yesterday but hadn't been with it enough to consider the scope of the repair to her fascia. No wonder her entire abdomen was black and blue. The incision was jagged, leaving a zigzag down her skin with a puckered center where the entry wound was. She also had an exit wound when the bullet had left her body and slammed into the back of her vest. It took her a minute to realize she would have to rely on Efren to check that incision. The mirror didn't go low enough, and she couldn't twist around without pain to see it herself.

Her sigh was heavy, and he could probably hear it

out there, but there was little she could do other than re-dress the front incision and run a washcloth around her face and belly. After quickly brushing her teeth, she pulled her sweatshirt back on. "You've got this," she told the woman in the mirror. "It's just a Band-Aid. You can handle having his hands on you for that long."

The truth was, she couldn't handle having Efren's hands on her at all. Last night, when he held her hand and rubbed his thumb over it, she nearly fell apart on the spot. If she hadn't been so exhausted, she probably would have. It had been eight years since she'd encountered the intimate touch of a man who cared. That day, those few minutes of her life, had haunted her every day since then. Whenever she thought about Kai Tanner, her heart broke again. Vaccaro's venom poisoned more than just his victim. It traveled insidiously through their loved ones until they, too, suffered the wrath of the Snake.

Chapter Six

Eva watched and waited while the man she had known, and probably loved, finished the short climb up the bluff in the middle of nowhere, Wisconsin, and then bent over to catch his breath.

"I need your help, Kai."

His head snapped up when she stepped into the open, her dog Zeus standing steadfastly by her side. She saw the flare of love in his eyes. The same flare she'd seen for the last several years whenever they met up on a rescue. "I'll do anything I can, Eva."

"I have to run, Kai, and I'm going to need your help to get out of this alive." She spent the next few minutes outlining her plan.

"You want me to make a false report of your death?" Kai asked, taking a step back. "I doubt the authorities would appreciate that, Eva. If the ruse was uncovered, I could be charged."

"You won't be," she promised. "That's why I picked the bluffs. Falling into the river from up here is certain death, and a body would be washed away before a witness could even get to civilization for help. You're a search-and-rescue guy. If you tell them I never resurfaced, they'll

believe you. They won't try hard to find me and assume my body will wash ashore or end up in the Mississippi. Eventually, they'll forget about me and move on with life."

"I'll never forget about you, Eva," Kai said, his head shaking. "You've been the best partner a guy could have in this business. I'll never work with someone like you again. You lead with your moral compass, which is rare these days. I don't want to do this." His lip trembled when he put his hand on his hip in some form of defiance she didn't understand.

"Never say never, Kai. You're the kind of guy who attracts like-minded people. In my opinion, you're the best of the best. I hope you understand now why I always stayed hands-off with you. I will always love you even though I can never love you." She pressed Zeus's leash into his palm. "Take him for me. Give him the life I can't now."

"No," he said before she even finished. "No. You aren't leaving, Eva. Stay. We can work this out."

"There are only two ways of working this out, Kai. They both require me to die, fake or real. If I stay, the Snake will be certain my death is real." Eva wished she was wrong, but she wasn't. She'd crossed the wrong man, and now, if she wanted to stay alive, she would have to die.

"I'm not ready to say goodbye, Eva. There is so much left unsaid."

"There's nothing you can do for me now, Kai," she insisted. "Except to promise me you'll take care of Zeus and give him a good life."

She could see the terror that filled him, but he finally nodded. "And you're sure I won't get in trouble for this?"

"Positive," Eva promised. "You have to know I don't have any other option. I wouldn't do this if I did."

"I know, but Eva, he's going to be heartbroken. I don't know if he'll ever recover."

"Zeus will be fine." She hoped someday Kai would be, too. "As long as he's got you and Apollo and can search, he'll find his purpose."

He choked back a sob and nodded. "We'll take care of him."

"I left his papers and money for his care in my truck at the entrance to the park. It should get you through quite a few years. I'm sorry I can't do more."

"No," he said, trailing a finger down her cheek. "Don't apologize for doing the right thing despite knowing the right thing meant a bounty on your head. I'll do my best to give him the kind of life and love you would have."

She knelt and wrapped her arms around the German shepherd's neck, whispering into his ear and stroking his fur. The pain in her chest was almost overwhelming. She'd lost her family to the Snake, and now he was taking the final things she loved.

Eva stood, and Kai grasped her elbow. "When it's safe, check my blog. I'll post updates about Zeus and Apollo as they work together. There will be pictures. It's the best I can do."

"Thank you," she said, raising up on her toes to kiss his cheek. "You are a genuinely good human, Kai. Find someone to love who's deserving of yours."

He grasped her hand. "You are deserving of love, Eva." He held tight to her hand as she tried to turn away. "I'll go with you. Let me grab Apollo."

"No." The one word was firm and heartbreaking.

"For this to work, I need you to play your part. The Snake will know I took off if you aren't here to run interference."

Kai nodded, and she noticed him blink back the tears that filled his eyes. "Okay, I've got your back."

She threw her arms around his neck and held him momentarily before doing the same to Zeus. "You know what to do?" she asked, standing again and holding his gaze.

"I'll set the scene. You get out of dodge. I love ya, partner. Be safe."

Eva blew him a kiss, turned and ran like the hounds of hell were after her.

"Selina?" Efren's voice snapped her from the daydream, and she gasped, the sound loud in the concrete room. "I'm coming in."

When he opened the door, their eyes locked, and before she had truly returned to the world, he pulled her from the bathroom and into his arms. Efren held her lightly, one arm wrapped around her back and one holding her head to his shoulder. She couldn't help but catalog everything about him in quick succession. His muscular chest was warm and tight. His cheek smelled like cedar soap and shaving cream as it rested against hers. His arm wrapped around her waist was soft and warm against her skin. It took her a moment to realize she hadn't pulled her shirt down all the way, and it was trapped above his arm, allowing his heat to pour into her. What settled in somewhere deep inside was the way he held her against him gently, and while careful of her wounds, he still made her feel safe in a world she knew wasn't.

"You look like you've seen a ghost," he murmured. "Are you in pain?"

"Not physically," she answered, her words rough to her own ears. "I was thinking about the last time I had to run from the Snake." Rather than go any further, she snapped her lips shut.

"I can't pretend to know what you're going through, Selina," Efren whispered, squeezing her a bit tighter. "Just know that we all have your back and we'll stop at nothing to protect you from Vaccaro."

"I know." The two words were whispered, but they held so many emotions. Fear. Gratefulness. Regret.

"We don't hold a grudge at Secure One." He'd turned his head so his lips brushed her ear when he spoke. The sensations rocketing through her made her want to collapse to the ground, and she would have, had he not been holding her. "Have you ever held it against any of them when their demons attacked you unexpectedly?"

"No."

"The same is true for you, Selina. We'll get through this, and the team will be stronger for it."

She lifted her head, prepared to pull away, but instead, she laid her lips on his. They were warm, moist and open, as though they'd been waiting for this moment their entire life. She couldn't help but notice how perfectly matched they were as his settled against hers for a hairbreadth before he leaned into the kiss. He caressed her lips, keeping it tender but barely contained until she forced herself to step back out of the hug and stand on her own.

She didn't want to. Lord, how she didn't want to, and that scared her, too. Efren was the enemy. You didn't kiss the enemy. Because of him, she had been overlooked and cast aside as an operative by Cal and the rest of the team. She was supposed to hate him, not find refuge in his arms and lips. Even if the game had changed and he was no longer her biggest enemy, she had to stay hands— and now lips—off. She couldn't help but notice the way his gaze raked her from head to toe and back up again to rest at her midsection, where her shirt still hung haphazardly, allowing her pink and puckered flesh to peek out. His gaze warmed her skin and insides, sending heat spiraling through her at an alarming speed. She had to put the brakes on whatever this was before things got out of control and she started to like the man in front of her. She already liked that kiss way too much.

"I—I need some help with the wound on my back." She had no idea how to address what happened, so her game plan was to pretend it didn't. "Will you check it and rebandage it? I can't reach it from any angle."

"Sure." The word was growled, and she couldn't help but notice that his hands were in fists as he walked to the bathroom for the first aid kit. "I'm glad you mentioned it, because I'd forgotten about the exit wound."

"I haven't," she said, tongue in cheek. "It's annoying to sleep on that bandage. I'm hoping we can cover it with a regular Band-Aid at this point."

He swung a chair around and had her sit on the edge so he had a clear view of her back. After the supplies were readied on the table, he started working the bandage off her skin a little at a time. "The team is ready as soon as we are," he said, giving her something else to focus on as he worked. "They're anxious to put eyes on you so they can see that you're okay."

"I'm worried they're angry," she admitted. The truth was easier to speak when not staring directly into his eyes.

"That's one thing you don't have to worry about." He dabbed liquid around the wound. It stung for just a moment, but then cool air stole it away, telling her he was fanning her skin to avoid hurting her. "From what I can gather, Cal knew the truth?"

"Some of it, but not the full scope. He was going to run a background check on me, and there was no way that was going to work. He had a…reputation, so I leaned into that in hopes he'd understand."

"As the kind of guy you could trust with your secrets because he had a mountain of his own?"

"Bingo." She hissed as he probed the edges of the wound. "What are you doing?"

"Sorry," he said, popping his head around her shoulder. "It's a little pink, but your reaction said it's pink from healing and not infection."

"Take a picture of it," she said, waiting for him to grab the Secure One phone. He handed it around to her, and she inspected it closely, trying not to visibly grimace at how ugly it was. "Well, I've taken better pictures. Let's put some antibiotic ointment around the edges just to be on the safe side, but avoid the stitches."

He squeezed her shoulder. "You're alive. Remember that and use it to fight through this. Someone else tried to take you down, but you stood tall. That mark on your skin is a badge of honor."

"Change the narrative and change the world, right?"

"Not the world," he disagreed, as he swiped ointment around the wound and grabbed a large bandage from the pack. "Just your mindset. I already know you're a fighter,

Selina, so keep fighting. Don't let a Loraine bullet be the bullet that takes you down, physically or emotionally. They don't deserve to hold that kind of power over you. That much you know for sure." He pulled her shirt down over the wound and patted her back. "You're good to go."

Selina stood and stretched her back before giving a nod. "Thanks. It feels better to get that big bandage off there."

"Happy to do it." He threw away the old bandages and cleaned up the first aid kit before he washed his hands.

"Brenna," she said, and he turned, drying his hands on a towel. "I appreciate the pep talk. I got caught up in the past and you helped me refocus."

"Understandable," he said, tipping his head to the side. "It happens to all of us, which is what I like about working at Secure One. There's always someone there who understands and can pull you back before that rabbit hole goes too deep."

"Speaking of Secure One, I suppose we should make that call."

"Deep breath," he said, walking toward her until he was standing chest to chest with her again. She followed his order, and they took a deep breath together and let it out. "Good. You didn't even grimace with that breath. You must be feeling better," he said with a wink.

"I'm glad for it, too. The less medication I have to take, the sharper my mind will be."

"That's true, but you also have to be able to move quickly with little or no notice."

Selina tipped her head back and forth. "I'll take over-the-counter painkillers, but keep the other ones on me. I can always pop one fast if we have to go. That said,

I'd give anyone major props who can find the entrance to this place. Cal didn't even tell the team where it was or how to find it."

"He wanted it need-to-know, so I didn't find out until last night when he sent the location to my GPS."

"That's Cal for you. The fewer people who know, the better. Time to make that call," she finally said, settling herself down at the computer terminal. He sat next to her and leaned into her ear.

"You can pretend that kiss never happened, but it did, and I'm not going to pretend that I didn't feel the connection between us. Fair warning."

His piece said, he clicked a button on a device next to him without another word.

Chapter Seven

Efren's words replayed on repeat in her mind. "Fair warning." Was he implying that he planned to kiss her again? The very idea made her nervous. Not because she didn't want him to, but because she did. Getting involved with anyone could mean instant death for them. If necessary, she'd remind herself of that every second of the day. She couldn't be the reason an innocent person died at Vaccaro's hands.

Before she could speak, a familiar voice filled their concrete prison. "Secure one, Charlie."

"Secure two, Tango," Efren responded, and the screen flickered to life.

"Secure three, Sierra," she finished, and Cal's face filled the screen.

"You're a sight for sore eyes," he said without preamble. "How are you feeling?"

"Better. I've had worse injuries."

"Maybe, but our goal now is to get you through this without more." Cal set his jaw for a moment and then shook his head. "I'm going to flip the camera."

Selina nodded, and they waited until the conference room came into view. Mina, Roman, Mack, Eric, Lucas,

Cal, Charlotte and Marlise sat around the table. That was their core team, and Cal couldn't make it clearer he was sticking with them to get this job done. Awkward wasn't Selina's style, but staring into the faces of the people she'd lied to for years was exactly that. So much so that she didn't know what to say.

"We're a team," Eric said, standing and leaning on the table with his hands to peer into the camera. "We've been a team for years, and that doesn't change now. Is that understood, Sierra?"

Her nod was instant and quick. "Heard and understood, Echo."

Eric sat with a nod.

Mina spoke next. "Good to see you, Selina. We've been getting updates from Efren, but it's not the same as talking to you. Before we go any further, we all want to know the answer to one question." She motioned around the circle of people, so Selina nodded for her to ask it. "Going forward, do you want to go by Eva or Selina?"

"Selina." There was no hesitation in her answer. "Eva Shannon is dead. Do you all understand? She must remain dead and buried for more reasons than I have time to go into right now."

"He already knows you're alive," Marlise said. "No matter what name you go by, the bounty is on your head."

"I understand that, but if I'm going to get through this and figure out how Ava Shannon came back from the dead and why, I need distance. The only way to separate myself from my twin is to pretend I am someone else entirely."

"You are," Efren said, slipping his arm around her

back where no one else could see. "You may be twins genetically, but not in morals or anything else that matters."

"He's right," Cal said with a nod. "That's the reason I hired you eight years ago with the weak story that you were a domestic violence victim on the run. That's also the reason we've got your back today even knowing that story you sold was fiction." All the heads around the table nodded as he spoke, and it lifted her tired lips into a smile.

"Thanks, team. My greatest fear was my attitude over the last few months damaged our relationship and you wouldn't want to work with me."

"Never," Mack said before anyone else could speak. "We all have our own brand of attitude depending on the day and situation. That's accepted within this circle, as you well know. You've been on the receiving end of my attitude more often than not."

"I still feel bad about it," she said, biting her lip.

"That's because you're a good person in your heart, and you don't want to hurt people," Charlotte said. "You got me through those first few days after I turned myself in and I was too scared to speak. It was you who kept me calm and made me feel safe even when I wasn't. Let us do that for you now."

A breath escaped her chest as though she'd been punched. "Thank you, Charlotte. I needed to hear you say that. It shifted my guilt and brought the reason we're here into focus. Getting out of this alive."

"It was the least I could do," Charlotte assured her.

Cal drummed his fingers on the table, and all heads turned to him. It was magical how he made those metal and plastic fingers behave just like real ones. "It's time for full disclosure, Colvert. The moment someone said the Loraine name a few weeks ago you should have been in my office, but we can't go backward, so let's go forward. Tell us why you're in their crosshairs."

She took a deep breath, knowing she had to bare her soul if they were going to save it. Efren rubbed her hip, his warm hand what she needed to ground her in order to tell the sordid tale again. She did it with as little emotion as possible as she filled them in on her family's involvement with the Mafia and her crossing of them during her law enforcement career.

"You're saying your sister didn't die that night?" Roman asked when she finished telling them about the raid.

"That appears to be the case, since she showed up at the hospital asking for me."

Eric shook his head and chuckled. "When I told the charge nurse to watch for someone suspicious asking about you, I never dreamed that person would look exactly like you. I was expecting a hit man."

"Trust me, Eric, she was the hit man. If Efren hadn't gotten me out of there, you'd be attending my real funeral right now. My twin believes in the whole Mafia mentality of an eye for an eye, and when that eye is family, she will stop at nothing to make you pay. What I don't know is why she's not dead and how she knew I wasn't either."

"I've got some feelers out in regard to the Loraine family. Unfortunately, I don't have any answers," Mina interjected.

"Yet," Roman added with a wink.

"I've concentrated my efforts on Randall Loraine Sr.,"

she explained, clicking a slide up onto the screen for them to see. "As you know, he's resided at Federal Correctional Institution Pekin for the last eight years serving a fifty-year sentence for the counterfeiting scheme. Since he was convicted of a nonviolent crime, he is in a low-security institution."

Selina rolled her eyes. "The crime may have been nonviolent, but trust me, Randall Sr. knows how to be violent."

"I have no doubt of that, considering who he worked for," Mina agreed. "From what I can see of his records, he hasn't had any visitors since Howie Loraine was last there to see him shortly before his death almost a month ago. However, prior to that, Howie visited him once every two weeks for the entire time he's been there. Randall Jr. visited him once a month without fail."

"So maybe Howie and Randall were continuing Daddy's business on the outside?"

"More than likely," Eric agreed. "But we already suspected that was the case."

"None of that explains how my twin came back to life." Selina heard the frustration in her voice and tried to curb it. This wasn't her friends' fault, and she needed their help if she was going to come out of this bunker alive.

"I'm working on that as well," Mina promised. "I've pulled the information from that night, and I'm following the chain of people who were in contact with your sister from the time you shot her until she was pronounced 'dead.'" She used air quotes around the word, considering the circumstances. "My hope is to follow the money. If any of them got a large influx of cash, I'll find it."

Selina leaned forward, partly to free herself of Efren's warm hand on her side and partly to be seen better, so no one misunderstood what she was saying. "If Ava didn't die eight years ago, there's a connection somewhere between her and Vaccaro. We need to find that connection and follow where it leads."

"That's easier said than done," Mina answered. "The Vaccaro organization is one organization I can't hack. I can use back channels to find out what the organization is doing, but anything personal is off-limits to me."

"The Snake doesn't allow anyone into his den who he doesn't invite in as a warm body or a meal." Selina shivered involuntarily. "Is there a way to find out who Randall Jr. talked to the night he was arrested?"

"Like, did he make any phone calls?" Mina asked, her hands poised over the keyboard.

"Or have any visitors," Selina said. "I wonder if Randall Jr. knew she wasn't dead since he hung out so much with his father in prison. If he did, he may have been the one to report to her or Vaccaro that I was alive."

"He knew it was you since he already knew that Ava was alive and where she was," Efren finished, nodding immediately.

Eric spoke up. "Honestly, Eva and Ava are impossible to tell the difference when lip reading. It was dark and we were all moving. Randall Jr. could have said Eva and I wouldn't know. That would explain why he shot you."

"There was a lot of law enforcement there that night. If one of them was a plant by Vaccaro, they could have reported back that they saw Selina," Roman suggested.

"Since Randall Jr. already knew Ava was alive, he knew it was me." Selina clenched her jaw in frustration.

"We're assuming that Randall, and thus Vaccaro, knew Ava was still alive," Cal said, holding up a finger. "Until we know that for sure, we can't assume anything."

"Easiest way to find out is to start with Randall Jr. I can hopefully have an answer in a few hours," Mina said without taking her hands off the keyboard.

Selina smiled at her friend and nodded. "I know it won't be easy, but until we know why she's back, our hands are tied. That said, I assure you that Vaccaro is aware that Ava is still alive. I would go so far as to say he's the *reason* she's still alive."

"You think she's been working in his organization all these years?" Mack asked.

Selina's nod was exaggerated. "Without a doubt."

Cal waved his hand in the air. "What I don't get is, why Vaccaro was building an organization outside of his family. Our basic understanding of him says he's over the age of sixty. Shouldn't his children be the ones layered up into his organization? Isn't that how the Mafia works?"

"You're correct." Selina pointed at the screen with a smile. "Here's where things get interesting. Vaccaro is the last of his line. His swimmers didn't swim if you catch my drift?" Heads nodded around the table. "Since he never had children, he made his wife his second-in-command. A queenpin if you will. She was ten years younger than him, but she died of cancer about ten years ago. I have no idea what's transpired since, whether he's remarried or not, but that's beside the point. There are no children, so his only choice was to find other families he could corrupt and pull in to build his organization."

"It seems that his choices were a bit off?" Roman asked.

"In hindsight," Selina agreed. "My father and Randall Sr. were his buddies from college, so it made sense for him to pull them in. He trusted them to have children and raise them to be part of the business. He forgot that children live what they learn, and corruption doesn't always swing in your favor when the chips are down."

"He also forgot that some are simply not corruptible," Efren said, giving her a gentle shoulder bump. "All of that said, it's time for us to get back to Secure One."

"No." Selina's objection was loud and precise when she stood on the two letters.

"Selina, we're safer behind the layers of security at home than we'll ever be anywhere else."

"Maybe," she said, spinning to stick her finger in his chest. He stood, which made her smile inside. He was not going to be the beta male in this game if he could help it. "But I won't risk opening Secure One to the Vaccaro organization. That would be certain death for every single person sitting around that table. Is that what you want?"

"You're overreacting." She noticed him grit his teeth and make a fist before he spoke again. "We can't stay here. We have to move, and the most logical place is back to Secure One."

"I disagree with you, Tango," Cal said from the head of the table. "We already put Secure One at risk by going into the Loraine mansion to get Kadie and Vic. It was the right thing to do, but it opened us up to an attack that even our security measures may not be able to withstand. All I can do is hope they're too busy scrambling to get Randall Jr. out of jail and find Selina to worry about what we are doing. The last thing I want is for them to get wind that Selina is here."

"To that end," Marlise said, "I've made you disappear. Your credit card was used to buy a ticket to Hawaii and you were seen getting on the plane with a male resembling Efren."

"I doubt that will buy us much time," Selina said. "Thanks for trying, though."

"That one may not," Cal said, wearing a smirk. "The other five will probably slow them down, though."

"You bought six different plane tickets?" Efren asked, laughter bubbling out of him. "That's diabolical level stuff."

"This is life-or-death level stuff," Cal said. "I know Vaccaro won't believe you're on one flight, but if he's suddenly faced with six, he has no choice but to check them out, just in case. My goal is to keep the heat off you long enough to get some healing time in and to buy me time to find you somewhere else to go. When I built that bunker, I didn't have hiding an operative from the Mafia on my bingo card."

"That's my fault, I know," Selina agreed. "I can tell you until I'm blue in the face how bad I feel about that, but I'd rather get through this alive so I can make it up to you on the next case."

"There's the spirit!" Mina exclaimed, giving her an air high five. "Hang tight there and get some rest. Let us work on things on our end and before you know it, you'll be back in your lab doing your thing."

Efren looked like he was about to object when Cal spoke. "I'll contact you on the secure line if I need you to call in. While you wait, rest, and if you think of anything more to help us find your sist—" He held his hand up. "I'm sorry, find Ava Shannon, let me know immediately. We'll be in touch again at 2100 hours for an update. If you have to move before that, you know the drill."

Efren gave him a salute right before the screen went dark. Selina paced to the other end of the bunker in silence. "The Snake will know it's a ruse." The words were muttered rather than spoken. "He won't take the bait. He'll know I'm still here. We have to move."

"No." Efren grasped her arms and held her in place. "We have nowhere to go."

"We can't stay here." She looked up into his eyes and wondered if hers told a louder story than her words. "He will find us and he will kill us!" Before she could say another word, his lips were on hers.

Chapter Eight

Stop kissing her. Efren's inner voice demanded he listen, but he wasn't. He dug in deeper, drawing her into him with a hand at her waist and his other hand buried deep in her long, silky hair. She was butter under his lips and sagged against him as they stood in the silent room. She poured her pain, anger, fear and guilt into him, and he willingly swallowed it all. He'd been with plenty of women over the years, but none of them could bring him to his knees with a kiss the way Selina did. And she would always be Selina to him. He would fight for her and with her until his dying breath, if need be, but he'd rather make love, not war. That was all he was thinking about as his lips stroked hers. Selina slid her arms around his waist and moaned softly, telling him she was as into it as he was, despite the danger they faced from Vaccaro and what getting personally involved might bring down on them.

Too damn bad.

"We have to stop," she murmured against his lips before pulling away. "We can't let this distract us and leave ourselves open to an attack."

"You're right." The words were as heavy as the breath in his chest. "I just can't deny this spark between us any longer. We've fought against it for months, but this was inevitable."

"Was it though?" she asked as she walked to the bed and sat. "I'm still mad at you. Don't think for a minute that I've forgotten how you became part of the team at Secure One."

"What does that mean, Selina?"

"I can't do this right now, Brenna. I need to rest." She'd scooted under the blankets and closed her eyes by the time he approached the bunks.

"It's interesting how you call me by my last name as soon as I get a little too close or you feel a little too vulnerable. Sleep now, but know there will come a day where we'll work out this grudge you've got against me. The way you kiss me tells me it will be worth it."

He waited, but she never responded, just kept on with her fake sleep. He'd allow it, for now, but he'd spoken the truth. One day, they'd have it out and once the air was cleared, he had every intention of exploring this heat between them. For now, he had to do what he could to get them out of this bind. To do that, he'd have to understand the enemy.

Efren waited for Selina's breathing to even out so he knew she was actually sleeping and then grabbed the Secure One phone. He typed out a message to Mina, whose response came within minutes. Sure thing. While Selina slept, he intended to learn everything he could about Vaccaro and the Shannons. Not so much about Eva as much as Ava. He would have to have a handle on what her sister was capable of if he was going to stay one step ahead of them. If that was even possible. If Vaccaro was half as powerful as they said he was—and he had no reason to doubt them—then his only choice might be to go stealth mode and literally stay one step ahead of them until the team could figure out how to bring them in.

He grabbed a bottle of water and a package of trail mix, then fired up the direct link computer. He'd have to wait until the satellite passed over to get the transmission, but with any luck, the info Mina was sending would be what he needed to get to not only know the enemy but better understand the woman he one day wanted in his bed. That truth hit him in the gut. If they somehow managed to cut off the head of this snake, he'd stop at nothing to prove to Selina that letting go of her anger and making room for him in her life was worth the risk.

He glanced at her and couldn't help but smile. That may be easier said than done, but he was up for the challenge.

SELINA WOKE SLOWLY, her head pounding and her belly sore when she sat up. "Oh Lord, end me." The words were grunted in pain. Efren was beside her almost instantly, helping her stand.

"I'll do no such thing, but I think you may have hit the seventy-two-hour hell."

"I couldn't agree more." She couldn't stand up straight, so she just sat back down. The seventy-two-hour hell was a place no one wanted to be after surgery. It was always the third day that everything hit you like a ton of bricks. The pain, fatigue the healing, and for her the fear, combined to make the next few hours miserable until she got everything under control again.

"Take this," Efren said, handing her a pill, but she pushed it away. "Take it. This is not up for argument."

He held out a bottle of water and she grudgingly took the pill and forced herself to drink most of the water.

"I can't keep taking the heavy stuff," she said, leaning over on her thighs. "I have to shake this pain off and get ready for battle."

"Not treating your pain is going to make that impossible," he said, pulling the chair over to sit across from her. "You had a bullet in your belly, and it did some funky stuff to your body. Acknowledge that and accept it, so we can stop having this same argument every time you wake up."

"Why did I get trapped in a bunker with a smart-ass?" Her words were tongue-in-cheek, but she also meant them.

"More like a badass," he answered with a wink. "A badass who made you more soup and crackers and wants you to feel better because he knows how miserable you are right now. Speaking in generalities of course, since my last surgery wasn't gut surgery."

"What was your last surgery?" He helped her up and walked with her to the table where she sat again and waited for him to bring her the soup that he'd been heating up for her. He knew when she woke up, she was going to need food.

"Limb revision." He set a bowl in front of her with rice and chicken in broth. "That was about six years ago."

"How long ago was the original amputation?"

"Ten. They originally left my knee, but that limited my options for prosthetics, so I opted to go above the knee when the original amputation had to be revised anyway."

"They should have gone above the knee to start, right?"

"It would have saved me a lot of headaches, but traumatic amputations, as you know, are tricky. They did the best they could, and I was functional with a through the knee, but I'm outstanding above the knee." He winked to tell her he was joking, but she shook her head.

"You actually are outstanding above the knee. Considering what you've been through, you've come back from it well. I just wish you gave your limb more time to rest. I never see you without the prosthesis. Do you sleep with it?"

"No." He lowered himself to the chair across from her. "After the revision, I developed strong phantom pain. With the original injury, it was there, but it was more a minor annoyance in the background. This is not that. It's mind numbing and distracting, and the only way I found to deal with it is to keep compression on the limb at all times. It feels good in the socket, so at night, I have a soft one I wear to help with the pain while I sleep. The medication I take helps as well."

"Do you have your meds with you?" She asked the question with the spoon halfway to her mouth and a brow raised. Once the question was out, she finished spooning in the soup while keeping a close eye on him. She would know if he was lying.

"Some."

"Not enough, right?"

"Not for an extended period, no. I'm rationing them for now."

"And if you run out?"

"Not an option, so if we can't get back to Secure One,

Cal may have to make an unexpected airdrop. We'll cross that bridge when we come to it."

"I want to say it won't come to it, but I am all too familiar with this game. We aren't going back to Secure One anytime soon."

"After what I read, I have to agree." He tapped his fingers on the table. "I knew from the moment I met you that you were someone special, but all of this leaves me speechless."

"All of what? My hot mess express?"

"No, that you willingly took on a kingpin knowing you were signing your own death warrant. There aren't many people in the world who would do that."

"They would if they'd seen what I had in life." Her shrug at the end probably told him more than her words, but she couldn't worry about that now. Her secrets were no longer secrets, but she still wasn't comfortable with him knowing even the little bit she'd told him.

"I spent the night reading through the articles Mina sent me, and I stand by my statement. Not many people would do what you did."

"Articles?" Selina laid her spoon down, the soup threatening to come back up at the idea that he had information outside of what she'd given him. If she couldn't control the narrative, then she had no control left whatsoever. For someone like her, that was more terrifying than facing off with a kingpin.

"Mina dug through the archives and found some old articles about the Snake. His moniker is fitting."

She exhaled a bit at his words. Old articles on the Snake were okay. Old articles about her would leave her open to more questions than she wanted to answer.

She was no longer the woman who fell off that cliff eight years ago. He couldn't get that idea in his head or it would be too hard for him to consider her an equal going forward.

"I thought I had a lot of medals. Then I read your bio."

Selina's heart sank. "I don't know what you mean. I don't have any medals."

"Not what I read. Sounds like you were not only a decorated Chicago PD cop, but you were an up-and-comer in the search-and-rescue world as well. Did you know they awarded you the valor award posthumously?"

Selina stood, no longer caring about the pain in her belly. The pain in her chest overpowered it. She wanted out of this bunker and away from Efren Brenna. She'd gotten used to hiding out in the lab at Secure One to avoid him and his damn tempting eyes, but here, there was nowhere to go, and she suspected he was taking full advantage of the situation. He liked making her uncomfortable. It was probably something they taught them in the military, like, live on the edge of your comfort zone, and soon you'll be comfortable in all the zones. She snorted at herself and offered herself a mental high five for that gem.

What was she supposed to say? No, she had no idea they bestowed upon her the most respected award in law enforcement after she faked her death.

"It's okay, you know," he said from directly behind her. "They didn't award it to you because you died. They awarded it to you because you lived."

Her shoulders sank, and he wrapped his arms around them, holding her against his chest. Every time they touched, his settled her somewhere deep inside that even she couldn't pinpoint. Or maybe she didn't want to pinpoint it and admit that his touch had power over her.

"Maybe I lived honestly, but I died dishonestly. I bet they wouldn't have considered that so medal-worthy."

"It's no different than going into WITSEC and falling off the face of the earth. The difference is, when you go into WITSEC, you don't get to shape the narrative. At least you did it your way. You did it in a way that reminded people, sometimes the heroes that go out to save them don't always come back."

Selina grabbed his forearms and held on tight, letting his heat warm and relax her. "I suppose that's true, but some might call what I did taking the coward's way out."

"Anyone who thinks that hasn't read the articles I have on Medardo Vaccaro. You took the only out you had at the time. Never consider your contributions to taking that man down as less than because of the choices you had to make after the attempt. You had no good ones, so you took the one that hurt the fewest number of people."

"How do you figure?" She was curious to know why he thought that was the best choice she could have made.

"Listen, you're talking to someone who ran a lot of missions in a lot of hostile places. Our first instruction if we were caught was to take any opportunity to end our lives before they could get information from us. The movies make it look like you can escape any situation when captured in a war or hostile territory, but the truth is, no one escapes. The enemy gets the information from you in the most painful way possible, and then you die. Make no mistake. You were in a war with no team and no one willing to protect you from the enemy. You already knew the police department suspected you of being involved with the Snake. They weren't likely to bend over backward to protect you from him, right?"

"If I'd thought it was likely, I wouldn't have run."

"Then you did what soldiers do. Sure, you didn't die, but you've spent the years since you disappeared doing good for other people. You've continued to rescue those in need, even if the way you do it looks a little bit different."

Selina said nothing, she just leaned her head back and let the words he said settle deep inside her where she could call them up whenever she doubted the decisions she'd made over the years. There was one important thing she had to do before they spent any more time togeth—

"Secure one, Whiskey."

Efren dropped his arms and hurried to the console with Selina on his heels. "Secure two, Tango."

Mina's face popped up on the screen, and she eyed them both. "I have an update, and you may want to sit down for this."

Chapter Nine

Efren's gaze darted to Selina for a moment, and then he pulled out a chair, motioning for her to sit, which she did without argument. Whether it was fatigue from the surgery or opening up to him over the last few days that made her feel weak, he didn't know, but whatever Mina had to say was sure to change the game again.

"How bad is it?" Selina asked, her shoulders stiff as though she was preparing for battle.

"You'll have to answer that question. I learned through some back channels that Randall Sr. could be released on a technicality."

Silence. Efren counted to ten before he slid into the chair next to Selina and hooked his arm around her waist. He didn't care if Mina saw him do it, either. He could see in Selina's eyes that her world was spinning and she needed someone to ground her. While he couldn't be everything for her, as the only one here, he could support her.

"Do you know why he's being released?" Efren asked since Selina had opened her mouth, but only a puff of air escaped.

"I'm working on learning that and what his release date will be."

"That explains why Ava is back now." Selina said her sister's name as though it were venom on her tongue she had to spit out. "Still doesn't explain where she's been all these years."

"Working on that, too," Mina answered. "But if she's within the Vaccaro organization, I won't find much."

"I have no doubt she is," Selina said with conviction. "Did you get anywhere with Randall Jr.'s arrest?"

"I have a few feelers out. The information is fresh, so it will take a bit longer to get."

"Understood," Efren said. "Thanks for the update. At least we know why Ava has shown her face again."

"Ever the loving wife. Give me a break," Selina muttered. "Are you sure there were no unnamed visitors visiting Daddy Dearest in prison?"

Mina smiled the smile she wore when she was a dog with a bone. "Great minds think alike. I broke down his visitor list, and I'm looking into the names individually. If she was there, I'll find out."

"Thanks, Mina—"

Before he could say more, Cal loomed over Mina's shoulder. "My surveillance indicates our attempts to throw off anyone looking for Selina has failed. Someone has been sniffing around the Jeep, and I haven't been able to get it out of there. Stay on your toes."

"I've always got an eye on the trail cameras," he assured his boss. Did he feel guilty for lying since he spent half his time staring at Selina? Not even a little bit.

"Good. We'll be in touch as soon as we know Randall's court date and the technicality."

"Selina," Mina said before Cal could end the transmission. "Would Vaccaro put out a hit on you, or do you think this is purely Ava's axe to grind?"

Selina was silent longer than necessary to think about the question, which told Efren she was hiding something. "If the Snake knows I'm alive, he would want me as dead as Ava does, so a hit would be pointless. He'd send my twin after me."

Mina turned and smiled at Cal. "Told ya."

When she turned back, she winked at Selina.

"You're saying the real person we need to track is Ava?" Cal asked, and this time, Selina nodded immediately.

"I have no question. Ava has her own agenda, but this time, it lines up with the Snake's, so he's probably given her his blessing to take me out by any means necessary."

"All because you were a cop?" Efren asked.

"If you cross Vaccaro, no matter how small, you will pay. I knew that going in, but I held on to hope that if we could bust Randall and Ava for counterfeiting, that trail would lead us to Vaccaro and we could finally arrest him."

"You don't know if that happened, right?" Mina asked.

"If they found evidence leading to Vaccaro?" she asked, and Mina nodded. "If we know he's not in prison, then they didn't find anything. I assume since Randall was tried and sent to prison, the police were able to prove he was running the ring."

"There's nothing you can think of offhand that would be a reason they'd be releasing Randall now?"

"No," Selina said. "This is so frustrating!" Her fist hit the table and bounced until Efren grabbed it and held it between his hands.

"Take a deep breath." His whisper calmed her immediately, and she inhaled and then exhaled.

"Sorry." She glanced up at Mina and Cal, still on the screen. "It's hard to be here and not there. It's like watching someone save your life, but you aren't a participant in it."

"You very much are, though," Cal said to reassure her. "Your job is to keep your wits about you there and to answer our questions as information comes in. I know it feels like you aren't doing anything, but hang in there. We've all got your back, and the one who has your physical back is the best in the business. If he says jump, you don't ask questions, got it?"

Selina gave him a salute, and Mina promised to be in touch soon before they signed off.

"I can't believe they're releasing that lying sack of human flesh," she said in a sudden gush of fury and vitriol. "I gave up my life for this, and now he's going to walk free again!"

Efren was still holding her hand, and he massaged it until she relaxed the fist and let him caress her palm. "We don't know that yet. Don't jump to conclusions."

"What other conclusion can there be?" she demanded.

"It could be a retrial situation or house arrest. Let's give Mina a bit more time."

"Time, time." She muttered the words as she stood and paced the room. "We have so much time and never enough time. We're trapped here with nothing but time that we're wasting doing nothing to help them."

"We can't help them." Efren grasped her waist and held her in place. "But we aren't wasting time. We're biding our time. There is a difference. You need to heal and once I think you're ready, we'll leave this place and spend our time clearing your name."

Selina stared him down for the longest time before she spoke. "First off, I'm the medical professional here, not you. Second, there is no clearing my name. I'm either alive, and Ava is dead, or I'm dead and Ava is alive. Those are the only two outcomes."

"As a forever optimist, I believe there's a third option and that is you're alive and Ava is in prison next to her husband and the monster who is pulling her strings. We can do that at Secure One if we work together."

She reached up and patted his face, letting her fingers linger as they trailed away from his skin. His cheek heated from her touch, and he forced himself to stay focused on calming her enough to sleep. There would be time to explore this connection between them when her life wasn't on the line. He feared if he didn't convince her to rest, he'd use the time in this bunker unwisely, and that would cloud his decision-making process going forward.

"You're so innocent in the ways of the Mafia. I wish you could stay that way, but by the time this is over, you'll see the only proper place for these people is ten feet under. There is evil in this world that can't be reformed, and Vaccaro is the captain of that bus."

"You're saying the movies got it all wrong?" His words were light as he walked her backward toward the bed.

"There have been a handful of movies I could relate to as someone who grew up on the fringes of that lifestyle. Understanding the Mafia is impossible unless you live it, which I don't recommend. Unfortunately for you, you're about to live it."

"Don't feel bad for me, Selina Colvert." His words

were an order, and her eyes widened a touch as he lowered her to the bed. "I've taken out a lot of that evil you speak of. Mafia of a different kind, you could say. If I had guilt about it, that ended when I found scores of villagers dead with their tongues cut out. Those are the images I'll never unsee, but I don't lose any sleep at night over the men who I made sure never walked this earth again. I'm not afraid of doing the same thing to Vaccaro if it comes down to you or him. Understand?"

He waited for her to get comfortable, but she didn't—she pulled him down onto the bed next to her. "You're going to war for me?"

"Yes. Only because I want to, Selina." Efren turned and cradled her face in his hands. "Not because I have to."

"I'm sorry," she whispered, her hands grasping his wrists.

"For what, darling?"

"Asking you to wade into another war you didn't ask to fight."

His smile was gentle when he ran his thumbs across her lips. "You didn't ask. I offered. Those other wars I fought, they were faces I didn't see or know. This war... Well, this war has a name and a face of someone I care about, so I'm standing in front of you now asking for a gun and a chance to march beside you. Together we can end this war swiftly. First, you need some rest." His thumbs stroked her temples as her eyes drooped, despite how she fought to keep them open.

He leaned in and placed a gentle kiss on her lips. "Sleep now, my beauty. That is time not wasted while you heal your body."

"Lie with me," she murmured as he lowered her head to the pillow. "I don't want to be alone."

Before she finished the sentence he'd scooted her to the back of the bed, kicked off his shoe and lain next to her. After arranging his prosthesis so it didn't hurt her, he pulled her against him tightly and gently splayed his hand across her belly.

"Sleep now. Clear your mind and let it rest, too. I've got your back."

Selina may have drifted off to sleep, but that was the very last thing on Efren's mind. The thought of losing the woman in his arms to an animal like Loraine or Vaccaro filled his mind. He was trained to hunt animals hiding in a hole, smoke them out and then end their lives. He vowed he'd do the same thing with Vaccaro so Selina could have her life back, even if he had to sacrifice himself to do it.

An hour later, as he peeled himself away from her and walked to the cabinet where the go bags waited, he refused to look too deeply at why he was willing to sacrifice himself for a woman who had treated him with nothing but animosity since the day they'd met. Maybe it had something to do with the look in her eye when she did it, or maybe it had something to do with the way she touched him when her guard was down, but whatever the reason, when this job was over, he'd have to leave Secure One if he wanted solidarity again. A team was great, until someone got too close and opened you up to emotions you didn't know how to deal with after what you'd been through.

Death and destruction were the emotions he understood now. The soft caress of a woman desperate for a connection as her world spun out of control was something else entirely. The first one he could prepare and plan for. The second could only lead to one thing, and he'd already had enough heartbreak in his life to add more.

The touch of a woman was okay when it was no strings attached and no expectations, but it could never be that with Selina, and he knew it. The cost of being a hero was one he'd paid dearly for over the years. He may have saved six men that day, but only three of them remained all these years later. The scars of war went deep, and he was not immune to them just because he'd been the one doing the saving. What he learned was, you could rescue someone, but it was up to them to save themselves. Some could and some couldn't, but that wasn't his job. His job was to rescue or protect and then walk away, and that was exactly what he'd do again, even if it broke him to say goodbye to the brotherhood he'd found at Secure One.

He glanced behind him at the woman he considered part of that brotherhood, even if no one else on the team acknowledged the contributions she'd made to the business at a significant cost to her soul. That was the part that scared him the most. He understood that she suffered in silence out of some misplaced idea that stoicism was required to be part of the club. To be part of the inner circle that allowed you to do more than fix battle wounds and babysit. What surprised him the most was how angry it made him that she had to. He wasn't supposed to care. He wasn't supposed to get angry. He was supposed to do his job and move on to the next one. For the life of him, he couldn't figure out when that had changed. That was a lie. He knew the exact moment it changed, but he couldn't, and didn't want to, give it space in his head.

Efren turned away from Selina with determination. Once they made it through this battle, he was done pretending that protecting people would bring back those he'd already lost. It was time for a new path, and no matter how much he wished it were different, that path would not include Selina Colvert.

Chapter Ten

Selina woke with a start, immediately registering that all the lights were low. On guard, she sat up and searched the room until her gaze landed on Efren's back. He stood at the consoles in deep concentration.

"There are tactical clothes at the end of the bed. Get dressed in place. I'm not looking."

"Do we have a problem?"

"Potentially." His words were clipped and quiet. "Someone is sniffing around topside."

Selina stripped off her sweats and pulled on the black ripstop pants. They were a little big, but they'd have to do for now. She strapped on a belt that came complete with a holster and 9mm. After she adjusted them to protect the incisions on her front and back, she stripped off her sweatshirt, pulled on the black T-shirt and covered it with the sweatshirt, and then a lightweight black coat. She eyed the boots and before she could decide on a way to put them on, Efren was kneeling in front of her, tying on the boots for her.

"I can put on my own boots."

"I'd rather you save the energy for what's ahead of us. Grab your pills and take one. Just in case."

"I'm fine." She stood and stretched side to side to

prove it. "We've been here for a week now and it's nothing more than a slight twinge." His disapproving glance made her sigh, so she took two over-the-counter painkillers to satisfy him. "What are we dealing with here, Efren?"

They hadn't gotten an update from Mina since yesterday afternoon, which meant she wasn't breaking through any of Vaccaro's firewalls put up to keep her out, and keeping Mina Jacobs out was no easy feat.

"My eyes in the sky are showing me that the guys who found the Jeep didn't give up there. They've been poking around in the woods, too."

"Damn it. Have you let Secure One know?"

"Not yet. I'm not sure that they'll hang around if they don't find anything." He pointed at the camera where two groups of two guys moved through the woods, silent as ninjas. They wore night-vision goggles and carried big guns.

"How far out are they? Are we safe in here?"

"For now," he answered, his gaze still on the console. "They won't find our hatch in the dark if they don't know where it is. The daytime is a different story."

"You're saying we won't be here if they make it that far."

"Not if I have anything to say about it. Our go bags are packed. I made a small one for you to carry. It has the first aid kit and the little bit of tech we can take with us. I don't want you carrying anything heavier than that until we see how you do."

"Do you have a destination in mind?"

He turned and took her in, his gaze dark, intense and focused. "Somewhere that isn't here."

"Secure one, Whiskey."

Efren put his finger to his lips and then turned and answered the console quietly. "Secure two, Tango. Hush mode."

Selina waited until Mina's face popped up on the screen. She spoke, but it was impossible to hear what she was saying; all she could do was read the captions on the screen. Her first questions were, "Are you in danger? Should I get Cal?"

Efren sat and put the foldable keyboard on his lap, dulling the sound even more. She thought he was being paranoid. There was no way Cal didn't make this place soundproof, but she supposed, considering his job, safer was better than sorry. She waited while he typed out what he'd seen and then asked her if she had an update.

What was written had her seeing red. "His lawyers filed a writ of habeas corpus?"

Efren turned to her. "What is that? I'm not a law enforcement person."

"Unlawful imprisonment," she answered. "Ask her if she knows the content of the writ."

After typing, they waited for Mina to answer. It wasn't one Selina liked, and Efren must have sensed it. "She may not know yet, but give her time, and she will find out what it is."

"It won't do us any good if we aren't in contact with her by the time she knows." The words were hissed through her teeth. She wasn't mad at him, it wasn't his fault, but she was mad that Randall's lawyers were playing games. The man deserved to rot in prison for his crimes—both the ones they knew about and the ones they didn't. Letting him out of prison was a surefire way of having him disappear, leaving her on the run forever.

Selina grabbed the keyboard from him and typed her own question. "When does he go before the judge?"

"Monday."

Selina did the math in her head and realized they were coming up on early Thursday morning. "That doesn't give us much time," she whispered, her lips in a thin line as she typed back to Mina. "As soon as you know, I have to know." Mina gave her a thumbs-up and then stood, moving aside so Cal could sit down.

Selina paced the room. She wanted to pay attention, but her mind was still focused on Randall. If his law-yers had proof that he was being unlawfully detained, he could go free as soon as Monday. Since she hadn't been present for the trial, she had no idea if that was a possi-bility. Then again, she knew the Snake, and chances were good that money was changing hands as they spoke.

"Colvert," Efren whispered, and she snapped to atten-tion. He was motioning her over and she leaned in next to him. "You and Cal need to talk strategy."

"Strategy? Isn't that your call?"

"This is your life, you should have a say in it, yes?"

She took his seat and pulled the keyboard onto her lap. Cal was speaking, and she waited for the captions to come up.

Avoid going west. Once you leave the state, it will be harder for me to help. You're much closer to the western border, so go east or southeast.

Do you have another safe house in any direction of this location?

Negative. You have experience with avoiding Vaccaro.

*in the past. Fall back on that. Once you're clear, call in
and we'll have a plan in place.*

Selina frowned as she stared at the man who had
given her a home, sharpened her skills and treated her
like family the last eight years. *Is leaving the bunker the
right decision, or should we stay put?*

What does your gut say? Cal asked.

Run. Three letters. One word. The story of her life.

Now you're in your element. Good luck, Sierra. Charlie, out.

Before she could wrap her head around the fact that
might be the last time she ever spoke to her friend, a low,
guttural curse came from Efren's side of the console.
He pointed at the top left camera where one of the four
guys was spinning the hatch open inside the old cabin.
He held his finger to his lips, and she nodded, watching
in silence as one of the men climbed down the ladder
and inspected the small space. There was barely room
for him to turn around, which meant he wouldn't see the
camera hidden inside one of the pipes. They didn't miss
the shot of his face, though. They captured it and Efren
sent it to Mina for identification. The night-vision goggles might make that more difficult, but if Mina could
get his name, she would.

The guy climbed the ladder and shook his head at
his buddies. After whispered conversation they weren't
privy to, the men broke off into teams of two again and
spread out through the woods, headed back in the direction of the Jeep. Once they disappeared, Efren let
out a breath.

"Chances are they're going to regroup at the Jeep and
fan out in the next direction," he whispered.

"Which will make it hard to know which way to go, right?"

He waited another few minutes until the teams were past the second set of cameras in the woods, then he waited a few more minutes after that, she assumed to make sure they didn't come back again. Once an adequate amount of time had passed, he started unplugging and unhooking several devices.

"These are going with us. They're our only tie to Secure One."

Selina held her bag out for him to stow away the folding keyboard and receiver. Once safely tucked away in protective pockets, she closed the bag and lowered it to the ground. "What's the plan, Brenna?"

"You tell me. I'm following your lead."

Her nod was almost imperceptible, but it gave her the push she needed to make the decision. "I don't know how you feel about it, but I don't want to be here if they come back during the day and find our hatch."

"Same. Walk me through the plan."

"We know they're out there, but this is our only window. We'll give them a thirty-minute head start. It took us an hour to get here from the Jeep, but I was moving much slower than they were tonight. We know they're headed north. We can't be sure where they'll go from there, but my bet is north or west, thinking we'll head for the closest border. If we head southeast, we'll be clear of them before daybreak. What say you, Brenna?"

"I say, I'll follow you anywhere, Colvert."

Before she could react, he dragged her toward him by the back of her head until their lips collided in a kiss that heated to boiling instantly. If they were going to survive this, she would have to keep her lips off his. When he tipped his head to take the kiss deeper, she knew that was going to be easier said than done.

THE SUN WAS breaking on the horizon, and they'd been walking for nearly five hours. Efren could see Selina needed to rest sooner rather than later. She'd been a trouper keeping pace with him all night, but as 6:00 a.m. approached, she needed food, a place to sit down, and a few more Advil before they could continue their journey.

He followed her down along a shallow creek and started edging her closer to the road. They needed to find a restaurant where they could sit for a bit and give her side time to rest. First, they had to get close enough to the road to watch for civilization. He hoped she was tired enough that she wouldn't notice what he was doing. It was easy to let her lead. She was an excellent leader who thought of even the smallest things that could trip them up, but she wasn't good at admitting when she needed rest. She would push herself until she crossed the line, and then he'd be finding a hospital instead of a diner.

Their walk had been in silence, and he'd spent the majority of it replaying that last kiss they'd shared in the bunker before risking their lives to save them. He hadn't held back that time and moved it past closed-lipped and into territory he wasn't sure she wanted to go, until she'd willingly joined him in the hot tangle of tongues. When the kiss ended and they made their plans for leaving the bunker, he'd vowed to keep his hands and his lips to himself going forward, but nothing turned him on more than a strong, independent woman who could take care of herself. Selina Colvert was that and so much more.

Maybe that was how he should look at his time with Selina. Whatever happened between them happened because the feelings were mutual, but that didn't mean there were strings attached when the case ended. His hard and fast rule had always been never to get involved with anyone he was guarding, but Selina wasn't just anyone. She was a teammate, an equal, dare he say a friend now that they'd put their trust, and lives, in each other's hands.

"Brenna," Selina hissed from his left. "You're too close to the road. Fall back."

Well, he should have known she wouldn't miss his migration east. "We need to find someplace to rest. I'm watching for signs to a diner or a gas station."

"Negative," she whispered, grabbing his backpack to pull him to a stop. "What part of 'we can't be seen' do you not understand? We may have left those guys behind, but they aren't the only guys. Vaccaro has scouts all over this state, I can assure you."

"That may well be true, but you aren't going to make it much farther without resting. We need food and to check your incision."

"Fine," she said, pointing ahead. "We'll cross the creek up there and stop as soon as the sun is up. That will allow us to rebandage the wounds without using a flashlight and we can grab a protein bar and some water."

"Or," he said, taking her hand and keeping her level with him as he continued to walk closer to the road. "We can find someplace big enough that we can blend in and grab something hot to eat. It would be good to have hot water and soap so we don't get your wound infected."

She held up until he had to stop or risk pulling her over. "What happened to 'you're in charge, Colvert. You know this guy best'?"

Efren spun on his heel and tipped her chin up. "I stand by that until I see you pushing yourself too far. Then you start making bad decisions that can make your situation worse. I've watched you go from a five to a six to a seven on the pain scale in the last two hours. It's time to rest your body."

"Now you're an expert on my pain scale?"

The sarcasm dripped from the sentence when she crossed her arms over her chest and waited for him to respond.

"Yes, because I saw you at ten when I forced you to walk through the woods for an hour after a perilous ride less than a day after surgery. I've cataloged in my mind what level of pain you're at when you take medication and when you don't. I may not be an expert on you, but I'm observant, and that's what keeps people alive when I protect them. While I stand behind you running the show with how Vaccaro will behave, and knowing the best way to avoid him, keeping you safe is still my job. I will override you with a snap of my fingers if I think you're putting yourself at risk." He snapped his fingers in front of her face and she jumped, but not before he noticed the smoke in her eyes catch a flame.

Good. Let her get fired up. That would keep her going until they got somewhere to rest.

Selina stepped up to him and put her finger on his chest. "If you think I can't deal with a little bit of pain, you're dead wrong. I'm going to hurt much worse if Vaccaro gets hold of me—"

A stick snapped to the left of them, announcing in no uncertain terms that they weren't alone.

Chapter Eleven

Selina slowly removed her finger from Efren's chest and reached for her gun as he did the same. The woods had fallen silent again and they waited, their only communication their eyes. "Could be an animal," he mouthed, and she nodded. It could be an animal. It could be a snake.

She motioned with her eyes to a tree less than five feet behind them. They just had to make it there without alerting anyone that they were so close. The detritus on the forest floor was going to make that difficult, but they needed cover in case whatever was in the woods was an animal that walked on two legs and carried a big gun.

His nod was slow and deliberate as he brought his hand up to point from his eyes to the woods, telling her he'd watch while she went first. There was no way to argue with him, and he was supposed to be her body-guard, so she looked down at her feet and slowly inched her way toward the tree. It was a giant oak that would easily hide them from anyone walking past, as long as they didn't get too close. It felt like forever before she had her back plastered to the tree. She inhaled a breath, then slowly turned and stuck her gun around the side of the tree, a sign to Efren to move.

He had taken his first step when the first shot rang out. Efren used it for cover and tore at her, rolling behind the tree as the second shot hit the dirt not too far from where they were standing.

"Not an animal," he hissed as they each braced their gun around opposite sides of the tree.

"What's the plan, bodyguard?"

"As much as I hate to say it, we wait." He eyed his bag. "You're going to need a bigger gun."

He'd been carrying an assault rifle through the woods, while she'd kept her sidearm on her only. Carrying an extra eight pounds around her shoulder would wear her out too quickly, so he'd kept it on his pack. Selina slowly holstered her sidearm and reached for the gun as another shot peppered the ground to the left of the tree.

Haste had her grabbing the gun off his pack and bringing it up to her shoulder in one smooth motion. "Where are they shooting from?"

"I can't tell. The vegetation is too thick this time of year. Until they show their face, we can't shoot back in case it's an innocent."

"They're shooting at us!"

"They could think we're an animal."

Selina couldn't stop the eye roll. "It's not even hunting season. We need to move."

"Not until we know where they are," he hissed, his words barely audible in the silence of the forest. "We could be surrounded."

She hated that he was right, but he was. Just because the bullets were coming from in front of them didn't mean there wasn't a team on every side. They didn't have enough ammo for a gunfight of that size, so she had to hope that wasn't the case. There were four last night, and she had to pray there were only four this morning. She glanced at Efren, who had his gun up without a waver as he waited, sweeping the dark vegetation in front of them.

"Slowly bend down and find something to throw to your right," he whispered.

Drawing fire was an excellent way to determine their location. She searched around the tree for something to throw until she encountered a hefty rock. With a nod to him, she tossed it to the right, and it landed and rolled a few feet before someone lit it up. She wasn't expecting the pop-pop from next to her but was happy he had a shot. Then she heard a grunt, and a heavy object dropped to the forest floor.

Her eyes wide, she glanced at Efren, who used the suppressor on his rifle to point at the ground, and then he mouthed, "throw another."

The man was going to pick them off one after the other to protect her. She felt around and came up with a piece of bark. It wasn't big, but at least it wouldn't sound the same as the rock. Efren gave her a head nod and she tossed it to their left. The morning was immediately lit up by gunfire, and he used the illumination to send a few bullets their way until they heard another body hit the ground.

"They aren't the smartest blokes in the forest," he muttered.

"That's Vaccaro men for ya," she whispered with a grin. The situation wasn't funny, but leave it to Efren to ease her fear a little bit.

"Throw something else. I doubt they'll take the bait again, but we have to try."

She grabbed a rock and tossed it far to the right. They waited, but this time, nothing happened. They stood in silence another five minutes, but they couldn't wait all day. They had to make a decision.

"We need to move, Brenna," she said, gun in hand. "Last night, there were two teams of two. Maybe they split up."

"That's what I'm thinking, too. Back-to-back until we know for sure."

"What direction?" she asked, lining their backpacks up and sweeping her gun across the trees in front of her.

"To find the hunters who became the hunted."

Efren moved forward, and Selina followed, struggling to walk backward without falling on the uneven terrain. Her trained ear listened for footfalls or any sound to indicate another human in the woods. They were barely across the creek and into the deeper vegetation again when moaning reached their ears. He tipped his head twice to the right, and they sidestepped toward the sound, watching for an ambush. It wasn't likely, or the bullets would have rained down on them already.

She nearly tripped and fell on the first body until Efren tossed his arm back to grab her. Once she was solid again, he stuck his left leg out while he crouched on his right to check the guy's pulse.

"Dead." He put his finger to his lips and tipped his ear to the side to indicate they should listen.

Selina heard a soft gurgling and motioned forward and to the right frantically. The guy was still alive, but he wouldn't be for long. Efren held her back and followed the sound at the same pace, sweeping his gun across the brightening forest as the sun rose above them. The light revealed the man they were looking for as he lay against a tree trunk, blood running from his neck and mouth with every labored breath.

Efren motioned to the left, and she turned and brought her gun up as he knelt by the man. "Who are you and what do you want with us?"

"Her," he said, his hand slowly raising to point at Selina. "He wants her."

"Who's he?" Efren asked, but Selina didn't wait with bated breath. She already knew the answer.

The man hissed, then laughed, blood bubbling out of his mouth with the action. "He's coming for you, little Eva Shannon. You once were lost, but now you're found."

"How many more are there?" Efren asked the question but the man just smiled, as though his secret was her death sentence. Efren pressed the butt of his gun to the guy's neck wound. "I'm going to ask you one more time. How many are there?"

"None today," he croaked as Efren eased off on the gun. "Tomorrow, more than you can count and the next day, even more. You can't escape the Snake, sweet Eva. Tag, you're it. Run, run, as fast as you ca…"

The sentence hung in the air as the guy's head lolled to the side and a final breath left his body. Efren cursed and grabbed his flashlight, shining it across the body frantically.

"GPS," she whispered and ran to the other guy, searching his body for the tracker he likely wore. If they had activated it before they went down, Vaccaro would send reinforcements. It took a moment but then she spotted it. "Left side of the vest!"

Selina pulled his off and ran back to Efren, who was

struggling. She helped him and then motioned for him to follow her. He did without question, this time taking the back position while she walked forward at a fast clip. She held up her fist in a stop motion and slung her gun around her chest. A fast dig through his pack, and she came up with a condom. They used them at Secure One for all types of things from water containers to boot liners. She had something else in mind as she rolled the condom over the beacons, blew air into it, and tied it off. Once she was satisfied with the vessel, she lowered it to the creek and let it go.

"Brilliant," Efren said with a chuckle as the beacons floated downstream at a leisurely walking pace.

"All that does is buy us time." Selina stood and shook her head as the sun came up. "The guy was right. This place will be crawling with snakes faster than we can kill them. We have to find a faster way to move."

"Agreed. For now, let's move as quick as we can the opposite direction of those beacons."

He took off at a pace that was going to be tough for her to match, but she dug deep and reminded herself if she didn't find a way, she would find herself in the snake's den, and the pain would be greater than anything she had dealt with thus far.

HER BODY WAS screaming at her, but she wouldn't stop. Couldn't stop until they had a place to hole up long enough to take a shower and contact Secure One. A little food wouldn't hurt, either. Efren was trailing her, not demanding answers, which surprised her if she were honest. He had been incredibly supportive of her plans, only pushing back when he wanted her to stop long enough to think about things from all angles. They hadn't had time for her to do that when they hopped a ride in an old potato truck about four hours ago. They didn't know where he was going, but it was better than where they were at the time. It afforded them time off their feet to rest their bodies while getting as far away from the two dead guys as quickly as possible. When the truck stopped to refuel, they opted to jump out and find a place to contact Secure One. Mina was their eyes in the sky, and they needed more information. Hopefully, she had it.

"Where are we going?" Efren asked, his voice nearly drowned out by the rushing of the Mississippi River. The Mighty Miss was raging today, and that told Selina a storm was coming. Actually, more than one storm was coming for them, which was why they needed to regroup and get better prepared.

"I'll know it when I see it." That was the only answer she could give since she hadn't found what she was looking for yet.

They'd taken a few more steps when her arm shot out in front of them. "There."

"A cabin?" He pulled her to a stop and forced her to make eye contact. "Why?"

"It's November, so the cabins are closed for the winter. At least that one is. With any luck, inside is a shower, food and a place to call home."

"Fine, but let me scout it. Better I'm caught on camera than you."

Selina wanted to argue, but she couldn't. He was right. She had to be a ghost if she wanted to survive long enough to clear this area and get back to Secure One alive. He tugged his gaiter up around his face to hide it the best he could before he leaned in to whisper, "If it's safe, I'll owl call."

With a nod from her, he took off, approaching the cabin from behind where cameras would be less likely. Selina watched the way he moved across the yard. Considering he'd been on his leg for almost a full day and still moved like a dancer, it was impressive. He disappeared around the end of the cabin, and she waited for him to pop back up at the front of the place. When he did, he was low and angled away from any cameras that might be pointing right at him. He moved in slowly, knowing that any doorbell with a camera would be easy to spot on a cabin this old.

She moved closer, her trained eye already knowing the cabin was as low-tech as they come. Her validation came in the form of an owl hoot from the porch of the small structure. By the time she joined him, he was holding up a key.

"Guess they aren't afraid of theft." He had the door open and held up his finger, doing a quick sweep of the three-room cabin before he motioned her in. "Shades."

In quick succession they pulled the shades and then dropped their packs. "I'm glad we found this place. A storm is blowing in." Selina unzipped her coat and pulled her gaiter off as she took a look around. "Doesn't look like anyone has been here for quite a few seasons."

"That was the vibe I got, too, by looking in the windows. Let's just hope no one decides now is the time to take a trip to Grandpa's cabin."

"Not likely this late in the season with a storm brewing. We need to get a call into Secure One now before we can't." To make her point, a gust of wind rattled the windowpanes and made her jump.

"Hey, it's okay." Efren walked over and rubbed her arms before he pulled her into a quick hug. "You did good, Colvert. I'm proud of you for not only hanging on but finding the opportunities we needed to get clear of that mess. Let's use this time to regroup and make our next plan."

"I'm glad we got the best of those two in the woods, but there will be more."

"I know." He kissed her cheek before he stepped back and held her out at arm's length. "We're a team, and we'll face whatever comes at us the same way we did with those guys. Together."

"I'd be screwed without you, Brenna."

"Did it hurt to admit that?" he asked, his lips quirking in humor.

"Surprisingly, no. I've taken many of my frustrations out on you for too long. You didn't deserve it, but you were convenient. When you went to bat for me with Cal in the bunker, I realized you didn't deserve attitude from me."

"Apology accepted." He winked while he set out the equipment to call Secure One. "I'm a big boy and always knew there was more to your dislike of me than met the eye."

He fell silent as though he were waiting for her to tell him what that was, but she had no intention of doing that, now or ever. Admitting that she didn't hate him was hard, but admitting that she cared about him in ways she shouldn't could be dangerous to her heart and her life.

Chapter Twelve

She had bigger fish to fry than Efren Brenna's ego, and his name was Vaccaro. Selina made a vow to remind herself of that every minute of every hour if need be. The console linked up, and Efren spoke.

"Secure one, Tango."

"Secure two, Whiskey," came the voice of an angel.

Selina dropped to the small couch in relief. "Secure three, Sierra."

The small screen came to life, and Mina's face reflected at them, grainy and barely visible, but smiling. She panned the camera out, and four other faces stared back at them. Cal, Mack, Roman and Eric also sat around the table. "So good to see you guys!" Mina said. "We've been cautiously optimistic you'd call soon."

"Is that your way of saying you've been worried?" Efren's question was in good fun, but Mina nodded immediately.

"More than worried, especially when you missed your check-in," Cal said.

"Sorry about that. We were in the back of a potato truck moving too fast for the phone."

"A potato truck? Never mind, I don't want to know. Fill us in."

Efren was about to speak when Selina did. "We ran into two of Vaccaro's guys about four hours south of the bunker. Mr. Sharpshooter over here took them both out with a shot."

"Before they died, one confirmed they were working for the Snake and that more were on their way."

"That's when we jumped on the potato truck," Selina said to clarify. "We had to get out of the area quickly and without being seen."

"I'm relieved you found a way out," Roman said. "What's your location?"

"The Mississippi is right outside the window. That's all I know, other than the name of the gas station the truck stopped at. We borrowed a cabin until the storm passes."

"Borrowed," Mina said with a snort. "I'm glad you found shelter. We have much to discuss and little time to do it. First, tell me the name of the gas station."

"Go for It Gas," Selina said as Efren laughed. "What?" She punched his arm playfully. "It was easy to remember."

Mina clicked the keyboard a few times and then smiled. "You're on the outskirts of Winona to the north. That's a good place to be. Now, let's fill you in on Daddy Dearest."

Selina leaned in toward the console. "Do we know why he's being released?"

"We do, or at least why he's going before the judge. I'm glad you're sitting down. The writ of habeas corpus they filed pertains to you."

"Me?" she asked, and Mina nodded with a grimace.

"Randall's original trial lawyer allowed your written

testimony to be included in the trial paperwork despite it not being signed. He also didn't ask the prosecuting team to do the due diligence of finding your body."

"Is that a thing?" Efren asked, glancing at her.

Mina nodded. "It is, but I don't buy it. I suspect money has changed hands here and this is just a way to get Daddy Dearest out of prison."

"Why now, though?" Efren asked in confusion. "It's been years."

"Because Randall Jr. was arrested." Selina's answer was resigned. "Vaccaro probably planned this all along, and we walked right into the trap he set."

"I don't understand," everyone said at once.

"Explain it if you can," Efren encouraged her, and she stood, pacing back and forth behind him as the winds intensified.

"The Snake was setting Randall Jr. up to take a fall by killing Howie. There's no way to know for sure, but if Junior wasn't running the counterfeiting business the way Vaccaro wanted, or heaven forbid, was skimming off the top, he would make an example out of him. Since Howie was already cheating on the Winged Templar's daughter, it was easy to kill him. They drop his body in the storage unit since Sadie works there and set up Sadie to take the fall, already knowing that Randall had Kadie."

"He had no way to know we would be there that night, though," Eric said.

"As I said, we fell into his trap. We played his game perfectly. In the end, Randall was arrested on kidnapping charges, which will put him away for life. With Randall Jr. and Howie both out of the picture, Vaccaro needs someone to run the business. Now it's time to get Daddy out after having served just enough years to make it look like an injustice was corrected rather than a criminal walked. The original trial attorney left that unsigned statement of mine in there on purpose. It was planted for this very occasion. I'm honestly surprised Vaccaro didn't just kill Randall Jr. and be done with it."

Cal's gaze darted to Mina's, and Selina cleared her throat. "What?"

"They found Junior unresponsive in his jail cell this morning. He's not dead, but he's also not expected to live."

Selina threw her arms up. "More reason for Daddy to get out of prison. Now he's lost two sons since he was so unjustly incarcerated. I should have signed that statement before I started writing it!"

"Was there a reason you hadn't signed it?" Efren asked, taking her hand and leading her to the couch to sit. "Rest. You're still healing."

"I didn't sign it because I wasn't finished with it. I had it on my desk and was working on it when I got called in and suspended for the shooting. Once that happens, I'm not allowed back into the area for anything. They must have found it on my desk, but I don't know anyone who would have put a half-finished, unsigned statement in a trial packet, cop or lawyer alike."

"Remember when we talked about someone being a mole for Vaccaro?" Efren said, and she nodded. "This smells like a mole."

"It smells like a rat." Cal's voice was angry. "And snakes love nothing more than a rat for a snack."

"I'll look into it," Mina said, writing it down on her pad.

"Did you find anything about Randall Jr.'s arrest before his unfortunate accident?" Efren asked.

"He used his one phone call for his lawyer. That was it."

"Vaccaro likely pays his lawyer, so any mention of the missing twin being in his basement that night would easily flow back to the snake's den," Cal said. "For now, that's our working theory. We assume he knows Selina is alive from the lawyer and sent Ava to clean that mess up. Since she couldn't, he's hunting you while trying to free his head capo."

"Just another day in the life," Selina said with an eye roll.

"We have the information. What's our next move?" Efren asked, sitting beside Selina and putting his arm around her waist. She glanced at him questioningly, but he didn't seem bothered by his PDA in front of the team. Thankfully, only Mina seemed to have noticed the interaction when she looked back to the console.

"There's more," Mina said, holding up her finger and pointing at Roman, who held up a map of Minnesota. "It turns out, the house in Bemidji isn't the only property titled in Randall Sr.'s name."

"What?" Selina asked, leaning in to see the grainy video.

"I did some digging and discovered a house in Caledonia that Randall owns." Roman held the map up to the screen so they could see the house marked near Highway 44.

"Wait," Efren said, his eyes roving in his head for a minute. "If we're near Winona, that puts Caledonia somewhere around fifty klicks from here."

"It's close, for sure," Cal said, leaning forward, ready to take over. "We can't be certain, since we can't do much recon on the place, but our guess is that's where Randall Jr. moved the operation after the trial. He couldn't keep anything in the Bemidji place, but as long as he lived there, he could make authorities believe he was clean."

"Did Randall Jr. travel to Caledonia frequently?" Eric asked, suddenly interested in the conversation again.

"Not as often as Howie Loraine did prior to his untimely beheading."

"Interesting," Selina said. "Maybe Howie was the gopher to keep Junior's nose clean."

"Possible," Cal agreed. "What are you thinking? I can see your instincts are locked and loaded on this. You know the family and how the Snake runs. We're counting on you to tell us our next move."

Selina was silent for a moment. She hoped they thought she was thinking of a plan instead of trying not to cry. She'd longed to hear Cal say those words. To treat her as an equal. To acknowledge her skills as a cop and law enforcement professional. Now that he was, she was afraid to screw it up. All she ever wanted was for them to see her as an equal. Suddenly, she was at a loss for words.

"Follow your gut," Efren whispered in her ear. "It's telling you the right answer."

His words broke her internal freeze-up, and she nodded. "If he's released by the judge on Monday, and you think he will be?" She was addressing Mina, who nodded. "They'll do one of two things. Go to one of Vaccaro's places and regroup, or go to Caledonia."

"Which do you think is more likely?"

"Hard to know if I can't see the place in Caledonia."

Mina held up her finger and dug around in a pile by her computer, coming up with a paper she handed to Roman. He held it up to the camera. "I could only get a view from above, but as you can see it's—"

"Sprawling," Efren said.

"There," Selina said without conscious thought. "They'll go there. Ava's a spoiled brat. When she showed up at the hospital in a fur coat, it was obvious to me she hadn't changed her spots. She wants the cushy lifestyle, and that place affords them her every whim. Of that, I'm certain."

"Now that's your gut talking," Efren whispered, squeezing her hip.

"I'm inclined to agree with you," Cal said. "Not regarding Ava, but that Randall will want to check his operation immediately."

"Vaccaro will demand it," Selina said, standing to pace again. "It's been unattended or left in the care of an underling for too long. What time on Monday?"

"The docket says 11:00 a.m."

She paced a few more times, and an idea came to her that was dangerous but diabolical. "What if I was also there at 11:00 a.m. to give my sworn statement to the court? Signed, sealed and delivered."

"Not going to happen!" Efren said, jumping up and grasping her arms as though he forgot they weren't alone in the room. "Are you trying to get yourself killed?"

"The court would protect me. Is it dangerous, yes, but it would keep Randall Sr. in prison."

"Which doesn't solve our problem." It was Cal's voice, this time from behind them. She couldn't break eye contact with Efren. What she saw in his eyes said maybe he cared about her as more than just a job. "Randall is still in jail, but Ava and the Snake won't be. Doing that signs your death warrant, too."

"He's right," Efren said between clenched teeth. "You know he's right. We've fought too hard to keep you alive. We think this out. We make the plan and then we follow it. If we don't, you won't make it out of that courtroom alive. We both know it. You always want to do the right thing, and I'm proud as hell of you for even suggesting it, even knowing you'd be giving up your life for it, but you'd be giving up your life for the low-hanging fruit. We need the apple at the top of the tree, and the only way to get that is to let the rotten apple out of prison."

"As long as Ava is free, she will hunt me, Efren. We can't live that kind of life. I've been hiding for years from Vaccaro. I can't hide forever."

"If that's the case," Cal said from behind them, "Brenna is right. Let Randall out of prison, get him back to Caledonia. If they're both there, then we have evidence that Ava knows about the operation."

"What did you just say?" Selina asked, spinning on her heel.

"That we'd have proof Ava knows about the operation."

Selina smacked herself in the forehead. "Of course she does! That's where she's been all this time."

"You think Vaccaro was letting her run the operation all these years?"

"Hell no." Her laughter was enough to make Efren smile, she noticed. "There's no way he'd trust a Shannon to run any of his operations. Even one who had proven herself to his organization. That doesn't mean she wasn't living there all this time and helping. It's the only thing that makes sense."

"You think there's proof there that she knew the operation had continued all these years?" Roman asked, and Selina nodded. "If that's the case, and we can find it, it would take one assassin off your heels."

"Just not the most dangerous one," Selina said, gnawing on her lip. "There's no 'we' here, either." She dropped her hands and leaned into the console. "I won't put any of you at risk again. This is not your war to fight, and God knows you've all lost enough fighting other people's wars. This is my problem and my problem alone. From the moment I saw Ava standing at the nurses' station, I knew my days were numbered. There is no escaping the reach the Snake has when your time comes. My time has come to face off with this cobra, and I accept that. I can't accept anyone else getting hurt because of me."

"He's a man," Cal said, standing to his full height and leaning into the camera. "Not a god. He is not untouchable, Selina Colvert, and this team is damn good at its job. We protect and we serve, we just do it a bit differently than you're used to. That doesn't mean we don't get results. The storm is ramping up and we're about to lose connection. Stay put. Rest. Prepare. As soon as the storm is over, call in. We'll have an actionable plan. Do you understand me, Sierra?"

Selina wanted to argue, but knew it would do no good. "Understood."

"Good. Charlie, out."

The screen went blank, and she looked up into the

eyes of the man who had gotten her this far, but could end up a casualty of her past. She wasn't okay with that.

"I'm okay with it," he said, as though he were reading her mind. "I've fought less just wars than the one we're about to wade into, Colvert."

"Vaccaro has an army of soldiers, Efren." She was desperate to make him understand. "This is another war you can't win, but this time you'll pay with your life. If you send me alone, then no innocents have to die."

His finger came down on her lips to hush her. "He may have an army of soldiers, but they protect him for money. We protect you for love. That's why he will fail and you won't. Never forget that."

Chapter Thirteen

He shouldn't have used the L-word. He saw it in her eyes the moment he'd said it. She was dealing with enough, and that put pressure on her that she didn't need. Not that he meant it in a romantic sense, not using "we" before it, but she was an intelligent woman who was good at reading between the lines after working with men all her life. There was nothing he could do about it now other than continue to reassure her that the team was behind her and not going to let her face Vaccaro alone.

When Selina disappeared into the small bathroom to clean up, Efren had rummaged around the kitchen in hopes of finding some kind of canned good that was still edible. He wasn't expecting to pull open the fridge and encounter someone's canning stash. Why it was in the fridge, he had no idea, but he wasn't going to look a gift horse in the mouth. Admittedly, he held his breath when he tried to light the stove, fearing the propane tank in the backyard had long been empty. He was pleasantly surprised when it lit up and he was able to warm their dinner. The temperature was dropping outside, so rather than freeze the entire night, he'd also started the small propane cabin heater on low. He didn't know how long the propane would last, but it was better to warm up the cabin for as long as possible. If the propane ran out, they'd stay warm the rest of the night with the blankets from the bedroom. Always a gentleman, he'd give her the bed to sleep while he kept watch. He wasn't worried, though. The storm raging outside wasn't fit for man nor beast, but most especially not Vaccaro's men. The wind whipped against the cabin walls, and the river roared her way past them. Anyone out there tonight had a death wish.

"What smells so good?" Selina asked as she walked into the room. She was wearing a sweatshirt and pants that were too big for her, but she had the shirt tied in a knot to show her midriff and the pants cuffed at the ankles.

The sight of her bare midriff had him staring rather than speaking. "Uh, dinner," he was finally able to stutter. "What's with the outfit?"

"I found clothes in the dresser in there that were warm and clean. Saved a pair for you, too. I was surprised that there was warm water."

"Propane tank," he said, his throat still dry as he stared at the incision on her belly. "I thought it would be empty, but it's not. Shouldn't you have a bandage on that?"

Efren motioned her to the table where he had two sets of silverware waiting. She sat and he carried the hot pot of stew over, with veggies and brown bread for their feast.

"Dang," Selina whispered low when he set out the food. "Did you make a run to Winn-Dixie?"

He snorted as he slid into his seat. "I'd have to go pretty far to find a Winn-Dixie around here. I found all of this in the fridge. They were storing it in there. I thought that was a bit odd."

"Mmm," she said, taking a bite of the bread and chewing. "Not odd. An unplugged fridge will keep the canned goods from freezing in the winter if there's no heat. Then you just move them back to the shelf in the spring."

"I thought if there was no heat then there was no water? Why is there running water?"

"Insulated pipes," she answered around a bite of beef stew. "These cabins are mainly for summer, but a lot of trappers and snow lovers use them throughout the seasons. I feel like whoever owns this place isn't one of them. They come early spring through late fall."

"We can hope." He glanced at the door again, and she laughed.

"No one is coming out tonight. Was the barricade necessary?"

He glanced at the door again, where he'd shoved a heavy chest full of raincoats and other fishing equipment against it. "Yes. It won't stop anyone, but it will slow them down enough for us to bail out the bedroom window. We still need to avoid light hitting any of the windows. I'm sure the neighbors are also long gone, but we can't risk it."

"Penlights only, aimed at the floor. Oh, this is so good," she moaned as she took another bite of the bread. "I haven't had canned brown bread in years."

"I'll admit when I saw that I thought it was one of those fake cans where you hide your valuables or something. Never saw anything like it when that bread came out onto the plate."

"Are you from Mars?"

"California," he answered, and her lips tipped up on one side.

"That explains it."

"California explains why I've never seen bread in a can?"

"It's a Boston thing that's moved west, but probably not quite that far west. We keep it handy for power outages and snowstorms. The carbs keep you going, and you can eat it straight out of the can."

"I've eaten much worse meals ready to eat." He pointed at her belly. "Why isn't that bandaged?"

"I'm letting it get some air," she explained between bites. "The skin is red around the stitches, so after dinner, we're going to have to remove them."

"Remove them?" He propped his spoon in his bowl. "It's only been seven days since the surgery."

"Plenty long for my skin. I heal fast. If I let them go too long, they'll fester until they're infected. Trust me. I've had enough stitches in my life to know."

"I'm going to need more than a penlight to get them out."

"The bathroom doesn't have a window," she said. "We can close the door and get it done. I can do the front ones. You'll have to do the back ones."

He shuddered, drawing a laugh from her as she finished her stew. "The big bad bodyguard can't handle a few stitches?"

"Reminds me of my military days. Getting stitches in the field, or watching them desperately try to stitch a friend's body part closed long enough to get them to safety before they bled out." He cleared his throat and stood. "I found some cinnamon applesauce for dessert. Let me grab it."

As he walked away from her, he shoved the memories bubbling up inside him back behind the black curtain. Every so often, they liked to peek their head around the corner to remind him why he didn't *care*. Caring led to pain. He'd had more than enough of that for a lifetime.

EFREN PACED THE front porch, holding the sat phone in his hand. He'd left Selina inside to stay warm with the excuse that he needed to check the phone for messages. The storm had slowed for a bit, but there was still no way to get coverage inside the cabin. Would there be any messages? No, but he wasn't looking for them. He wanted to call Secure One when she wasn't within earshot so he could suggest a plan he knew she would never agree to.

The cold sleet pellets pounded on his back as he dialed Cal's secure phone. The phone didn't even ring before he heard, "Secure one, Charlie."

"Secure two, Tango," he answered. It sounded like a greeting, but it wasn't. It was a go-ahead between team members that it was safe to speak. If they answered any other way, they knew the team member was being tracked or held by the enemy. Considering what Cal used to do before he started Secure One, it was a legitimate way to ensure everyone's safety.

"Everything okay?" Cal asked. "I'm surprised to hear from you again, but I'm glad you called. I need your opinion on how Selina is doing after the surgery."

"Storm is raging here, as I'm sure you can hear. We just finished removing her stitches."

"Already? It's been seven days."

"Exactly what I said, but she's completely healed. Most bizarre thing I've ever seen. Do you know how many times she's been shot?"

"I suspected this wasn't the first," Cal said with a chuckle. "She was way too calm when she climbed out of that hole."

"To answer your question, she's in decent shape considering a bullet to the gut. She has a good appetite and has semi-okay stamina. The less walking we have to do, the better, though, for me and her."

"Noted. I know you don't have your other leg. How are you holding up?"

Efren bit his tongue to keep from telling the truth about his limb. They had bigger problems to solve, and his whining wasn't going to help. "Good. I can wear both legs interchangeably, though the blade can tire me out faster if I wear it too long. I'll be fine until this is resolved. Before we lose our connection, I need to talk to you about something when Selina isn't around."

"Of course you have my permission to date her. Not that you need it."

"I'm sorry?" He couldn't hold in his laughter.

"You aren't calling to ask me for her hand in marriage?"

"Smart-ass," Efren grumped as the cold wind whipped hard against his neck. "No, I'm calling to suggest we keep the cops out of the situation in Caledonia."

"What's your reason?"

"If the chance is given, we need to take out Vaccaro and Ava. Cops make that messy."

"Not untrue, but also, we aren't cops, and that's breaking the law."

"Oh, come on," Efren huffed, burrowing deeper into his coat to block the rain. "How many times in your life have you had to do bad things to benefit the greater good?"

"Too many, but does killing the Snake and Ava benefit the greater good or does it benefit Selina?"

Efren bit his lip and stepped closer to the cabin to keep from getting drenched. He was glad he'd saved his shower until after he made the call. He was going to need it. "It can't benefit both?"

"That depends on who comes out better off. Selina or the greater good."

Efren took a deep breath to keep from losing his temper with his boss. "It's like you want this guy to kill Selina, and he will, if we don't get to him first."

"Listen here, Brenna. The very last thing I want is to lose Selina from the team. She's paramount to everything we do here and while she may not see that, the rest of us do. I would take Vaccaro out with my bare hands if given the chance, but I can't risk the reputation of Secure One and what I've built here. What's the saying, cut off the head of a snake and a new one will take its place?"

Efren wasn't giving up. If they brought the cops in on this mission, Selina was going to die. "If the head of the snake is removed, you can bet the rest of the heads will be too busy scrambling to wonder where Selina Colvert has gone. All I'm asking is to wait and loop the cops in on this operation after the fact rather than before."

"Does Selina know you're asking this of the team?"

"Not yet."

Cal was silent, and Efren had to wonder what he was thinking. It was a big ask, but Selina would never be safe if they didn't stop Ava and Vaccaro. She deserved more out of life than constantly looking over her shoulder for the next bullet.

"I'll keep the cops out of our plans for now," Cal finally said. "For now. That could change depending on what we find when we get to Caledonia. Understood?"

"Loud and clear," Efren said, letting out a breath.

"Selina has always been the one to demand we bring the cops in. I'm not sure how she's going to feel about you going behind her back like this."

"Let me handle Selina. Do you have an actionable plan?"

"Working on it," Cal answered. "As soon as this storm clears, we're headed your way for backup."

"Is that safe? What if he's watching Secure One?"

"Let me worry about us here while you do your job there. Keep Selina safe tonight. Eat. Get rest. Try to remember we're a team and we do better working with each other instead of against each other. We'll be in contact in the morning. Charlie, out."

Efren dropped the phone to his side and turned to stare out at the storm. The wind whipped and howled, and the sleet pelted down, changing direction with each turn of the wind. If his soul were an image, that would be it. This had become more than an assignment the moment he'd put his lips on hers. If they were going to get out of this alive, he was going to have to keep his head in the game. It was his job to convince Selina that this was one time the cops didn't need to be involved until after Secure One had gone in and doled out a bit of karma to the two people who deserved it most. After spending the last few days with her, he suspected it wouldn't be a hard sell. This was one time Selina Colvert might agree that manipulating fate was the right thing to do.

Chapter Fourteen

The stitches were out and Selina was feeling much better about life, even as a storm rolled around outside their tiny wooden structure, a madman and her twin were after her, and the man she was trapped with had flipped a switch and turned into king jerk of the universe. There was nothing she could do about the storm, the madman or Ava, but she could talk to the man who had switched into defense mode to protect himself. He'd helped her with the stitches begrudgingly, more than a little surprised when her skin was perfectly healed as she'd predicted.

What he didn't know was that her trained eye picked up the bounce he did every three or four steps on his blade as he paced the small room. That was something he didn't normally do. They'd decided to stay in the main room for as long as the heater stayed running. Eventually, they'd take turns sleeping and keeping watch until the storm passed and they could connect with the team again. In the meantime, she was going to have to convince him to let her look at his limb and treat any problems with it before they became major ones. Considering his attitude over the last few hours, she suspected that would be easier said than done.

Efren was dealing with some internal battle Selina wasn't privy to. She could see it in his body language and the way he set his jaw. What he couldn't control was the look in his coffee-brown eyes every time he glanced at her. Every so often, he'd run his hand through his short, curly hair and sigh. An hour ago, he'd moved the wardrobe away from the front door and gone outside. She could see he was talking on the sat phone, but he refused to answer any of her questions about why he had to call Secure One. He paced, huffed and sighed like the entire world was on his shoulders. Considering the circumstances, it was a real possibility that was how he felt as he sat trapped in a cabin with her. They both knew what was coming, and their war would likely include fatalities. They just had to hope those fatalities were on the enemy's side.

She'd call him out about his phone call later. For now, she had a bigger problem to solve. "Stop." She stood in front of him so he had no choice but to. "You have a situation with your leg. Sit down so I can look at it."

"My leg is fine." He growled the words more than he spoke them, and she lifted a brow.

She wasn't new to dealing with surly guys who didn't want to take the time to deal with an injury. "It's not fine. Every four steps you're doing an unusual bounce to take pressure off the anterior side of the socket. Now, would you like to sit down so I can check the skin or would you like to stand here and argue about whether or not you have a problem when you know you're going to lose the argument anyway? I'm good either way. I have nothing else to do."

Efren glared at her with his lips pursed and his eyes

flaming. "You need to understand that I'm not comfortable with that idea. Let it go."

"Not happening. I don't care if you're uncomfortable. You're going to be more uncomfortable when you can't walk and we need to run. Pretend I'm a nurse at the VA if you have to, but sit down and take your socket off."

"I can't pretend you're a nurse at the VA," he said between clenched teeth as she dragged him to the couch near the heater. It put off a bit of light, and she'd need it to find the problem and repair it.

"Why not? You don't think I have the chops to be a nurse at the VA?"

"Oh, you have the chops, but I'm far more interested in you as a woman than any nurse I've dealt with at the VA."

He sat and she knelt in front of him, zipping off his pant leg to turn them into shorts. It was Mack who had found creative ways to dress the crew, who all had different braces and prostheses to wear. These pants worked great for getting their clothes changed quickly without taking their devices off. No one realized what a pain that was until they no longer had to do it. She removed the valve in the prosthesis to release the suction and glanced up at him. "I can be both and separate myself as each. Take it off."

His sigh was heavy, but he finally grasped the socket and pulled, carefully working it back and forth until it was off and he could set it aside. Selina took in the limb as a whole. His skin bore the typical changes that came with wearing a skin-fit prosthesis for years. The scar at the distal end of the femur was well done and shaped the limb nicely, but there was an area where a sore had developed.

Selina glanced up at him. "There's a hell of a blister on the scar."

"Kind of figured," he said, grasping his thigh and rubbing it. "The longer I wear the blade, the worse the phantom pain gets, and that changes my gait."

"Yet you refuse to let me take care of it when I have the skills to do it. Someone told me you were smart." Rather than wait for a response, she grabbed the first aid kit from his bag, and a clean towel from the bathroom cabinet. They'd both showered, which wasn't easy for him, but he'd managed by using a kitchen chair to sit on. The fact that he showered, saw the problem and refused to do anything about it really jacked her pickles. "You could have a little respect for what I do at Secure One." She tossed him the towel in anger, and he caught it midair. "Do your massage while I work on the blister."

"What are you so peeved about? I'm out here trying to help you, and you're giving me attitude."

"I'm giving you attitude because you showered, saw the problem and still didn't ask for help!"

He slung the towel under his thigh and moved it back and forth in a pattern he'd mastered, while she readied the first aid supplies she'd need to treat the blister and keep it from getting bigger. "I don't like coming to you for help."

"Well, thanks for the vote of confidence." Her eye roll punctuated the sarcasm in the sentence.

"Not because you're incompetent, Selina." He grabbed her hand, and she glanced up at him. "I'm supposed to be the one protecting you. How do you have confidence in that when I show you my weakest link?"

"It's not your weakest link, Efren. This doesn't stop you." She motioned at his leg. "What stops you is this." She tapped her temple. "You overthink things instead of following your gut. You're the one whispering in my ear to follow mine. Why aren't you doing the same?"

"Following my gut would be a dangerous thing for you, Selina Colvert. If you were wise, you'd rethink telling me to do so."

"I can hold my own with you, Efren Brenna." Without waiting for his response, she inspected the scar while he held the limb up with the towel. The blister had already popped, which made the cleaning and bandaging easier, but they'd have to watch for infection until they could get back to Secure One.

"Mina said you were injured by an IED but saved six men that day?" It was time to change the subject before she told him how much she wanted him to follow his gut when it came to her.

"For what it was worth, yes," he agreed.

"Purple Heart?" She swiped antiseptic over the wound. His next words were hissed. "Yep, and Bronze Star."

"What does it feel like to be a hero? Like a real hero?"

"Don't be condescending, Selina." His words were cold, and she glanced up to meet his clouded gaze. Whether it was pain or anger clouding it, she couldn't be sure.

"I'm not, Efren. It's a sincere question."

"I could ask you the same thing. You did an awful lot of saving when you were Eva Shannon."

"Not like you. Not missing a limb and bleeding out

on the field. That's next-level stuff right there. Besides, I wasn't a hero. I was a cop doing my job, and in the case of search-and-rescue, that was something I enjoyed doing that benefited others. That's it."

"I'm sorry for being short, but you made my point. I don't like the word *hero*. It sets my teeth on edge."

"Because?" She wanted to keep him talking so he wouldn't notice what she was doing with his limb. Keeping his mind focused on something other than her messing with the sore would hopefully keep him from having worse phantom pain when she finished. The nervous system and mind were so closely connected that it was difficult for amputees to train their brains not to focus on the pain, which was understandable. Unfortunately, messing with his limb was going to make it worse for a few days.

"I don't believe in heroes. Heroes are people we inflate in our minds as being more than human, and that's not right. Did I save six men that day in the field? Yes. Are they all still here on this earth? No. Since returning that day, we've lost three—one to his injuries and two to the scars the event left on their mind."

"I'm sorry. That's a tough reality, considering you went through the same experiences."

"It is, which is why I agreed to be a bodyguard when the opportunity came my way. I could protect people in danger for any number of reasons and deliver them safely to the other side. Score another soul for Efren that he managed to keep on this earth, at least for a little while longer. I know it isn't a healthy way to deal with the aftermath of the war, but I haven't figured out any other way."

"I wouldn't say it's unhealthy." Her fingers deftly applied a special transparent skin to the limb, and she held it gently while it settled in. "There are much worse ways of dealing with it."

"I've seen those ways, too, and didn't want to go down that road. I thought going back over there as a contractor would be better. It would give me more power to help those people, but it didn't. If anything, it gave me less power. I didn't like it, so I came back stateside and started protecting witnesses and domestic abuse survivors. That's where I found satisfaction in using my skills to help others."

"Why Secure One, then?"

"I came running because Mina called. That was the only reason. Mina, Roman and I worked together quite frequently when they were FBI. As one of the main bodyguards for WITSEC witnesses, we did a lot of co-ordinating."

"Ah, that explains why you were so concerned I was part of the program." Selina lowered his limb to the couch for support and pulled off her gloves to clean up the mess.

"That explains why I was so surprised to find out you did this on your own. Most people struggle to do it with the government behind them. I could only imagine how hard it was without them."

"It was a struggle, but I always knew that one day I might have to run, so I had planned for the contingency in the way I lived my life."

"What was it like growing up with a dad who was part of the Mafia? What did your mom think about it?"

"My mother died in childbirth. I was born first, but

Ava was breech. They saved Ava, but my mother was gone. Dad named me Eva because it means life and her Ava because it means to live. My mother was Italian and her name was Bibiana, which meant full of life. Dad always said we carried her life. All of that said, he had no idea how to raise two baby girls, so he hired a nanny who cared for us until we were old enough to go to school."

"Your dad never remarried?"

"Thankfully, no. We found out shortly after he died that my parents had only been married eight months before we were born."

"A shotgun wedding?"

"Apparently, and not one based on love. Uncle Medardo had insisted he make an honest woman out of her. He wanted my father to play the part of the family man to bolster Medardo's attempt to change the face of the organization."

"Uncle?"

"That's what we called him growing up," Selina said with a shrug. "Looking back on it, it was weird, but we didn't know that he was a cold-blooded killer who used people like napkins and threw them away when he was done. Hell, we lived with a man who would kill on command."

"Did you know what your dad's job was? Seems like an odd thing to tell your kids."

"He didn't tell us. According to him, he was Uncle Medardo's business partner. I was twelve when I learned what he did for a living." She pointed at his socket. "Do you have pads you can put in there to protect that spot?"

"The small black bag in the front zipper. What happened when you were twelve?"

Selina walked to his go bag and knelt, pulling out the smaller supply bag and carrying it over to him. "I was supposed to wait in the car that night." She sat next to him and took his limb onto her lap, starting the towel massage so he could fix the socket. "He was taking forever and I was hungry. Since he'd gone into a pizzeria, I figured I'd run in, grab a snack and be back before he missed me."

"Instead?"

"Instead, I walked into the restaurant to see my father aiming a gun at a man who was on the ground groveling for his life. The man next to him already had a bullet between his eyes. My father said, this is done by order of the Snake, and then put a bullet between that guy's eyes. Thankfully, they were in a side room and my father never knew I was there. I got back in the car and waited for him like I hadn't just witnessed him kill someone. Intrinsically, I knew it would be dangerous to my life if I let on about what I saw, so instead, I spent six years plotting out a way to take him down when I got old enough. I saw police work as the only way, so as soon as I graduated from high school, I went to the academy. I had dreamed of one day being in the FBI, but I knew a dream was all it would ever be. What about you? Are your parents alive?"

"Yep, alive and well," he said as he added a pad to the socket. "My dad is from Italy, and my mom is from Bolivia. My dad worked for the UN, so I was born here in the States. They eventually became citizens when they retired."

"That explains the exotic skin tone," she said, running her hand up his forearm. "Mina always says you're the epitome of tall, dark and handsome."

"Do you agree?"

"It would be hard to disagree with that statement. Do you talk to your parents often?"

"Nice pivot, Colvert," he said, chuckling. "I talk to them every Sunday and keep them updated about where I am. I got a message to them while you were at the hospital that I was on a new case and didn't know when I'd call next. They've always been supportive of what I do, but they've enjoyed me working at Secure One. They like that I've found a way to do what I love and have a brotherhood again. They've seen how the loner lifestyle changed me, I suppose, and as parents do, they worry."

"Is that why you've stayed at Secure One? For the brotherhood?" Selina was trying to concentrate on doing the massage the way he did while they talked. It was her fault he was in this bind, so she would do what she could to give him some relief.

"That's one of the reasons I've stayed. It's refreshing to work with a team of people I trust where we're doing good things to help people. Even if we have to operate under the law a bit to do it."

"I try to avoid that," she said with a bit of a lip tilt. "Sometimes we can, sometimes we can't. When it came to Randall Jr., we couldn't. When it comes to the Snake, we will, and I fully support that."

His brows went up. "Seriously? You're okay with not bringing the cops in on this?"

"There's a certain finesse that will be needed on this case. No one knows that better than me. Is that what your little tête-à-tête was about out there? You could have talked to me about it before you went to Cal."

"I was going to, but I wanted his approval before I presented it as an option to you. It doesn't matter what our plans are if Cal's are different. He runs the show."

"True. We'll have to bring the cops in, but it can be after the fact."

"After what fact? After Ava and Vaccaro are dead?"

"If that's what has to happen," she answered. "Are you going to leave Secure One after this and go back to bodyguarding?"

His laughter was quiet as he shook his head. "We'll have to discuss the plan in further detail, but I'll let it go until morning when we meet with the team. As for what happens after this case, no, I'm not leaving Secure One." He finished with the socket and set the leg down. "Cal has hired me on full-time. He's starting the cybersecurity division now with Mina, and he needs a strong team for the rest of the security work. I'll be bodyguarding, but for Secure One instead of the government. It will be a tighter team when this op is over."

"What does that mean?" She paused with the towel, confused by his statement.

"It means that it's time for you to set your stethoscope aside and pick up your gun again. You proved yourself last week as an invaluable operative. If Cal wants me to stay, we're a package deal."

"You're going to quit if he doesn't move me to operations from medical?"

"Without a moment's hesitation. My goal in life is to right wrongs, and you're a wrong that Cal needs to make right. You have the training and the chops to do what all those other guys do, the only difference is, you're a woman. I would hope by now, Cal has seen the difference all the women who have joined Secure One have made to his business. If he doesn't, then I don't want to work for him."

"Despite how I've treated you?"

"Partly because of the way you treated me. It intrigued me. I wanted to know why you were so upset that I was there when the team so obviously needed help. I understand now." His finger traced her cheek, and the sensation sent a skitter of desire through her. "You didn't hate me. You hated what I represent."

"It wasn't fair to you." Her whispered admittance released a tightness in her chest she'd been carrying for too long. "I hated you for coming in and stealing my chance to take down the Red River Slayer."

"That's nonsense. I had nothing to do with that capture. I was there to guard the senator's daughter."

"But had they needed another person, they weren't going to pull the nurse off the injured woman, were they? No, they were going to go to the tall, dark and handsome stranger who had proven himself in the same war they'd fought."

"That's fair, and logical. Coupled with what you were dealing with as the caretaker of these women, I can understand the hostility you felt toward the newcomer. The Red River Slayer case has been over for almost a year. Why the continued animosity?"

"I'm always nervous when Cal brings someone new in. The Snake's reach is far and wide."

"I'm not a Vaccaro plant. I've only been to Chicago once."

"I know. And that's not why I've kept you at arm's length. There's this draw between us that's too hard to fight if I don't put up a wall." He gently pushed her hands aside and rolled on an elastic sock.

"That will control the nerves for now. As much as I love having your hands on me, I can't handle having your hands on me." He tugged her up onto the couch next to him and grasped her hands. "I feel the draw, too. Why do you want to fight it?"

Why did she want to fight it? That was a complicated answer to a simple question. "For starters, I'm a woman in a man's world."

"That's not the reason," he said, grasping her chin and forcing eye contact. "Mina is a woman in a man's world. So are Charlotte and Marlise."

"I'm not them." Her words were defensive. "I've had different life experiences. I don't know how to connect the way they do. Even if we wanted to explore this draw, I wouldn't know how."

"Wrong. You're scared. Just admit it, and then we can move on. We have to stop being afraid to be afraid. We have to stop letting the fear control us and use the fear to motivate us. Do you want me to admit it first? Okay. I'm scared of what this draw between us could mean. Every look, every interaction, every time I kiss you, it's a reminder that I can still feel. After I lost my leg and the men I cared about, I swore that I would never fall in love or have a long-term relationship. Life can change in an instant and someone you love can be taken just as quickly. Then I met you, and your attitude toward me hurt. Suddenly, I cared that you didn't like me even though you didn't know me. Those were dangerous feelings. I'm not supposed to care, but when it comes to you, I do. I care what you think about me, and I worry that this—" he motioned at his leg "—makes you think that I can't protect you as well as Roman or Cal could."

"No." The word was said quickly and with conviction. "I would trust you to protect me as much or more than I'd trust Cal or Roman."

"Why?"

"You've proved your mettle, Efren. You've kept me alive longer than I ever thought possible when Vaccaro entered our lives again. You haven't just kept me alive, but you've included me in the decisions that affect my life. That's more than anyone else at Secure One has done. You demand respect for yourself and the same respect for me. The only time the amputation is a factor is when you're limping and not taking care of yourself. That doesn't mean you can't protect me. You would lay down your life for me, which, while misguided, is the true definition of protection."

"Misguided? Why would dying for you be misguided?"

"Because no matter how much you give, you can't save me, Efren. You'd lay down your life and he'd slither right over you to get to me."

"Maybe you're right. Maybe I can't save you, but I can support you while you save yourself. You don't need a hero, Selina. You can fight Vaccaro and win as long as you have the right team behind you. Secure One is the right team. Every single one of your friends back home is busy making a plan to defend you. Find that woman inside you who stood on the top of a bluff and asked a man who loved her to support her one last time. Find the woman who survived and thrived on her own despite having the deck stacked against her. Let her guide you again, and the rest of us become soldiers in *your* army."

She was straddling him now to get closer. To be closer to the man who saw things in her that she didn't see in herself. "What if I want you to be more than a soldier?" Her question was soft as she lowered her head toward his, their noses touching as she waited for him to answer.

"I thought you were scared to be more with me."

"You told me to stop being afraid of being afraid. It sent me back to the woman who stood on a bluff and broke a man's heart in order to do the right thing. She used fear as motivation. Right now, that fear is motivating her to kiss you, Efren Brenna."

"Then she should quit talking about it—"

He didn't have a chance to finish the sentence before her lips were on his and the storm inside was stronger than the one knocking on their door.

Chapter Fifteen

"Selina, we have to stop," Efren said against her warm lips. Lord knew he didn't want to, but he also knew if he had this woman once, he'd want her every day for the rest of his life, and that was not in the cards for him.

Stop being afraid of being afraid.

He inhaled a breath, hating that voice for being right and being wrong at the same time. This wasn't being afraid of being afraid. This was protection. This was the way he protected himself from having to live in a world where his failures as a man and a soldier were always with him.

"We don't." Selina leaned back and took his face in her hands. "This connection between us has already been made. Trying to fight it will only be a lesson in frustration."

"Oh, trust me, I'm frustrated," he assured her, shifting under the sweet warmth of her draped across his lap. "That doesn't mean it's a good idea. Emotions complicate everything."

"You're right," she said, kissing the right side of his lips. "The biggest thing they complicate is our internal fight to protect our hearts from the pain of losing someone. It's an unfortunate side effect of the jobs we've done in the past. Those memories stay with us and shape every decision we make in the future. If we let them." She whispered the final sentence in his ear, and it sent a shiver of anticipation, expectation and desire down his spine. "How long are we going to give it that power before we pull it back and control our future again?"

"Up until a year ago, I'd planned to give it the power for the rest of my life. Tonight, here with you on my lap, I'm rethinking that plan."

"I bet I can make you rethink it quicker," She lifted a brow, and it transformed her from the beautiful woman she was to a sexy vixen whom he wanted to make love to for the rest of his life. Selina slipped her hand between them and caressed his undeniable source of frustration.

He grasped her face and attacked her lips, thrusting against her hand while he searched for relief from the sweet torture she doled out. "Let me put my leg on," he said against her lips. "We'll go to the bedroom."

She leaned out of the kiss and lifted herself on her knees. Her shirt came off in a slow striptease, offering a full frontal that turned him on and hurt him at the same time. He traced the scars that marred her skin while he held her eye. It wasn't until his hands moved toward the clasp on her bra that she spoke. "We're not going to the bedroom. I want to make love to you right here, being open and honest with each other with all of our scars visible. These scars are part of us and will remain that way forever. I accept yours, Efren. Do you accept mine?"

He didn't answer with words. He deftly twisted her until she was on her back on the small sofa and he was kissing every scar across her belly, his featherlight touch raising goose bumps across her bare skin as he moved farther north. It wasn't until those kisses landed on her nipples that she inhaled deeply. "Efren, make me yours. Now."

Her words shot fire through him, and he finished relieving them of their clothes until every painful scar and emotion was laid bare. "I have to grab some protection," he whispered as he kissed his way up the inside of her thigh.

"We don't need any."

The way she said it made him lift his head to meet her gaze. Her eyes were open and honest, and he chastised himself for forgetting something so important in the moment. He slid alongside her until he was able to kiss her lips. "I'm sorry. I forgot. Can we even do this? It hasn't been that long since your surgery."

"I'm fine," she assured him, running her hand through his hair. "I just want to feel something other than scared tonight. I'm not afraid of being with you anymore. I have no control over the storm outside, but I have control of the one inside me. That storm says only you can calm it, but first, you're going to have to fight through the waves threatening to take you under."

"I'm not afraid of those waves," he promised, scooting back on the couch and lifting her gently by her waist to sit across him. "Let's dive in and let them take us under together."

Selina leaned forward and took his lips with hers, kissing him senseless while her warmth settled around him. It was a moment before the sensation broke through the high he was on from holding her sweet body. When it did, he thrust upward with a moan nearly as loud as the ones from the storm outside.

"Selina," he hissed, thrusting his hips against hers until they were locked together in harmony and ecstasy.

She leaned back and braced herself on his thigh, taking him under the waves for a moment before she brought him back up, setting him on top to savor the pleasure. She paused, their heightened senses meshing as they entangled their hands and rode out the storm. With a satisfied sigh, they rested together in the calmness of their connection.

SELINA PACED THE small cabin as she tried to put together in her mind a way to make Vaccaro and Ava disappear from her life. She paused near the couch where the man she'd made love to three times in the same number of hours now rested. She'd insisted he catch a nap since she knew she wouldn't sleep. She was energized by the great sex but riddled with anxiety about what was to come—both with Vaccaro and her life now that she'd admitted she cared for Efren.

Stop being afraid of being afraid.

Those six words echoed through her head as she kept an eye on the perimeter of the cabin. The lesson she took from those words was to live life afraid. Playing it safe means the only winner is fear. In this case, playing it safe with Vaccaro meant he would be the winner in this decades-long game of cat and mouse. Playing it safe with Efren meant they'd both lose. They were good together, both as work partners and as life partners.

"Life partners?" she muttered. Back up the wagon. They shared some secrets and made love—no, they had sex three times. Not the definition of life partners. The question she kept trying to block from her mind—the one where the answer made her afraid—was, could they be life partners given a little more time and trust?

She was afraid because the answer, at least for her, was yes. She had always had feelings for Efren that went beyond basic colleagues. This night made their lives so much more complicated, especially considering she was still being hunted by a madwoman with an axe to grind. And she had no doubt they were still being hunted. This little interlude had been too good to be true, and as soon as the sun came up in a few hours, a memory was all it would be. A memory was all it would ever be if she didn't figure out a way to get Vaccaro and Ava off her back and keep Randall Sr. in prison.

Selina's heart pounded hard in her chest at the thoughts running through her head. If she could get that witness statement signed before Randall went before the judge, she might be able to keep him in prison. Efren's words came back to her then, and her shoulders slumped. He was right. Even if she did get the statement signed, if Vaccaro had already paid off the judge, she was risking her life for nothing. There had to be a better way.

Fear was keeping her from thinking through the better way. The fear she'd carried for so long wanted her to run back to Secure One and hide behind the fortress while someone else fought her battles. The other side of the fear told her she'd done that long enough. It was time she stepped up and took control of her own destiny again. When she was Eva Shannon, she was the kind of person who didn't hesitate when a decision had to be made, fear or no fear. She faced the fear head-on in her job so many times that it had simply become how she lived her life until her entire life became a calculated risk.

Selina had spent too long not taking any risks, calculated or otherwise. That, she realized, was why she hadn't pushed Cal to make her part of the core team as something other than medical. While she was mad about it, she was also afraid to rock the boat. If Cal did make her part of the team, then the safety she'd found in the med bay would be gone. She'd have to expose herself to the outside world again. Her life had become a yin-yang that she couldn't break. She wanted something she couldn't have but didn't want what she already had.

Selina recalled the woman who stood on that bluff eight years ago. That woman had an actionable plan that put her in complete control. That woman wasn't afraid to ask for everything from someone when she couldn't repay him. That woman was not afraid of the fear that engulfed her because the fear kept her alive.

She paused and gazed at Efren, his hair tousled in sleep and a deep five-o'clock shadow covering his chin. She wanted him more than any man she'd wanted in her lifetime. Fear rocketed through her at the idea of asking someone to be part of her life when her life was always a calculated risk. She'd let fear stop her from asking Kai. She couldn't make the same mistake with Efren, right? They had survived bombs, bullets and pain to get here. Those bombs and bullets didn't take their lives, which meant they shouldn't let them take their future.

Determined to get her life back, she grabbed a notebook and pen, then stood to the side of the window to use the light of the moon to write. The storm had blown out of town about an hour ago, and as happened in Minnesota, the sky cleared off immediately, dropping the temps to a teeth-chattering cold. The rain and sleet that had fallen was surely going to freeze, turning everything into an ice-skating rink until the sun came out to melt it. They'd have to be extra careful when they left the cabin so Efren didn't slip. His limb was already in rough shape, and falling could mean life or death for them. Thankfully, he had his spiked sole and his all-terrain sole with him.

What was that sound? Her brain registered it and dropped her to the floor under the window. She crab-walked to the other side of the cabin to peer out the window on that side from under the curtain. Her fear had been confirmed. A drone hovered around the yard, obviously trying to get a look inside the cabin. They had turned the propane heater off and with no lights on, as long as they stayed low, the drone would show its pilot nothing but an empty cabin.

Still in a crouch, Selina moved to the couch and put her hand on Efren's chest from where she sat on the ground. His eyes opened immediately and met hers. "Drone," she mouthed, and he slid off the couch onto the floor, curling himself around her as they listened for the faint sound of the flying spy to disappear—if it disappeared.

"How did they find us?" he whispered into her ear.

"Vaccaro has eyes everywhere, but this is a stretch even for me. We've left no digital trail and made no purchases."

"That's not entirely true," Efren whispered. "The sat phone leaves a digital trail when it goes to the service provider for billing, but Cal assured me it was safe to use."

"Nothing and no one is safe from Vaccaro. You used the phone what, five hours ago? They already found us. I'm surprised all we have is a drone in the air and not ten guys knocking down the door."

"Only because a satellite phone can't pinpoint where the call is coming from. It will give them a quadrant to search, so they know we are in the area, but they don't know our precise location. Using a drone makes sense. As soon as it's gone, so are we."

"To where?" Selina asked, rolling over to make eye contact.

"Anywhere but here. We need to get free of this place and then get connected with the team. I'm done letting this idiot control our lives."

"Me, too," she whispered with a nod. "I have a plan, but it's going to require backup from Secure One and a dance with a devil who's the spitting image of me."

"Wrong," he hissed, slamming his lips into hers to quiet them. "You may be identical twins, but that woman wears her evil like a fine linen cloak. You're like night and day. Remember, your fear feeds the devil, but if you stay strong, you'll starve her for good."

"That's where you're wrong," she whispered. "The devil gets her power from a snake, but once we've shredded his scaly body and buried him ten feet deep, the devil will become mortal once again. I no longer fear Ava or Vaccaro. I fear giving up another second of my life to them. Eva Shannon may be dead, but before she went over that cliff, she transferred her power to Selina Colvert. The time to bide is over. The time to do is upon us." She paused and they listened, but the night was silent again. "Are you ready to act rather than react?"

He pushed himself up and then held out his hand for her. "Secure one, Tango."

Selina slid her palm into his and let him pull her up. "Secure two, Sierra."

Quickly, they dressed for the weather and readied their bags. Selina held up a fist at the door of the cabin and they listened for several moments, but heard nothing but silence. "When we get out there, follow me and don't ask questions."

"Ten-four."

Efren pressed against her back, but she paused. "Ten-four? No arguments?"

"I knew from the moment I met you that I'd follow you anywhere, Sierra."

A ghost of a smile played on her lips as she opened the door. Today was the day she took her life back.

Chapter Sixteen

The night was as cold as Efren was expecting it to be, but he'd stayed close on Selina's heels, his gun out and his head on a swivel as they worked their way downstream, following the river. She had a plan, so he was going to let her lead until she asked for help. Selina didn't need anyone to save her. She could save herself as soon as she channeled the woman she'd hidden away so many years ago. That must have happened during the hour he'd been asleep, because the woman leading him now was completely different than the one he'd known over the last year.

Then again, as he thought about it, he'd been watching it happen over the course of the last week. Slowly, she was coming to realize that waiting around for someone else to help her out of this jam wasn't the answer. If she wanted to be free of Ava and Vaccaro, she was going to have to do the saving herself, even if it scared her.

And it scared her.

He could see it in her eyes when the drone was flying over their heads, but she hadn't buckled to the fear. She'd used it to spur her forward, and something told him she was just getting started. Their lovemaking came back to him, and he couldn't help but smile, even as they trudged along the cold, wet banks of the Mississippi. He loved nothing more than when a woman was willing to dominate him in the bedroom. Did he always allow it? No, but last night, he sensed that it was a first step for Selina to be in control again, and he was all too happy to give her that power. She deserved it. She harnessed it, and now she would use it to find her twin and put an end to this game of hide and seek.

For him, the most challenging part would be to put the image of her sweet, hot body on top of his out of his mind long enough to help her get the job done. Especially since the things his body told him about his time with her confused his mind and heart. Selina deserved a better life than she'd lived the last decade, but that didn't mean he could be the one to give her that life. Damn if he didn't want to, though. He couldn't remember the last time someone turned him on with a lifted brow and a snide remark, but Selina did every time.

His body contracted at the memories of the way she turned him on. His mind was blown at the number of times he'd made love to her last night and still couldn't get enough of her. He wanted her now. Cold, tired, hungry and sore, he'd still lay her down on the beach and frolic in the sand with her.

"Almost there," she whispered through a huffed breath as they hurried through the woods.

"Almost where?" He hoped she knew where she was going, because he was utterly lost. They'd been running parallel to the river, but other than that, it looked like trees and not much else.

"We need to get somewhere safe to call into Secure

One before daybreak. We can't risk turning on the emergency tracking beacon, even if Cal says it's hidden from everyone but him. Vaccaro has bested us at every turn."

Selina was right, and Efren ran the crew at Secure One through his mind, looking for a mole. Their newest hire, Sadie Cook, had suffered at the hands of the Loraines, which was what prompted all of this just a few weeks ago, so there was no way it was her. He made a mental note to suggest to Cal that he check his people again. Efren hadn't been at Secure One long enough to know everyone well, but if there was a Vaccaro mole in play, Cal would find them.

"That drone could still be out here," he whispered as they pulled up to a tree and stopped. Selina leaned over to give her side a break and take a breather. He rubbed her back, hoping to relieve some tension there from the injury she was still dealing with despite her rapid improvement. "I haven't heard it again, though, so Vaccaro doesn't have a lock on us yet. My gut says that could still change."

"That's why we moved as fast as we did," she agreed. "We couldn't get picked up by their drone, but I also didn't want to miss our ride out of here."

"Our ride out of here?"

After straightening again and doing a bit of a side stretch, she pointed at the area in front of them that was still pitch black. "What time is it?"

He flipped his wrist to check his watch. "It's 4:37. Daybreak will be coming soon."

"So will our ride."

"Did you hire a rescue chariot? Because all I see is darkness."

"What you don't see are the train tracks in front of us," she whispered with a satisfied glint in her eye. "There will be a train coming along in the next few minutes. It's our ticket out of town."

Efren slid his hand into hers and turned her to face him. "We can't jump a train, Selina. That's crazy dangerous. I've already lost a leg. I can't afford to lose an arm, too."

"Why do you think I picked this spot? We could have picked up the tracks not too far from the cabin, but the train would be going too fast. By the time the train gets to this part of the track, it's slowing for a junction ahead. Your grandma could get on it at that point, so jumping the train will be safe and easy. Finding an open boxcar will be harder. Worst case, we take the stairs on the caboose, but that will leave us open to sight once the sun comes up."

"How do you know all this? We don't even know exactly where we are."

"Last night, while you were sleeping, I heard a whistle off in the distance. Mina said we were north of Winona, so that meant there was a cargo train moving through the area. All I had to do was be here when one went by. Luckily, we won't have to wait long. I'll have to thank Vaccaro when I see him for sending that drone up and getting us out the door early."

"How do you know all of this?" he asked as she kept her head turned up the track.

When she turned back, she wore a sad smile. "This is my old stomping grounds for search-and-rescue, Efren. We did a lot of work on the Mississippi and the surrounding areas. The bluffs near La Crosse are just downriver from here a bit."

"Are those the bluffs you—"

"No," she said with a shake of her head, already knowing what he was thinking. "But it's the same type of topography. Being here, it makes me nostalgic for those days and the days I used to spend with Zeus and Kai tracking the lost and wounded. On the other side of the coin, it makes me angry that Vaccaro stole my passion and turned me into someone else entirely."

"That's not true," he said, stepping up and taking her face in his hands. "You're still the same caring person who wants to rescue others. You just do it in a different way now."

Her head tipped in his hands, and her beautiful navy blue eyes turned confused. "I put Band-Aids on scrapes and hydrate grown men who push themselves too far?"

"You also nursed hurt and scared women back to health to the point that they can now lead healthy, happy lives with a man, which is a testament to the care they got at Secure One. Just a few weeks ago you took on the role of caregiver again when you took care of a scared baby and his aunt, while terrified of the man after them, I may add. Then you set the fear aside and stepped up with the information the team needed to prepare for a mission. A mission you went on to rescue two people in danger where you paid heavily. If that weren't enough, over the last year, week and last night, you rescued me." He leaned in to kiss her softly without lingering, but did allow his thumb to keep caressing her temple.

"Rescued you from what?"

"The need to be everyone's savior. The self-hatred I

carried about the men I've lost since returning to friendly soil. The fear that I would never be enough for anyone and the loneliness I've been drowning in for years."

"My catty attitude toward you did all of that?" She tipped her head up to make eye contact, and he saw the truth in her eyes. She needed to know that he didn't hold any of that against her.

He hoped what she saw there was more than his words could convey. "It did, sweetheart. That attitude set an ember burning in my chest again. It gave me a reason to fight when I no longer had the spirit. This past week, when you've put your trust in me to keep you safe, it reminded me that I can still do the job. Last night, when you put your trust in me as a woman, it reminded me that I still have something to offer the right person, even if we come from different experiences in life." She gazed at him, as though she was unsure what to say, so he dropped a soft kiss on her lips and then tipped his head upstream. "I think I hear the train."

That sentence snapped her out of her trance, and she whipped her head to the right, listening for a moment before she nodded. "It's coming. We need to get in position, which means still in the trees, but once the conductor is past, we get as close to the cars as we can. As soon as we see a workable situation, we go for it."

"The conductor won't see us?"

"Not in the dark and on his flank." She moved to the edge of the trees and flipped down her night-vision goggles. "You with me, Tango?"

After flipping his goggles down, he nodded with a smile. "Right behind you, Sierra."

Somewhere between the time the train passed and the

time he followed her onto an empty train car, he knew he'd always be behind her, rooting for her, and probably, if he were honest, loving her, even if from afar.

THE TRAIN RIDE had been slow, but Selina was happy for a chance to sit down and give her side a break. It was healing, but her stamina was minimal, which meant pushing herself when all her body wanted to do was rest. Preferably rest in bed with the man who had held her during the train trip so she could lean against his chest and be comfortable.

Physically, she'd been comfortable, but emotionally, she'd been fighting against the things he'd said to her in the dark woods. His words made her rethink her place at Secure One again and what she wanted when this mission was over. Then again, wanting and getting were two entirely different words in the English language; no matter what she wanted, she would get what Vaccaro wanted her to have and nothing more. Unless they could take him and Ava down, she'd only get another ticket to run.

Selina shook off those thoughts and hung her legs over the edge of the doorway, motioning for Efren to do the same. "As soon as it starts to slow a bit more, push yourself off, drop and roll. Don't try to land on your feet."

"Got it, boss," he said, readying his hands to copy hers.

Jumping on and off trains was dangerous business that no one should be doing, but when it was a matter of living another day or falling into the Snake's hands, she'd take her chances with the train. At least she could walk away from the train with her life and limbs. The same couldn't be said of the Snake. She felt the slowing of the train under her and glanced at Efren. "See that opening in the trees?" Her finger swung out to the right, and he nodded. "Let's aim for that."

"You jump first. I'll follow once you land. That way, we won't land on each other."

Her nod was quick as she scooted to the edge, waiting for the right moment. Selina had no doubt that sticking this landing would hurt, but landing in the Snake's den would hurt worse. With a deep breath in, she pushed off the car, being sure to land on her right side, not that it mattered much when the hard earth smacked her ribs and sent a ricochet of pain through her entire body. Her momentum rolled her once before her backpack stopped her on the second roll. Selina scrambled to her feet, barely breathing, and ran for the opening in the woods as she watched Efren do the same from his southern position.

"You okay?" he asked as soon as he'd joined her, grasping her elbows to steady her. "I saw you land pretty hard on your side."

"There wasn't a choice, but I'm fine," she said between hissed breaths as she tried to make that statement true. "How's your leg?"

"Better than your side." He was eyeing her closely, probably trying to decide if he needed to carry her.

She forced herself to stand straight and then stretched side to side, trying to work out any last cramps from the fall and to keep new ones from starting. "We missed our check-in time with Secure One. It couldn't be helped, but we need to call in."

"Using the sat phone means another pin of our location for Vaccaro."

"Do we have a choice?" she asked, pulling the phone from her bag. "Last time it took him five hours to get the info. We'll be long gone in five hours."

When the screen came alive, Selina turned it so Efren could read the message. "Shady Lakes Campground. Number 117. ASAP. How are we supposed to know where that is? We don't even know where we are right now."

"You don't, but I do, and Cal knows it." Selina lowered the phone, but she couldn't keep her hand from shaking. Twisting to face south, she pointed to her left. "Ahead half a klick is the marina near Brownsville, which means we're about four klicks from the campground."

Without another word, Selina took off through the woods, knowing he would follow her without question. She had her compass out, following it south and then jogging west, praying her stamina held long enough to get to the campground. A mile and a half in, she slowed to a walk, bending over to catch her breath while Efren came up behind her, rubbing her side the way he did when she was hurting. Before she could speak, he relieved her of the backpack and carefully slipped his hand under her jacket to massage her side until the cramping eased.

"You gotta take it easy, sweetheart," he whispered in her ear. "This is a marathon, not a sprint."

"I know," she said, her breath still coming in spurts. "But the sooner we can link up with the team, the better. Wasting time because I'm weak could be a death sentence." She kicked the ground in front of her in frustration.

Efren wrapped his arms all the way around her and held

her to him. "You're not weak. A weak person wouldn't have jumped a train, jumped off a train and then run for two miles without stopping. You're recovering. You're not weak. There's a difference. Now, before we go any farther, are you familiar with the campground?"

"I've been there a few times for search-and-rescue, and it's a mix of modern and remote. The number he gave us is remote. We can bypass the campground through the woods and come at the site from the back side."

"When you're ready and at your pace," he said, releasing her, but slinging her backpack over his shoulders.

He would lighten the burden for her any way he could. She offered him a smile and then took off again, at a slower pace, not wanting to go too far past the campground. She was running blind without the convenience of a map or GPS, so she had to use her memory of her past to guide her. Those were painful. Those memories conjured the face of the man she'd left behind and the companion who had loved her unconditionally and understood her completely. How she had missed them both.

Memories of last night played through her mind, and she couldn't help but smile. She couldn't live in the past. She could only learn from it. She made a vow to herself right there as she slowed, sidestepping toward the edge of the trees and motioning for Efren to follow, that she'd take her life back. She'd find a way to be Selina Colvert and Eva Shannon for the benefit of others again.

She waved her hand at her throat as Efren stepped up to her. "That's 117, but it's empty. Did they leave?"

"Not without sending another coordinate," Efren answered, his eyes firing all around them. "The hair on the back of my neck is standing up, though, so we need to make a decision."

With clarity comes wisdom. That was a line Kai always said when they couldn't find their target on searches. "With clarity comes wisdom," Selina whispered. "Watch my back."

Before he could stop her, she broke through the brush and jogged to the wooden sign that said 117. She felt the thin ledge under it near the stake it was attached to. Sure enough, there was a piece of paper waiting. She grabbed it and ran back to Efren, who had his gun out and was sweeping the woods intently. Something had him spooked. He held his finger to his lips and waved his hand at his throat as he pointed at the note, then motioned for her to go south again.

She read the note as she pulled her gun from her holster and started forward. One klick west. That was it. Something told her getting one klick west was going to be hard won.

Chapter Seventeen

There had to be a mole in Secure One. Nothing else made sense. Efren motioned for Selina to move behind a tree, where they paused, listening for footsteps. If there wasn't a mole, then Vaccaro had a beacon on their location without Cal's knowledge. Considering the lengths Cal went to in order to ensure their security, that was saying something. Then again, if you ran a large crime organization, it was doubtful anyone could keep you from getting what you needed in a timely manner.

"What did the note say?" The whisper into her ear was barely audible.

She didn't speak; she held up one finger and then three. He nodded. One klick west. That wasn't far, unless they were ambushed on the way, and the hair on the back of his neck said that was a real possibility.

He leaned in closer again, keeping his gun pointed forward. "They're breaking through Cal's security layers. We can't lead them to Cal's front door."

"We can't have a gunfight this close to the campground," she hissed. "Too many civilians."

"I'm afraid that choice may not be ours. Let's move southwest and see what develops. Stay close. We don't have the big guns." Selina glanced down at her handgun and grimaced, which was exactly how he felt. The bad guys had the big guns this time, and they were at a deadly disadvantage.

They hadn't made it ten steps when motion caught his eye. "Behind you!" They yelled in unison, both swinging around on instinct with their guns, right into a hulking body in black.

Efren threw a punch blindly, hoping to connect with the assailant who had knocked his gun away already. His fist glanced off the guy's shoulder but when he brought his knee up, it landed square in the nether regions. The guy grunted and doubled over, stunned long enough for Efren to finish him off with a hit to the trachea. The dude dropped and Efren recovered his gun and rolled, coming up in the shooter's stance, searching for Selina. A grunt whipped his head around and he saw Selina stumble backward as the guy pummeled her in the kidneys, rendering her motionless. She couldn't take much more, so he waited for her to drop to the ground and then fired off one perfectly placed round. The guy spun like a ballerina before he dropped like a rock, his carotid emptying his lifeblood onto the ground.

"Selina!" Efren whisper-yelled, scrambling to the woman who was now writhing on the ground. On his way, he scooped up her weapon and grabbed her by her jacket, pulling her behind a tree. "Talk to me, baby." He knelt over her, his lips near her ear as he waited for her to breathe normally again.

"I'm okay." The words were huffed, and he knew she wasn't okay, but she would be. "I'm real sick and tired of these guys popping up like Whac-A-Moles."

He smiled. Yeah, she was going to be fine. "Can you sit up? Lean against the tree for support." He helped her into a seated position, but his gaze darted around the woods, searching for more goons. "We will have to move as soon as you're able. There could be more out there."

"Two or four but never more," she recited as she rubbed at her side with a grimace. "Uncle Medardo used to say that to my father all the time. Dad told us it was a rule about nails and how many go in a board. How dumb was I?"

"You weren't dumb," he whispered with half a chuckle. "You were a kid. The theory being more than four leaves room for capture?"

"That's my assumption," Selina said, pushing herself up when they heard a pop.

They dropped, both waiting for a bullet to slam into one of them or a tree above their heads, but there was nothing. Efren glanced at Selina and motioned her to him, just as another pop reached their ears, followed by a growly moan.

"Secure one, Echo."

Efren let out the breath he was holding and stood. "Secure two, Tango."

"Secure three, Charlie," Cal said as he broke through the trees, dragging someone behind him. "Welcome back. Good to see you. We were getting a little worried." He tossed the guy in front of their feet and knelt. "This can go one of two ways," Cal told him. "I can finish you off and leave your corpse to rot in the woods, or you can tell me how many more of you undertrained, uneducated, technology-reliant infants are out here, and I'll give you a fighting chance with that gut wound."

Efren noted the guy was barely old enough to drink and the color of paste. Cal better get him to talk fast, because he had no fighting chance against that gut wound. Hopefully the kid didn't realize that yet.

"If I talk, I die," he murmured.

"The Snake has his ways, right?" Cal asked, turning chummy with the kid. "You just follow orders and keep your head down so you aren't the next target. How'd you get tied up with this jackass anyway? You seem like a nice kid."

Efren couldn't help but snicker, willingly playing along with Cal's technique. "Did you just call the kingpin of Chicago's Mafia a jackass?"

"If the shoe fits," Cal answered without looking at him.

"Vaccaro wants her," the kid said, lifting his arm to point at Selina. "The first guy to bring her to him gets promoted."

"Promoted?" Cal said, acting impressed. "To what? Head henchman?"

"Something like that," he said with a groan.

"That doesn't answer my question. How many more are coming?"

"If we don't come back, another team will follow, and another. It's impossible to escape the Snake once you're in his sights."

"That's true," Selina said, crouching beside the kid. "How about if I save you all the trouble and turn myself over to the Snake?"

"Only if you want to die, Eva," he said, spittle and blood starting to bubble up from his lips. "That's your real name, right? Your sister is good and tight with the

Snake now, if you know what I mean." He turned his head and spit, more blood bubbling up as he did so. Efren saw the moment he realized he was dying. There was no fear, just resignation. "I don't know who you all are, but if I were you," he said, pointing at Selina, "I'd run as fast and as far as you can, and I would have left ten minutes ago." He coughed, blood flowing freely from his lips as it also flowed over his hands, holding his stomach. "The next round will reach this location in thirty minutes. Less once I hit this." His bloody hand reached for his vest, but Eric stepped down on his stomach wound, stopping the guy cold.

"But you're not going to hit that," Eric said, his tone cold, hard and angry.

Cal searched the guy and found a beacon that he carefully unhooked from the vest.

"How many were there?" Selina asked, motioning toward the woods with her head.

"Two. The other guy is taking a dirt nap for eternity."

"Same for us," Efren said, motioning at the guys on the ground.

"We need to move," Cal said. "But first." He handed the beacon to Eric. "Get the rest of them and set them off somewhere before you double back."

Selina pointed upstream and to the right. "About a quarter mile back, a creek runs east toward the river. Toss them in there. It will buy us some more time."

With a nod, Eric disappeared into the trees like a ghost. Laughter bubbled up from the kid on the ground, though weak. "Tag, you're it. Run, run as fast as you can, sweet Eva…"

His words trailed off as his head lolled to the side,

his eyes staring blankly at the ground. Efren shuddered and looked away. "That's the second guy to say the exact same thing as he was dying."

"This is a game to Vaccaro," Selina said, holstering her gun. "It's the same thing Randall said to me the night I shot Ava eight years ago. Vaccaro makes the game rules, and he expects everyone to play."

"Well," Cal said as he started forward. "I don't know about you, but I'm not in the mood to play games with this idiot. I'd rather end his reign of terror the good old-fashioned way."

"With a bullet or brawn?" Efren asked as they hurried along behind him.

"First with brains, then brawn, but a bullet if necessary."

"Trust me," Selina huffed. "A bullet will be necessary."

CAL PULLED THEM up short near a gravel driveway. He reached for his phone, but Selina noticed Efren stop him. "Somehow, he knows your every move. Either you have a Vaccaro mole in Secure One or he has a mole in your communications company."

Cal sighed and shook his head. "I reran specs on all my people, and no one has connections to him other than Sadie and Selina, which we already knew. The communications company? Really?"

"I made that call to you last night on the sat phone and five hours later a drone was hovering over our cabin. You sent us the coordinates for the campground and an hour later, guys are in the woods looking for us."

"Damn it. Someone is inside my carrier, and they're supposed to be the best."

"The Snake's tentacles are many and wide," Selina said. "If you owe him a debt, you repay it when he comes to you. If you don't, you're dead. Even if you do, you're dead. As soon as you're no longer useful to him, he'll make sure you find a way out of his life for good."

"Comms are out then," Cal said with a shake of his head. "We'll have to use burner phones. I hate to do it, but by the time he figures out what we're doing by not using the carrier, we'll be knocking on his front door."

As they crept up the driveway, Selina was glad he'd had the forethought to bring burners with him, but then again, if he had mobile command, they had everything they'd need at their fingertips.

She had never been happier to see her friends show up when they did. If they hadn't, it would have been a dangerous endeavor to take on four guys by themselves. Especially worrying about civilian injuries if bullets started flying. The moment Cal tossed the guy down in front of them, dread filled her. People were dying, and her friends were going to be next if she didn't do something.

Her spine stiffened as she went back over the plan that she'd prepared this morning. She would have to stand her ground and force them to listen to her if they were going to come out of this alive as a team.

"Roman and Mina are waiting for us at mobile command," Cal said as he grabbed his birdcall from his pocket. He brought it to his lips and blew until a clicking, almost drumlike, sound filled the air.

A shudder went through Efren, and she stepped up against his back. "You okay?"

"Yeah," he whispered, shaking his head a bit. "The call of the white stork sends me back to the sandbox every time. It's how we called to each other since there were so many storks there. That's the first time I've heard it since I left."

Cal pocketed the birdcall and held their position, waiting and watching until they heard, "Secure one, Romeo."

"Secure two, Charlie," Cal answered, and Roman stepped out of the brush.

"It's good to see you guys," he said, shaking Efren's hand before he hugged Selina to his side. "Where's Echo?"

"He's running some interference for us."

"Why the birdcall?" Roman asked as they walked up the driveway, keeping an eye on both sides.

"Vaccaro has compromised our comms. I'll explain once we're inside."

When the vehicle came into view, Selina started. "This is new." The RV was white and had a rental company logo all over it.

"It's less conspicuous than mobile command," Cal explained. "I couldn't roll into town in that and expect Vaccaro not to notice. That's why it's tucked back here on private property. It's rented, so let's avoid putting any bullet holes in it."

They climbed the stairs and instantly, Mina was running toward them, grabbing Selina in a bear hug. "I'm so glad you're here. I've been worried sick about you guys."

"We're fine, Mina," Selina promised before she released her from the hug.

Mina eyed her carefully. "You don't look fine. You've got a bruise on your jaw and a black eye. Oh, wait, don't forget the busted lip."

Selina touched her lip and grimaced. "Better than getting punched in the gut." That was her only response.

When Selina glanced at Efren, she noticed he'd received the same treatment from their friends in the woods. His beautifully sculpted face now sported a black eye and a bruise across his nose. She'd have to check that it wasn't broken.

"Those guys aren't going to bother us again," Cal said, stripping off a few layers of clothes. "We do have a problem, Mina. Our comms are compromised."

Mina lifted her brow. "By Vaccaro?"

Cal motioned to Efren, who filled Mina in on what they'd experienced the last few days.

"That's not good," Mina said, her hand in her hair. "No wonder they could find us so easily. Burner phones?"

"Yep," Cal answered. "We'll use a burner phone app."

"A burner phone app on a burner phone?" Roman asked, digging out a bucket from under the table.

"A double layer of protection by using numbers that go away each time we make a call or send a text," Cal explained. "Best we can do under the circumstances."

Roman jumped up and ran for the door. "Eric doesn't know not to use comms," he said halfway out the door. "I'll find him and be back."

He was out the door and Mina was already shutting off her phones and equipment in a mad hurry. "This is going to cramp my style," she muttered. "It's going to be hard to track you guys with burner phones."

"You won't have to," Selina said, stepping toward Cal. "I have a plan. If we follow it to a T, most of us come out of this alive and unhurt. I will lay it out, but first, I need to tend to our injuries and address his leg."

"Everyone will come out of this alive and unhurt,"

Efren ground out, his eyes flaming when he looked at her. "Most especially you."

Mina raised a brow, but Selina ignored it. She didn't have time to argue with them. She'd lay out her plan, convince them it was the best way and then divert at the last minute. Sacrificing her life was worth it if it meant Secure One could continue to help people when this was finally over. They had their mission, and she had hers. As she walked to the back of the RV with Efren, his hand sitting naturally in hers, Selina knew the hardest part of the mission would be coming to terms with never feeling his touch again. It was just another item on her long list of things she hated Uncle Medardo for—a list she'd been keeping for twenty-three years. Now it was time to face the man, read him the list of sins and let him atone for them one bullet at a time.

Chapter Eighteen

Efren pulled Mina aside after Selina had set his broken nose and added a couple of butterfly bandages to his cheekbone. He probably needed stitches, but he wasn't interested in taking the time to do that right now. The rest of the team was preparing for battle, while he was preparing not to lose the woman he'd come to care about.

"Have you heard anything more about Daddy Dearest? Is the hearing still scheduled for tomorrow?"

"It is, but it won't be an in-person judgment."

"I don't understand."

"Randall will remain at the penitentiary and be connected via closed-circuit television. The prosecution is afraid that taking him out of prison for the judgment puts too many people at risk."

"They're naive enough to think that the judgment will go their way?"

Mina shrugged. "I can't tell you what they're thinking, only what they're doing."

"If the judgment goes his way, when will he be released?"

"The following day," Mina answered. "There's paperwork to be done and filed before he can be released."

"Which means they won't return to the Caledonia house for two more days. That's if they come at all."

"It appears so. At least the best that I can figure. Now, not being able to use my equipment, I'm limited with what I can do."

"Understood," Efren said with a nod. "We need to do recon and then be prepared to move on the place as soon as they show up, and they will. They have nowhere else to go, and there's not a chance in hell Daddy Dearest is returning to Vaccaro's den. He'll want to separate himself as though he's an upstanding citizen who was wrongly accused, tried and convicted."

"All orchestrated by a madman who wants one of our own dead. We cannot let that happen," Efren emphasized. "Are we on the same page with that?"

"You can be assured of it," Mina said firmly. "Selina has been part of Secure One for longer than either of us has, and the teams' loyalty to her runs deep. They respect her and what she does as much as what Cal does. She may not see that, but it's the truth. Besides, it's not like her interactions with Vaccaro in the past made her a bad person. Just the opposite is true. She tried to stop Vaccaro once and never got the chance. Now she's got the chance again. Let's do everything we can to make it happen."

Efren held up his finger. "While keeping her safe."

"As safe as we can without taking away her power," Mina said, lowering his finger.

"Power means nothing if you're dead, Mina." The sentence was rough and revealed all the emotions inside him. "We have to protect her."

"You love her, I understand that feeling, but she's not looking for a hero. She's looking for a partner."

"No one said anything about love." The words were tight and clipped, which made Mina smile. He didn't care. His only goal was to get across to her the importance of keeping Selina tight to them so she didn't get hurt.

"They didn't need to. I can see it all over that handsome, if slightly dented, face." Her grin was wide as she waved her finger around his nose. Then she turned and walked back to the front of the RV, where everyone was gathered.

Everyone but one.

Selina was cleaning up and changing in the bedroom of the RV. Efren walked to the back and slid the door aside just in time to see her shirt fall over a nasty bruise across her ribs.

"Selina," he said, slipping through the door and sliding it closed. "Did you see that bruise?"

Her laughter was soft. "Didn't need to see it. I can feel it."

Efren lifted her shirt again and inspected the damage to her side. "This is from the train. Did you land on a rock?"

"Probably the backpack," she answered, pulling the shirt from his hands. "You threw yours, but I kept mine, hoping to use it to break my fall. It is what it is."

"Is it broken?"

"No," she assured him, sliding her arms into a black windbreaker. "It's sore, but I can breathe just fine." Selina turned and put a hand to his chest. "I'll live to see another day, Brenna."

"Let's make it many more days, okay?" he asked,

pulling her to him by her coat and planting his lips on hers in a kiss he hoped would remind her why she wanted to.

"Keep kissing me like that," she whispered when he pulled back, "and I won't want to leave this room for many more years."

"That's kind of the point." His wink was playful but was underlined by nervousness. She patted his chest and then walked past him, slid open the door and went to the front where everyone was gathered.

"I want to say thank you for having my back," Selina said to the group assembled around her. Cal had brought Roman, Mina, Eric, Mack and Lucas, but Mack and Lucas were currently setting up closer to Caledonia so they had a command station ready when they arrived. It was less than fifteen minutes from their current location, but he felt like they'd fight for every mile. "Mina, do you have an update on the Randalls?"

"Yes." She shuffled some papers around and came up with one. "Randall Jr. is still in a coma. They can't pull the plug until a direct relative signs off on it."

"How convenient," Selina said, rolling her eyes.

"Exactly. I would guess that means Daddy Dearest has to sign the papers. Maybe from prison, or maybe he has to go there to do it. I wasn't able to find that information before we went dark."

"That may delay their arrival to Caledonia," Selina said, pacing in front of the small table.

"Or, he will leave his son in a coma and play the part for the cameras."

"While likely, that doesn't help us make a plan to take them down."

"But it does," Selina said, pacing the floor. "I tried to think of every way possible to sign that witness statement before Daddy Dearest has his hearing, but there's no way to do it without exposing me and the entire team. Instead, we'll just have to get him here and catch him in the act."

"You're thinking paperwork with his name on it, or...?" Mina asked, her head cocked in confusion.

"If it's there when the cops raid the house, then sure. In the meantime, our plan of action starts way before that."

"We're all in agreement that we keep the cops out of this," Cal said, his gaze darting to Efren, who nodded once.

Selina stopped pacing. "At least until I've gone in with the wire and gotten some confessions."

"Are you kidding me?" Efren exclaimed. "I didn't keep you alive for the last week to have you walk to your execution!"

"First of all, you didn't keep me alive," she said, stalking over to him. "We kept each other alive. That's what partners do. The other thing partners do is support each other. You're the one who told me to stop being afraid of being afraid and harness the woman who used to use fear as motivation. That's what I'm doing, so you can either respect that and participate in the planning of this mission, or you can disrespect it, stand here and keep your trap shut, but you can't have it both ways."

Mina was nearly biting her tongue off to keep from laughing by the time Selina stalked away from him, but he wasn't amused. What was she thinking? She was going to get herself killed, and none of their fancy guns or tactical skills could stop that from happening.

"She could shoot you on sight," Cal said, playing the devil's advocate. "Then we've got nothing to take them down with, their business stays open, and we all become Vaccaro's targets."

"You don't know my twin, Cal," Selina said, facing him. "She's dying to have it out with me. Ava wants to spew all her hatred for me before she kills me. She won't shoot me on sight. Will I get out of there alive? Depends on how good your snipers are." She glared at him, and he stepped back. Selina wanted him to take out her sister right in front of her?

"This time, I'll make sure she's dead, make no mistake." His words were firm, and even Cal lifted his brow. Efren didn't care what they thought about him and Selina at this point. Let their tongues wag; he had more important things to do, like protect Selina.

"What about Vaccaro?" Roman asked, putting his arm around Mina's waist. "It's bad enough that Secure One is on his radar. We don't want to be his targets."

Selina leaned against the table and crossed her ankles. Efren knew she wasn't nearly as relaxed as she looked, but she wanted the team to focus on what she was saying and not how she was feeling. He noticed she was always good at that, especially when an injury was in immediate need of care and the patient resisted. "Ava isn't the only target on the table. Anyone in the house is fair game as far as I'm concerned, including Vaccaro."

Cal's brows went up. "Now you're talking about a lot of death hanging over my head. I'm not sure I'm superbly comfortable with that."

"Let's be real here," Selina said, eyeing each one of them. "You've all been special ops at one point in your life. You all understand that sometimes we have to do bad things for the betterment of society. I can live with their deaths if the Snake stops hurting people for money. If it means the Snake stops destroying families and traumatizing children. If it means the Snake stops selling drugs that are killing people and making millions doing it. We are not above the law, but we do have a responsibility to the country, even if they walk around in their lives completely clueless about the things we're faced with in this job. That's how I want it. I've taken that burden on myself in the past and been okay with it because it meant good, honest, innocent people could continue to help others in the light, untouched by the darkness we see."

You could hear a pin drop in the small space when she finished speaking. Efren's chest had swelled the longer she spoke, and he stepped forward, finally joining the rest of the group. "She's right. It kills me to put her in danger, but she's right. Our entire mission at Secure One is to keep people safe. You've done that for a countless number of people already. We can do it again, safely, so we all go home at the end of the day. No one knows this man like Selina does, so I say we follow her lead." His gaze caught hers, and she smiled then mouthed "thank you." It was killing him inside to put her in danger, but he had told her to take her power back and let her fear motivate her. He couldn't turn around and tell her she was doing it wrong now. All he could do was make sure she was protected from harm, the one way he was best at.

Cal took a step forward. "Sierra is the mission commander. I expect you to have assignments ready when we get to Caledonia."

"Already done," she said, standing up and moving beside Efren. "Everyone has a specific role in making this a happy ending, but I've played to your strengths."

"Mina does not leave home base," Roman said without room for argument. "She's desk duty now for oh, at least the next six months." He put a protective hand on her belly and kissed her cheek.

Selina squealed and ran to hug her as everyone started talking at once. As Efren shook Roman's hand and hugged Mina, then pulled Selina into him, he was sure of one thing. He had found his home, and now it was time to protect it from evil.

Chapter Nineteen

The trip to Caledonia had been surprisingly uneventful, even if they had to hide in the back of a food truck headed for a Caledonia bar and restaurant. Selina would have ridden a horse if it meant they could end this decades-long feud between the Shannons and Vaccaro—at least the only Shannon who mattered. Ava may have sold her soul to the devil, but Selina would take a bullet before she did. Hopefully, the man sitting beside her would ensure that didn't happen.

Once there, they met up with Lucas and Mack, who had set them up in a small cabin just outside the Loraine property. They had set up a communications system to rival no other, only to learn they couldn't use it. Instead, they'd have to rely on flip phones to communicate. If one took too long to send a message… Selina hated to think about the consequences of that, so she shook it off. She had to keep her head in the game or she risked losing it to the Snake.

"I'm still not sure about the wire," Cal said as he leaned against a table in front of them. "You're the cop, so you know more than I do, but I didn't think you could submit a hidden wire as evidence."

"Depends on the state," Selina answered. "Minnesota allows it as long as one person in the conversation is aware of the wire." She pointed at herself. "In Illinois, laws are a bit tighter, but we aren't in Illinois. We're in Minnesota, and I'm technically still an officer of the law. That's why I'm wearing the wire and no one else."

"Run it down then," Cal said, motioning that she had the floor.

"The mission objective is to take Ava Shannon and Randall Sr. into custody after getting their confessions on tape to implicate them both in the counterfeiting operation."

"What about Vaccaro?" Roman asked from where he stood by Mina.

"Vaccaro doesn't come into play here," Selina said, facing him. "He won't return to Caledonia with the happily reunited couple."

"I'm aware, but the question was more geared at how do we stop him from coming after us?"

"We don't." Selina turned and leaned on the table to look them all in the eye. "Once we have Randall and Ava in custody, Vaccaro will cut all ties with them and anyone around them."

"I don't buy it." Roman shook his head with his lips in a thin line. "He's had thugs out searching for you for over a week now, and if this counterfeiting operation is as important as you say it is, he'll be looking for revenge that we shut it down."

Selina held her finger up as she stood. "We aren't shutting it down. We took two people into custody. We didn't burn down the house. He'll have that place cleaned out and the operation moved faster than we can book

Ava and Randall into jail. At that point, he slithers back to Chicago never to be seen again." She glanced at all of them one at a time and could see they didn't believe her. "You're going to have to take my word on this, team. I've known Medardo my entire life. I've seen how cold, calculating and evil he is. One day you're his favorite person in the world and the next you no longer exist to him. Are there thugs hunting me right now? Yes, but not at Vaccaro's direction. Ava is behind all of this. I'm surprised Vaccaro bought in, but then again, I'm not. Ava can be—" she motioned around in the air for a bit as she searched for the right word "—convincing? Relentless? If Ava Shannon wants something, she gets it. Right now, she wants me dead."

"Well, she's not going to get that," Efren growled from the corner.

Selina shook her head. "No, she's not, but we can let her think she is. Imagine her face when I waltz through the front door and into the study while they drink to Randall's release."

"She could have a gun," Lucas pointed out. "Then what?"

"Then I put my hands in the air and start talking. I know her. She will not shoot until she's had a chance to spew all her hatred at me. I'm the root cause for everything that's wrong with her life." She added an eye roll to assure them it was sarcasm. "Besides, if she gets trigger-happy, we'll have people in place who have a faster trigger finger than she does."

"That makes it complicated." Cal's grimace was felt by all of them, including Selina.

"That makes it attempted murder on her part and self-defense on mine. Case closed."

Eric looked up from his notebook. "What happens if you don't get anything incriminating on the wire?"

"We take them into custody anyway," Selina said with a shrug. "Then we call in the cops and let them tear the place apart to find the evidence they need to send them to prison."

"Where Vaccaro will get them out again?" Mina asked, a brow raised.

A sigh escaped Selina's lips. "Not likely. Again, Vaccaro has a line, and if we capture Ava and Randall, he will be done with them. They will pay for his crimes, which is always the way he likes it."

"Even if the cops come in and take the evidence before he gets there to get it?"

"I assure you, there will be no information in that house proving Vaccaro is involved in the scheme, just like last time. Randall went to prison, but Vaccaro was never even mentioned, even though we all knew he was behind it. The same thing will happen this time. The only way we could get Vaccaro for the counterfeiting is if Ava or Randall confirm it on tape. Even then, his lawyers will get him off."

"And if they both end up dead?" Lucas asked.

"Then we turn their cameras back on after I walk out the door and we walk away. Someone will find them and assume Vaccaro took care of his problem. Case closed."

"Except that the evilest one of the three is still walking around sucking air and ruining people's lives," Eric hissed. "I don't like that idea."

"You were a cop, Eric. You know that we can't get all

the bad guys. All we can do is our best and let the law take care of the rest."

"We aren't cops, though," Efren said. "If I think for one second that woman is going to get trigger-happy, she's going down. Messy or not, she's going down. I don't like any of this."

"Neither do I," Cal agreed. "Like it or not, we're between a rock and a hard place. We can't call the cops in since we have no proof of the operation being moved here. They can't get a warrant on 'we think this is what they're doing.'"

Selina shook her head. "There is no rock or hard place here, Cal. There is only one choice and we've made it. I will reprise my role of Eva Shannon long enough to take my twin and Randall down, and then Eva dies again."

"As long as Selina lives," Efren said between clenched teeth as all the heads around the table nodded.

She gave the final nod. "I apologize for putting you all in this position. If I could do it over, I would, but all we can do now is play the hand we were given."

"Don't apologize to us," Roman said with a shake of his head. "We've all done much worse things for the betterment of the world than what we're facing here tonight. My conscience is clear. It will be clearer if we can get Vaccaro, but two are better than none."

"With that decided, it's time for assignments." Cal pushed off the wall where he was standing and walked to the center. "You must memorize what Sierra tells you. I want no written evidence." Cal pointed at Selina's notebook. "Once the assignments are given, Mina will burn that."

"Ten-four," Selina said, spreading the notebook open on the table. "Let's walk through it."

As she handed out assignments and went over the plan of attack, Selina couldn't keep her gaze from drifting to the man who sat with his lips in a thin line and his arms crossed over his chest. He wasn't happy. Neither was she, but she understood one thing he didn't. If they ever wanted a chance to be together. To really have the chance to make a life together, then Ava had to die. Selina would squeeze the trigger without hesitation if she had to, and all she could do was pray he would do the same.

AVA SHANNON IS on the property.

Those words had sent a chill down Selina's spine when the scout team had reported in. They were surprised to find her look-alike sitting in the den sipping sangria when they did a sweep of the property. Like it or not, she had to act now, even if they all said it was too dangerous. If she could apprehend Ava, and then do a video testimony to send to the judge before the trial tomorrow, she could keep Randall in prison and send Ava there, too. Maybe she was being too idealistic, but she was using those ideals as her motivating factor. It was time to bring all of them some peace. If the only way to do that was to clash with her twin, then so be it.

Selina lifted her shirt, threaded the black leather belt through her pant loops, and buckled it in the front. There was a small recorder inside the buckle with an antenna running through the belt. It was voice activated, so it should easily pick up any conversation she had with her twin face-to-face. Since they wanted to avoid a digital signal, she couldn't wear a transmitter that would send a signal back and allow Mina to listen in. It would be all on her to get the audio they needed to put Ava behind bars with her husband. This was one time she was lucky that they had to go low-tech. The team didn't see the bigger picture, but she did, and the picture was ugly. It would be up to her to erase the past and start over.

Selina grabbed a secondary voice-activated recorder to ensure she got the recordings she needed. It was the length of a paperclip and slid into her pocket without leaving an outline on the material. She positioned her concealed holster at the back of her pants and tucked a small 9mm into it. She wasn't going in unprepared, and wasn't afraid to use the gun if push came to shove, and it just might. Her only goal was not to put that decision or action on any of her friends, especially Efren. "I killed for you" didn't feel like a winning basis for a healthy relationship.

Were they in a relationship, though? That was a question she couldn't answer without consulting Efren. She suspected any theoretical relationship they may have had would be destroyed when she left this cabin. It couldn't be helped. Selina was the only one who understood how volatile her twin was and how any plan wholly depended on Ava's choices, not theirs.

Knowing Ava was here meant the plan disappeared, and instinct kicked in. The Shannon twins were finally in the same place again, and in an hour, this would all be over. If they waited until after the trial and planned the mission down to the very last detail, it would be too late. Selina would text them she was going in right before she approached the front door. She felt bad that the team would have to scramble to get into place, but she'd tried to reason with them. Once again, they all disregarded her knowledge—despite the lack of their own—when it came to her family. She planned to buy them time by talking to Ava to get all the dirt she could on Vaccaro and Randall.

More than likely, Ava was at the house to destroy anything tying them to the counterfeiting operation. Once that was done, she would return to Chicago to join her husband before they disappeared for good. Selina couldn't risk it. Her past was her past, not the team's, and she would do whatever she had to do to protect them even if that meant dying. That was a real possibility, and even though Efren refused to address it, Selina was honest with herself at all times. These could be her last few minutes on this earth. She'd fight like hell to make sure that didn't happen, but if it did, she was taking Ava down with her.

The only thing she regretted was not kissing Efren before he left to scout out his sniper position, and not whispering three words in his ear after the kiss ended. She'd hold on to the emotions and those words, using it all as motivation to walk out of that house alive tonight. Efren may not want to hear it, but if she made it out, she'd tell him anyway. For the first time in her life, she'd be honest with a man about her feelings, even if he rejected her. And he might. She wouldn't blame him if he did, either. She was breaking his trust by going rogue, but what none of them understood was, she had no other choice. It was now or never if they wanted to apprehend Ava Shannon and put this to rest.

She slid her arms inside the sleeves of her Secure

One jacket and zipped it to cover the holster and the belt. After slipping past the closed bathroom door, where Mina was cleaning up, she slid out the door of the cabin silently. This would be the shortest and longest walk of her life, but one way or the other, the game would be over tonight.

Chapter Twenty

Efren swung through the cabin door and immediately switched out his all-terrain sole on his blade for his spiked sole. He'd found the perfect spot that would allow him to cover Selina when she was inside the house. He was more than surprised when he looked through his scope, and Selina's face stared back at him. He had to remind himself that the woman inside that house was nothing like her sister. Selina had a soul and she wasn't afraid to do the right thing, even when the right thing was the hardest thing to do.

Temptation had called to him when he had Ava Shannon dead to rights under his rifle scope. He could have ended the whole thing right then and there, and the desire to squeeze that trigger and make it look like an assassination so they could all go home was almost overwhelming. Instead, he did the right thing and took his finger off the trigger. The satisfaction he'd get in taking out Ava Shannon would be short-lived when he screwed up the rest of the mission by not hearing what she had to say.

"Selina?" he called, walking to the back of the cabin where several beds sat in a row. This was obviously someone's hunting cabin, as it was well cared for but utilitarian.

There was a figure on one of the beds, but it wasn't Selina. "Mina? Are you okay?"

"Hey, yeah," she said, sitting up and rubbing her eyes. "I was just catching some sleep. I was sick earlier, and the long hours are taking a toll on me. We couldn't have picked a worse time to get pregnant."

Efren chuckled as he leaned against the door. "I didn't know you guys were trying."

"We weren't," she said, sliding her leg into her prosthesis. "It was, what do you say, a happy surprise? Heavy on the surprise in the beginning. Our work doesn't lend itself to having a family, so I'm glad Cal is starting the new cybersecurity division *and* hired Sadie. She's going to be a godsend in more ways than one."

Efren held his hand out to help her up. "It's a great idea, honestly. We have more requests for cybersecurity than we do physical security now. Cal is lucky to have you at the helm. You're the reason it will be a successful endeavor for Secure One."

Mina playfully leaned into him. "You are good for my ego, Efren Brenna. As soon as this mission is over, I'll start looking for others to join the team. We'll have to recruit, and how we live at Secure One will be a tough sell, but if I can build a solid core team, we can always expand if needed."

"You mean like satellite offices?"

"More like the way Elliot works security around the upper portion of Minnesota. We'd have people who live off Secure One property who can go into businesses and fix systems that have been hacked, then build new security in. Remote, but still doing Secure One business."

"So needed, too," Efren said as they walked back into the main room. "Do you want me to flip through my Rolodex to see if anyone is looking for a change?"

"Yes, thank you! You have connections everywhere, so I know Cal would appreciate it as much as I do."

"No problem, I'll do it as soon as we get back to base." He paused and glanced around the empty room. "I thought Selina was staying with you and out of sight."

"I did, too. After I horked my guts out for fifteen minutes, I passed out on the bed. I thought she was out here."

Efren got a bad feeling in the pit of his stomach. "Did anyone report back what we found at the house when we did our recon?"

"You mean about Ava Shannon being on the property? Yeah, Cal, Mack and Roman checked in to let us know. They wanted us to arm ourselves but stay in the cabin. Selina argued with them for a while before they left again."

"What did they argue about?" A bad feeling filled the pit of his gut to overflowing.

"Honestly, I was sick, but I think it had something to do with them not listening to her?"

Efren cursed and ran for the back where they'd set up a makeshift equipment area. It didn't take but a second for him to see that her jacket and boots were missing. He jogged back to the front of the cabin. "What kind of wire is Selina wearing into the house?"

"We decided on the belt recorder. It's voice activated, so she doesn't have to worry about it not coming on when she needs it to." Mina pointed at the table but then cocked her head. "The belt is gone."

Efren cursed again. "She's going in alone tonight."

"You're jumping to conclusions, Efren," Mina said. "She's probably just out getting some air and you missed her on the way in."

"She's out getting air after Cal told you to stay hidden? No, she's going to have it out with her sister before we have anything in place to protect her—"

He was interrupted by a sharp report that had him jumping in front of Mina. When he realized it was too far away, he grabbed his jacket and ran for the door. "Text Cal! Tell him Selina's inside that house."

Efren pumped his legs as fast and as hard as he could as he ran to where his rifle was hidden. That shot could mean it was too late, but he had to try. He wanted to plow through the house's front door, grab Selina and then shake her silly for going off alone, but he couldn't risk it. For all he knew, Selina was the one to do the shooting, so it was better to get in place and assess the situation than go off half-cocked, the same way she had.

He scrambled up the ladder against the small shed, then army-crawled toward where he'd left his gun. The entire time he prayed to anyone listening that when he looked through that scope, the twin he loved was still standing. He'd planned to tell her how he felt before the mission, but now he was glad he hadn't. This little stunt was proof that trust was easily broken and that losing someone you love can happen in the blink of an eye. He couldn't, wouldn't, get involved with someone he couldn't trust, and Selina had proved that here tonight. She was the mission manager. If she'd wanted to change the plan, she could have easily called everyone in and prepped them for the change, but she hadn't done that. Instead, she decided she would handle this herself, without so much as the courtesy of a heads-up, and that told him all he needed to know about Selina Colvert.

SELINA SLIPPED THE phone in her pocket after texting the team. Get in position. I'm going in. Six words that would shape her future from here on out. She'd either walk out alive or be rolled out dead, but either way, this nightmare would be over for the rest of the team.

After a deep breath in and out, she walked to the front door, assured by the team that there were no cameras they could see on the house's perimeter. She found that odd at first until she remembered they had to fit into small-town Caledonia, and you don't do that by making your house a fortress. Selina had no doubt there were cameras somewhere, so rather than ring the doorbell, she tried the knob, not surprised when the door swung open. Her twin was expecting her. Good. That meant she wanted to talk. If she knew Selina was here and wanted her dead, she would have done that already. No, Ava wanted to have a chat with her, so she'd welcome her to her home.

Selina strolled through the house leisurely, giving the team time to get in place after getting her text. Before long, she found her twin, a replica of herself, sitting on the couch in a small den.

"Well, well, if it isn't big sister," Ava said without standing. "So glad you could stop in. I'm sure you've been dying to know how I'm still breathing. Considering, you know, you shot me."

"You don't give me enough credit, Ava," Selina said, inching her way into the room, but standing to the side of the window, just in case Efren needed a clear shot. "It's not hard to put your return from the dead squarely on Uncle Medardo's shoulders."

Ava smiled, and it chilled Selina to the bone. They may share the same features, but Ava's twisted into evilness with every expression. "Good old Uncle Medardo. We aren't blood related, but he's been better family than my own. He's taken care of me and made sure I had a roof over my head all these years. That's more than I can say for you."

"Considering I thought you were dead, I'm unsure what you expected me to do."

"Funny how that turned out. I thought you were dead, too. For over seven years, I lived in bliss, knowing I had not only done the heavy lifting to get rid of our father, but you had fallen to your untimely death just days after mine. Maybe I should say timely, at least as far as I was concerned."

"You killed our father?"

"Of course. He had to go. Uncle Medardo was too loyal to him. Daddy needed to be out of the picture so I could take his place. Funny how that works. He sold me for the price of a debt, but in the end, he was the one who paid."

"The debt he incurred trying to make you happy!" Selina exclaimed, anger filling her as she listened to her deranged twin. "You're the problem, Ava."

"No, you're the problem, Eva. You keep turning up like a bad penny, which has to end. That's why about a year ago, I happened to be in Seattle on business for

Uncle Medardo. Did you know your old friend Kai Tanner lives there now? Well, not in Seattle, some little town around there, but he wasn't hard to find."

"You saw Kai?" Selina asked with her hands in fists at her side. She wanted to pull her sidearm and end this right now, but shooting an unarmed woman was murder.

"Such a lovesick fool," Eva said, brushing at her skirt. "He sure had a lot to say when he thought I was you, though. A chance meeting, a couple of spiked drinks and a roll in the hay gave me all the information I needed to know that my intuition was right. Your fall off the cliff was nothing more than a swan dive."

"Did Randall Jr. know you were alive?" Selina asked, forcing her mind away from Kai and concentrating on asking the right questions to get the answers they needed to put her away.

"Of course he did. Howie and I were running the operation here at the Caledonia house while he kept his father's other businesses going."

Selina finally understood why Randall had shot her in the tunnel. He knew his stepmother was still alive, so when he came face-to-face with someone who looked like her, but was working with the law, he knew it had to be her.

"How did you manage to keep the counterfeiting operation going when Randall was in prison? He was the brains behind the operation."

"Wrong," Ava said haughtily. "My husband is nothing more than a puppet who makes Medardo look good. Medardo wanted to get rid of Randall before he even made it to trial, but I talked him out of it. I showed him the operation here and that I was the mastermind behind its success, not Randall. Keeping Randall in jail took the pressure off me and let me continue with the business here, while keeping him somewhere safe for use at a later date, if need be."

"And suddenly, because I'm alive, now is the time to use him?" Selina knew she was getting it all on tape, and wanted to keep her talking for as long as she could before she had to face down the inevitable gun her twin had somewhere in this room.

"More like a lucky coincidence. You see, the business here has run its course, and Medardo has a different assignment for us."

Selina smiled with satisfaction. If they'd followed the original plan and waited until after Randall was released from prison, they would have missed their opportunity to take them down.

"That's why you sent all the goons after me?" Selina asked, refusing to splint her side despite the pain. There wasn't a chance in hell she would give Ava the satisfaction of knowing she'd hurt her. "So I didn't screw up your new assignment?"

"I sent the goons after you based on nothing more than revenge," Ava spat, standing to get in Selina's face. She dug her finger into her chest. "You tried to put me in the grave, so tit for a tat, big sister." Ava's eyes were wild as she shook with vengeance. "You always thought you were so important, so righteous. The truth is, you're just like me, but you hide behind a badge to make your revenge heroic."

"I didn't realize you were so close to Uncle Medardo," Selina said, the words sticking in her throat. "What's it like letting that snake make love to you at night? The idea makes me sick," she hissed, the sound loud in the room.

Ava hauled off and slapped Selina across the face, but Selina didn't flinch. "Don't you talk about him that way! He loves me!"

The report of gunfire was so close to Selina's left ear that it sent her spiraling backward for several steps. She righted herself and dialed in on the scene in front of her. Ava was on the ground, blood bubbling out of her mouth as Vaccaro stood over her with a gun.

"You talk too much." That same voice from childhood drove a shiver down her spine. It had been so many years since she'd had the displeasure to be in his company that seeing him again was doing weird things to her equilibrium. "For the record, I never loved you, but you sure were easy to manipulate with those three little words, you poor misguided woman. Your daddy issues were your downfall, but I happily manipulated them to my advantage. Did you hear the news? Randall Jr. didn't make it out of the coma. He passed just an hour ago. So sad." He shook his head as though he had a heart. "I suppose the news will come out in the morning that his father died by suicide in prison when he learned the news. What a sad, sad family you all were."

Medardo swung the gun in Selina's direction. "Speaking of sad families, how lucky am I to get a twofer? In my opinion, it's more than time to make sure no more Shannons walk this earth. All the bickering in this family is exhausting—first, your father, then your sister. You were refreshing, Eva. You never kowtowed to your father, and you always did your own thing. I could respect you as an adversary, but my respect has limits.

This whole mess has to go away." He motioned around the room with his gun while Selina slid her gaze to her twin. Blood pooled around her on the couch where she'd fallen. Blood no longer bubbled from her mouth, and her eyes were fixed on the ceiling in the stare of death. There was no doubt that this time, Ava Shannon was dead.

"Eva Shannon is already dead," she said, and Medardo snapped the gun and his attention back to her. "As far as I'm concerned, we can come to an agreement."

"An agreement?" The question was filled with curiosity, so Selina shrugged as though none of it really mattered to her.

"We both walk away from here tonight and forget the other exists. I have a new life now that I'd like to continue to live, so I'm happy to strike a deal with the devil in order to do that."

Medardo laughed the laugh she remembered from their Sunday dinners when she was a child. "You always could make me laugh, little girl. Unfortunately, I won't be able to forget you exist. You're far too noble to pretend that I don't exist, either. No, the only way to make sure my interests are served is to dispatch the Shannon twins and be on my way. Especially since this place is about to go up in flames. It's a shame there's no fire hydrant way out here. When the house becomes an inferno, they'll have no choice but to let it burn itself out."

Medardo smiled the smile that reminded her of the snake he was. His gun lowered to her center mass, and she had to make a split decision. Try to run or go for her gun. Before she could do either, Medardo jerked backward with a shriek.

They both looked down at his arm to see half of it had

been blown off, and the gun was nowhere to be found. Medardo grabbed his elbow as he fell to the couch next to her sister, blood pouring from the destroyed tissue.

"You shot me," he said, shock setting in. "I can't believe you shot me."

"I didn't shoot you," Selina said, a smile tugging her lips up. "You see, I have friends who don't take kindly to bullies who threaten other people. They shot you. I'm surprised it took them as long as it did, to be honest."

Selina pulled her gun from the holster and glanced around the room. "An inferno, you say?" She sniffed the air, and the scent of accelerant reached her nostrils. It was hard to distinguish it over the coppery smell of her sister's blood, but it was there, and she had to get out sooner rather than later. He probably had the system on a timer to ignite on his way out the door. "You know, they say in life, you get back what you put in." Selina aimed at his kneecap and pulled the trigger. Medardo yowled in pain, unsure what to grab with his only free hand.

"That was for stealing my innocence," Selina said, backing toward the door. She couldn't risk being in the house when it went up. She didn't want any of her team seeing the flames and running in to save her.

"You can't leave me here!" he screamed. "My bodyguards are just outside the door."

"Are they, though?" Selina asked with a smile. "I suspect they're taking a nap just like all the other guys you sent out to find me. When they wake up and discover the house on fire, do you think they'll come running to save you? I'm going to guess no. I can't think of a better place for you to die, Uncle Medardo," she said with enough venom to poison the man in front of her. "You see, I right injustices regardless of the consequences, and that is something I will continue to do while you rot in hell right next to my sister."

Selina smiled, turned and gingerly walked to the front door. One spark and this place was going up. She didn't want to be in it when it did. With a final smile, she tucked her gun in her holster, pulled the door open and slammed it behind her. She'd seen the spark, and as she ran for the woods, she heard the telltale whoosh of the accelerant igniting. It was then that she knew it was over.

Chapter Twenty-One

The team was back at Secure One and gathered in the conference room. Last night had been a blur, and Efren hadn't had a second to breathe since they'd pulled in, all in separate vehicles. They didn't have time to talk, much less argue, about anything that had happened if they wanted to be out of the area before the fire engines arrived. They'd emptied the cabin and been on the road in under fifteen minutes, which was when they passed the fire engines heading to the inferno on the outskirts of Caledonia. All of them had watched that house go up and knew there would be nothing to save by the time they got there. Not the house and not the people inside it.

"Well, that was not our finest hour," Cal said to open the meeting. All heads turned to Selina, who sat at the end of the table in silence.

"I accept full responsibility for that." She stood and pulled off her belt and tossed a small device on the table.

"What's that?" Cal asked, pulling it toward him.

"Proof, should we ever need it."

"Unless his bodyguards wake up and decide to tell the police all about their involvement with a Mafia kingpin, I doubt that will be necessary, but I'll log it in."

"No, you're going to listen to it. Now." She pointed at the computer Mina had in front of her, and Mina hooked up the small device and did some fiddling. When she was done, she glanced at Cal, who nodded. Mina clicked the mouse and the room filled with Ava's voice. They listened in silence to the information unfolding.

Efren couldn't help but notice the expressions on their faces as they took in and processed the information. He also noticed how Selina subconsciously grimaced when the first shot rang out and then how she flinched when Medardo howled. Efren had hit his target dead-on. He could have killed the man, but that wasn't his goal. He wanted to get rid of the weapon and give Selina the upper hand to get out of the situation herself. In the end, it hadn't mattered, since Vaccaro was now dust.

When the recording ended, Cal glanced up at Selina. "What were you thinking?"

Efren noticed Selina's jaw tic once, and she blinked several times before she spoke. "We're supposed to be a team, but not one of you listened to me. You heard her," she said, pointing at the computer. "She was leaving Caledonia and never coming back. Had we waited until after the hearing, they would have disappeared. As soon as you said she was in the house, I knew. She was waiting for me. That entire game, her showing up at the hospital and pushing us farther and farther south, was on purpose. She wanted me to die tonight, and her ego was too big to consider it would be her who died."

"You both could have died!" Cal exclaimed. "I can't even wrap my mind around what happened. Not only did you break rank and go rogue, but you put yourself and this entire business at risk! If anyone figures out that we were there tonight, I'm done. Do you understand me? This business is over. We have protocols and plans for a reason!"

"You're right," she said, standing and walking to the front of the room. "This is my fault, and I take responsibility for it. If I wasn't willing to, I wouldn't have done it. You will have no legal trouble from what happened tonight. There is nothing left, and if they figure out Medardo died in that fire, you won't see the FBI crying about it. As you heard, Randall and Randall are no more, so this case is closed." She lifted her lanyard from her neck and set it on the table in front of Cal. "I hereby resign my position as chief medical officer at Secure One. I committed too many inexcusable offenses tonight to be trusted as an operative again. I will clean out the lab of my personal belongings and head out in the morning. Thank you for everything. I mean that," she whispered as she wrapped her arms around the man in front of her.

Cal hugged her awkwardly, his gaze holding Efren's in a look of terror and desperation. Efren wondered if he wore the same look. Was he angry at Selina for what she had done? Yes. Did she put them in a tough position? Yes. Did he want her to leave Secure One? His head said yes, she was a liability they couldn't keep around, but his heart said he'd follow her wherever she went and that was his internal battle now.

Selina ended the hug and turned to the team. The tears on her face had clearly surprised everyone as they glanced at one another around the table. "I owe all of you my life, and that is something I can never repay. The only thing I can do is say thank you for everything and for understanding that all of this—" she motioned at the devices on the table as she wiped a tear away "—started long before I ever had a say in how any of it would end. For the record, it ended the best possible way, and that's because all of you took it on your shoulders to do the right thing by doing the wrong thing. I'll never again lose sleep knowing that Vaccaro is still hurting people and I could do nothing to stop it. We stopped it. We did the wrong thing for the right reasons. That's enough for me."

"That's enough for me, too," Lucas said, standing and saluting.

"It's enough for me, too," Roman said, following Lucas.

"It's enough for me, too," Eric and Mack said, standing and saluting.

"I won't lose any sleep tonight," Mina said, standing and giving Selina a smile.

Efren stood slowly, pushing the chair back with his knee and meeting Selina's gaze right before he walked out of the room.

SELINA BLEW OUT a breath as the man she'd fallen in love with walked out on her. She expected him to be upset, but she also expected him to act like an adult. She was right about only one, apparently.

"Give him time," Cal said, resting his hand on her shoulder. "He's stared fear in the face a lot over the last week, and came to the realization too many times that he might lose you. Quite a few of us in this room have gone through it. Right?" She glanced up to nodding heads. "Give him some time, and he'll come around. Now, about your job."

"I'll head to the med bay and clean out my things." Her heart was heavy now that she was faced with the realization that this team would no longer be her team. "If you don't mind, I'll need to take care of my wounds, too." She lifted her shirt to show him her abdomen, but it was Mina who gasped.

"How are you even upright?" she asked, coming around the table to look at her ribs. "You need a hospital."

"Nothing's broken." Selina lowered her shirt. "I'll tape up my ribs and fix my incision before I head out."

"You're not going anywhere." Cal handed her the Secure One badge back. "You may have pulled rank tonight, but in hindsight, you did what had to be done. We, as a team, failed to listen to you about a lot of things when it came to Vaccaro, and that's on us, not you. When the going got tough, you walked in and took care of business. Do I like having an operative on the team who does her own thing, whether it's right or wrong? No. We will have to talk about that, but I do like having an operative on my team who is quick on their feet, competent and perceptive. You're all of those things, which is what made you a good cop back in the day. I think it's time we move you onto the team as the valuable op that you are, as I know you've been unhappy in your position for some time now."

"You want me to stay?" She lowered herself to the table in surprise. "As an operative?"

"Yes, but we can talk about it later when we're all rested. Promise me you won't go anywhere until we've talked, and you've talked to Efren. He deserves that much if nothing else."

He deserved so much more, but suddenly, Selina wasn't so sure she was the woman to give it to him anymore. She understood how he felt, and couldn't pretend that she didn't. She'd betrayed him by going after her twin by herself. It was a chance she had to take for the betterment of the entire world, but whether he believed that or not was up to him.

Cal dismissed everyone with instructions to get some sleep and meet up in the morning for a debriefing once the news reports about the Caledonia house, and the two Randalls, started to generate.

"Mina, could I ask a favor?" Selina asked before the woman could walk out of the room. She didn't know how to ask her this question without looking like she didn't care about the man who didn't think she'd done the right thing.

Mina smiled and pulled a piece of paper from her pocket. She handed it to Selina without a word and disappeared with a wink.

Selina looked down at the paper and all it said was, *Kai Tanner, Cliff, Washington. 425-555-4577.*

BEFORE SHE LOST her nerve, she knocked on Efren's door and waited. Selina had followed Cal's advice and given him an hour before she followed him, but she wondered if even that was enough. What happened in the next ten minutes would direct Selina's life going forward. If she and Efren couldn't come to an understanding, she would leave Secure One, despite Cal insisting otherwise. While she had screwed up the mission, she had also done the right thing, and that was something none of them could argue with.

The door cracked open, and Efren looked out. "Not into talking tonight, Selina."

She stuck her hand in the door before he could close it. "How about listening, then?"

Selina heard his heavy sigh, but he opened the door the rest of the way and let her into the room. "I'm sorry." Those were the first words out of her mouth, and he lowered his brow.

"Are you, though? It doesn't seem like you were too sorry when you were defending your actions in the conference room."

"I'm sorry for breaking the planned mission," she clarified. "And I'm sorry you were put in the position to shoot Medardo. I'm not sorry that they're dead."

Efren tipped his head to the side in agreement. "I don't have a problem that they're dead either. I took out his hand to give you a chance to do the rest. I do have a problem with my trust being broken."

"I know." She stared at her shoes for a moment before she glanced up into his deeply troubled eyes. "When I made the decision to do it, there was no question in my mind you'd feel betrayed. The problem was, no matter what angle I argued from, no one was listening to me."

"Including me," he admitted with a sigh.

"I spent a long time with the team after you left, helping them understand that what I did put my life in danger, but I did that so that they'd remain safe. If Ava had disappeared, I shudder to think how long it would have been before she turned up again, but I do know we'd all be looking over our shoulder. I want you to understand that is the reason I chose to betray your trust and risk my life. Better my life than any of yours, considering this was my fight. Did I play into Ava's game? Yes. I bit hook, line and sinker into it, but there was no other choice. I just hope you all see there was no other choice." Her voice was barely above a whisper by the time she finished her impassioned plea. Her hands fell to her sides, and she lowered her head. "You risked your life to keep me safe this last week, and for that, I'm eternally grateful, Efren. I'm sure when you got that text that I was going in, you felt as though it had all been for naught, but it wasn't, I promise. I will continue to do good things to help other people because that is who I am."

"Wait. Text? You sent a text?"

"Of course I did. I sent it right before I went in to tell you to get into position. How else would you know I was going in?"

Efren gripped her forearms gently and held her gaze. "I didn't get a text message. I was in the cabin with Mina and heard the first shot. I ran like a man possessed to where I'd left the rifle and looked through the scope to see Vaccaro holding the gun on you. You don't know how badly I wanted to end him."

"Why didn't you?"

"You needed to take your power back. You needed to be the one who made the decision you could live with. Doing anything else was being a hero you didn't need. That's why."

"I love you, Efren," Selina said the words in a rush of breath and tears. Her lips trembled as she tried to form words, but she hiccuped and had to start over. "You were the only thing on my mind the entire time I was in that house. How mad you were going to be at me and how I was going to lose you, but how I had to protect you. I had to protect you from those people so you could continue to help others. My decisions tonight meant I would lose you, but I couldn't leave Vaccaro on your doorstep for the rest of your life. That would have been wrong and the exact opposite of what it means to love someone."

Efren ran his hand through his hair as he stared at her. "You went into the house for me?" Her nod was shaky as she sucked up air, but she didn't speak, just lowered herself to the bed and tried not to sob.

He didn't say anything, just paced back and forth in front of her with his hands in his hair until finally, he joined her on the bed and tipped her chin toward him. "Do you know how I know that I love you?" Her eyes widened, but she didn't answer. "I let you see my leg. I made love to you without my prosthesis. I let you see me. The other night in the cabin was the first time I let anyone see me in twelve years. That's when I knew that I loved you."

"You love me, too?" Her voice was shaky, but she noted a little hope in the words.

"Probably since the first day you made a snide remark about my ability to guard someone. Do I love what you did tonight? No. Can I respect it for what it was? Yes. Do I ever want you to do something that stupid ever again? No. No. Never. Do you understand me?"

He had grasped her upper arms and held her so close she could feel his warm breath on her cheek. "Never again," she whispered.

"Did you really quit?" he asked, his gaze holding hers as their noses touched.

"I tried, but Cal wouldn't let me. He said we're going to talk about it tomorrow, but as long as I don't go rogue again, I earned my spot as an operative. I may take it, I may not. I'll talk to him first and then decide. That is, if you are willing to continue to work with me despite what happened between us."

"Despite what happened between us? Do you mean making love to you? Kissing you? Loving you?" She nodded against his forehead, and he smiled. "I'll only continue to work with you as long as we can still do those things, Selina. Do you think we can still have a relationship with all the baggage we carry?"

She gazed into his clear, open, accepting eyes. "I'll carry yours if you'll carry mine."

"That sounds like a mission we can work together on."

"Are you okay with knowing I can't have your child?"

"You're all I'll ever need in this life. Our lifestyle doesn't lend itself to little ones, and I'm okay with that if you are. I love you, Selina." He lowered his lips to hers.

"Not as much as I love you, Efren Brenna," she said against his lips right before he captured them for the first kiss of the rest of their lives.

Epilogue

Selina flipped through the news stories about the death of "known Mafia kingpin Medardo Vaccaro." It had taken authorities almost a week to identify the bodies in the house. The fact that it took so long told her that Vaccaro's bodyguards had indeed dipped rather than try to rescue their boss. Conspiracy theories were already rampant less then twelve hours since it was determined that the body found in the charred home in Caledonia was Vaccaro. The second body found next to him had been identified as Ava Shannon, a woman the world thought was already dead. While Selina's bullet eight years ago hadn't killed her twin, it had done enough damage to her heart that she required a pacemaker and defibrillator to keep ticking. Those devices were registered to the patient, and that was how they determined which Shannon twin had been found dead…again. As far as Selina was concerned, Eva Shannon was dead and she was happy to let it remain that way.

True to his word, Vaccaro had taken out both Randalls as well. To think Randall Sr. was so overcome with grief about his son that he hung himself with his bed-sheets in his cell just hours from being released. The first thing Secure One had done was make sure that the only living Loraine son, Victor, was still alive and well in Bemidji, where he was recovering from being kidnapped by his brother just a few weeks ago while trying to save his fiancée. They were fine and rejoicing that Vaccaro, his father and his brother were dead. Now he could live an everyday life with Kadie and his son without leaving Bemidji. Since the Loraine home was now empty, they'd sell it and use the money to start their life together. Selina had never been happier to hear that something good would come from this debacle. Sadie, Kadie's sister and aunt to Houston, was even more thrilled. She worked at Secure One now as the chef, but if her sister and nephew remained in Bemidji, she could maintain her relationship with them easily, which was important to her.

There had been multiple times over the last week when she had to stop and ask herself if she had done the right thing. Each time, she got another sign that she had, so she decided to bury it in the box where she kept all the memories of her life as Eva Shannon. All but one part, that is. There was a thread dangling that would have to be tied up, but she had yet to find the courage to dial the number Mina had given her.

Cal had come to her a few days ago to talk about her job. He began by apologizing for treating her as an afterthought when the business took an unexpected turn. He admitted he should have asked her if she was comfortable caring for the women who had found their way to Secure One for safety, and not assumed she was a robot who could continue to care for them without help or someone to talk to about what she was going through as their caregiver. Selina had taken some of that responsibility on her shoulders, as she could have spoken up and told Cal of the toll it was taking.

In the end, he offered her a full-time operative position, which, after much thought, she'd turned down. After the last case, she realized she was far more valuable to the team as a floater. She would remain the chief medical officer at the compound, ensuring the men were healthy and eating correctly by working with Sadie. When they went on cases, she would also go, using the mobile command as her home base where she would be their medic or jump in as an operative if the occasion called for it. She would also be the medical informant for the new cybersecurity division. She'd help out when something came up with a medical clinic or hospital that the team needed help translating. It was a lot of hats to wear, but that had been her life for as long as she could remember, and she wouldn't want it any other way.

"Selina?" She turned and made eye contact with the man who had been there to hold her up through each new revelation over the last few days. Efren had spent some time in the med bay with her. His limb had been damaged more than she was happy with, but he assured her he had hurt it worse in the past. He came in for treatment of the skin twice a day and was unfortunately using his fancy wheelchair rather than his prosthesis at the advice of his medical team. He took it unexpectedly well when she told him he had to stay off it if he expected the damaged skin to heal, which told her that it was bothering him far more than he was letting on.

"Hi," she said, walking to the door. She bent down and kissed his lips in a work-appropriate buss. "Did you need something? How's the limb?"

"My leg is fine, but Cal sent me down to get you. He needs you in the comms room. I'm here to give you a ride."

Her laughter filled the hallway after she locked the med bay door. "I can walk, but thanks."

Efren grabbed her hand and pulled her down onto his lap. "I know you can walk, but if you walk, I don't get the pleasure of having you on my lap." They wheeled down to the comms room where she kissed him and then hopped off his lap, walking into the room.

"Cal?" she asked, but the room was empty. She turned back to the hallway. "I thought Cal wanted me."

"He did, but he also wanted you to have some privacy, so he sent me to get you. Sit." He motioned at the chair in front of a bank of computer screens.

She took the chair and he rolled over, hitting a button and waiting until the screen illuminated. Selina's gasp was loud when the face staring back at her was the only happy part of her past.

"Kai!" she exclaimed, leaning in closer to the screen.

"Eva," the man said, his voice awed for a moment until he held up his hand. "Sorry, Selina. I'm just so stunned to see you again."

"Same," she said with a smile. "I never checked your blog, I'm ashamed to say. I was too afraid to want a life I couldn't have. I was afraid I'd do something not to the benefit of my health. Yesterday, I spent the day going through your posts from the first ones to the last. Thank you for being so good to Zeus."

"He was my buddy," Kai said with a smile. "From the day you handed him to me, he never left my side. It was like he knew I was his only connection to you and he was my final connection to you. Until the day he died he made me walk him with the leash you left him with that day."

Selina had her hand to her heart with a smile on her face and tears in her eyes. "I never doubted that you would care for him better than I could in my situation. You did such great things as a team. I'm so proud of your accomplishments. Look at you running your own team. I always knew you could and would do it one day. That's why I left. Had I stayed, I would have held you back and put you at risk."

"I can see that now," he agreed.

"Listen, about the elephant in the room," she said, glancing at Efren, who slipped his hand in hers.

"It wasn't you," he said before she could. "She approached me in a dark bar, and I'm embarrassed to say I fell for it in the beginning."

"Don't be embarrassed," she interrupted. "My twin was manipulative and calculating. You didn't stand a chance."

"Still, part of me knew. All of me knew when she barely touched my dog's head, much less loved him up the way you would have. By then it was too late. She'd drugged my last drink with ketamine."

"So she got her answers, but you don't remember a thing."

"Nothing other than bringing her home and then waking up naked and alone, with this feeling of being gutted all over again."

"Kai, I can't begin to tell you how sorry I am. When I left, I thought she was dead. I didn't know she was alive until a week ago."

"That much I figured. Part of me knew that you would have somehow let me know she was alive if you knew. It wouldn't be hard for her to find your old relationships and leverage them, especially since I took Zeus. I was more than a little surprised when someone named Cal reached out yesterday."

"I wasn't aware he had." Selina rubbed her hand on her leg nervously. "I was going to, I wanted to apologize for Ava. I just had to build up the courage I'd need to see you again."

"You always were my one who got away, but I hear you've found the one you're meant to be with."

"This is Efren Brenna. He's the only reason I'm sitting here talking to you. The last few weeks have been tumultuous."

"From what I heard, you did some search-and-rescue of your own kind. At least that's what I understood from reading between the lines. Let me offer my congratulations on that search. It was more than time. I'm proud of you for staying in the light and fighting the darkness with integrity."

"I don't know about all that, but I'm glad their reign has come to an end."

"He's right," Efren said, kissing the fingers of the hand he held. It felt to Selina a bit like a power play for Kai, but she'd allow it considering what they'd been through. "Your integrity in the face of bad odds is the reason the country is a much safer place."

Selina smiled at him for a moment before she focused on the screen again. "Gosh, it's just so good to see you. I want to hear about the Cliff Badgers and how you started the team!"

"Let's just say you weren't the only one looking for a fresh start. This was mine. I won't bore you with the details, but let me say this, friend. If you two are ever looking for a new line of work, you've always got a place on my team."

Selina lifted a brow at Efren, who lifted one right back.

* * * * *

INTRIGUE

Seek thrills. Solve crimes. Justice served.

Available Next Month

Tracking Down The Lawman's Son Delores Fossen
Twin Jeopardy Cindi Myers

....

Cold Case Protection Nicole Helm
Wyoming Christmas Conspiracy Juno Rushdan

....

Danger In Dade Caridad Piñeiro
Holiday Under Wraps Katie Mettner
Larger Print

6 brand new stories each month

INTRIGUE

Seek thrills. Solve crimes. Justice served.

MILLS & BOON

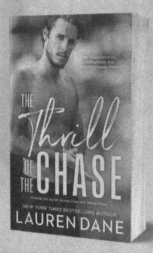
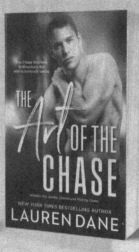